ASHLAND PRICE

VIKING ROSE

ZEBRA BOOKS
KENSINGTON PUBLISHING CORP.

ZEBRA BOOKS

are published by

Kensington Publishing Corp.
475 Park Avenue South
New York, NY 10016

Copyright © 1993 by Ashland Price

All rights reserved. No part of this book may be reproduced
in any form or by any means without the prior written con-
sent of the Publisher, excepting brief quotes used in reviews.

Zebra, the Z logo, and the Lovegram logo are trademarks of
Kensington Publishing Corp.

If you purchased this book without a cover you should be
aware that this book is stolen property. It was reported as
"unsold and destroyed" to the Publisher and neither the Author nor the Publisher has received any payment for this
"stripped book."

First Printing: January, 1993

Printed in the United States of America

The shining splendor of our Zebra Lovegram logo on the cover of this book reflects the glittering excellence of the story inside. Look for the Zebra Lovegram whenever you buy a historical romance. It's a trademark that guarantees the very best in quality and reading entertainment.

A STRANGE AND SENSUOUS CUSTOM

"I shall bathe in my tunic, sire," Alanna stated. "I am sure it needs cleaning as much as I."

"Oh, don't be daft," snapped Storr from the warm water of the tub. "You cannot get clean with that flea-ridden frock hanging about you. Take it off at once, before I do so for you!"

His sudden impatience took her by surprise, and she found her fingers trembling as she turned her back to him and pulled off the garment.

"Besides," he added " 'Tis pleasant, this bathing. 'Tis one of our most treasured pastimes in my land. We build houses for it, where great hearths are kept burning and one can bathe in comfort, even on the coldest days. Do come try it," he invited, as she turned to face him with her tunic clamped in front of her.

"Drop it," he whispered.

Modestly, she turned her back to him again before letting go of the tunic; then she lowered herself to a sitting position in the deep tub.

He was right about the pleasant feel of the water. This Viking type of bathing was warmer than any blanket. Her thoughts were interrupted, however, as she felt him wrap his arms about her waist and slide her farther back . . . into the vee created by his legs.

"Don't!" she exclaimed.

"Why not. I am seeing you bathed, not bedded," he declared. "When it is my intent to claim you, believe me, you will know it. There shall be no question in your mind!"

PUT SOME PASSION INTO YOUR
LIFE . . . WITH THIS STEAMY SELECTION OF
ZEBRA *LOVEGRAMS!*

SEA FIRES   (3899, $4.50/$5.50)
by Christine Dorsey

Spirited, impetuous Miranda Chadwick arrives in the untamed New
World prepared for any peril. But when the notorious pirate Gentleman
Jack Blackstone kidnaps her in order to fulfill his secret plans, she can't
help but surrender—to the shameless desires and raging hunger that his
bronzed, lean body and demanding caresses ignite within her!

TEXAS MAGIC   (3898, $4.50/$5.50)
by Wanda Owen

After being ambushed by bandits and saved by a ranchhand, headstrong
Texas belle Bianca Moreno hires her gorgeous rescuer as a protective escort. But Rick Larkin does more than guard her body—he kisses away her
maidenly inhibitions, and teaches her the secrets of wild, reckless love!

SEDUCTIVE CARESS   (3767, $4.50/$5.50)
by Carla Simpson

Determined to find her missing sister, brave beauty Jessamyn Forsythe
disguises herself as a simple working girl and follows her only clues to
Whitechapel's darkest alleys . . , and the disturbingly handsome Inspec-
tor Devlin Burke. Burke, on the trail of a killer, becomes intrigued with
the ebon-haired lass and discovers the secrets of her silken lips and the
hidden promise of her sweet flesh.

SILVER SURRENDER   (3769, $4.50/$5.50)
by Vivian Vaughan

When Mexican beauty Aurelia Mazón saves a handsome stranger from
death, she finds herself on the run from the Federales with the most dangerous man she's ever met. And when Texas Ranger Carson Jarrett steals
her heart with his intimate kisses and seductive caresses, she yields to an
all-consuming passion from which she hopes to never escape!

ENDLESS SEDUCTION   (3793, $4.50/$5.50)
by Rosalyn Alsobrook

Caught in the middle of a dangerous shoot-out, lovely Leona Stegall falls
unconscious and awakens to the gentle touch of a handsome doctor.
When her rescuer's caresses turn passionate, Leona surrenders to his fiery
embrace and savors a night of soaring ecstasy!

*Available wherever paperbacks are sold, or order direct from the
Publisher. Send cover price plus 50¢ per copy for mailing and
handling to Zebra Books, Dept. 4030, 475 Park Avenue South,
New York, N.Y. 10016. Residents of New York and Tennessee
must include sales tax. DO NOT SEND CASH. For a free Zebra/
Pinnacle catalog please write to the above address.*

To Earl and Vince Carlson,
my tall blond, "Viking" uncles
and students of Scandinavian
history. Thanks for your love and support!

And to my dear, old friend,
Paul Olson—fellow artist and Swede.
May our paths never part.

Special thanks, too, to author,
Cathy Lane, for her great
knowledge of the Middle Ages.

One

"Nothing is so strong as gentleness; nothing so gentle as real strength."

De Sales

The southeastern coast of Erin (Ireland) — 815 A.D.

Alanna reached down and clutched her dog to her, gasping at what she saw. It was a monster! A tall, blond, naked male rising from the splashing waters of the brook, like a sea serpent! She crouched in the nearby thicket and clamped a hand about her harrier's muzzle, in an effort to prevent him from barking and betraying their presence. She was painfully aware that such a betrayal could mean death for them both.

Her heart was racing like a frightened rabbit's. Its beating seemed so loud, in fact, that it occurred to her it might actually be heard by the stranger. Yet, he continued to seem unaware of her in the seconds that followed. He simply went on with his bathing, stooping with cupped hands and pouring the brook's water down the length of him again and again.

7

He might be a countryman, a voice within her offered hopefully. The horse he had tied to a nearby tree looked to be of fine, Erse bone and breeding. But the Norsemen were known for their horse thievery, she reminded herself; and one look across to where the stranger's clothes were strewn, on the opposite embankment, told her he was definitely an outlander. Ersemen, be they commoners or privileged, didn't go about in crisscross leggings and ankle-length breeches. Nor did they, as a rule, carry swords as ominous-looking as the one this man had shed with his garments.

Then, too, there was his dog, a huge red-coated creature who bore an unnerving resemblance to the lions Alanna had seen depicted on religious tablets. She was getting a fairly full view of the animal, while it sat on the other bank, methodically licking its wet legs and paws; and she acknowledged that no Erseman had ever been seen with such an enormous beast. It wasn't much of a watchdog, though, she noted, for it seemed as oblivious as its owner to her presence.

As she continued to hold her own dog fast and quietly shush him, Alanna's eyes returned to the unclothed body of the stranger. He was, *indeed,* a Norseman, she finally admitted to herself, one of those horrible raiders from some distant, northern land, come to attack the tribes of her people and enslave all who were not killed in the process.

She should make a run for it, a voice within her warned. She should hoist Faolan, her harrier, up in her arms and dash homeward, while she still had some hope of going unseen. She knew this was the wisest course, yet she couldn't seem to bring herself to move.

Something kept telling her that this sort of opportunity, to study and subsequently report upon one's enemy, came only once, if ever, in a maiden's lifetime; and she truly wanted such a claim to her credit. What was more, the stranger held an almost mesmeric fascination for her. She'd never seen the like of him: so golden-haired, muscular, and threateningly large of frame. He was, by any Erseman's standards, a heathen, a brute, and, yet, by those same standards, surprisingly handsome. Even more comely than she, with her commonplace, dark features.

She noted that his hair was much longer than that of most of her countrymen, almost shoulder-length as it was swept back now in the northerly breeze. And, though she'd been told that the foreign raiders usually wore moustaches and beards, this one was clean-shaven, with only the bluish shadows about his cheeks and chin to hint at the beastly hairiness she'd been given to expect.

Far from beastly, in fact, there was an indisputable beauty in his face, in the dimplelike recesses beneath his sharp cheekbones and the natural shadowing of his broad eyelids, as he continued to stare down into the cooling water of the brook. Indeed, the only flaw she saw in him was what looked to be a long, sutured wound in one of his upper arms. And this was so overshadowed, so dwarfed by his breath-stopping height and brawn, that it seemed almost as insignificant as a bug bite.

Try as she might to fight it, Alanna's eyes again lit upon the most private parts of him; and, though she knew there was no one but herself to bear witness to this impropriety, she felt her face grow warm with embarrassment. Nakedness was a sin, according to the

9

Christian Church, one that had greatly discouraged such full-body bathing among her people. Yet, seeing the musculature of this stranger, the lovely ripples of water spilling down his sun-bronzed chest, she thought this no more a sin than watching a prize stallion high-stepping about a croft, its hindquarters riding high and firm.

But he wasn't a horse, she silently scolded herself, and he was no Erseman either. He was nothing less than one of the devils her fellow citizens had been falling prey to for over twenty years; and she knew that, if she managed to slip away undetected now, she was sure to be deemed a heroine among the people of her tribe. She would be a blessed herald, warning of a raid to come. And, more importantly—though she knew such pridefulness to be an offense to God—she would be the bearer of a tale that would make each man, woman, and child in her clan hang upon her every word at that evening's fireside gathering.

Storr was being watched. He could feel it, as surely as he felt the warmth of the afternoon sun on his naked shoulders and back. After eleven summers of spying on others he'd come to know when he was being spied upon in return.

He slanted a look towards the thicket that stood just off to the right of the brook in which he was wading. He squinted, searching for any movement within it, any fluctuation of light or shadow that might betray a presence. But there was none; so he simply continued to bathe in the chilly, calf-deep water.

His gut, his instincts, had him convinced that there

was someone nearby, someone in that very thicket, in fact. Yet his trusty dog, Biorn, was offering no warning of this, as he lay drying himself on the sun-drenched bank of the brook — having just indulged in a bath of his own. Storr glanced backward and confirmed that the big hound hadn't so much as perked his ears in the past few seconds. But, then again, Storr knew that Biorn, his "Bear," was getting old. He had definitely lost some of his alertness, after so many years of serving Storr as both a hunting and raiding companion.

A bird, perhaps, Storr thought fleetingly, knowing that couldn't possibly have been the explanation. The sound he'd heard suggested something heavier. A hare or otter, maybe, rustling about on a quest of its own . . . It was possible, he supposed, that a creature of that sort could have produced such a crackling of twigs underfoot. Yet it stayed with him, the nagging sense that a pair of eyes, *human* eyes were watching him.

He would have to cross the brook and investigate, he decided. The lives of his warriors might depend upon it in the days to come. He'd learned the hard way that he simply couldn't afford to let word of their presence be carried back to any of the Erse tribes they planned to attack. It was just that kind of forewarning, after all, that had nearly gotten him killed on their last raid — that and the fool-headed actions of Earl Sigurd's second-born son.

The thought of the mishap made Storr reach up and run his fingertips over one of his huge upper arms, the one that still bore the suturing his chief freemen had had to administer after an Erse arrow had been dug out of it. Storr drew a pained breath in through his

11

clenched teeth. Even though the wound was now eight days' old, it still hurt like the blazes when it was touched. It hadn't festered, however. At least that could be said for the cowardly men of Erin; it didn't appear that they'd resorted to using poisoned arrow-heads.

He must seem unhurried and calm, he told himself, as he concluded his Saturday bath and began wading back towards where Biorn lay. He must dry his body with his cape and then dress, without giving his observer any hint that he was aware of his presence and intended to act accordingly.

Storr realized now what a fool he'd been to have left his weapon so far up on the bank. Though he hadn't seen a soul for days — outside of the tribes he'd spied upon — he had learned, from his family's Erse slaves, that Erin's natives were as given to hunting and raiding as his own people. He, therefore, acknowledged what folly it was to have let his guard down while alone like this.

He had allowed himself to be so lulled by the almost tropical warmth of this southern region and its sparkling brook, that he'd forgotten what every Viking boychild knew by rote: never to place one's sword out of reach, never to leave one's self open for a surprise attack. But he'd done just that, and he knew, as he again donned his trousers, pulled his tunic over his head, and stepped into his shoes, that he would pay the price for it. His observer might be just yards away now, but Storr was fully aware that, with any sign, the stranger might be off like an arrow.

It was widely known among Storr's people that the Erse, with their love of footracing, could be remarkably quick. What was more, for all of Storr's scouting, this native doubtless knew the surrounding terrain — its straightaways and hiding places — a great deal better than Storr did. So he was acutely aware that he couldn't afford to do anything that might cause him to spook and, consequently, lose track of his watcher. Such a false move was sure to result in the knave returning to his tribe with the forearming news of a Viking raid upon the area.

But what if he didn't charge across the brook with his sword drawn? Storr's mind raced, snatching at the threads of an idea . . . another, more subtle way of handling the situation. What if he simply put his belt-strap, scabbard, and sword on, gathered up his leggings and cape, and led his horse back across the brook as though intending to return to some encampment or tribe at a nonchalant pace? That *did* seem a better plan than giving his opponent the forewarning that would come with a head-on assault.

He, therefore, began to carry it out, part of him grateful that he still sensed his watcher's presence and part of him sorry about it. The last thing he'd wanted, after all, on such a peaceful, sunny day as this, was a fight to the death with some nosey Erseman. But, as with so much else in his life of late, the bitter was again being thrust upon him.

Biorn stopped licking his forearms and stared up at his master questioningly, as Storr ordered the dog to rise and follow him and the horse southward once more. They had been travelling towards their camp in the north since dawn, and it was as if Biorn knew that Storr was attempting to lead him in the wrong direction.

"Come," Storr again said sternly in his native Norse, turning to glare back at his pet, as he bent down to roll up his trousers for the wade across the water. "Come hither, you witless hound, or I shall leave you here to starve!"

Before coming up from his hunched-over position, Storr caught sight of a long stick that lay on the bank. Fighting a smile at the fine opportunity it would afford him for a stealthy flushing of his prey, he picked it up and waved it at his "Bear."

At this the old dog, always one to find sudden energy for such sport, struggled to his feet and began rushing towards him.

"Fetch!" Storr shouted, flinging the stick towards the thicket.

Biorn bolted into the brook, drenching his master's trousers as he passed. To Storr's amazement, it wasn't a person who came dashing out of the cloaking copse and into the mouth of the adjacent woods, but another dog! Its symmetrical markings appeared to be tan, black, and white, almost lost amidst the shadows of the forest floor, and the great speed of its retreat caused its long ears to fly comically backwards.

Spotting the hound, Biorn instantly lost interest in the stick his master had thrown. With a snarling bark, he set out after the strange dog at a dead run.

Nothing more than a harrier, Storr concluded, shaking his head and laughing with relief. The worthless little snoop *deserved* to be chased for a while, for having brought Storr's bath to such a discomfiting end! The accursed mutt had earned a scare in return; though it was probably already clear to both animals, as they disappeared completely from Storr's line of sight, that Biorn had no hope of overtaking him. Old Bear was, after all, at least three times the harrier's size, and probably twice his age; Storr felt certain the latter would emerge the victor in the chase. But Storr really couldn't fault Biorn for trying. It was just that sort of spirit that had compelled Storr to pick the red hound from the many litters of pups their farm's bitches had produced through the years.

There was no doubt about it. His Biorn could be counted upon to give it his all, trailing after the harrier for several minutes more. Then, once he lost track of his quarry, he would head back to his master with his usual shuffling gait, his long tongue hanging out of the side of his mouth.

Storr chuckled again at the lingering image of the long-eared hare-hunter. The Erse and their damnable lapdogs! What a frivolous race they were, keeping some hounds, not for the hunt or even for herding, but simply for their own amusement and pleasure! Storr had learned enough about Erin's natives to know that they routinely fed good-for-naught terriers from their dining tables, while, every year, hundreds of Norse *infants* were put to death at birth for lack of food!

They were a fainthearted, overindulgent people, Storr decided once more, his previous amusement with the situation turning to rancor. They'd become shamelessly spoiled by their temperate weather, abundant land, and their lavishly long growing season. So, they had no real right to object if those less fortunate came and gathered up some of their surplus from time to time. And, with that discourse of reason firmly in mind again, he headed back up the northern bank of the brook, retied his horse to the tree, and sat down to await his hunting dog's return.

Just as he was getting himself comfortable, however, there came a peculiar noise from the woods into which Biorn and his prey had disappeared. It was a haunting sort of howl, like the cry of a wounded animal; and, though it didn't strike Storr as a sound Biorn was capable of producing, he knew he should look into it.

He got to his feet once more and, choosing to leave his newly acquired horse behind for the time being, he began heading back into the brook.

Alanna winced and stopped dead in her tracks, as she heard the howling in the woods. Faolan was hurt! She just *knew* it! In the five years since the harrier had been whelped, she'd come to know his different outcries as well as a mother knows her child's, and she was certain that this one meant Faolan was in dire straits and that, in spite of the raider's presence, she must return to the woods and rescue him.

When the Norseman had thrown the stick for his dog minutes earlier, his eyes had been intent upon the thicket, and she'd realized that he knew there was someone hidden there. So she'd chosen the only course that had come to mind. She'd used Faolan as a lure, sending him off into the adjacent woods with a whispered order that he run home. An instant later, seeing that the warrior and his dog were sufficiently distracted by Faolan's getaway, she'd snuck off to the left, letting the edge of the woodland cloak her as she began a more southerly route back to her tribe.

It should have worked. Surely Faolan was fast enough to have shaken the lumbering hound and its

16

master by this time. But then the awful, gut-wrenching howling had filled the air, as it was again now, and she knew that she had no other choice but to go to her harrier's aid. He was, after all, her constant companion, the only real, immediate family she'd known since her parents had died some eleven years earlier. He seemed to trust her completely, and, if he was to suffer the consequences of her having wandered too far afield on this hot, summer day, then, by God, so would she!

She turned around and began rushing back towards the woods. She hated herself for having ignored her aunt's warnings about straying too far from their ringfort. Her paternal uncle and his wife were, after all, her legal guardians, and she was filled with remorse for having disobeyed them. Nevertheless, she knew they'd have to agree that losing Faolan was just too dear a price to pay for what had started out as a prospective wade in the brook.

She picked up her pace to a breathless run and silently prayed that that horrible heathen she'd seen hadn't somehow caught up with her poor harrier and thrown a dagger or axe at him for sport. Given what she'd heard about the Vikings, however, she knew she shouldn't be surprised to find that he'd done just that!

Two

The dogs had veered from the woods' central path and off towards the south, so it took Storr several minutes to place the piteous howling and finally overtake Biorn and his prey.

To Storr's amazement, it appeared that his Bear had done the impossible. He'd somehow managed to get hold of the harrier, and he had him pinned to the forest floor by the throat. Storr, therefore, gentled Biorn, as he came up behind him. Then, kneeling down to have a better look at the strange dog, he softly assured his pet that he didn't intend to deprive him of his prize. Biorn wagged his tail slightly at this, as though he was quite relieved to hear it. Nevertheless, he kept his mouth fixed about the harrier's throat, as Storr attempted to examine it.

The hare-hunter was lying on its back, its male gender now abundantly evident, and, as Storr reached out to still the flailing lower half of him, his pitiful yelping became all the more intense. For some reason, he seemed to fear Storr even more than Biorn. But this close look at his body indicated that it wasn't just fear, but pain that was causing him to carry on so.

There was a long, hide-deep laceration running from the harrier's right underarm all the way down to the middle of his rib cage, and Storr realized that he'd never seen the like of it on an animal. It was as though someone had slashed the poor creature with a scythe.

It certainly wasn't a wound that Biorn had the means to inflict. Nor, as far as Storr could tell, was there anyone else in the woods who could have caused it. So he was forced to conclude that the ridiculous hound had caught himself on a stick or some undergrowth, as he was making his hurried getaway, and finally, in too much pain to run anymore, he had simply sunk to the ground, allowing Biorn to catch up with him.

Storr considered drawing his sword and putting the dog out of his misery, but looking down into the creature's entreating brown eyes, he suddenly felt compelled to take even greater pity upon him. He would knock him out with a rock, he decided. Then he'd suture the slash wound with the bone needle and thread he carried for just such emergencies.

He looked about the forest floor and finally spotted a rock that seemed large enough for the task of rendering the hound unconscious. Before he could rise and fetch it, however, something came running at him from the west, something that was moving so fast that he didn't even have time to turn and look at it before it hit him. With his peripheral vision, he saw only that it was short and verdant, like

19

an uprooted bush being whisked along in a violent windstorm.

The next thing he knew, he was toppled over on his left side with his wounded, right upper arm burning, as though it had been opened anew. He nearly fainted for the pain, yet, as he looked upward, his vision blurring, he could have sworn his attacker was nothing more than some little Erse maiden in a long white tunic and green cloak.

By the gods, that's just what he *was* seeing! He was sure of it now, as she glared down and began hollering some choice Erse curses at him. Storr's vision was impaired, but his hearing still seemed to be functioning, and, even with what little he knew of the local language, it was clear that she was calling him a bully, a ruffian for some reason, and that her next move would be to lunge for his sword and try to run him through with it.

He managed to struggle up to a crouch before she did so, however, and, still stunned with pain, he staggered away from her, getting his weapon and himself well out of her reach.

Biorn, meanwhile, had relinquished his hold on the harrier and begun to growl at the girl. It was his fiercest of growls, the sort that usually preceded his most savage attacks. But again, to Storr's astonishment, the chit seemed unfazed, indomitable. She simply lifted her calf-length tunic and kicked Bear in the side of the head with her sandaled right foot.

Storr's pet appeared stunned by her blow. He issued a yelp and wisely chose to stagger away from their apparently crazed assailant, before she could kick him again.

In the midst of all this, Storr reached up and tried to assess the damage she had done to his already-wounded arm. To his dismay, he discovered that he had, indeed, been pierced again. There was a curiously shaped metal object embedded in his sutured flesh. He winced as he dug it out of himself. Then he lifted it to see that it appeared to be a long-stemmed brooch—now coated, from its point to its head, with his blood.

He studied it with almost morbid interest. In a land where the law dictated that one's brooch be proportionate in worth and size to its wearer's rank, he knew he could safely assume that this maiden was an aristocrat.

He snarled to himself, dashed the brooch to the ground, and continued withdrawing until he backed up to a tree, against which he could brace himself.

From the privileged class, was she? The little shrew! Well, no matter how lofty her station in life, there was no denying the fact that she was a maniac! A woman possessed!

However, as she removed her now-unbrooched cloak, spread it out beside the harrier, and carefully began transferring the wounded beast to the garment, it dawned upon Storr that he might be wrong about the state of her mind—that she might actually be the owner of the dog and that she blamed *Storr* for the animal's present condition.

She'd obviously been somewhere nearby and heard the harrier howling, Storr deduced, still trying to make sense of the attack. Clearly, she'd had the element of surprise on her side, and she'd certainly used it to her full advantage. But there was something more about her approach, something that had made both Storr and Biorn choose to back down. It had been filled with *rage,* Storr realized, an unmitigated, righteous rage that had come at them like a funnel cloud.

Storr couldn't help continuing to be awed as he went on watching her. He'd never seen such a display of emotion from a woman, let alone an Erse woman. He found himself half admiring her, as she lifted the harrier in the makeshift stretcher and began to walk away with him.

Biorn, on the other hand, seemed to hold no such respect for the maiden. Apparently having recovered from her attack, he got back to his feet now and began stalking her, as though planning to pounce from behind. Storr hissed an order for him to stop, however; and the huge dog, looking displeased and a trifle confused by the command, turned around and slunk back to his master.

Storr knew that, like Biorn, he should have been angry. He should have wanted to lash out at the girl, as she had at him. Oddly, though, respect was all he continued to feel, as he went on observing her steady stride, her determined pace. She wasn't running away from them, as Storr himself probably would have in her place; she was simply walking. She was sidling along with her heavy burden and glancing down to comfort the harrier, rather than gazing fearfully back over her shoulder, as he might have expected her to do. It was as if she felt she possessed some divine right to carry on as she had. Some god-given impunity!

Storr shook his head slightly and directed his gaze downward. It was going to be a shame to have to stop her, but he knew he had no choice. She'd seen him. She'd surely had enough of a look to have noticed his Norse attire, and she could not be allowed to return to her tribe and inform them of his presence.

Were she a man, Storr would have chosen to kill her. But she was a maiden, and it was Viking practice to spare the Erse women and children, whenever possible, and take them as slaves. If the truth be known, however, Storr wasn't really interested in capturing any more slaves. There were already so many of them on his family's farm that he'd begun to fear an uprising against his mother and younger siblings, while he was away on his summer raids.

He could always sell her, he supposed. Women of her fine stature were bringing a pretty fair price in the trading town of Hedeby these days . . . But, no, he concluded. This one was just too interesting, too plucky to sell off without having some misgivings. He would simply keep her for a while, he decided, bearing up against the continuing pain in his arm and crossing to the rock upon which he'd set his sights earlier. It wasn't just the harrier he must knock out now, but its guardian as well.

Storr was, of course, aware that she might prove more bother than she was worth in the end; but, for the time being, anyway, he would plan to keep her.

She had true spirit, after all, and that was something that had been sorrily lacking in his life for quite a while.

Storr took the time to suture the harrier's wound, before seeking a hiding place for the night. Then, leaving Biorn to keep watch over their unconscious captives, he had gone back to the brook for his horse. Once he had the girl and her dog slung and tied over the Erse stallion, he had begun heading northward again, with old Bear at his heels.

When they reached some lowlands an hour later, a point that seemed wooded enough to allow Storr to build a campfire without its smoke being readily detectable, he decided to stop. He took the maiden down from his horse, tied her wrists behind her, and propped her still-limp form up against a nearby log.

Biorn supervised all of this, of course, still looking skeptical about how far the Erse woman could be trusted. It was obvious that he disapproved of Storr's decision to bring her and her harrier with them. But, if they *were* to come along, it was equally clear that Bear felt they should be watched most closely; and he sank down beside the girl now, as if to do just that.

Storr, meanwhile, noticed that his captive's tunic was badly torn at her right shoulder, causing its bodice to flop over and reveal what he found to be an unnerving amount of cleavage. He instantly bent down and did what he could to close the baggy garment about her, but he didn't have much success with it. He'd just never been very good at dealing with raiment — especially the foreign female variety. Even when he'd been required to manage more familiar apparel, to help his little brothers get dressed on cold, winter mornings, he'd always fumbled horribly. His fingers were simply too large to handle such things as tiny pull-through straps and tie closings, and he had, in the end, always been forced to enlist the aid of one of his sisters in order to get the youngsters clothed.

Well, no matter, he concluded, finally giving up on the effort. He would simply toss the girl's cloak over her and cover her nakedness that way. With that decided, he circled down to her feet, took hold of her ankles, and tugged until her supine body slid out fully upon the ground. Her head and neck came to rest on the log, against which he had propped her, as though it were a pillow.

He then crossed back to his horse and took the harrier down from the saddle as well. He carried the still-sleeping dog over to the maiden and set him on the ground, just to her left. Then he slipped the girl's cloak out from beneath the little beast and turned to lay it over her.

He'd become rather skilled at knocking out Ersewomen through the years, and he knew that this one would only be out for a few minutes more, at best. But, before she turned back into the furious she-wolf she'd been earlier, he should try to drink in her peacefulness, he told himself, stooping down to behold her once more.

Almost a year had passed since he'd been alone with a woman, and, though he knew he must go off and scare up a hare or two for their evening meal before darkness fell, he felt he owed it to himself, to his soul, to simply kneel beside her once again and take in her loveliness. She was like a forest flower beaded with drops of summer rain. And, on this particular day, Storr sensed that the gods meant for him to stop and appreciate her as he would such a bloom. It somehow seemed their will that she be relished, rather than simply crushed underfoot.

He suddenly recalled that there had been a dark bird overhead as she'd attacked him and Biorn earlier. He distinctly remembered it now, though he'd only been vaguely aware of it at the time. It had been quite large, and it had cawed down upon the scene and swooped from one treetop to the next, as though the girl's frantic approach had interrupted its business, as surely as it had Storr's.

It was a huge black bird of the sort that the war god, Odin, had at his command. A raven, perhaps, come to act as a messenger, Storr concluded. But it couldn't have been meant to warn him of the girl's attack, for that had been under way before Storr had become aware of the bird.

To warn? Storr asked himself again. To warn of the obvious: that she would return to her tribe with word of him, if he didn't stop her? . . . Yes. That could have been all the bird was meant to convey. But now, seeing at this close range how beautiful his captive was, Storr couldn't help thinking that Odin had meant for him to have her, to take her and keep her close to his heart, as he might one of the golden amulets he'd looted from the bodies of fallen Ersemen through the years.

He drew closer to the maiden and continued to study her features. Her long hair had looked almost black to him when he'd first seen her. But now, up close, he realized that it was actually auburn, her dark brown mane streaked throughout with the color of flame. It wasn't hanging loose, as Norse women wore theirs. Rather, it was swept up in a knot of curls that was supported by two colorful cloth bands. These encircled her head, extending from just above her hairline to the nape of her neck. Here and there, some ringleted wisps had fallen free of the bands, and they seemed to Storr to create a perfect frame for her peachy complexion.

A wry smile tugged at one corner of his lips. His face had been as lineless and filled with dewy innocence as hers once, he thought wistfully. Perhaps *that* was what Odin wanted from him, that he extract the youth from this maiden, as he would nourishment from a hunted kill, that he sacrifice this newly acquired slave to Odin—the god who had not stopped at sacrificing even *himself* to himself in his quest for the wisdom of the dead.

Storr swallowed dryly and drew back slightly at the thought of it, of ending her short life before she'd even had the chance to regain consciousness and say a proper farewell to the harrier and her homeland.

What a cruel message! What merciless irony to offer a heart-shattered man like himself: a hope of recovering his appetite for living by crushing the life from one as callow as this!

Blast Odin, an outraged voice shouted within him. To the nether regions of ice and darkness with a god who had no more compassion for one of his followers, than to offer him yet another death, when what Storr really needed was life and a reason to go on living it!

He felt his fingers closing angrily about a fistful of grass and earth, as he continued to kneel at his captive's side. Then he dashed it back to the ground with a snarl. His throat ached with the jumble of emotions he'd kept sealed deep inside himself since Freyja's death. He'd had enough of warring! Enough of putting others in their graves!

Valho'll help him, all he truly wanted now was to escape into places and times such as these, into a sun-washed land like Erin and into the peaceful, unhurried life of this maiden and her droopy-earred harrier. Sadly, however, he knew that his sense of duty to his widowed mother and his role as leader of his clan would always call him back to his frigid homeland.

The girl began to stir a bit, and Storr reflexively moved away from her, reaching up with his tunic sleeve to blot the tears of frustration that had welled up in his eyes.

She still appeared to be unconscious, but her movement had caused her cloak to fall away from her, and Storr now noticed the silver crucifix that hung about her neck.

"A Christson," he silently acknowledged. But,

28

no. That wasn't quite how the word was said, he remembered. "Tian," he corrected himself. She was what his Erse slaves called a "Chris*tian*."

His curiosity got the best of him in those seconds, and he moved closer to her once more, so he could take hold of the odd little pendant. It looked like an alphabetic letter. Rather like the Norse rune for *n*. But the truth of the matter was that he'd never cared enough about the Ershry's craven beliefs to inquire any further about it. It could well have been nothing more than an Erse letter, he imagined. Or it could have been an emblem of some kind, like Thor's thunderous hammer or Odin's sacrificial tree.

It was probably a ridiculous faith, in any case, he again concluded, lowering his fingers so that the crucifix came to rest upon the girl's chest again. And, yet, even having decided anew that this Christian religion was foolishness, he found himself unable to release the pendant and pull his hand away.

But it wasn't any magical power on the part of the cross that kept him frozen there, he realized in the minutes that followed. It was the girl herself. It was the warmth of her flesh beneath his own, the gentle rise and fall caused by her breathing. And again Storr recalled that, save for hugging his mother and his sisters goodbye before this summer's raids, he hadn't touched a female in nearly a year. In what now felt to him like a lifetime, he hadn't had occasion to smell the sweet scent of perfume, of flowers and spice gracing a woman's flesh and hair. And, perhaps his mind had gone completely, but he could have sworn, as he leaned closer yet to his captive, that she smelt of scented oil.

He knew that the Erse weren't much for bathing—let alone in anything as carnal as perfumed water. Nevertheless, there it was, at the pulsing hollow of her throat: a scent that was very much like honeysuckle or, perhaps, hyacinth. But, whatever the fragrance, whether real or imagined, it didn't compel him to strip or rape her—as he was certain his fellow raiders would have in his place. Rather, to his surprise, it simply made him want to gather her up in his arms and clutch her . . . and *weep*.

She'd had time to spot the wound in his arm and prey upon it earlier. But it was a far greater wound she was unwittingly piercing now: the aching region deep within him that had been bleeding incessantly for so many months, and he knew it was threatening to drain out what life there was left in him.

By the gods, it was happening once more: the horrible choking in the back of his throat, the hot, wet welling in his eyes. He wanted, more than anything, to reach down, slip his hands beneath his captive, and simply hug her to him . . . as though she were nothing more threatening or aware than one of the wooden dolls his sisters carried about. He wanted to bare his soul to her unhearing ears, and tell her what it was like to have one's spouse taken away for an eternity.

But, on the off chance that she was half listening, half able to understand his tongue, he knew it was wisest to simply take his hand from her and quietly rise and back away. No one, not even a groggy slave girl, must ever be allowed to know of his pain, his vulnerability. Such folly would surely be his undoing, and, even worse, his family's!

Continuing to be mindful of this, he finally let go of the crucifix. Then he rose and took a few steps away from her. Like Biorn, he would simply keep watch over her now, as she began to awake.

Alanna's eyes fell open, and she was aware of a shady, green coolness all about her and a painful throbbing at the back of her head. Her vision was blurred at first, but she could see well enough to know that there were treetops on high and that she was presently in a forest. The *forest*. The forest she'd been in when she'd gone to rescue Faolan, she surmised . . . And that explained her torn tunic. She now felt the drafty gape where she'd heard it tear earlier, when she'd lunged at the stranger with her brooch. She looked down to see that someone had apparently attempted to drape her bared flesh with her cloak.

Faolan! It all came rushing back to her in nightmarish detail. That terrible heathen had slashed her poor dog's chest, and would surely have finished him off, if not for her intervention.

She felt a wave of panic run through her, and she began struggling to sit up and look for her pet. But something was wrong . . . Where were her hands? How could she sit up without the use of her hands?

They were tied behind her, she realized with a gasp, and, as she strained to push herself upward against the log behind her, she was able to see the very culprit who'd bound them.

The raider's face was almost level with hers now. He sat just a few feet before her; and, at this close range, she saw that he was truly an outlander, a man with eyes too extraordinary to be an Erseman's. They were, in fact, as luminously blue as the sky on a cloudless day.

Alanna swallowed tensely, feeling terrified, but sensing that it was wisest not to show it. He'd chosen to let her live, after all, she reasoned. He hadn't killed her, as she might have expected after her attack upon him. So, obviously, her offensive approach had worked on him and might continue to be successful.

"Untie me," she suddenly heard herself ordering. "Untruss my hands forthwith, you great, wretched bully!"

She had hoped to see him flinch at the sternness of this command. She'd heard that the Norsemen hailed from so far away that their tongue was very different from Erse, but she couldn't help praying that she would see at least some indication that her acidic tone had taken him aback. Unfortunately, however, there was none. In fact, his eyes were actually crinkling a bit at their outer corners now, as though smiling at her demand.

"Where's my dog?" she continued, doing her best to appear undaunted by his seeming imperviousness. "What have you done with him, you . . . you *monster?*"

To her further dismay, his lips gave way to a subtle, but unmistakable smile, an instantaneous flash of snow-white teeth. Then he lifted a finger and pointed just to the left of her.

"There," he said, in the oddest, most guttural tone she'd ever heard. It was, nevertheless, the Gaelic word for "there." There was no mistaking it; and, as Alanna looked to the left and saw her poor harrier lying at her side, she realized that this stranger had not only addressed her in her own language, but had somehow understood her well enough to have answered her question.

"My God, you've killed him," she exclaimed, seeing how still Faolan was lying.

"Nay. Nay. Asl—asleep," the stranger stammered, as though both lost for the Erse word he needed, and feeling defensive at her accusation.

"Asleep?" Alanna asked, not sure, given his queer pronunciation, if that was what he'd meant to say. But it didn't really matter what he'd meant, she thought, gritting her teeth with anger. It was evident to her now that the pitiless barbarian had knocked Faolan unconscious, just as he had her.

He nodded, looking pleased that she'd understood him. "Asleep. Aye."

"But he was bleeding. Slashed. Cut on his chest," she countered anxiously. "He may have bled to death by now!"

The stranger's eyes narrowed confusedly, and it was obvious that he'd had very little luck with deciphering all of this. "Blee—bleeding?" he repeated blankly.

She gave forth a furious cluck. "Aye. Bleeding,

33

you fool! Bleeding—as in 'to death'!"

"Ah, death," he replied, nodding. "Nay. Not dead. Asleep."

To Alanna's horror, he rose in that instant and began approaching her, and, though she felt certain it wasn't wise to show him any fear, she couldn't help recoiling slightly.

To her relief, however, it quickly became apparent that it wasn't her he was crossing to, but Faolan. She looked on cautiously, as he reached out and carefully rolled the groggy harrier onto his back.

"I . . . weaved? Weaved him," he explained, running his fingers along a now-sutured ridge of flesh that had earlier been torn open.

"Weaved?" she repeated, inwardly breathing a sigh of relief at seeing that he'd at least had the decency to try to set right what he'd done to her pet. "You mean sewed?"

He gave forth a soft laugh and pointed at her as if she'd taken the word right out of his mouth. "Sewed. Aye," he repeated, smiling again. "I sewed him."

"Which is as it should be, considering 'twas *you* who wounded him," she retorted. "Now, kindly untie me, will you, so we can be on our way."

The stranger seemed to ignore this request. He simply reached down and picked up a stick from the forest floor. "Nay. I did not wound him. This," he declared, shaking the stick at her, "this. Coming from the dirt." And, with that, he jabbed one end of the stick into the ground at her feet.

She eyed it, then looked up at him skeptically.

"Oh, nonsense! I won't believe he did such a thing to himself. 'Twas you who slashed him," she maintained, looking squarely at him.

He fixed his jaw, as if angered by this rebuttal. "Nay. *Stick,*" he repeated in a tone as resolute as her own. "Run . . . run very fast over stick," he added with a note of finality that warned her not to go on contradicting him.

"Very well, then," she conceded after several seconds. "I shan't sit here and wrangle with you. Profound thanks to you, sire, for sewing Faolan. And now, if you will please untruss me, we will be off and not trouble you and your good dog any further."

He understood her. She could see it in his eyes in that instant, and, yet, all he did in response was to toss the stick aside and turn away.

"Hungry," he said, walking to his horse and withdrawing what looked like a throwing spear from the pack that was tied behind his saddle. "I go hunt hare to eat."

"Oh, none for me, thank you all the same," she answered gingerly. "I shall eat when I return to my family."

He turned to face her again, his expression quite sober. "Nay. You stay here. You may . . . may not return."

"Oh, but I *must,*" Alanna blurted. "They shall be terribly worried about me . . . my aunt and uncle. It grows dark, and I must return, or they will come looking for me."

He stared at her for several seconds more, his eyes

35

shifting a bit as though he was having some difficulty making out all that she'd said. Then he glared at her with such intensity, that she felt as if she were being riveted to the log against which she still rested.

"They will not find you. You are Storr's now," he said, tapping his chest emphatically. "Storr's slave."

She swallowed uneasily at this proclamation and, more particularly, at the firmness with which it was delivered. "So . . . that is your name?" she asked, her voice quavering. "You are called Storr?"

He nodded.

"I am called Alanna."

"Alanna," he interjected, as if trying to commit it to memory.

"Aye," she confirmed. "And I am the daughter of a jurist and the niece of a physician. Thus I am of the privileged class, the *aes dana,* and I cannot be any man's slave."

To her surprise, he looked amused by her words, as though he half believed she was saying them merely to entertain him. Suddenly his smile faded, and another sentiment seemed to come to the fore . . . *admiration,* Alanna realized, as he began walking towards her once more, this time with the spear in hand.

He kept his eyes fixed upon her, though she, herself, chose to drop her gaze when he finally stood just before her. The weapon made her even more aware now that he could simply run her through, right then and there. Or, perhaps, he would force her down and rape her, as she'd heard such raiders did—and all of this where there would probably be no one for miles to hear her screams.

She had been mistaken when she'd regained consciousness. This wasn't the forest in which she'd encountered him earlier. She'd seen enough of her present surroundings by this point to know that they were completely unfamiliar to her, and that these woods were too low-lying to be part of the region from which she hailed. What was more, the sun was considerably farther down in the sky now, so he'd obviously had plenty of time to hie her off to some distant location; and that, by all appearances, was precisely what he'd done.

But why was he alone? she finally asked herself. She had heard that the Norsemen usually travelled in scores, dozens of them leaping from their monstrously carved ships and onto Erin's beaches. Yet this one had been on his own from the moment she'd spotted him at the brook.

He was acting as some sort of scout, she suddenly realized. She had, in fact, also heard it said that the Vikings were no longer just raiding and retreating to their homeland, but had actually begun setting up hidden camps along Erin's shores—bases from which they could launch their attacks. And, given the obvious difficulty of attempting stealthy navigation about her country's rocky coasts, it did stand to reason that such a solitary warrior might be sent out by land to scout for prospective raiding sites.

He was upon her now, she acknowledged again with a terrified gulp. He had dropped to one knee before her, and he clearly expected her to look up at him once more. When, after several seconds, she still failed to do so, he placed a finger beneath her chin and lifted her face until she was meeting his eyes with her own.

"The *ces dana*," he echoed with obvious approval, and his regard was so engaging in those seconds, so paternal, that she half expected some sort of helpful, fatherly advice from him.

But she shouldn't allow herself to be guiled by his fine countenance, a voice within her warned. He was no kinsman. He wasn't even a countryman! He was some sort of outlandish raider, intent upon forcing her into a life of servitude, and she knew she should resist him at all costs.

"Aye. This is good, such pride and cour . . . courage in a woman," he continued, a faint smile dancing upon his lips. "But you are Storr's now," he added in a growl, and it was apparent that he was finished discussing the matter and that, if she knew what was best for her, so was she.

"Understand?" he asked after several seconds.

She understood well enough, but she'd be damned if she'd agree to it. She simply clenched her jaw and let her gaze drop to the ground once more.

Her heart started to race again in those tense seconds. She didn't have any idea what he'd do in response to her refusal to answer, and she knew that she'd just have to pray that his retribution wouldn't be too severe.

But then, to her amazement, he suddenly seemed to be doing precisely what she'd requested. She felt him turn her about and begin to untie the rope at her wrists.

"Understand?" he asked again, this time much more firmly.

And now, with the prospect of being unfettered so close at hand, she found herself willing to say just about anything, and she offered him a barely audible aye.

The coarse rope tightened about her wrists for several seconds, as he obviously strained to untie the knot he'd placed in it. Then, all at once, like a sunburst from the heavens, she felt it: the wonderful sensation of being free once more.

She brought her hands around to the front of her and sat rubbing the abrasion the rope had left on her skin. She was free again. Full use of her limbs had been returned to her, and, with it, seemed to come a new flood of hope that she would find a way out of her plight, that she could break away from this frightening captor and return home with Faolan.

Just as this hope was dawning, however, she felt the stranger pulling her up. The next thing she knew, her cloak fell away from her completely, and he swept her up onto one of his hips and carried her, like a load of firewood, over to a nearby tree.

She kicked and clawed against his powerful grip. She screeched and bent her head in towards him, in an effort to bite his torso. But he was so much bigger and stronger than she, that she felt as helpless and insignificant as a mite perched on the face of a windswept daisy.

He could do *anything* to her, she realized in those horrific seconds. He could crack her in half, like the wishbone of a game bird, and use her limbs for kindling, if he so desired! Fortunately, however, that didn't appear to be what he had in mind. Rather, he hurriedly set her down, backed her up against the tree to which he'd walked, and circled behind her to bind her hands about its trunk.

He was going to tie her to the damnable thing! a voice within her exclaimed. He was going to lash her there, like a witch to a stake, and go off to spear that hare he'd mentioned. And, should anything happen to prevent his returning, she would simply be left to die a slow death of starvation.

Realizing all of this suddenly made something snap inside her. Her fear of his reprisal seemed to fly out of her head, and she found her mind racing, searching for some way to stop him from tying her up once more.

His *shoes* His thin, summer shoes were what her eyes lit upon in those desperate seconds, as he stood, straddling the narrow tree. And, as he continued trying to fetter her writhing wrists behind the trunk, she brought her sturdily sandaled right foot down upon his flimsily shod one.

There was a gruesome cracking sound in that instant, as though she'd actually broken one or two of his toes against the exposed tree roots that rested beneath him. But she didn't let it faze her. With lightning quickness, she stomped his foot once more, and, as she hoped, he let go of her hands.

She turned to see that he'd bent down to tend to

his throbbing extremity, and she realized that she would have only a second or two in which to flee. So she snatched up the spear he'd leaned against the tree, and took off running towards the east, with his howls of pain and anger echoing after her.

"Faolan! Faolan," she called back as she ran. She knew, in her heart, that this was probably futile. In his groggy, injured state, the harrier wasn't at all likely to be able to scramble to his feet and out-course the raider's dog. But she had to try, she told herself. She had to encourage her pet to escape while they both could. Failing that, she would find some way to come back for him. Or perhaps there was hope that the Norseman would take mercy on the poor hound, as he obviously had when he'd su-tured him earlier, and would simply choose to leave him behind before going on to his encampment. Either way, however, she silently vowed to do all she could to recover her dog.

For now, though, she simply had to run, to *fly*, to make her feet carry her, as quickly as possible, back to familiar territory, where she would have the chance of enlisting the help of some countrymen.

Only a moment or two had passed since her escape, yet it already felt as if she'd been running for an eternity. She was breathless, and her lungs ached so intensely that she was forced to give up calling for Faolan altogether. What was more, she was convinced that her captor was close behind her now. Even over the frenetic swishing of her own breath, the deafening pounding of her heart, she could have sworn she heard his speeding footfall.

What on earth had made her think she could outrun him? And what would she do when he finally overtook her? She could stop and throw the spear at him, she supposed. But could she really kill him? She'd never been called upon to use a spear; so, in truth, she had no idea whether or not she had the strength to deliver a fatal blow with it.

Her mind continued to race with such questions. But, miraculously, her feet kept racing as well. Inexplicably, as if by God's own divine hand, she was making it through the maze of trees before her and continuing to speed eastward, as if being carried on a cherub's wings.

Maybe she could outpace the Norseman, after all, she thought with an ecstatic tingle running through her. Though her people rarely travelled out of sight of their respective ring-forts, and she had, therefore, never been as far away from home as she was now, she desperately needed to believe that it was still possible for her to find her way back to kin and safety.

But, just as she was beginning to hold genuine hope of this, she definitely heard someone on her heels. An instant later, she was falling forward as the result of a heavy blow in the middle of her back. To her surprise, however, it wasn't a human form that pinioned her to the ground in the seconds that followed, but that of a dog—the raider's snarling, panting, red beast.

The next thing she heard was the dog's owner calling after them both with words she did not understand. The hound apparently understood them, though, because he stopped his growling at once and relinquished his ominous, toothy hold upon the back of Alanna's neck. Pawky creature that he was, however, he continued to straddle her, until his master reached them.

The raider stepped forward and picked up the spear Alanna had dropped as she'd fallen. Then he stowed it under his left arm and turned back to glare down at her with his sword drawn. She lifted her face with what strength she had left. Then she let her eyes travel up the length of the blade, as well as that of the arm that gripped it, until she again met her captor's gaze.

He was about to kill her. She saw it in his now-steely eyes: a look that said she had pushed him as far as anyone had ever dared, and that she would know no further mercy at his hands. Realizing this, acknowledging that this conqueror against a twilight, treetop-framed sky would be the last earthly sight she would see, she let her face drop to the cool, sweet soil beneath her, and she kissed her beloved Erin farewell.

She heard him step slightly away, and she tensed, readying herself for the blow that would surely come, the swipe of sharp steel that would sever her head from her body. But, to her amazement, she was still alive several seconds later, and all she felt was a searing pain at the crown of her head.

He was pulling her up by her hair, and she had no choice but to spring to her feet in an effort to end the awful, tearing sensation. Fortunately, he let go of her auburn mane, gripped one of her shoulders, and spun her about towards where he had set up camp.

"Walk," he ordered, with what felt like the tip of his sword poking into her back. Alanna knew it was best to oblige him.

"Next time, you die," she heard him hiss from behind her, as she made her way along on most unsteady legs.

"I shall not spare you again," he continued; and this utterance, to Alanna's dismay, was punctuated by a burning slap across her buttocks. It was a resounding blow. One she was certain could not have been produced merely by his hand. As she staggered in response, fighting to regain her footing, she found herself not only praying he wouldn't strike her again, but wondering precisely *what* he'd used to do so.

The flat of his sword, she suddenly realized. He had actually resorted to spanking her, as if she were an unruly child! Of all the *gall,* she silently fumed, doing her best to keep up with his quick strides, as he finally moved ahead of her and began hauling her along by one of her arms.

Of all the abominable gall! As if *she* were the wrongdoer in all of this, and he was somehow in the right! She'd never been spanked in her life, and she'd be damned if she'd let such an indignity go unavenged!

What mattered most, though, was that he hadn't chosen to kill her. And she knew now, as he continued to pull her along after him, that, if she wished to remain alive, she was going to have to take a more artful tack with him hence forward.

She would simply have to conceive a subtler plan the next time around . . . Such as a surreptitious pinch of a naturally growing poison, perhaps. Something that would not only incapacitate him, but his monstrous dog as well. What was more, she would have to act fairly quickly — before she was led so far away from her region, that she could no longer find her way home.

Three

With the girl finally trussed to the same tree he'd tried to tie her to earlier, Storr could breathe a sigh of relief. He had planned to go off immediately and hunt them both up some supper, but the toes she'd stomped when trying to flee were throbbing to such a degree, that he was forced to sit down now. He crossed to the fallen log and tried to determine whether or not she'd broken any of his bones.

He could have sworn he heard his assailant snicker, as he sank down upon the rotting bole and began to take off his right shoe. But one murderous glare up at her apparently caused her to grow sober again, and he instantly returned his gaze to the task at hand.

His foot hurt so much that he had to remove his shoe with the utmost care, and it was not until he pulled his injured extremity up towards his face for closer examination that he realized how comical his hunched and bowed posture must have looked to his captive. Ordinarily, he might have laughed at such a sight himself, but he was simply in too much pain at this point to find anything he'd suffered since meeting up with the damnable maiden, humorous. He had, in fact, been so incapacitated by her latest attack that he'd doubted whether he could catch up with her when she'd run off. As he hobbled hurriedly after her, he'd simply found himself grateful that he'd had the good sense to bring his ever-reliable Biorn along with him to attend to such matters in his stead.

If he'd had more foresight, he would have chosen to have his most trusted freeman accompany him on this scouting expedition as well. Leif would have proven invaluable now, with Storr's foot feeling too shattered to do anything more than swell up to a ludicrous size and refuse to be stuffed back into his shoe. Long admired for his skill in hunting, Leif would have supplied the second set of hands, the extra pair of vigilant eyes that Storr so desperately needed. But Storr had wanted to be alone on this particular trek. Weary of his antagonistic companions, he had craved only solitude and silence, and for a time—until he'd been assailed by this demented girl—he'd been fortunate enough to know both.

Two of his toes were broken, he concluded, with an angry cluck, carefully lowering his foot back to the ground. He would have to use what was left of his suturing thread to bind them to the bigger digits on that foot. Then he'd have to hope that such immobilization would allow them to mend, in spite of the journey he still had ahead of him. So, with this decided, he rose and limped over to his horse and saddle-pack.

"Broken?" he heard his captive inquire gingerly from the nearby tree.

He glared up at her seconds later, as he withdrew his thread and tottered back to settle down upon the log once more. Fortunately for them both, there didn't seem to be a trace of taunting in her voice as she made the inquiry. Nevertheless, he decided not to dignify it with a response. He was simply too furious with her to risk speaking just yet. The answer must have been apparent to the stupid chit, in any case. Obviously, a man wouldn't sit about tying his toes together, if they were still intact!

"I'm sorry," she offered after several seconds in a hushed voice.

Storr knew the phrase. He'd heard it often enough from the slovenly slaves he'd had to confront through the years. They were always sorry. Sorry when they'd been caught chatting, instead of working on his farm. Sorry when they hadn't broken up and carted their fair shares of soapstone over the course of a day. Sorry, whenever they had cause to believe that their actions, or more often, their inaction, might provoke some punishment. And this one claimed to be sorry now, too.

From the moment Storr had first spotted her and her blasted hound, he had shown them nothing but mercy, and what had he gotten in return? In the course of just a couple of hours, the crazed little witch had torn open his arrow wound, kicked his dog in the head, and broken two of his toes! And now she actually had the audacity to believe that this paltry apology could atone for it all!

"Truly, sire, I am," she dared to say again.

At this Storr finally took his attention away from binding his toes and turned to stare at her, his eyes narrowed to an amply enraged and skeptical squint.

He saw her pale a bit in response, and, with hidden satisfaction, he returned his gaze to his foot. He knew that his glower had said what no amount of fumbling about in her strange tongue could have: that he flatly refused to be guiled by her. She had simply offered him too much offense, for there to be any hope now of his being lured into a web of her cajolery.

"Nay, you are not," he spat, and, to both his relief and displeasure, the wench offered no rebuttal.

"Now," he began again, wincing as he eased his injured foot back into its shoe. "I go hunt hare to eat."

He rose from the log, and, to Alanna's dismay, his pained stride was directed right for her. Fortunately, however, his gaze dropped just before he reached her, and he bent down to retrieve the spear, which he'd set next to the tree when tying her up earlier. Then he turned abruptly away and headed off towards the north, apparently in search of other prey.

"How long will you be?" she found herself calling after him; and, though she half regretted having asked it, she knew she desperately needed a response. She could only hope that, given the angry looks he'd been flashing her, this anxious inquiry wasn't enough to provoke him to come back and thrash her.

It occurred to her, in those sinking seconds, that he might not respond at all, that he might simply choose to leave her writhing there, tortured with worry. But, to her surprise, he answered with a swiftness that told her he was far more fluent in Erse than she'd thought.

"Longer for the broken toes," he growled back pointedly. He beckoned for his dog in that same instant, and the huge beast sprang to its feet and trotted after him.

As they disappeared from view, it occurred to Alanna to raise her voice and cry out for help, on the off chance that there was a ring-fort close by. She stopped herself from doing so, however. She'd seen enough of the Norseman already to know that he probably wasn't fool enough to have chosen to set up camp too near an Erse settlement. Then, too, there was the danger of angering him to the point where he might follow through on his threat of killing her; and she knew that, no matter how close a tribe of her countrymen might be, the raider was closer still. Surely close enough to do away with her before anyone could come to her rescue.

So, rather than screaming, she found herself silently praying, as she heard her captor's footfall fade. She beseeched God to go with him and assure his safe return. For all the lunacy there seemed in making supplication for one's enemy, she knew her prayer was more for herself and Faolan, because, without the return of their captor, she was sure to become carrion trussed to a tree. Her poor Faolan would simply have to look on and whine, as she was reduced to dead flesh for the passing birds to feed upon. That fate was just too horrible for her to allow herself to continue to ponder it.

Amidst the silence that followed, she again looked over at her dog and saw that he appeared only slightly less dazed than he had when she'd regained consciousness herself. His eyelids were opened a bit, but it was as if his vision was too blurred or his mind still too dulled for him to really make out what he was seeing.

Damnable raider! Leaving her dear pet in such a state, then binding her so that she couldn't go to his aid! She wondered what on earth had possessed her to apologize to him, when it was so clear that it was *he* who should have been remorseful!

Anger and fear. She was realizing that they weren't emotions she'd ever had much occasion to feel. Her life, up until today, had been so predictable, so carefree and filled with her tribe's sense of Christian fellowship, that there'd simply been no cause for such emotions. But now, as night's darkness was beginning to fall like a smothering shroud all about her, she was becoming sorely familiar with them.

The pain caused by the chafing rope about her wrists convinced her that all of this really was happening, that it wasn't just part of some unusually vivid nightmare. How, after all, could she have ever conjured up a captor such as he? One with so beguiling a beauty about him and such a seductive slant in her native tongue? And where could she have imagined that he'd learned enough of her language to converse so readily with her?

From his Erse *slaves,* she realized, even as the voice within her was finishing the question. Who else could have taught him the tongue of Erin, but her own countrymen? This realization sent a chill through her. That was why he'd been so emphatic when he'd declared that she was "his." Clearly, he was a man who had come raiding before and had taken others, like herself, prisoner. Clearly, he'd had enough dealings with his unfortunate Erse captives to order them about in their native language and to understand and rebuke them for any impudence.

She was just one more to him, she acknowledged with a dry, angry swallow, one more lamb being culled for whatever barbarous purposes he and his kind had in mind. As he had told her earlier, he didn't care how high her rank was among her people, how privileged she was as a freewoman, because, to his way of thinking, she was no longer free.

She felt herself on the verge of tears as all of this began to sink in for her, but she fought back the burning urge to cry. She reminded herself that, just as with the Israelites under Egypt's enslaving pharaohs, all tyranny began as one man's thoughts governing another's and she wouldn't allow herself to be lulled into accepting the fate this captor was so obviously trying to push upon her. She might be forced to eat the food he hunted and drink from his waterskin, but she would not allow his will to fill her mind!

And, now, as some of her fear began to subside and she was in control of her thoughts once more, she again recalled the plan that had occurred to her earlier. She would poison the Norseman and his huge hound at her first opportunity. She would keep her eyes peeled, as they journeyed, for the purplish flowers and black berries of the deadly nightshade plant which her physician uncle had taught her about, and, with it, she would send this presumptuous abductor into a winter sleep or beyond!

Storr returned nearly an hour later with a dead rabbit and some sort of game bird in hand. It was, by his usual standards, a meager kill. Given the state his right foot was in, however, he felt he and Biorn had done fairly well. It was, in any case, more fare than they would have been apportioned back at the encampment with his fellow Vikings. Given the cramped conditions on their longships, they'd had room to bring only sour milk and dried fish along from their homeland. Consequently, there never seemed to be enough fresh game to go around at mealtime. There were, of course, the fine quantities of food they routinely stole from Erse villages. But, due to their decision to begin focusing their attacks on the fairly untapped territory about which Storr was presently out scouting, they hadn't replenished their provisions for several weeks now.

It was quite dark by this point, so Storr knew that his first task must be to light a fire and, without a word to his captive, he set about doing so.

"What did you bring back?" the maiden ventured somewhat brightly, as he made his painful way about the campsite, gathering up what twigs and branches he could spot on the forest floor.

Still angered by the damage she'd done to his foot, Storr considered not answering her. The question was simple enough, however. He'd understood it and knew the words needed to form a response. So, in the interests of appeasing her, and, thereby, possibly obtaining a peaceful night's sleep, he deigned to reply.

"Hare, as I promised. And a bird."

"A goose?" she asked hopefully.

He scowled over at her, as he knelt down and

began arranging the wood he'd collected into a readily ignitable pile. "Just a large bird," he snapped. "I do not know what your people call it."

"Well, it will surely be savory none the less," she returned in an amenable tone.

He didn't look up at her after that. He simply continued to ignore her, as he proceeded to start the fire and skin his kills by its light. Alanna went on learning what she could from him, nevertheless. She watched how quickly and efficiently he prepared his game with the knife he had stashed in his belt-strap, and she wondered at his ability to see so well by the fledgling fire's low flame. But he was a predator, she reminded herself, from a land said to be filled with horrible, fanged creatures who did their preying by night. So she supposed this gift of vision in darkness should not have surprised her.

Even from as far away as she was, she caught sight of a golden glimmer on one of his fingers, as his large, sturdy hands worked. A ring, she realized after a second or two. A band of gold where most Ersewomen wore their rings of betrothal . . . Perhaps he was actually married — if, in fact, such savages had any notion of so sacred a state. Somehow, though, the tales Alanna had heard of the Norse raiders had led her to believe that they satisfied their fleshly urges simply by ravishing and raping; and she couldn't imagine what call they had to steal Erin's maidens, if they truly had lawful wives back in their homeland.

She wanted very much to ask him about this now, to come right out and inquire as to what significance this shimmering finger ring might have. But, of course, she stopped herself. He looked too hungry and tired to be bothered with such a question, and she forwent asking it, in favor of a far more pressing one.

"Do you think . . . Might you untie me now, sire, with the evening meal so near?" she stammered uneasily.

Again he raised his eyes to her, his light-colored orbs looking quite luminous by the firelight. "Nay," he answered simply and returned to the work of whittling some spits for the game.

It was, indeed, as curt and frosty a response as he must have intended it to be. Given her attempt to flee, however, Alanna supposed it was, in some right, deserved.

Her voice wavered as she spoke again. " 'Tis not your intention, then, to feed me?"

He had his eyes fixed upon the business of impaling the skinned rabbit. "When the food is cooked, you shall be fed."

"But I . . ." Her words broke off, as his eyes flashed up furiously at her daring to argue with him. She swallowed back her fear, however, and tried again. "I must . . . must *empty* myself," she explained. "It has been hours since—"

He raised a silencing palm to her, and it was clear that he didn't wish to hear any more on the subject. Then, to her relief, he set the skewered rabbit down on a nearby rock and got up with a resigned groan. He obviously understood what she'd been trying to say, and she had every hope that he was rising in order to help her remedy her situation.

Storr took up his bloodied hunting spear in those seconds and limped over to his captive. It had occurred to him to simply let her remain trussed there until she wet herself. But, on second thought, he decided to oblige her. It was he, after all, who would have to abide her stench, if he forced her to swash her clothing. Moreover, he'd learned, through many years of having to endure the habits of younger sisters, that when a female indicated such a need, there was usually precious little time in which to accommodate it.

He stood well away from her, not allowing either of his feet to come within reach of hers as he untied her, and he growled a warning of punishment by death in her ear, should she again attempt to escape. She wisely chose not to, however, and, with all due swiftness, he had her arms detached from about the tree and retied at her back.

"Go," he ordered, giving her a nudge with his spearhead. "Into the shadows and go."

"Here? Before you?" she asked, obviously horrified at the prospect.

"Aye. Just two steps more. Out of the light."

She did as she was told, taking a couple more strides away from the fire's glow and into the cloaking darkness cast by the surrounding trees. Then she stood struggling to gather up the skirt of her tunic with her trussed hands. "Alas . . . I . . . I cannot," she declared, sounding, for reasons that confounded Storr, very close to tears.

Why couldn't she? he wondered. The Erse slaves on his farmstead did it all the time, and quite unashamedly. Like the race of unclean cattle that they were, they rarely bothered to use the privy. Rather, they simply squatted wherever they found themselves when nature called . . . But no, she meant her tunic, he realized. She couldn't seem to raise it sufficiently with her hands bound. So, without a second thought, Storr bent down and lifted the garment for her.

Alanna froze with fear, as she felt the raider's hands at her calves. Then, all at once, her legs were exposed to the evening chill, and she reflexively issued a terrified screech. He was going to rape her! She wasn't entirely sure what rape entailed, but, in spite of her chaste Christian upbringing, she knew that it obviously began with the lifting of a woman's frock. So she was certain that it was what was in store for her now. Before she could give forth another cry of protest, however, her captor was once again snarling at her.

"Your tunic. I lift your tunic so you can . . . empty yourself," he explained in annoyance.

She heaved a sigh of relief. *Of course.* She'd told him she was unable to gather up her shift with her hands tied behind her, and he was just trying to help. But now, to her continuing chagrin, she found she was too upset by the misunderstanding to will her body to release its burden.

His hands were still upon her. She could feel them holding her tunic up in a billowy clump at the level of her thighs. And, suddenly, the practiced way in which he'd executed this move, his ready understanding of all she'd tried to say about this humiliating need of hers, made her breath catch in her throat, and she couldn't seem to bid any part of herself to function.

He'd done this before, she realized with a hot flush coming over her. Such familiarity with the opposite sex was barely imaginable to her. Yet this man had hiked up her tunic with such experienced agility, that she could only conclude that he did this sort of thing fairly often, and the very thought of it seemed to make every inch of her turn to stone.

"Well, make haste," he urged after several seconds. "Empty yourself, chit! I am hungry!"

He sounded terribly vexed, and she knew she shouldn't risk displeasing him further, but her body still seemed to disregard her command. There she had been, just seconds before, so swollen with the need to pass water that she thought she'd burst if her captor chanced to grab her about the middle, yet nothing, for the life of her, was happening now!

"On with it, wench," he exclaimed again. "If this is just another of your ploys, I shall—"

"Nay! Nay, sire. I swear to thee 'tis no trick. The need is real," she blurted anxiously. With that, she squeezed her eyes shut and concentrated, and, as if inspired by her flood of words, the warm liquid did, indeed, begin to flow from her. She heard it pouring forth onto the ground below, and, to her deep embarrassment, she knew he heard it, too. In those seconds of heavenly relief, she didn't care, however. Relief was all she felt or seemed able to feel. Emptying herself, after the torturous hours of aching to do so, brought an ecstasy that seemed to rub out all sense of anything else. And, perhaps, she thought, *this* was what carnal relations with a man was like. Maybe one felt so good in the midst of the act that all cause for self-consciousness was obliterated.

But now, as the last of her burden left her and she felt him release her garment and let it fall back into place, that horrible sense of embarrassment filled her once more. She, therefore, bit her lip and kept her gaze locked upon the ground, as he turned her about and nudged her back towards where he'd had her tied.

"Do not truss me to the tree again, I pray thee," she heard herself say in a feeble voice as they trudged along.

"Nay," he answered "Over on the log. By the fire. You cannot get far with your hands tied, I warrant."

He was probably right about that; but time would have to tell, she reassured herself. For the present, in any case, he was correct in assuming that she wouldn't try to flee. It was dark, after all, and, though she would never deign to admit it to him, she was, doubtless, every bit as hungry and thirsty as he.

She went to obediently sink down upon the log as she reached it, but she found him pushing her over to its left end. After several seconds, it became apparent to her that he simply wished to keep her in his line of sight as he returned to his cooking. And, as she finally came to rest upon the bole, she again felt the bruising pain of his punishing sword swipe . . . it served as an ample reminder to her. No matter what mercy, what civility he had shown her in allowing her to relieve herself, he was still a raider, a captor—one capable of great reprisal if she made another attempt to escape. Nevertheless, she couldn't help but sense that, as long as she obeyed him, he would do her no real harm. If he'd planned to violate her, after all, he would surely have acted upon it by now, she kept telling herself. She was also mindful, however, that all that might have prevented him from satisfying such needs by this point was the greater need for food and drink.

She watched his profile, as he knelt at the fire once more and skewered the game bird on the spit he'd prepared. Then he extended both kills over the fire and, as if by reflex, turned back to flash her a look that warned her against stirring from where she'd been put.

She didn't know what to say to him, but she felt an almost desperate need to converse in those seconds. Anything seemed preferable to letting her thoughts stray onto the unspeakable possibility of being defiled by him. She had learned enough to know that such acts often led to a woman finding herself with child, and the disgrace that would come with so dire a state was just too much for her to even contemplate. "I . . . I was wondering about the . . . the golden ring you wear on your finger, sire," she began, in as ingratiating a tone as she could muster. "Prithee, would you tell me . . . why it is you wear it?"

Storr raised an eyebrow as he heard her stammering out this mystifying question. He'd seen her rage at him just a few hours earlier. He'd spied the very fires of Hell burning in her livid eyes, yet her voice was now as dulcet as freshly ladled honey. What a curiosity she was!

He turned back to face her with his amazed brow still raised, and he could see in a glance that she realized this was absolutely the last question he'd expected from her. Then, without a word, he returned his gaze to the game he was roasting.

"Nay. Verily, sire. I do not jest, but truly wish to know," she assured.

He swallowed uneasily, suddenly acknowledging that he had absolutely no intentions of answering this particular question. *Freyja*. His beloved Freyja had given the ring to him on their wedding day, but the silly girl could not possibly have known that this was a forbidden subject. No one, neither serf nor chieftain, had ever had the nerve to broach so emotionally charged a topic with him, and this pesky captive couldn't begin to grasp what danger she'd placed herself in by doing so.

Storr was silent, fuming for several seconds more. Then he addressed her in a threateningly low voice. " 'Tis no concern of yours!"

"Very . . . very well," she replied. "I did not mean to accuse you of stealing it from an Erseman, of course. That was not my intent, you understand."

Again Storr turned and glared at her, wondering how much longer she would dare to go on digging her own grave with her tongue. To his surprise, however, his threatening look did not seem to dissuade her. She just kept on speaking.

"I simply wished to know if the ring means, as it doth here in Erin, that you have been wed."

"Have *you?* he countered bitingly, and he realized in that instant that there was yet another reason why he found this line of questioning so galling. It was he who was the captor, after all, and, since he hadn't been brazen enough to inquire about her marital state, he was hard-pressed to understand why *she* should presume to do so with *him*. Why, if she had fallen into other hands amongst his raiding party, those of Sigurd or his kin, she wouldn't even have been asked. She would simply have been forced down upon a spread cloak or blanket, and her captor would see for himself if virginal blood was spilt by his entry! So, *damn her,* Storr inwardly raged, she had better answer his question now or risk having all civility leave him, as well!

Alanna recoiled at having the inquiry thrown back at her with such ire. She didn't really know why, but she felt, for all the world, as though the raider had his sword drawn upon her once more. "Nay," she choked. "My aunt and uncle think me too young yet." This was not entirely true, of course. Anyone could see that she was of marriageable age. It seemed wisest, however, to attempt to keep the outlander from thinking of her as such.

Try as he might to fight it in those seconds, Storr couldn't help letting his eyes travel down to the voluptuous flesh revealed by her torn tunic. "You look to me to be old enough," he declared, suppressing a smirk as he turned back to face the fire. He allowed himself to smile more fully, once his expression was out of her view. Though it wasn't he who had brought up the subject, he was, in fact, relieved to hear that the girl probably wasn't pregnant, that he was stuck with bringing back only one more mouth to feed, rather than two. Had she been with child, he would, of course, be forced to kill the infant upon its birth; and that was definitely not a task to which he was feeling particularly equal these days.

Heaven knew, he had seen enough of it in his

youth: his father, as master of his steading, having to carry out the grim duty of ordering a newborn's death, as its enslaved mother screeched her protests all the while. But such was the responsibility that came with being a chieftain. It was simply the price a master paid for the pleasure of bedding his Erse concubines . . . And that was one of the reasons why Storr had refrained from indulging in the privilege since he'd inherited his father's position. That and his immeasurable love for Freyja, of course. With a woman as splendid as she at a man's side, what possible need would he have for seeking any other? But Freyja was gone, he reminded himself again, clenching his teeth with bitterness. She was gone, and it was all this accursed chit's fault for bringing the greatest loss of his life to mind once more!

"I am not wed," he suddenly hissed. "I was once, but I am not now. And, if you dare to speak to me of it again, those words shall be your last!"

The girl, looking both surprised and chagrined by his outburst, let her cocoa brown eyes study him for several seconds more, before dropping her gaze. Then she showed the good sense to allow a long silence to ensue, and Storr seized the quiet in order to calm himself and collect his thoughts.

He shook his head in wonder, as he continued to roast his kills. He was astounded at her uncanny ability to find his deepest wounds, be they physical or of the soul, and gouge them so unmercifully. First, it had been his arrow wound. She had spied it and closed in upon it with such rapidity that afternoon, that he was finally beginning to realize that she must have watched him from some hiding place before charging at him. Logic told him now that she could not have made such a shrewd and effective move without the time to behold him at length. Then, as if blessed with a witch's foreknowing, she had pinpointed the very subject that could destroy him, the only topic that had the power to shred his heart as a cat's claws might.

He could still feel the throbbing in his injured upper arm. He was, at last, aware of how the swelling, caused by its having been torn open anew, was making his flesh strain the suturing. His mind up until now had been occupied with having to deal with this plaguing captive and her dog. Then he'd had to focus all of his energy upon scaring up an evening meal in the day's fading light. But now, with the vexing maiden so near, like a thistle caught in his clothing, he was reminded, on every level, of all the damage she'd done.

He had heard the Norse *skalds* — ever fond of recounting the battles in which they never took part — refer to arrows as "the wounding bees," and it finally dawned on him why he'd always found that likening so annoying. Any true warrior knew that there was no comparison between a mere sting and the agony of having one's flesh sheared open by a speeding arrowhead. So, too, there was no expressing the torture of losing one's beloved bride by one's own, foolish hand—the hand that still wore the golden ring she had had wrought for him. And his suffering was being made all the more acute by the fact that this presumptuous Erse prisoner—a little dark-eyed wench who could never hope to offer him the same pleasures he'd known in Freyja's arms—had proven churlish enough to bring it all down upon him once more. What he felt now wasn't at all like the *skald's* single bee sting. Rather, it was as an entire nest of wasps ruthlessly jabbing at him, both inside and out!

She, this harpy of a captive, had been the human presence he'd sensed in the thicket as he'd bathed, a voice within him suddenly exclaimed. As he continued to reflect upon it, he was certain that there had been no one watching him in the forest, prior to her attack. Yet, he had definitely felt such an onlooker in the thicket near the brook. It was *then* that she'd had the time to study him at length and spot the wound in his arm, he concluded. And, later, when her daft little dog had torn himself open, she had returned to rescue him. So, she had, indeed, seen Storr disrobed, and perhaps that was what accounted for her blushfulness since he'd captured her . . . Yes. Most of his father's concubines were blushful at times, Storr silently conceded. But not like this one. Not so consistently and wittingly as she.

"You saw me earlier, as I bathed," he declared abruptly, turning away from the fire and staring at her invincibly.

Her eyes, still locked upon her feet, flashed up and met his for half a second. Then they quickly escaped to the ground once more. "Nay, sire," she whispered.

He turned more fully to her. To Alanna's relief, his tone was not accusatory, but simply one of realization. "Aye. You did," he maintained. "I felt there was someone in the thicket, and I was right. It was *you* hiding there, was it not? And that was how you knew just where to strike me with your brooch."

Again she was silent, as if she either didn't dare to argue with him or was simply too aware of his certainty to see any point in continuing to lie about the matter.

"You saw me . . . Nay, *studied* me with no raiment, and you made no move to flee," he went on, just grateful that her language was coming to him so readily now, that he was remembering enough Erse to confront her on this point and keep her in her place. He'd always relied upon his chief freeman to do the bulk of the conversing with his family's slaves but, to his surprise, he did seem to have absorbed more of the language than he'd realized.

"Nay, sire," she offered again in her own defense. "You must know, 'tis a sin to the Erse . . . such . . . such nakedness."

Her voice was almost pleading by this point, and Storr donned a knowing smirk and turned back to the fire. She'd seen him, most certainly. The little pry had seen him unclothed and unarmed. So, was it really any wonder that she'd known just where to strike him when the need had arisen? Was it truly surprising that she seemed to sense, as a lover would, what questions would best cut to the heart of him?

"You saw me wearing naught, and yet you screamed so when I lifted your shift and saw only your legs?" he continued in teasing amazement.

"Oh, stop," she blurted, sounding quite distressed. "I swear to you that I will not say a word more in your keeping, if you will only leave off speaking of this!"

Storr returned his attention to the browning rabbit and bird. "Very well," he agreed after several seconds. "But I do hope you were pleased by what you saw . . . You must have been, for I sensed you there for quite some time," he added, and he had to bite his lip in that instant to keep from laughing aloud. Such a look of horror from her, such dismay at having been caught nosing about where her ridiculous deity had supposedly forbidden her to. They were absurd, really: the Erse's childish views towards the ways of the flesh. They were preposterous, and it made some playful, boyish part of Storr want to continue to tease her about the incident—want to hurt her as much as she'd hurt him.

Deep inside, he realized that he took pleasure in seeing her blush, in hearing her voice waver and crack, as though he were actually one of Erin's clergy having caught her perusing his body. It had all been most entertaining: the way in which she'd sent her long-earred harrier darting out of the thicket, her infantile curiosity about matters that her parents had evidently lacked the dutifulness to speak of with her. It made Storr want to roar with laughter, and he was becoming sorrily aware that he hadn't known such amusement for a very long time.

Four

When, at last, the game appeared to be cooked, Storr withdrew both skewers from the flame and propped them against a nearby rock. Then he crossed to his horse, withdrew a wooden bowl from his saddle-pack, and returned to the fire to begin peeling the cooked meat from the carcasses. Biorn, in response, rose from where he'd been lying since their hunt, and lumbered over to claim his fair share. The harrier, obviously roused by the aroma of the roasted meat as well, struggled onto his belly and slowly lifted his head.

"Per chance, still too roiled by my questions to eat?" Storr inquired of his captive, as his fingers worked to quickly fill the bowl.

Alanna, also fully aware that supper was about to be served, had her eyes locked squarely upon him. "Nay," she replied without hesitation.

He smiled and raised an eyebrow at her. "I thought not."

"But you must untie me, sire, mustn't you, so that I might feed myself?"

Some perverse, impulsive part of Storr actually stopped to consider the advantages of attempting to perform this task for her—the parting of her pouty lips to his ready fingers. But he sensed that the time such an effort would require wouldn't be outweighed by its pleasures. She was, in spite of any folly she might have indulged in at the brook, probably too much of an innocent for his tastes. So, making certain that his spear was well out of her reach and resheathing his knife in his belt-strap, he rose and went over to the log to untruss her.

"Only for eating," he warned, as his hands worked behind her. "Then you're tied again."

She nodded. "Aye. I do understand."

Storr extended the serving bowl to her seconds later, watching now, with measured gazes, not her sensuality as she ate, but that she consumed no more than what he felt to be her due. That was the sorry way of the world, he silently acknowledged, as she carried out the plodding work of chewing and swallowing. It was one thing to fantasize about a wench when one's back was turned to her; it was quite another once she was self-consciously close.

"Might . . . might I have some drink as well, sire?" she asked after a moment or two.

Storr, having been squatting before the log as she partook of the kill, rose to his full height and went to his horse to retrieve his waterskin. "What is this 'sire,' you keep calling me? Do you dishonor me with it?" he asked, as he crossed back to her and handed her the skin.

"Oh, Heavens, nay. 'Tis a title of respect, I assure you," she replied, then tipped back her head and took a long drink of the liquid. "What, after all, do your people call you, if not sire?"

"*Master.* My slaves and my freemen call me master, of course."

She was drinking again, and she looked up over the skin at him with a furrowed brow. "Master? Sons and daughters of Erin call you master?"

Storr scowled. "Aye. 'Tis fitting, for I am the chieftain of the region."

She lowered the skin a second time and wiped her wet lips with the sleeve of her tunic. "Oh, but you must be aware, sire, that you are not their true master. Nor, I am sorry to tell, could you ever be mine, for only God can be thus."

Storr had the urge to bend down and slap her in that instant. Such impudence would surely not have gone unpunished in the company of others. But, since they were alone here and he was too hungry and tired for any resultant hysteria from the girl, he simply took hold of the serving bowl and jerked it from her grip. "You have taken your share," he snapped. "Norse law says 'tis Biorn and I, the *hunters,* who should have eaten first." With that, he turned away from her and strode to the fire.

"But what of Faolan?" she beseeched. "He must eat, too, mustn't he . . . with all the blood he lost today?"

Storr, clenching his jaw with annoyance stormed back to the log and slapped several slices of the meat onto her lap. "Feed and water him, then, wench! But leave enough for Biorn and me to drink!"

Alanna accepted the food from the raider with a mystified scowl. What on earth had she said to anger him this time? She'd merely explained that the Christian faith was such that only God could truly be called one's master, and she'd certainly meant no disrespect by saying so.

What a thin-skinned lot they were, these Vikings! Given their alleged ruthlessness and disregard for the lives and property of others, Alanna would never have guessed how easy it would be to offend one of them. However, she wasted no further time with continuing to contemplate this irony. She knew that she must see to Faolan's needs immediately, before the raider again trussed her hands. So, she slid down the log to where her still-dazed companion lay and knelt to begin ministering to him.

Meanwhile, her captor was doing essentially the same with his pet. In between his own bites of food, he tossed portions of the meat to the hound and watched with enjoyment as the creature caught them in his mouth. And, back and forth this alternation, this disgusting interaction went, until the savage pair had not only emptied the large bowl, but picked both carcasses clean as well.

Then, having accomplished this, her abductor came and towered over her once more. "The water," he demanded, thrusting one of his huge hands at her.

She hurriedly squeezed a bit more of it into Faolan's mouth. Then she gave the skin back to its owner and sank down to the ground, so she could hug and stroke her pet, while her hands were still free to do so.

"How is he?" she heard the raider inquire, after he'd taken a lengthy drink.

She didn't bother to look up at him. "Still a bit dazed by your blow," she answered with an edge to her voice. "But it appears you've stitched him well enough."

"Good."

"I think, though, that you would do him even greater service, if you would kindly allow me to hold him for a few minutes more."

Storr, feeling, as always, much more amiable after having eaten, settled upon the log and continued to look down at the maiden and her pet. "Very well. A few minutes."

"My thanks, sire," she replied, her sweet tone only partially masking the rancor she felt. No matter how innocuous the circumstances, she deeply resented being made this monster's after-supper entertainment. Yet that, clearly, was what she and Faolan were at this point!

"What is that you call him? Fay . . . ?" the Norseman broke off questioningly.

"Fay-lin," she pronounced, again with an edge to her voice. "Faolan."

"What does it mean? Faolan? I have not heard this name before."

"Little wolf."

Storr laughed. "Little wolf?" he echoed with surprise. "Who gave him such a name?"

Alanna glared up at him indignantly, hugging the harrier more tightly to her. "I did. He is my dog."

"Aye, but, how did he come to *earn* such a noble name? Does he bite? For we have seen that he can run and hide. But that more befits a hare, than a wolf, does it not?"

Alanna fixed her jaw and narrowed her eyes at this cruel, mocking stranger. "Aye. He bites well enough, when fairly matched . . . And so do I, for that matter," she added in a warning tone. She hoped that this threat would help to wipe some of the aggravating smirk off her captor's face in those seconds, but, instead, he looked all the more amused.

"I doubt it not," he said, clearly enticed by the challenge he seemed to perceive in her words.

Though his sportiveness made a shiver run through Alanna, she continued to feel that an abrasive tack was wisest at this point. She sensed that he would better be dissuaded from forcing himself upon her, if she continued to keep him bantering . . . Those eyes, those penetrating blue eyes of his were so disarming, that she knew instinctively that any distraction she could offer was better than allowing a seductive silence to take place between them.

"And what of *your* dog?" she countered. "Is he any better named? Is he, per chance, called savage or monster, as he should be?"

A smile tugged at the corner of Storr's mouth, as he looked over at Biorn. The big hound was busy with his usual, after-supper grooming, and Storr couldn't help picturing him as he'd been in his puppyhood: toothless and tiny as a baby otter. Having known his dear companion from so tender an age, it was, even today, difficult for Storr to understand why others were often so afeard of him.

Still keeping his eyes fixed on his pet, Storr issued a light laugh as he answered. "I call him Biorn. 'Tis our word for bear. Many Norsemen name their sons Bear. 'Tis meant to give them strength and courage when they grow up."

Alanna furrowed her brow. "I do not know this word bear, as you use it. In my tongue it means only to endure. Or to bear a child . . . to give birth."

The raider looked at first as though he thought

77

she spoke in jest. Then his expression grew more serious. "Oh, of course not. For there are no bears in Erin, are there?"

Alanna shook her head slightly. Then, to her surprise, her captor suddenly dropped to his knees on the ground beside her. Again he unsheathed his knife, and she reflexively drew away from him. She realized she had nothing to fear, however, as he bent forward and began scratching about in the dirt with the weapon. *He was simply drawing something with it,* she acknowledged with a relieved sigh. Though she couldn't make out much of what his scratches were producing, with his body blocking the fire's light, it was instantly clear to her that it was some kind of script or picture which he intended to have her regard. And, seconds later, as he finally pulled back from the crude rendering, she saw that it was a burly-looking creature that walked on all fours.

"Very large," the Norseman stressed, reaching out to augment the drawing by adding great, puffy strokes to its coat. "Many times bigger than a man."

Alanna continued to study the furry form. "And they are fierce, these bears?" she inquired, her eyes wide with an interest that Storr found strangely charming.

"Aye. Fierce both of claw and tooth," he replied, curling the fingers on his right hand, as if to simulate such a creature's paw, and pretending to swipe at her with it. "Known to kill and eat entire clans."

Alanna couldn't help recoiling at the bestial gesture. "Oh, well, then, this land of yours cannot be very pleasant, can it? Surely not one that I would want to visit."

Again looking genuinely displeased by her words, he withdrew from her, got back to his knees, and rose to his feet. "But you belong to me now," he stated once more, wiping his dirt-coated palms on his breeches. "And you *shall* go there with me."

Clearly not wishing to allow her further opportunity to argue this point, he crossed to his horse and, after rummaging around in his saddle-pack, withdrew what looked to Alanna to be a small sheet of rolled-up parchment. Then he returned to the fire with a duteous air and sat down to unfurl and study whatever it was.

Storr's teeth were still clenched with anger, as he proceeded to peruse the map he'd created on this scouting trip. It was pitch-black outside now, and the chit's infernal insistence that she still possessed free will had made him decide to end their discourse and use the remaining firelight to add what he'd learned today to his charting. Despite his efforts to concentrate, however, he couldn't help continuing to fume. His captive was obviously bright and had shown signs of being able to prove good and entertaining company for him. But then her blessed headstrongness had come to the fore once again, and Storr had realized that he had much more important — and far less aggravating — matters to attend to, before bedding down for the night.

He studied his handiwork for a couple minutes more, doing his level best to put the girl out of mind, and determine where the map needed supplementation. Then, having decided this, he rose and returned to his saddle-pack in order to withdraw the quill and berry ink with which to do so.

"What is that?" he heard his captive ask, once he'd settled back down before the fire. He had tried to keep his back to her since he'd left her, but he was still aware of her stirring where she sat. She was, evidently, sidling about in an effort to catch a glimpse of what he was working on.

She certainly was the inquisitive sort! Even his simple rendering of a bear had seemed to pique more interest in her than he'd seen in any other maiden, and her claim that she was of Erin's learned upper class now seemed all the more substantiated. Storr's short stays in this land had already taught him that the Erse had even more of a love for things written than his own people did, and he realized how he must have been torturing the girl by not agreeing to let her come and have a look at his parchment.

" 'Tis a map," he grunted after several seconds. "But 'tis no concern of yours."

Her voice said she was undaunted by his gruffness. "A map of what, good sire?"

"Of here," Storr snarled.

"Of Erin, you mean? The whole of Erin?" she pursued, as though she had never had occasion to see such a thing and could hardly conceive of it.

"Nay. Of *here,* ye meddlesome wench," Storr exclaimed, beginning to pen in some lines that indicated the settlements he'd snuck up on that very morning. "Now, just pet your harrier, will you, and kindly grant me some silence!"

To Storr's surprise, a minute or two later, he actually felt the girl standing just behind him. He turned back to glare at her with fire in his eyes. He could scarcely believe she had succeeded in rising and striding across the short distance between them, without his having been aware of it before now! But here she stood—and such was the concentration needed to produce an accurate map, he silently excused. Such, too, was this foolish maiden's jeopardous curiosity! It had obviously gotten her into great trouble at the brook earlier. She'd lost her very freedom due to it, in fact, and it was about to see her penalized once again.

"I told you not to move," Storr bellowed, and, without a second thought, he reached up, grabbed one of her hands, and jerked her down to the ground beside him. "You are untrussed, and I might have thought you stealing up to attack me!"

"With what?" she asked, her voice cracking defensively. She couldn't seem to fight a whimper, as

81

she shifted to a sitting position and reached down to brush off the dirt that had smirched her tunic as he'd yanked her to her knees. " 'Tis you who has the knife and sword and spear. What possible harm could I do thee? I simply wished to see the map. Nothing more, sire."

"Oh, look then, if you must," Storr hissed, picking it up and holding it angrily out before her.

Without hesitation, she placed her hands near his on the parchment's furled edges. Then she drew up even closer to study it in the dim light. "And where are we now?" she asked after several seconds.

Storr was somewhat surprised by this question. "You do not know?"

She gave her head an innocent shake and her doelike eyes met his entreatingly.

Storr supposed this could be the truth. He had been told that his Erse slaves often seemed to know little of their own land, beyond the boundaries of their respective ring-forts. But how could a race be so damnably timid? he wondered. How could one possibly come to know one's potential enemies and allies, when one never dared wander beyond one's own fence? Even given this pitiful ignorance, however, he saw absolutely no advantage in orienting the girl. Clearly, it could only serve to facilitate any future escape attempts on her part. "This is your land, not Storr's. 'Tis you who should be telling where we are," he admonished.

The girl was silent for several seconds, as though choosing to ignore this reproof. Then, seemingly out of the blue, she lifted a finger and brought it down upon a cliff-sheltered cove, which was located along the southeastern coast. Storr had, in fact, penned the recess onto the parchment only minutes before.

"Here," she said triumphantly. "I know this stretch of shore. 'Tis where my family lives." She continued to eye it, almost longingly, for several seconds. Then she spoke again. "And, if you will kindly let me return to them, sire, I swear that I shall never tell of seeing you."

Her voice wavered wrenchingly as she made this pledge, yet Storr knew he must disregard it. Yes. Of course her eyes glistened with sincerity now, for she was his *captive*. But his common sense told him that a few days hence, when she was safely back with her people, she would finally succumb to the urge to warn them of a coming Viking raid. It was simply human nature to protect one's own, just as it was in Storr's nature to safeguard his men from the deadly forearming that would come with the girl's monition. He was sorely aware that, in the end, they would both be bound by their respective loyalties, and he did his best to let his eyes convey this important truth to her.

"But you *shall*," Alanna heard him answer, in an undertone that made her breath catch in her throat in those seconds. The flickering firelight was reflected in his eyes as she beheld him at this angle, and she couldn't help being taken aback by the certainty . . . nay, almost the *sadness* with which he'd said it. That instant seemed to freeze for her, and she saw for the first time, the age, the wisdom in his face, the subtle lines between his brows and under his eyes that bespoke all the years he had lived beyond her own. They somehow told of things too violent, too tragic for her to even imagine.

Strangely, though, his voice was no longer scolding. He wasn't annoyed or angry at her, as it seemed he'd been from the moment they'd encountered one another. Rather, it was resignation she sensed in him, and she realized, in that frozen grain of time, that he was, beyond question or pause, absolutely right. Despite any efforts she might make to convince him that his presence would remain a secret, she knew that she would, indeed, tell her clan of him. It was, apart from all Christian considerations, just natural to do so, and no amount of pleading on her part would convince either of them otherwise. She was finally aware now that she could no more lie to his eyes — those sagacious orbs, as blue as the eternal sky — than she could to a clergyman of the Mother Church. Not about *this,* in any case.

So, she said nothing more on the subject, but simply bit her lip and tearfully relinquished her hold on the map. Then she pushed away from him slightly, drew her knees up to her body, and sat clasping them to her chest in the evening chill. To both her relief and dismay, it was finally dawning upon her that he was somehow just as much a captive in all of this as she. He didn't really want her. He was simply stuck with her, because he could not risk having her return to her people with news of him. She was just a burden to him, a thorn in his foot on this scouting trip of his; and, for some mystifying reason, he had chosen to spare her so far. He had actually troubled to feed her and had worked to converse with her in a tongue that was not his own. She didn't understand it, but she knew it was for the best not to question such mercifulness any further. The terror inherent in imagining that each moment, each hour might be her last, would surely drive her out of her senses, and she realized that she had to do everything in her power to keep her wits about her.

Even given all of this, however, an odd sort of peace began to wash over her, as she continued to hunch against the night's dampness. While there had been little hope in his voice, in his eyes, there had also been no malice or lust. Having seen this for herself, having dared to look at him long enough to recognize that whatever carnal designs he had were buried deeply, safely within him, she could rest easier in the darkness. As the fire died, she could dare to let herself fall asleep.

"Cold?" the raider asked, interrupting her thoughts.

She nodded.

"Go fetch your cloak then," he said, pointing back towards the log, where the garment had fallen away from her earlier.

Alanna seized the opportunity to do so. She threw the cloak over her shivering shoulders, and tied it about her the instant her hands came upon it. Then she stopped to gather up Faolan in her arms and bring him closer to the fire as well.

The Norseman, meanwhile, had returned to his saddle-pack. He'd apparently finished working on his map, as she'd sat ruminating, and was now tucking it and his writing implements away for the night. Alanna watched him, as she sank down before the fire once more. She noted his continued methodicalness, as he went on to finally relieve his stallion of its saddle and to offer him food and water.

A seeming adjunct to these Norseman being such a warlike lot, she realized, was the fact that they were clearly so resourceful and disciplined. They had found need to create great, ranging maps of lands which her own people had never bothered to chart, and their raiding ships were said to be awesomely crafted and carved. They were obviously a very vigilant and thorough race — two traits that she knew weren't, by any means, offensive to the Church. Such character, at least, helped to assure that she wasn't apt to fall into the hands of any Erse raiders while in this man's keeping, and she did find an odd sort of comfort in that.

On the other hand, she acknowledged with a soft groan seconds later, it was that same vigilance that was making her captor gather up the rope that he'd had tied about her wrists earlier, and return to her with it to do so again. Fortunately, however, he did not carry out this task with his previous brusqueness, but seemed almost gentle to her, as he walked behind her and drew both of her hands back in his own. His knotting, too, seemed more lenient somehow, leaving her wrists more give in which to move about.

Then, almost as if to make up for the binding, he crossed back to his saddle-pack and returned to her with a small, folded blanket. To her surprise, however, he didn't drape it over her as he reached her, but rolled it into a bolsterlike shape.

She looked up at him questioningly. "A pillow?"

He nodded and knelt to set it down behind her.

"But what will *you* lay your head upon?"

"The same," he answered matter-of-factly, giving the wide roll-up a pat on the end nearest him.

She was unable to hide her trepidation at this. "Right beside me?"

He smiled at her uneasy response and offered her a shrug. "Well, I've only one blanket. Would you have me take up my sword and cut it in half?"

"Nay. I suppose not," she conceded after several seconds, using her forearms, as best she could, to close her cloak about the front of her. Then she slowly reclined until her head reached the makeshift bolster.

Sweet Jesus, he intended to sleep with her, a panicked voice exclaimed within her. *Sleep with her!* A grown man, a total stranger huddled up next to her in the night with his head resting upon the same pillow! It would have been a horrendous proposition under any circumstances, but it was made all the worse now by the fact that her hands, her primary means of defense, were trussed behind her!

She wanted to cry, to offer some sort of protest; but she knew there would probably be no point in it. He had already proven himself to be a man who did what he said he was going to, and there seemed no reason to believe that the sleeping arrangement he'd just set forth would be any exception.

But he was probably right, she tried to tell herself. There was only one pillow to share and only the warmth of their huddled bodies to be had, once the fire died. So, what possible harm would there be in it? He was still fully clothed, and, as long as she was careful to keep her tunic and cloak anchored about her, she was relatively certain that she would not wake to find herself a sullied woman.

A moment or two later, however, as he finally lay down next to her and spread his heavy cape over them both, her efforts to calm herself seemed obliterated. It was as with his raising her tunic for her earlier. His manner was just so nonchalant, as he wrapped one of his brawny arms about her and drew her and Faolan up against him — into the hollow of his curled-up form — that shock was all she could feel for quite some time afterwards.

It wasn't so bad, though, she realized, as the minutes passed and she finally began to relax a little. He was very warm, very large, and enveloping, and these sensations weren't altogether unpleasant, when compared to the cold which now emanated from both the earth beneath her and the forest-darkened sky overhead. He was from Thule, after all, she reminded herself, a land said to be frightfully cold throughout most of the year. So, it was probably just reflexive for him to snug up with the nearest body at nightfall, in an effort to keep warm.

Then, though she wouldn't dare to turn back and confirm this for herself, Alanna heard her captor's big hound come and settle just to the right of his master. And there she and her abductor lay, pressed between their respective pets, sharing in all the heat four bodies could generate in the night.

"How far to your encampment?" she found herself asking, finally breaking the silence between them in a meek tone.

"Two days," her captor answered. "Per chance three with you and Faolan along."

She stared out into the darkness to the left of her and continued to listen to the fire, as the last of the burning wood crackled and fell. For the first time since she'd been captured, Alanna began to consider her aunt and uncle, and how terribly worried they must have become about her by now. For the first time, too, she allowed herself to ponder the horrible possibility that she might not be able to break away from the Norseman and return home.

But her fate was not sealed just yet, she told herself with a brave swallow. By the raider's own admission, two to three days still lay ahead in which she could turn the tables on him, and, as the good Lord was her Maker, she had every intention of doing so!

Storr lay listening to the gentle respiration of his most recent acquisition and her dog. She had certainly fallen silent when he'd predicted that, in spite of any claims she might make, she would indeed warn her people of his presence, if he set her free. And, while grateful for her apparent acquiescence now, he was also suspicious of it. Women with her sort of spirit simply did not back down so easily. Freyja surely wouldn't have, were she in this chit's place. Nor, for that matter, would any other self-respecting Norsewoman. And that, Storr realized, was part of the reason that he'd felt compelled to take her captive in the first place. She did not look like a Viking maiden, and she certainly didn't speak like one, but she conducted herself as such. She was clearly proud of her station in life. She was confident, determined, and willful, and those traits, beyond question, were what Storr had come to require from any woman worthy of his attention and respect. She was—this little, seven-stone spitfire, with her seemingly boundless curiosity—as plucky a female as any he'd encountered on Erin's shores or his own. And he knew he would be a fool not to expect at least a ploy or two more from her, as they continued their course to his camp.

But maybe this was just the sort of titillative challenge Odin had had in mind for him, when sending the black bird to goad him into abducting her. "Praise not the day until evening has come," was how the old Norse saying went. Yet, as sagacious as this counsel was, night *had* fallen, and Storr still couldn't make any further sense of his god's intent in all of this. Beyond the girl's vivacity, however, Odin's bestowment might simply have been enabling Storr to share the warmth of her body as he slept. It was, after all, the first time, since Freyja's death, that Storr had had occasion to lie with anyone, and he had to admit to himself that, no matter how innocent and forced the circumstances, it did feel good to have another human being so near.

Again, as his thoughts continued to flow, Norse words of wisdom filled his head. They were the hallowed utterances of the god, Frey, at hearing that he was soon to meet his bride. *"One night is long, Two are longer, How can I endure for three? Often a month seemed to me shorter than half this night of longing."* A mere nine days. That was all the time Frey had had to pass without his betrothed. And, after a year without a consort of his own, Storr could certainly attest that it was not the days that were so torturous in their emptiness, but the *nights*.

Five

Buried somewhere in the rankling, unhealed depths of Storr's memory, was his wedding night with Freyja; and it all came rushing back to him now in provocative detail. He again saw her lying in their nuptial bed, as he was led to her by his best man. She was naked beneath a fur blanket that she'd drawn up to her cleavage, and her blond hair was no longer pulled back, but falling loosely about her shoulders. There was a fire in the hearth of Storr's curtained-off bedchamber, and, in its orange glow, her flowing blond hair looked almost like flame to him.

She had been the shy little girl from the neighboring clan to the west, and he had known her for as long as he could remember. In summer, he had teased her with the occasional captured field mouse or snake. During the winter, he'd sought her love and admiration by hurling snowballs at her or showing off on the ice their fathers' freemen had cleared for skating.

Storr had known, from the first time he'd laid

eyes upon her, that he would have done almost anything to impress her. He had even broken his wrist one day, while wrestling for her benefit on a jagged seacliff that separated their families' respective farms. And, knowing she was watching as it happened, sensing she would spot even the glimmer of a tear, he had somehow found the fortitude to resist his boyish urge to snivel at the terrible pain of it. He had gone on and finished his contest with her older brother, then trudged home, soundlessly, in the burning winter wind . . . He would have died for her—even then. Even before he'd had the chance to kiss her, to hug her, to hold her naked flesh against his in their bed.

He regretted now how relentlessly he'd chaffed her in their youths. Yet, somehow, any response from her, even one provoked by his devilry, had seemed better to him than being ignored by her. And when, finally, their adolescent years had arrived, and he could express his great feeling for her in more gentlemanly ways, what relief he had felt. But what terror, as well. He was petrified at the possibility that she might decline his invitations to take her sledding, or sailing in one of his father's boats.

But, Odin help him, she *hadn't* refused. The gods be lauded, she hadn't rejected him, and, in the fullness of time, a marriage was arranged between them. It was a union that made Storr's heart want to soar to the mountaintops and sing Odin's praises for all of Norse tongue to hear.

Then, finally, the long-awaited day . . . nay, *night* had arrived, and there Storr stood, at the mouth of his bedchamber, weak-kneed with longing and anticipation. What folly! What an ugly truth for any maiden ever to be allowed to discover: that it was not in other males that a man found his ultimate vanquisher, but in the fairer, "weaker" sex. For spears and swords would never have the power to break a warrior's heart, and that, to Storr's mind, was, by far, the worst fate one could suffer.

Now she was his, at last, he acknowledged. She was no longer running from him, teasing and playing her coquettish games of hide-and-seek on some picnic near a fjord. She was *his,* promised and delivered. She was sworn to him for a lifetime, and reclining willingly in the bed that was part of her wedding offering to him.

For the first time in his life, he knew that the dawn would be loathsome to him, that he would actually bemoan the ending of the night with all of its imagined evil spirits and wicked, bloodthirsty trolls. Because, for a grown, married man, as he was now, night would become a haven from the day's striving, a paradise of darkness in the arms of a beautiful woman who would soothe away his cares. It would prove a sanctified escape from the constant company of dependent slaves and kin, and he realized, even on that first night, even before having been allowed to view his precious Freyja disrobed, that he would never,

95

never know his fill of nights with her.

Once he was sure his best man had left them and was well out of range of hearing, Storr slowly crossed to her. He was irritated with himself, all the while, for having allowed his nervousness, as well as his reveling guests, to urge him to drink so much wine at the wedding feast. But his step was steady enough, he told himself, as he made his way to her dowered bed; and, the instant he reached its huge wooden frame, he was careful to use it to guide his way along to where Freyja lay.

He kissed her, as he finally stood before her. He reached down, gently drew her face upward, and bent to press his lips to hers with a lingering kind of reverence. Then he sat down at the base of her curled-up legs, took one of her hands in his, and asked, in a whisper, if she was afraid of what was about to take place between them. She'd nodded, and, to his eternal chagrin, he'd actually gone so far as to confess that he was, too!

Heaven help him! What could have possessed him to do such a thing? He'd never admitted to a timorous thought in his life, and he instantly wished that she'd seen him lying naked and beaten by thieves in a ditch somewhere, rather than having heard him confide so unforgivable a sentiment!

But there was such acceptance in her eyes, such warmth, as the gold of the hearth's flame was reflected in those beautiful blue orbs, that he knew he still had her love. So he eased his hands behind her naked shoulders and back, and he pulled her into his arms. Such was his thankfulness for her understanding and her marriage vow.

What followed was still a jumble, a blur of passion and ecstasy in his memory. In order to return his embrace, his bride released the blanket that covered her, and, as her naked breasts pressed against him, his manly instincts came racing to the fore. He'd taken his obligatory turn with enough harlots in Hedeby, enough newly captured Erse maidens, to need no further priming in such matters; and, even as he continued to kiss her, his hands worked, in a blind rush, to free himself of his clothing as well.

Freyja had been utterly artless in the ways of love then. She scarcely knew how to return his kisses, let alone how to pleasure any other part of him; and on that first, sacred night, Storr knew better than to try to instruct her in the ways of the flesh. He simply allowed her to lie back and enjoy, as he slowly, savoringly ravished her. Every inch of her—from the crown of her golden-tressed head to the tips of her small, lilylike feet.

She was so silky and perfumed, so covered with the seductive scent of floral oils, that Storr knew, from the start, that this would be the most breath-stopping, life-altering experience he would ever have. And he couldn't have been more right!

The sounds she made, the enraptured gasps and sighs she issued, as his lips, his tongue made their passionate pilgrimage over her, were what he would remember most clearly. Soft and dulcet, they filled his ear, as he arched over her, and, and he knew full well that, even if she had been begging him to stop, he would not have been able to do so.

When the time was right, he slipped a hand downward and discovered how tiny and tight the sheath within her was. His fingers were suddenly careful scouts, sent forth to explore her recesses — just as he, himself, had been sent to do many times before his clan's raids upon Erin. He felt, he probed the welcoming wetness and narrowness; and, even realizing how much pain his entry would surely bring her, he went on with his resolve to lay total claim to her.

He would gentle her, he told himself, as he lay over her seconds later. He would do his best to distract her from the deflowering, by busying her with a breathless kiss . . . But, as he finally nudged his way inward, her sighs turned to muffled whimpers beneath his lips, and he knew that the pleasure she'd been feeling was turning to unavoidable distress.

He had to keep going, nonetheless, he acknowledged stolidly. It was his duty to see that their nuptial vows were culminated, no matter what strain the act put upon his bride's diminutive form. What was more, he knew that Freyja could never really respect him as her chieftain and master, if he failed to be insistent in this realm.

It had been this way before, he reminded himself. He had encountered a virgin or two who seemed almost to tear at his stoutness. But they had survived the coupling, and he was certain that his beloved would, too. Indeed, she *must,* if she was to fulfill her role as his wife.

And slowly, gradually, her groaning and tenseness did subside, and her flesh began to give comfortable way to his. He was actually able, in fact, to visit the reflexive rhythm and force of lovemaking more fully upon her . . . until his body could surrender to it as well.

When it was over, and he felt the dampness of her virginal blood on the linens beneath them, he again did the unspeakable. He allowed his eyes to well up at the thought of this wedding wound, at having caused his dear Freyja even a moment of discomfort. And, as if to atone for it, he showered her face and neck with kisses.

Only this once, never again, would their lovemaking cause her pain, he explained. Her body would grow accustomed to his and his to hers, he assured in a murmur, reaching up to brush the passion-swept strands of her golden hair from her face.

Then he did the most noble thing he knew he ever would. He vowed not to enter her again, until she invited him to do so. He would wait for days, weeks . . . even months, if necessary, he said. If it be her will, he would abstain, tortured all the more now for having already had a taste of her. And though he choked at the very prospect of speaking these words—of being tormented by the lovely, radiant sight of her by day and knowing he was not permitted to have her by night—he had every intention of keeping this pledge.

Fortunately though, she had chosen not to make him wait long. Within a day or two, once the soreness of their first joining had apparently left her, she signalled her willingness once more. She climbed into bed, all kittenish and blushful, with nothing but her waist-length tresses shielding her breasts from his view, and she again permitted his body to glide over hers like a relentless tide. And, for days afterwards, Storr found himself silently thanking Frey, the god of sexual intercourse, for allowing Freyja to find their first night together pleasurable enough to come seeking more.

Gradually, though, Storr's early-morning arousal—these stirring images of bedding his bride—was starting to give way to an awareness of the cold hard ground beneath him. And he woke to find that the sweetly scented neck he'd been kissing as he'd slept, the rounded bottom his aching male hardness was pressing up into, were not his wife's, but those of a total stranger! A dark-haired Erse girl who was looking back at him with terror and repulsion in her eyes.

"Please *nay,* sire! I pray thee," she pled in a voice hoarse with sleep.

Storr felt a flush come over him, and his hands instantly relinquished their hold upon her. Then he pushed himself well away from her and sat bolt upright. "Alas!" he said under his breath, searching his slumber-addled brain for recollection of his present circumstances.

He was not at home now, but in Erin. It was not winter, but summer. It was the summer following his dear Freyja's death—not the marvelous nights following their wedding. Most importantly, however, it wasn't his bride he'd been attempting to seduce in his sleep, but a young woman he scarcely even knew and with whom he could barely communicate.

The girl looked almost as aghast in those seconds, as he must have. She got to her feet and moved away from him as quickly as she could. It wasn't until she came to rest, several yards away, that she dared to turn back and look at him once more.

Oddly, though, it wasn't just fear that Storr spied in her eyes in those seconds, but questioning. *Questioning.* What on earth could she be puzzling over, at so disconcerting a time for them both? Then, even as Storr was asking himself this, he saw her eyes descend, like a fluttering butterfly, and light, for just an instant, upon the level of his loins. And even without aid of language, he realized what was causing her brow to knit so quizzically. She wished to know what it was she'd just felt pushing into her . . . what ineffable "weapon" was hidden in his breeches.

But he would be damned if he'd tell her, he inwardly exclaimed. He was far too humiliated at this point to attempt to explain such intimate workings to a virgin — let alone one who required that he fumble about in a foreign tongue!

He simply responded by scowling at her. Then he pressed a fist to his mouth, issued a cough to further mask his abashment, and pushed to his feet. He turned away from her abruptly and pretended to be looking for his dog. Unfortunately, however, Biorn wasn't far away. He had, apparently, just risen at Storr's stirring and gone off to some nearby trees to answer nature's call. So, failing this excuse, Storr strode directly to his horse and began detaching it from the tree to which it was tied.

"There is a stream nearby," he declared, continuing to avoid his captive's gaze. "I shall lead my horse to drink." *And I will soak my swollen foot in the cold water, while I am about it,* he wanted to add. He decided, however, that what had just transpired between them was certainly humbling enough. Rather, he simply concluded with an ominous, "I shall be back forthwith." Then, confident that Biorn would prevent her from fleeing, Storr was off, hurrying from view with the fervent hope that his flush would fade by the time he returned.

He was *embarrassed,* Alanna realized, as she watched him take his horse off towards the west. He wasn't truly angry or annoyed with her, as he would have his curtness lead her to believe. Rather, he was shamefaced. But whatever about? she wondered. It was she who had been the victim just now, the one pleading for mercy as they'd awakened. She was the one who was trussed and forced to endure his unutterable nudging. So, for the life of her, she couldn't imagine why he was casting himself as the sufferer in her stead.

She gave her head a perplexed shake and stared down at her torn tunic, where its gaping flap of ripped cloth peeked out from beneath her cloak. Her posterior was still sore from his blow of the day before, and it dawned on her now that his curious impingement was what had distressed her bruised flesh enough to wake her.

It had hurt. It had been uncomfortable. But she was realizing that it was her fear of what was happening, of not being able to stop his advances, that had been the worst of it. What, she wondered, still feeling panicky, would she have done, if he hadn't desisted at her imploration? What if he had somehow penetrated her garments with whatever it was he was attempting to push into her?

The very thought of it made her heart start to race anew, and, in spite of herself, she began to search her memories of seeing him naked in the brook. Could *that* truly have been part of his body? Her eyes had, admittedly, come to rest, more than once, upon the mysterious terrain at the apex of his thighs; but she certainly hadn't seen aught so hard and long as that! Surely her terror at being abducted was not so very strong that it could have razed all recollection of anything so unwieldy and threatening as what she'd just felt!

It hadn't been altogether unpleasant, however, she silently conceded, unable to fight a shame-filled gulp. For there had been something else. Something so gratifying, so engaging, that she half hated herself for recalling it. He had been *kissing* her, she acknowledged. Not on the cheek, as her aunt and uncle always had. Not even square on the lips, as her female cousins often claimed men would one day. But at the nape, at the spine-tingling curve of her neck. And the whisper-lightness with which he'd done it, the titillative wetness and warmth of his lips and tongue, had been what had kept her from crying out sooner.

Heaven help her, a voice screamed from within, *she had actually enjoyed it!* He was an enemy of her people, a ransacker of their sacred monasteries, and yet she'd allowed herself to revel in his carnal touch! But she had, at last, offered protest, another part of her begged to defend. For whatever fleshly weakness she had just discovered in herself, it did have to be duly noted that she hadn't let it go on for more than a moment or two.

Was *that* the way the Vikings "raped"? she wondered, hating herself for continuing to ponder so sinful a happenstance. She had always been told that such violations were violent and painful. Yet, this Norseman's unwitting attentions to her had seemed . . . well . . . almost *loving,* for want of a better term. His hands, his mouth had grazed over her with the gentleness one might accord the petals of a rare and delicate flower — as though he actually cherished her!

But that simply wasn't possible, she reminded herself. He scarcely knew her, and, indeed, upon waking, he'd returned to treating her every bit as brusquely as he had the day before. So, how could he have felt anything for her?

There'd been a word he had whispered, as he'd hugged her so tightly to him, and, even though Alanna didn't recognize it, she sensed that it held the answers to her present stream of questions. "Freyja," he'd said, again and again. First by itself, then preceded by several other foreign terms. They'd been reverent, murmured utterances that had told Alanna, even in her half-sleeping state, that this Freyja, whatever it was, was very dear to his heart.

A *name,* she suddenly realized. It was probably the name of someone he adored . . . Quite obviously a female, she deduced. With this conclusion came a flood of understanding. He'd thought she was someone else, a lover from his past, perhaps, or some woman back at his encampment or in his homeland, for whom he yearned. Night's darkness had blinded him to Alanna's features, and he had dreamt that she was someone he treasured!

This, in turn, accounted for the embarrassment she had seen in him. Sleep had lulled him into believing that he was opening his arms, his innermost self to a confidante whom he felt was worthy of such intimacy. But the dawn's light had finally arrived to reveal that all he held was an Erse bondswoman.

Alanna squared her shoulders at this realization. She suddenly felt as vexed and indignant as her captor had seemed before leaving. She had been many things in her short lifetime, but never the cause of such blatant disappointment! Yet, she reminded herself, it hadn't really been disappointment she'd seen in his eyes as he'd pulled away from her More than anything else, it had simply been surprise. Followed by unmistakable chagrin. Then he'd scowled, as though trying to play the part of the disapproving master with her; and, when she'd met his gaze with like intensity, he had fled out of the clearing and into the woods that adjoined it. She couldn't remember when she'd seen such a mortified expression, in fact, and she was forced to conclude that this Norse raider was even more vulnerable than he'd revealed himself to be on the previous evening.

Storr waited till he was certain he was out of the girl's line of sight. Then he proceeded to the nearest tree and pressed his face against its trunk with a thoroughly humiliated groan. How, in the name of the eternal fires of *Hel,* could he have managed to make such a fool of himself before a slave? He lifted his face slightly and continued to whisper a stream of Norse obscenities into the deeply furrowed bark of the bole. His throat positively ached with his continuing sense of embarrassment.

It was one thing to seize a maiden and rape her like a warrior. It was even acceptable for an earl, like himself, to go proudly forth to his slaves' quarters and claim the female serf he wanted to bed. But to have actually allowed himself to be lulled into to carrying on with a captive—as though she were some sort of goddess—was nothing less than scandalous! And he knew he could only pray that the girl would simply find herself too shaken by the incident to remember much about it in the days and weeks that followed.

He should explain to her, part of him counseled. He should go back and just admit that, in his sleep-drunk state, he had mistaken her for his dearly departed wife. He should make it clear that his kisses, his fondling, his worshipful words of love, had not been meant for her at all.

Admittedly, Vikings of his stature probably did fall in love with slave girls from time to time. Perhaps they even secretly held them in as high esteem as their lawful Norse wives. But that was only after they had come to know the wenches very well, he inwardly admonished. Well enough to be certain that they wouldn't speak of such matters with others, that they would exercise the good sense and taste to keep quiet about what went on in their master's chamber. Only the test of time could tell whether or not they should be trusted with a chieftain's deepest, most jeopardous secrets And Storr was sorely aware that he couldn't even trust this maiden to stay put when his back was turned!

But it was simply the dream, he rationalized again, doing his best at self-consolation. It had been the first time he'd slept with anyone since being widowed, and it was only natural for his longing, his aching for relations with a woman, to have led to such a sticky occurrence.

If the truth be told, the chit probably wasn't half as interested in understanding the emotional workings behind his actions, as in how it was that his brook-chilled member—so dwarfed by the cold of his bathing the day before—could have transformed itself into what she'd surely just felt from behind. Storr now recalled the wide-eyed, questioning look she'd offered him only minutes earlier, and he realized that it had held only a childlike inquisitiveness. As with his map on the previous evening, she simply wanted to know what was what and *what went where*. And, finally convincing himself of this, Storr couldn't help but chuckle a little at her naivete—at the blasted ignorance that ridiculous religion of hers seemed to insist upon imposing!

She was so much like his younger sisters in that regard. Such an innocent. She was so blessedly unaware of what would surely have happened to her by now, if she'd fallen into less tentative hands. She was aggravatingly oblivious to her great fortune in having found herself in the arms of a man whose love for his dead wife continued to be stultifyingly strong.

He would simply have to sleep with his back to her henceforth, he resolved, finally finding the strength of will to pull away from the tree trunk and face the harsh light of day once more. No matter how trying, he would just have to keep her safe and intact, until Odin's will in all of this was made more clear.

When Storr returned to his captive a short time later, she was still sitting just as he'd left her. The only change was that her wounded harrier had ventured off a yard or two, and was now busy sniffing and relieving himself upon every under-shrub in his path.

Storr lifted his chin with an unabashed air, as his eyes met the girl's once again. He went on to address her in a tone that said he had completely stricken the sorry scene of half an hour before from his memory. "I see your dog fares better to-day."

The maiden offered him a tremulous smile and nodded. "Aye. Thanks to your stitching, sire. But his master could use some morning relief, as well," she added pointedly, jerking upward on her still-trussed wrists.

Just as Alanna had hoped, the raider seemed not to want to repeat the task of lifting her tunic for her as she unburdened herself. He, therefore, crossed to her and stooped down to unfasten the rope that bound her.

"Oh, thank you," she said, turning around for him. Then she brought her freed hands forward and used them to push herself up to her feet. "By my word, I shall not go far. Just behind a tree for a moment."

Storr shrugged resignedly at her entreating tone and gestured toward the heavily wooded edge of the clearing. Then he turned and headed in the opposite direction, bending to gather up their bedding as he went.

Two or three more days, he thought with a dry swallow. It was, in truth, a short time; but he knew it would seem an eternity before he could return to his Viking encampment and hand this Erse charge over to one of his freemen. She was such a handful, such a dead lift, that a couple days would surely become thrice their length with her in tow.

He would just have to stop speaking to her, he suddenly resolved, reaching into his saddle-pack to put away the bedding and withdraw his comb. Except for when absolutely necessary, he would simply cease trying to stumble over her language and thereby put further halt to the awkwardness between them. But, even as he was deciding this, even as he was running the comb through his long, windblown hair, her chirpy voice rang out again.

"Oh, what have you there?" she asked, as though quite intrigued.

She'd obviously concluded her business and come back to the clearing. He turned to face her now with a perplexed expression. "Where?"

"In your hand, sire," she replied, coming towards him at what Storr found an unnervingly fast clip.

He took a step or two back, drew his hand forward, and eyed the comb for a second. "What? This?" he asked in amazement. The *comb*. She had, evidently, never seen one before. But then he shouldn't be too surprised by this, he realized. Most of the Erse his clansmen had taken through the years looked as though they'd never combed their hair; so perhaps, they truly didn't know the like of such an implement here.

" 'Tis called a 'comb,' " he explained, extending it to her.

She reached out somewhat hesitantly, as though half expecting it to bite. Then she accepted it and stood cradling it in her palm. "Oh, 'tis lovely," she observed, passing the fingers of her free hand over its coarse teeth and decoratively engraved spine. "Prithee, do show me once more how 'tis used," she added, giving it back to him.

Storr, unable to fight his amusement at her infantile delight with such a simple object, reached up and again ran it through his hair.

She watched with intense interest as he did this, as though she expected his blond mane to be transformed by it somehow. When, after several seconds, this did not occur, however, her expression sank into one of puzzlement. "But what does it do?"

Storr frowned at this question. The answer struck him as self-evident and, what was more, he doubted that he knew the Erse words necessary to explain it to her. "Well, it *combs*," he said with an impatient cluck. "You know, it . . . it straightens. Un . . . unknots."

"Does it hurt?"

"Nay. Of course not." He pressed it back into her hand. "Take a try." Her sleep-disheveled nest of curls looked as though it could use some coifing.

Again she was hesitant. But, after a second or two, she reached up, freed her locks from the bands that bound them, and began using the implement as he'd indicated. "Oh, it . . . it feels rather pleasant, doesn't it," she noted with marked surprise. "Pray, may I keep it?"

Storr was caught off-guard by this request. It was the only comb he had with him, and, though he was certain he had another back at the encampment, he knew he would be needing it again before they got there. "Aye," he answered finally. "But I will ask for it, mind thee, when I have need of it."

"Oh, aye. Aye," she earnestly agreed, stopping

her combing to again examine this new wonder. "I shall guard it with my very life," she pledged, raising her brows with glad sincerity. Then, as if having known of such practices all her life, she bent from her middle — as Freyja always had — and began combing out her dark tresses to their full, waist-length magnificence.

This must simply have been some sort of womanly instinct on her part, Storr concluded, reflexively stepping back from her in those same seconds. And, in spite of himself, he stood drinking in the velvety redness of her hair in the prevailing glow of sunrise.

Though he wasn't sure why, the sight of it made a lump form in his throat. Her mane was so different from his wife's, so thick and curly. Yet it was also undeniably similar: shiny and resplendent with its harmonious streaks of jewel-like color.

Nevertheless, he did manage to find the wherewithal to tear his gaze away. She was, after all, just a child in many ways, an unworldly chattel who'd never even been taught about bathing and grooming. What was more, he sorrily remembered, he'd already made enough of a passion-crazed fool of himself with her to last an eternity. So it was crucial to him that he not fall prey to her charms a second time.

"I wonder," she began again after a moment, returning to an upright stance and letting her flood of curls spill back over her shoulders. "Would it

113

offend thee, sire, if I wore my hair unbound to-day?"

Storr's expression was once again a confounded one, as he deigned to look at her.

"My aunt doth think it unseemly for one of my class," she explained. "But I've no mirror in which to style it, you see."

"You may set it afire, for all I care," Storr retorted, his steely delivery conveying how ridiculous he found the inquiry—as well as how hell-bent he now was upon remaining impervious to her feminine allure.

She appeared, for an instant, wounded by his response. But then she straightened her posture, as though having considered the source of it, and hurriedly stuffed the comb and her hair bands into the belt of her tunic.

"Will there be no break fast before we take our leave?" she asked, obviously fighting to keep her voice steady.

Storr fully expected her insolence to finally make him fly into a rage in those seconds. But he somehow kept himself from doing so.

By the gods, she certainly was a demanding thing this morning. First it was, "Untie me." Then, "May I keep your comb?" And now, "Feed me!" She was most assuredly in for a surprise, once they reached his encampment and she discovered that it was *she* who would be waiting upon his every need!

"Nay. No 'break fast,' " he answered coldly.

"I could gather some nuts and berries before we away," she suggested. "I know much of what Erin's woodlands bear." *Nightshade,* Alanna thought with an exhilarated chill running through her. Here, at last, was her chance to go in search of it. Her people rarely consumed more than a drink of water at the start of the day. But, on the off chance her captor could be made to believe that she required a break fast, she would try to wangle him into allowing it now. With any luck, she might actually succeed in finding some of the poison and slipping it into one of his waterskins. Then, with God's blessing, she could have him flat on his back by midday.

To her dismay, however, he answered with another unswayable nay, and she went and sank down dejectedly upon the nearby log.

"Come. Make haste," he called after her irritably, reaching up and giving his saddle a couple emphatic pats. "You will ride with me, and the dogs shall follow."

She looked dumbstruck as she lifted her gaze to him once more.

"But, surely, Faolan's in . . . in no state to walk such a ways, sire," she faltered.

"He shall, none the less," Storr decreed, mounting his horse and again gesturing for her to rise and join him. "I sewed him well, as you said . . . And we will find means to carry him, if he lags," he added reluctantly, when his captive failed to get up as ordered.

At this assurance, Alanna rose and slowly walked over to him and his horse. She wanted to offer more protest to this plan, but, as she reached the raider and felt the strength with which he grasped her and swept her up onto the stallion, she knew she should not. She landed behind him with such a stinging plop on her sword-swept backside, that she needed no further reminder of the possible consequences of his wrath. Moreover, he'd neglected to retruss her hands, when she'd returned to the clearing, and she feared that any additional resistance from her might be all it would take to remind him of this apparent oversight.

Even if he was guilty of slashing Faolan the day before, he was also responsible for having sutured him, she told herself consolingly. It stood to reason, therefore, that he probably wasn't the sort to let such a defenseless creature fall too far behind now. Alanna knew she must make herself believe this, in any case. Her sanity seemed to depend upon it.

An instant later, the raider was whistling for the hounds, and she had only a second, before he reined off towards the west, in which to take hold of his waist. Given the unnerving attentions he'd forced upon her earlier, she really didn't wish to touch him; but it was clearly unavoidable. *His* feet were in the stirrups, of course, so, short of clutching Storr and squeezing her thighs about the stallion, there was no other way for her to stay mounted.

To her relief, he kept the horse to a trot, as they made their way through the woods and began heading north. Several long looks backward confirmed that both of the dogs were having little trouble keeping up. It was a blessing, she realized, that the raider's hound was obviously so far along in years. At such a lumbering weight, the only speed he could maintain for any length of time was the measured one his master had chosen, and this, in turn, was making it possible for Faolan to keep pace as well.

She was careful nevertheless, to keep glancing back as they rode. Her hands were now free, after all, to go in search of poisons when next they stopped, and she wanted to make certain that her pet would be with her when she finally escaped from the raider.

In late morning, the Norseman brought the horse to a merciful halt along the bank of a river. He ordered Alanna to dismount and go off to take care of her inevitable needs. Then he got down from the saddle as well and led his stallion to the water to drink. The dogs, surely every bit as thirsty by this time, followed them. But it wasn't long before faithful Faolan came in search of his owner in the nearby woods.

After bending down to give him a pat, Alanna attempted to shoo him. She wanted him to return to the riverbank, before the Norseman noticed his absence and felt compelled to come looking for them both. But this was in vain, of course. Given all he'd been through, the harrier had no intention of leaving his mistress's side again. So Alanna was forced to rush her search for nightshade all the more, in the hopes that they could both return to the Viking in advance of his suspicion being aroused.

A minute or two later, however, she discovered that she hadn't succeeded in preventing this. Her scan of the forest floor was suddenly interrupted by the raider's booming voice, and she turned to see that he was standing just a few feet behind her. He'd struck a careless pose against a tree and was demanding to know precisely what it was she was doing. As if to echo this sentiment, his enormous hound stood beside him, with his head at an inquiring cock.

"I . . . I have . . . have lost a ring, sire," she stammered, inwardly praying that he'd believe her. "A . . . um, finger ring of silver which was given to me by my father."

Storr's eyes narrowed skeptically. "I saw no rings on your hands when I took you."

"Oh, aye. Verily. I was, indeed, wearing one. It is just that, with so little to eat and drink in the past two days, it seems my finger shrank and the blessed thing fell away from me. So, prithee, might you help me find it?"

This question, as she could have predicted, brought a decided frown to his face. He clearly had no intentions of joining her in rummaging through the underbrush. "Nay. We must away again now, while there is still enough light for riding. There are many such rings where we go," he concluded, and, without allowing for an instant of objection from her, he pushed away from the tree and headed back to where he'd left his horse.

After a second or two, Alanna and Faolan followed. As with Storr's leaving her hands untrussed earlier, she was simply grateful that he was choosing not to visit any more of his will upon her, and she knew better than to cross his bounds. Besides, she told herself hearteningly, this really wasn't the sort of soil in which nightshade was most often found. It liked shadowy areas, admittedly. But, she now recalled, it also seemed to prefer scrub, rocky ground, and this forest was probably too moist for it.

She would simply have to try again later, she decided, thankful that her captor had, at least, allowed her to relieve herself before stealing up on her. And, more importantly, that he had seen fit to believe her claim that she'd simply lost a piece of jewelry.

As she and Faolan trudged after him and his hound, the words he'd just spoken resounded in her head. *There are many such rings where we go.* Judging from all she'd heard of these foreign raiders, she didn't doubt this claim for a moment. God only knew, after all, just how many *dead* fingers one could wrest such riches from in the course of a summer. What struck her as surprising, was that he'd actually seemed to be offering to pass such a defiled item on to her, and that she would somehow be expected to accept it as ample compensation for a gift allegedly presented to her by a beloved parent.

They were a strangely dispassionate race, these Vikings, she acknowledged again, shaking her head. And, to her dismay, she knew that she could now add yet another detail to her knowledge of them: even maimed to a limp, a Norseman could be astonishingly quiet of foot!

Six

The Norseman allowed them to stop twice more before nightfall, and, to Alanna's dismay, neither respite yielded the poison she so desperately needed. She was careful on their journey to take thorough note of the land they traversed, every glen and expanse of woods, so that she'd be better able to find her way back home. Yet she was painfully aware that, without nightshade, she simply wouldn't get the opportunity to make her escape, and by late afternoon it seemed her only recourse was merely to shut her eyes in prayer.

Indeed, it wasn't until they were setting up camp for the night, that she finally detected a glimmer of the fact that her need was about to be met. She was hidden from her captor's view, again relieving herself within the cover of a nearby copse. And, exhausted by the day's seemingly endless riding, she was staring mindlessly into the undergrowth to her right. It was then that she caught sight of them out of the corner of her eye: a cluster of berries, black as death itself, hanging heavily from a tall, bushy plant with oval leaves. She squinted, not believing her eyes. Then, upon finishing what she'd started and letting her tunic drop back down to its full, calf-length, she lunged for a closer look.

It had already flowered, she realized. The blessed perennial had apparently put forth and lost its lovely, bell-shaped blossoms, and here, at last, was the fruit that evidently followed! And *that,* she acknowledged, may well have been her problem all along. In what little time she'd been able to steal away from the raider that day, she had looked not for the berries that she truly sought, but rather for nightshade's distinctive blooms.

She pulled a handful of fruit-laden stalks from the plant row, and stood clutching them to her chest with a triumphant sigh. Then, knowing that she didn't have a moment to waste, she took one of the hair bands from her belt and used it to bundle the fruit into a more easily concealable bunch. She then reached behind her and slipped it underneath her belt, at the center of her back, where it would be readily hidden by her cloak.

God had come to her aid! He had actually heard her prayers and finally delivered, in stunning abundance, that for which she'd asked. In very sooth, there looked to be enough berries here to vanquish an entire legion of Vikings! And, though she knew it was too risky to do so, she wanted to begin jumping about with glee. Her exaltation came to an abrupt halt, however, as she finally permitted herself to ponder the next hurdle: if and when she would get the chance to crush the berries and slip some of their colorless juice into her captor's food or drink?

But the time would come, she told herself, with a courage-gathering swallow. Maybe he would allow her to remain unbound for a while longer. Perchance she could even persuade him to let her help in the preparation of whatever game he scared up for their supper. Nightshade berries were fairly resilient, after all, a voice within her continued to hearten. She felt certain they could be counted upon to keep their potency for at least a day or so more. And, provided she and Faolan could survive that long, as well, there still seemed to be hope for remedying their plight.

"Alanna?" she suddenly heard from just a few yards away. She started with surprise. The raider had spoken her *name!* Since capturing her, he'd only deigned to call her chit and wench. But now, for some reason, he'd used her name. He'd actually remembered it, and she found herself a bit agape, as she hurriedly reached back to make certain her cloak was hanging loosely, providing ample concealment for her deadly find. Then, having convinced herself of this, she took a deep, calming breath and returned to the adjacent clearing to see what he wanted.

"Aye?" she asked, in her most artless tone, as she reached him.

He was sitting on a large flat rock, near where his horse was hitched, and he was whittling a sharp end onto a long sturdy-looking stick he'd apparently found. This perplexed Alanna, because the stick was clearly too big to be used as a spit for small game, so she couldn't imagine what else he planned to do with it.

"Know you aught of spearing fish?" he asked, stopping his work and raising his commanding blue eyes to her.

She shrugged. "I have done it once or twice, sire. But I must confess to being inept at it."

"Inept," he echoed as though confused. " 'Tis your word for poor? For bad?"

She blushed slightly and nodded.

He continued to look terribly serious. "Then you must become good, for, with my foot scotched," he added, glowering first at his swollen and bound toes, then back up at her, "I fear I cannot hunt for us."

"So I am to spear alone?" she asked, with an uneasy rise to her voice. The truth of the matter was that she had never, in all her seventeen years, been required to do anything as momentous as bringing home a meal, and she seriously doubted her ability to do so.

"Nay," he replied, returning his gaze to his whittling. "I will join thee . . . But, mind, you *shall* spear," he said firmly. And Alanna sensed that it was the nagging hunger they were both suffering

124

that was making him seem so humorless.

It was *high* time, Storr thought, putting the finishing touches on the spear with a weary sigh, then rising and resheathing his knife. It was she who had maimed him, so it certainly followed that she should begin at once to assume some of the responsibility for meeting their needs on this damnable trek! What was more, he reasoned, she was much less apt to embarrass him with her disobedience, once they reached his fellow Norsemen, if she was taught to do his bidding without undue question now.

"Here," he began again, thrusting the makeshift lance into her hand. "And do not prove fool enough to try using it on me! You lack the strength for it."

With that, he stepped over to his horse, took his throwing spear down from his saddle, and began heading out of the clearing with an order for her to follow.

Alanna stood still for several seconds, her hand moist with nervousness against the wooden spear, and her heart beating loudly. This was it, she realized: her opportunity to press some of the berries into one of his waterskins without him seeing. But, as she rushed to his stallion and her fingers raced to unloop the strap of one of the bags from his saddle-pack, he called out for her again. Realizing she had only an instant or two in which to leave the campsite and catch up with him, she reflexively

125

slung the skin's strap over her shoulder. Then she hurried after him with the winded claim that she was thirsty and wished to take a drink, as they made their way to the nearest fishing hole. The two hounds followed at her heels, of course . . . happily oblivious to her ominous plan.

Alanna succeeded with the spear fishing, managing to lance two, good-sized trout to the raider's three. Far more importantly, though, she succeeded in surreptitiously squeezing the syrupy contents of several of the berries into the waterskin she still carried. She simply waited until Storr was amply busied with building a fire and filleting the fish, to do so. What she feared now, however, as their supper crackled near the flames, was that she might not succeed in persuading the Norseman to drink in the near future and, more specifically, from the *right* bag.

He'd shown no interest in anything, since they'd returned, but getting their meal cooked, and Alanna could only hope that, after he'd eaten, a post-meal thirst would develop and he would partake of the water as heartily as he had the night before. In the meantime, she saw no other way to take her mind off the incalculable sin that lay before her, than simply to try to make small talk with her captor as he cooked.

"You called me Alanna earlier," she began, unable to hide the gratefulness and surprise she felt at this. "You remembered my name."

He looked up from over the aromatic smoke and met her eyes, where she sat down now, across from him. "Aye. Of course," he said, as though he saw no reason why it should have surprised her.

"I thank thee, sire. It doth please me to hear it used once again." *For I miss my home and tribesmen terribly,* she wanted to add. But, not wishing to roil him anew, regarding his plans to keep her, she left that part unspoken.

"What does it mean? Alanna?" he asked offhandedly, returning his gaze to the fire.

Because he'd conversed so little with her over the long hours of riding northward, she'd begun to feel quite lonely. She, therefore, found herself relieved to hear this question—indeed, *any* question from him.

"Bright one. Fair. Beautiful," she replied with a slight blush. She'd never had occasion to respond to such an inquiry, and she realized in that instant how immodest the answer seemed.

He was silent; but she could see a subtle smile tugging at one corner of his lips, as he worked to flip the fillets over on the stone upon which they cooked.

"Aye," he said, after several seconds. "It doth suit thee, then."

It was she who dropped her gaze now, staring down at the waterskin that rested in her lap. She couldn't help feeling taken aback by the compliment. Nothing he had said or done so far had given the slightest indication that he thought of her as anything more than a troublesome vassal, and she found herself almost speechless at this wholly unexpected praise.

But, perhaps, it was the fish, she told herself. He'd seemed impressed with her lancing earlier, when she'd helped him procure nearly half their kill, and, maybe that was why he was treating her with greater regard.

"Why, sire," she began again, lifting her eyes with as much daring as she could summon, "may I ask, have you now decided to address me as such?"

He looked up at her with an expression that said that the answer to this was obvious. "Because we will reach my people in a day or two, and, lest you be claimed by one of them, you must be addressed as part of my stead."

"So, all of your bondsmen are called by the names given to them at birth?"

"Aye. A good master must have such familiarity with them. 'Tis the only way they or their children can one day be made freemen."

Alanna furrowed her brow. "I don't understand. You mean you enslave them with the intent of setting them free?"

He nodded. "One day. Aye. 'Tis our way . . . for we have found that no man works well without respect and hope."

Alanna leaned back, feeling a chill run through her at the wisdom and compassion implicit in this curious practice.

"So, I am always to be called Alanna in your keeping?"

"Alanna of the stead of Storr," he amended, and she recalled in that same instant that he had, indeed, told her his name, as well, the day before.

"And what does Storr mean, pray?"

"Great one," he answered simply, as though quite comfortable with this grandiose—indeed, even sacrilegious appellation.

She wished, for a fleeting second or two, that she could do him the kindness of returning his compliment regarding her name. But, in view of its preposterous magnitude, she found she could not.

"Great one?" she echoed in a wavering voice. "But surely . . . surely, sire, you have a God whom you hold as being greater." She bit her lip, as she finished this question, afraid that, in spite of her cautious delivery, it might provoke him.

Instead, he looked as though he couldn't imagine what such a name had to do with one's deity. "Aye. There is Odin and, for the serf, Thor."

"You have more than one God?" she asked incredulously.

"Of course. Any man with eyes can see there is need for many. One for the sky and one for the land and so forth. The world is far too big to be tended to by but one."

His tone was so resolute that Alanna knew better than to offer any argument. It was clear that there would be no profit in it. Nevertheless, his response was propitious in one way, she realized in those seconds. Such wholehearted paganism on his part only seemed to offer further justification for her distasteful plan. How much sin could God see, after all, in the poisoning of such a dyed-in-the-wool heathen?

In spite of her efforts to hide it, however, her silence must have betrayed her disagreement with what he'd just said, because his tone was unmistakably combative as he spoke again. "You Erse claim to believe in only one god, but, in truth, you do not," he declared. "You believe in the lesser spirits of the forest and glen. In fairies and leprechauns. Is that not so?"

Alanna hesitated before answering, never having even thought to relate such folklore to the teachings of the sacred Mother Church. "Well, aye . . . but—"

"So, we have our 'little people, too,' as you call them. We have our Norns, Valkyries, and trolls, just as you have yours. And, forsooth, even your *one* god takes the form of three, I am told."

She knit her brow in confusion. What, in the Name of Heaven, was he speaking of?

"The tri—trin—" he stammered, as if trying to clarify.

"Oh, trinity?" she asked after a moment. "Do

130

you mean the Holy Trinity?"

He nodded.

"But the Trinity is yet one God, sire. I fear you simply did not understand."

He glared at her, as he used his knife to slide the browned fish into the bowl from which they'd eaten the previous night. "I understood," he said vehemently. "For any man knows that no one, not even a god, can be, at the same time, a father, a son, *and* a ghost! 'Tis lunacy," he exclaimed, waving his hands for emphasis.

Alanna bit her lip again — in part to keep from laughing at his exasperation. This dichotomy, which he'd apparently learned of from his other Erse captives, had obviously bothered him for quite some time; and she sensed that nothing she could say would truly clarify the matter for him. He was, all things considered, a confessed pagan, and, given what she had slipped into his waterskin, there seemed no real advantage now in trying to bring him round to the Christian perspective.

"Well, explain to me how this is possible," he demanded after a moment, rising and thrusting the filled bowl towards her with a huff.

She was so hungry by this point that she realized she would have done or said almost anything to keep him from withdrawing the fish before she'd taken her fill. " 'Tis . . . 'tis troublous sire," she said between chews. "For it 'surpasseth all understanding.' "

"Why?" he demanded. "Does your god not love you enough to explain to you his ways?"

She managed to swallow the bulging mouthful she'd just taken, and she quickly replaced it with another "Well, aye," she answered, nodding. "He doth try . . . He and His heavenly hosts. But, I fear, we are far too mortal to fully comprehend," she concluded in a pained tone. It seemed he had scarcely spoken two words to her all day. So, why on earth was he catechizing her now? *Now,* when she felt so ravenous that all she wanted to do was devour as much of the food as possible!

His eyes narrowed discerningly, and he bit at the inside of his cheek, as though pondering all she'd said. Then, as if becoming as nettled by the conversation as she, he walked around to her side of the fire, sank down on the ground next to her, and set the serving bowl between them with a telling thump.

"You need a more mortal god," he retorted, beginning to partake of the food as well.

"Such as yours?" she asked evenly.

He nodded.

"Then, pray, do tell me of them, sire," she prompted. Naturally, she didn't care to hear a word of what he'd have to say on this subject. But she figured this tack would both help mollify his aggravation over her mystifying faith, and keep him too busy talking to eat more than his share of the coveted fish.

Fortunately, he obliged her, launching into a surprisingly colorful speech about red-bearded Thor, the thunder god, and some deity named Ty who'd apparently suffered the misfortune of losing a hand to a wolf somewhere along the way.

Alanna listened with as much interest as she could feign, nodding her understanding of his broken Erse where appropriate, and secretly finding his descriptions quite amusing. But, in the midst of his eating and expounding, the raider started working his jaw rather oddly, and Alanna realized—even before he seemed to—that his mouth was dry, and *now* was the time to hand him the fateful waterskin.

He looked pleased by this gesture, as if such a show of helpfulness from her somehow indicated that he was succeeding in breaking her in as his future slave. Then, without another word, he uncapped the bag, lifted it to his lips, and took several long swallows from it.

Alanna's breath caught in her throat. Then she bit her lip as she anxiously awaited his response, if any, to the aftertaste that she'd learned accompanied this natural sleeping potion. *Would he know, somehow?* Was there any way for him to deduce what had caused the odd flavor?

To her relief, however, his expression was anything but accusatory, as he finally lowered the skin. Rather, it was simply one of boyish disgust.

"What is it? What troubles thee?" she asked guardedly.

He reached up and wiped his lips with his tunic sleeve. Then he grimaced once more. "Bit . . . bitter," he replied after a moment, as though searching for her race's word for this.

She continued to act confused. "What? The water?"

He extended the bag to her. "Aye. Here. Taste."

A horrified chill rushed over her at having the noxious liquid thrust back in her direction. "Nay, sire. I believe thee well enough," she assured, reaching out and recapping it for him. "Perhaps it was some mineral from the stream in which we fished. I drank from the skin before we reached it. Then refilled it there."

He set the bag down and offered a shrug. Then he began stuffing his mouth with fish once more, as though wishing to kill the awful flavor that had been left by the water.

"Some for the dogs, sire?" Alanna prompted gingerly.

This reminder, as she'd hoped, brought his gobbling to a halt, and she proceeded to call both of the drooling hounds in closer to them.

The raider fed them, tossing each what he evidently felt was his fair portion. Then he set the bowl down, and, to Alanna's dismay, uncapped the waterskin once more and began pouring its contents into the bowl. *For the dogs,* she realized in

134

those horrendous seconds. He was about to offer the deadly stuff to her precious Faolan! And, without an instant more to think, she whisked the bowl off the ground and sprang to her feet with it.

Her captor, of course, looked up at her with a perplexed glare.

"But you said yourself 'tis bitter," she explained. "Why give it to our poor unwitting hounds? I shall see to watering them and the horse myself, and you can tend to our bedding," she declared, hurrying off to the adjoining underbrush to dispose of the menacing liquid before he had the chance to get to his feet and stop her.

Storr sat watching the bewildering maiden for several seconds more, both puzzled by her sudden willingness to make herself of use, and glad about it. So the water had been bitter, he thought insouciantly; that hardly seemed reason to throw it away. What harm could there be, after all, in the occasional metallic-flavored stream water? He'd drunk rusty waters more than once in his many summers of raiding, and he'd never fallen ill as a result. So he couldn't imagine why the dear girl thought she needed to take such action now.

But she was trying to be aidful, a voice within him reminded. He'd seen this transformation in dozens of serfs through the years: the passage from rebelliousness to simple resignation to the fate of being captured. And he knew he shouldn't be surprised that even a woman of such purported stature was beginning to accept her plight. Considering how far away from home she was now, what choice did she truly have? What alternatives would he have in her place? The only sensible course was that of least resistance: making herself so invaluable to her master that he wouldn't find call to kill her or sell her off at the first trading town they reached. It was as simple as that, he concluded, rising from the fireside and crossing to his horse to withdraw the bedding she'd mentioned.

"Why do you raid in summer, sire?" his captive inquired, as she was rinsing and refilling his serving bowl with water from the second skin.

Storr was a trifle surprised that one as manifestly bright as she had asked such an asinine question. "Because the seas are calmer, of course."

She was kneeling now, holding the bowl out for their pets as she spoke again. "Nay. I mean, haven't you crops and beasts of the field to tend to in the summer, as we have?"

Storr walked back to the fire with his saddlepack in hand. Then he removed his blanket from it, spread it on the ground, and reclined upon it. Their hours of riding were finally catching up with him, it seemed. He was suddenly feeling quite heavy-eyed. "Aye. We do farm."

"Then how can you tend to that and yet be *here?*"

He laughed a little under his breath. She wasn't as predictable as Norse maidens. Not by any mea-

136

sure. There was simply no telling what line of questioning she might initiate next.

"Our women tend the farms . . . along with our slaves."

"Hmm," she said thoughtfully, getting back to her feet once both dogs had quenched their thirsts and walked away. "So, you come to Erin to steal bondsmen to tend your farms while you're off . . . stealing bondsmen?" she asked with a chary rise to her voice. It occurred to her that this pointed inquiry, however benign its delivery, might get his dander up once more. But it was, in fact, a question she and her kin had long pondered, and she knew that this might be her last opportunity to get it answered.

To her surprise, though, he simply chuckled again. It was a low, dull laugh that told her sleep couldn't be terribly far off for him. "Aye. That is one way to view it . . . But 'tis more," he continued. " 'Tis a way for our young warriors to prove their courage and strength. Seizing riches and slaves brings them fame."

Alanna, relieved that he was deigning to answer her questions with such forbearance, decided it was safe to walk over and join him on the blanket. "Prithee, did it bring *you* fame, sire? Is this how you came to be master of your stead?" she asked, reaching out to return the now-empty bowl to his saddle-pack.

Storr blinked a few times and let his gaze travel

up to the sky, as he continued to recline. His vision was a bit blurry, doubtless from all the hours of focusing upon the northern horizon as they'd ridden; and he found it easier now to lock his eyes upon the soothing twilight overhead. He choked a bit on his response, at the bittersweet memories it stirred. "It brought me fame once. Aye, as with the others . . . when I was young. But, alas, it is not what brought me my stead."

Alanna stretched out next to him, propping herself up on her elbow, as she continued to face him. "Then what did?"

"The . . . the death of my father," he replied, his voice wavering as though he found this answer wrenching. "All eldest sons get their holdings from their fathers.'

"So, your father is newly dead?"

Storr took his eyes from the sky to look at her, to again regard this creature whose insight continued to amaze him. And, to his surprise, he saw that, even though she was lying just a couple feet away, she was all a blur to him. Her face and white tunic suddenly had a halolike sheen in the firelight. "How would you know that?" he asked defensively.

" 'Twas the quiver in your voice. It bespoke the fact that this pain has not yet healed . . . I lost both of my parents years ago, sire," she explained, seeing, for the first time, solid proof that the nightshade was finally working its spell. The pupils of his eyes were unnaturally wide now — as wide and dark and empty as the sleep that surely lay ahead for him. And suddenly Alanna was filled not with delight at the prospect of finally being free of him, but with fear, with unbridled trepidation! How would she find her way home in the dark? How could she be certain she wasn't going to fall into hands far worse than his, as she and Faolan made their journey back to her tribe? How, given her limited hunting abilities, would she feed them both en route?

Panic. Sheer panic would have overtaken her right then and there, had some governing voice within her not succeeded in calming her with its assurances. She knew how to spear-fish, after all, it told her. She'd proven this to both her captor and herself, just a couple hours before. And she had his map, didn't she? She'd determined where her ring-fort was on it. So why, with it in hand as she made the trip back, couldn't she deduce how it related to the land she would be crossing and let it guide her to the coast? And as for raiders, wasn't she with one now? Wasn't she, even at present, subject to the tyranny of such a man? Yet slowly, gradually she was finding her way out of his clutches as the nightshade, her brain child, did its work. Hadn't she, in truth, already, faced and conquered all the things she now thought she feared?

She tore her eyes from his, suddenly feeling an odd sort of pity for him, for what might become of him, if her guess about dosage with the nightshade had been incorrect. Then she turned her gaze to the sky as well. "Thus, I know the pain of it," she concluded, certain that he was growing too drowsy now to even have noticed how long it had taken her to finish this thought.

He was actually going to do it: drift off without so much as trussing her hands for the night. And she realized — with a new sense of triumph filling her — that all she had to do now was simply lie beside him a bit longer and wait. Wait for his eyes to close and his limbs to become heavy with sleep.

Then, to her surprise, he spoke again. Groggily. In a drawl that made his Erse words almost indecipherable. "Are you . . . co . . . cold?" he asked, his gaze still fixed upon her.

She tried to smile, to conceal the inevitable guilt she was beginning to feel. But it was *his* fault, she told herself determinedly. If he'd only let her return to her people when she'd come to rescue Faolan, she would never have had to resort to this, to leaving him stiff with sleep in the woods. "Nay," she answered. "Are you?"

He gave half a nod and continued to stare at her. It was a glassy regard that was beginning to make her feel quite uneasy.

Unable to bear it any longer, she rose and crossed to his stallion to take his cape from where he'd left it, draped over his saddle. "Here," she said, returning to spread it over him. "This should help warm you."

He didn't move. He just lay there, gazing up at her as though already somehow aware that she'd gained a hold upon him, and it was she who was the master now. "Thank you," he said simply, as if too sleepy to say anything more. Then, to Alanna's relief, he finally let his eyes fall shut — those wrenching jewel-like orbs — and she knew that the time had come to test the waters with him.

"I am going to refill the skins at the stream, sire," she declared.

He did not respond; so she knelt down beside him and repeated this intention in a louder voice.

Again there was no reaction from him, nothing to indicate that he'd heard her or was even still awake. He was breathing well enough. His chest was rising and falling at a relaxed rate, and she could feel his steady heartbeat, as she reached out and placed a palm upon his huge chest. So she knew he wasn't dead or suffering unto death.

Nightshade just wasn't that sort of assailant, she again acknowledged with a relieved sigh. Thankfully for both of them, it wasn't known to make a person writhe in distress, for she didn't think she could stand to watch that. Rather it appeared that it was just as her physician uncle had claimed: a soothing conduit unto a still and dreamless sleep — and nothing more. Nothing worse.

She withdrew from him and slowly got back up to her feet. She *would* hurry to the nearby stream and fill the skins with fresh water, as she'd stated.

She would keep one for herself and Faolan, of course, and leave the other, completely rinsed of the poison, at the Norseman's side, where he could reach it when he woke. *If* he woke, a voice within her chided. She willed this thought away, however, knowing that her only concern now must be for her safe return to her tribe. This stranger had, after all, been attending to his interests and infringing upon hers from the first. So it was time that she coldly do the same.

He was still asleep when she returned with the refilled bags a short time later. He was lying just as she'd left him: motionless and heavy as a great rock. She set one of the waterskins down beside him, doing her best not to take too long a look at his corpselike form, where he rested beneath his cape—turned shroud? . . . She knew it wasn't an image she'd ever want to recall. What was more, she told herself stoically, darkness was fast approaching, and she wouldn't have long to go any distance on his horse, if she didn't away at once.

With that nagging realization again foremost in her mind, she wasted no time in moving to the other side of the raider and kneeling down to sift through the contents of his saddle-pack. There were all manner of things within it: some that she understood the use of, some, as with his comb, that she did not. She stuffed what she knew she would need on her journey back into the pack and left the rest, lying in a disheveled pile, at his side.

Then, as she crossed to the horse and refastened the pack behind its saddle, she took a silent account. She now had the Viking's throwing spear, saddle-pack, map, horse, and one of his waterskins. What more could she possibly need? His knife? she thought, weighing the benefits of possessing it against the disquieting task of having to walk back over to him and remove it from about his waist.

But she would need it, she sorrily concluded. It was sure to take a day or two of travelling to finally reach her ring-fort, and there was no escaping the fact that such a blade would be necessary in order to skin or scale whatever prey she was able to procure as she journeyed.

He would still have his sword she suddenly realized, feeling inexplicable relief at this. He would yet have the wooden lance he had crafted, and the sword in his scabbard with which to skin anything he might kill. So it wasn't as though she was leaving him utterly unarmed.

She crossed back to him and bent down to gingerly uncloak his torso. Then, with the utmost delicacy, she closed her fingers about the handle of his hunting knife and carefully withdrew it from its sheath—holding her breath for fear of his awakening all the while. He didn't, though. He simply went on lying there, as insentient as a sculptured effigy. She eased his cape back up to his neck and quickly rose once more.

But what of his dog? she suddenly wondered. Hadn't she planned to give him some of the nightshade as well? She looked at the big hound now, where he lay curled up near the smoldering fire. What on earth should she do with him? He seemed to have grown somewhat accustomed to her and Faolan, so she doubted whether he would cause them any trouble, as they fled. The fact of the matter was that she had just crept up on his sleeping master, getting so close as to relieve him of his knife, and she hadn't noticed that the beast had so much as lifted his head in response. So poisoning him in order to facilitate her escape did seem unnecessary.

On the other hand, which was more merciful? Leaving him here to forage for himself, if his master didn't wake up? Or putting him into the same carefree sleep which had enveloped his owner?

Alanna vacillated on this for several seconds, being, at heart, too much of a lover of hounds to make anything but what she felt was the kindest decision for him.

She would leave him as he was, she decided at last. She would let him alone and hope that he could take care of both himself and his ailing master, if the Norseman ever came to. The beast knew well enough by now where the nearest water could be found, and she felt certain that he would manage somehow, no matter what became of his owner. She knew she must try to convince herself of this, for the possibility of the animal starving to death because of her actions was just too much to bear.

But what if he tried to follow her and Faolan? What then? What if Biorn somehow sensed that his master was incapacitated and decided to tag after? She must try to discourage it, she resolved. She would have to scold him and make him understand that his place was still with his owner.

Such a fine, frightful hound would probably serve her well on her journey, scaring off attackers, perhaps, and helping her hunt game. But she wouldn't sink to theft of another's pet. It was bad enough that she was being forced to steal the raider's horse in order to gain the head start she needed. She wouldn't, she couldn't go so far as to leave him utterly alone.

And, with this last detail settled in her mind, she knew she could finally be on her way. She strode back to the stallion and stowed the hunting knife in the pack. Then she mounted him and snapped her fingers for Faolan to rise and follow. He, too, was lying by the fire at this point, and he lifted his head to her, as if wishing to be told where it was she was planning to lead him at this hour—after an entire day of his having been forced to trail along behind that same stallion. Alanna, naturally wishing to remain as quiet as possible, carefully guided the horse about the campfire and brought him to a halt at the eastern edge of the clearing. "Faolan, *come,*" she ordered through clenched teeth, her tone, in lieu of any volume, emphatic enough to make him realize that he must follow if he had any intention of remaining with her.

The two of them locked gazes, master and pet, and, after several grudging seconds, the wounded and obviously travel-weary harrier got to his feet and crossed to leave with her. To Alanna's relief, Biorn made no effort to join them, as she turned back to survey the campsite and the status of the raider a final time. The big dog simply raised his head questioningly for several seconds, then let it come to rest once more upon one of his forearms. She was, of course, greatly heartened at seeing this, at realizing that he didn't intend to respond to their leaving with that deafening bark of his. But he was, after all, the rightful property of the Viking. Alanna, on the other hand, was, at last, confirming that she was not.

Seven

Storr's sleep was a dreamless one. It was heavy and paralyzing, like being buried beneath rafts of black dirt . . . until the final hours. Then images began to come to him. Again, as on the night before, they were of Freyja, his beloved bride. But it was later now, months, perhaps a year, after their wedding. He knew this because she was clearly expecting their first baby. She was swollen with child — hopefully a boychild, who could one day assume the awesome task of becoming chieftain of scores of kin and serfs, and earl of the region.

Alas, how Storr had longed to possess these titles in his youth, to be master of the land for as far as his eyes could see, in all directions. Yet, once his father died, these roles, this power, were no longer just a legacy to be relished, but burdens to be borne. They were filled with incredible responsibilities and life-and-death decisions.

It would have been easier with Freyja at his side. Storr was acutely aware of that. But she was gone as well, having died with his father . . . Or *had* she?

Storr saw her now, vivid as day before his mind's eye. He was, once again, giving playful chase of her in their farmstead's western meadow. And, as she stopped and turned back to him, the noonday sun shone on her golden hair, and her ample chest rose and fell with her windedness. Indeed, the ring of her laughter was so immediate, her aqua eyes so inviting, that Storr couldn't seem to convince himself that she was anything but gloriously alive. She was vibrant flesh and blood anew, in her lovely, seed-rounded state.

"I have something for you," Storr heard himself say again. He was uttering it for the second time; but, oddly, this felt very much like the first.

He was keeping the gift hidden behind his back, and she, in her usual, gamesome way, had already tried more than once to slip around him and have a look.

She adored presents. Even when Storr was certain that whatever treasure he had just claimed, in raiding or trading, wouldn't be to her liking, her eyes twinkled with delight at what he brought forth. And her interest was equally piqued now.

"Then give it to me," she coaxed again, stooping to make her stealthy way behind him.

Storr backed up once more, dodging her lunges with his practiced speed at such maneuvers, and chuckling at how slow and clumsy she'd become in her delicate condition.

148

"Give it to me at once, or I shall not accept it at all!"

"Are you certain you want it?" he continued to chide, shifting the silk-wrapped surprise up over his head, up where he knew she couldn't reach it.

"Of course. Of course, I do," she assured, and Storr knew she meant it. Curiosity was her one great weakness, after all. It seemed he'd always known it, always played upon it. Always enjoyed both arousing and satisfying it.

He flashed her a look that said he was about to acquiesce, about to lower his arms and finally surrender it to her. She, in turn, stepped forward once more, extending her hands to receive it with another joyous laugh. Then she shut her eyes. Sweet Freyja . . . so close that he could actually reach out and touch her. He could cast away this gift, before it was too late, and pull her into his arms, just as she'd always been: warm and soft and vital. Not cold and hardened with death, as when he'd last seen her.

But, to his dismay, there seemed to be no changing the course of things. It was happening all over again. The inevitable. The unpreventable. He would step away now, angering her once more with his teasing, and she would do what she'd done before. She would turn in a huff and dash away, as best she could in her long skirts. She would run, and he would be compelled to follow, to follow and kill her. May the gods help him, *kill* her!

But Storr forced it all to stop, knowing he couldn't bear to relive the scene yet another time. Enough of it! Enough of the horrible, choking grief that always came with that image: Freyja's still, young body, sprawled far beneath him like a cloth doll's! Enough of reminding himself that her death and his father's had, indeed, been his fault, and that there was no one, not enemy nor rival, to blame for parting him from the only woman he had ever, *would* ever truly love.

He would will himself out of it! He would lift an arm now, in his dense sleep, and break the immobilizing spell that had somehow come over him. It would take great concentration, total mind over matter. But he would fight with every muscle, every drop of his strength to take another breath, to stay alive himself.

By the gods, he was dying, as well, he realized. That was why Freyja had seemed so inspirited to him just seconds earlier. She was actually beckoning him to the afterlife. He could presently die and abandon his responsibilities to his widowed mother and defenseless younger siblings. He could easily slip away, into Freyja's arms, and inadvertently allow his traitorous brother, Gunther—that ruthless, conniving swine—to take the helm!

But he couldn't let that happen! He owed it to his father, to all he still held dear, not to permit such a thing to come to pass! And, suddenly, he felt himself writhing, struggling as if he'd been wrapped, from head to toe, with great metal chains. He was bound and sinking to the bottom of some deep river — yet fighting, against all odds, to make his way back up to the air and life-affirming light at the surface . . . One hand, he acknowledged, one finger. If he could just move some small part of his body, he could probably save himself.

Then he heard it: a sound so real that he was convinced it wasn't just part of a dream, but actually occurring at present. What was more, he sensed that, if he followed it, it might be capable of leading him out of this ominous slumber.

But what was it? he wondered, as he heard it again . . . *Whining?* It was familiar, piteous whining that he knew he should be able to place. He stilled his thoughts, the frightened, panicking half of him, and strove to listen, to hear it again. And when it finally sounded once more, he was able to grasp it . . . *Biorn!* It was his dear hound whimpering at his side, crying, it seemed, for his master's return to life.

"Bi . . . Biorn." Storr heard only a garble of the word his lips were trying to form. Then, to his great relief, he felt himself heave a sigh, and he was at long last, able to draw in a wonderful, reviving breath. And, with the movement of his chest and lungs, came more strength, more hope. Hope that whatever had taken hold of him could somehow be completely shaken.

"Biorn," he forced himself to say again, this time more clearly. And, to his great relief, this summoning was met with a cool, moist sensation at his cheek. A cold nose and a tongue, he acknowledged. His dog was wetting his face with long, thankful licks.

"Biorn," he gasped, somehow finding the strength of mind to open his eyes slightly. He viewed the huge panting hound through fuzzy vision. "Odin be praised, Biorn!"

The dog backed up at seeing that his owner had finally regained consciousness, and he began to bark loudly, accusingly at having been so long neglected.

"Shh," Storr said in response, grimacing and closing his eyes once more. He felt as though he was waking from a night of too much revelry and drink. His head hurt. It burned, in fact, as if his brain were choosing, for some reason, to tear away from the inside of his skull. And he found that all he could do now was roll himself over, onto his stomach, and lie groaning against the blanket that was spread beneath him.

A hangover? Nay, this was no *hangover,* a voice within him growled. He had done more than his share of imbibing in his day, and he certainly knew enough to realize that this state, whatever it was, was far graver than mere sickness from drink. What was more, he acknowledged, beginning to recall his circumstances, he hadn't consumed any spirituous liquids in days. Only water. Only that ghastly, bitter water that had found its way into his waterskin. The skin that his Erse captive had apparently refilled . . . *Damn* her! She had somehow found means to poison him!

Where was she? a voice within him demanded to know, and he could feel the veins in his temples tightening all the more with rage. His hands closed into fists, and he strained to lift his head and torso, so he could look about for her. But she was nowhere in sight, and, with his vision still so inexplicably blurred, there seemed no point in exerting himself any further. He, therefore, let his weight fall back down to the ground.

She was gone, of course. He had half known it, even before he'd looked. The crafty little waif had slipped him some sort of venom and gone off, just as soon as he'd closed his eyes. He forced himself to turn his head to the left once more, and scan the edge of the clearing where he'd hitched his horse. It was gone, as well. Through clouded eyes he could see that his stallion was no longer standing next to the tree to which he'd tied it, and, little by little he was beginning to get a full grasp of his present situation.

Biorn, having dutifully refrained from barking at Storr's command, continued whining where he still stood behind him. It was an abandoned whine, a hungry whine, one that told his master that it hadn't been mere hours since their captive had left, but a day or more. And, to Storr's chagrin, as his blood again began circulating and the feeling started to return to his extremities, he suddenly became aware that so much time had passed that he'd actually wet himself as he'd slept.

He moaned and turned his head back towards the right, hoping against hope that the campfire he'd built was still burning, but seeing, in a glance, that it was not. There was no flame, no heat by which to dry his clothes, once he found the strength to rise and wash them. It appeared, in fact, that there wasn't so much as an ember left with which to rekindle it.

He reached up and ran two fingers over his chin and cheek. Just as he'd suspected: there was a beard that felt to be at least a day and night's growth. And the accursed wench, having obviously taken both his stallion and saddle-pack, hadn't even left him a razor with which to shave!

He wanted to let his arms go slack and his head return to the blanket; but, this time, filled afresh with rage at the devious maiden, he made himself roll onto his back once more and rise to a sitting position.

The clearing spun all about him, and his head continued to feel as though someone had run a blade through it. Nevertheless, he gripped the blanket with determined fists and fought the urge to recline again.

How dare she! How dare she prove disrespectful enough to poison a chieftain, an *earl?* Indeed, Storr was as near in rank to a king as the likes of her would ever know, and *this* was how she had conducted herself towards him! He chanced, in that same instant, to look down and see that she had forgotten to steal his sword, and he acknowledged that, had she remained, were she within reach, that sword would be severing her head from her neck at this very moment!

A death sentence! That was what any of his countrymen would have given her for her crimes—for stealing from and attempting to kill so esteemed a man! Yet, as miserable and furious as he was, Storr realized that he couldn't be certain that killing him had been the girl's aim. For, if it had been, why hadn't she succeeded? Why on earth was he yet drawing breath? And what sort of poison could have done what hers had?

It was miraculous, really. Simply astounding! It had submerged Storr in a couple day's sleep, then allowed him to wake almost *unscathed*. He remembered its early effects now. There'd been no pain in his stomach, no burning as he'd swallowed. Just sudden slumber. A weighty, inescapable sleep that sought to lead him into the afterlife as a lover might: gently, seductively—promising an existence that would be utterly free of feeling and cares.

How could so backward and lazy a race possibly have stumbled upon such a remarkable potion? And how could he, having known scores of Erse slaves in his day, not have heard tell of it? Not have gotten wind of this seemingly god-sent balm that could, with more kindly application, ease a wounded warrior's suffering to untold degrees, and deaden even the torturous pain of childbirth?

His mind was a whirl with such questions. And, as he tried to make himself more comfortable on the blanket, shifting his weight, so he could better ponder all of it, one of his hands came to rest upon a curious pile of articles to his right. He looked down and saw that his captive, had, for some reason, not only left one of the waterskins for him, but many of his personal effects!

He furrowed his brow with perplexity. Here, right at his side, were all of his map-drawing implements, his soap and various other sundries, and last, but certainly not least, the razor that he'd only just silently accused her of stealing. And, in spite of himself, in spite of his determination to stay angry with Alanna for poisoning him, he began to feel his wrath waning.

He was starting to realize that she hadn't simply stranded him there with nothing, but had, for some reason, troubled to sort through the contents of his saddle-pack, taking only what she'd thought she would need as she journeyed. The absence of his knife, but not his sword, of his saddle-pack, but not everything in it—all of this told him that there had been some benevolent forethought in what she'd done. Though he couldn't imagine why, her actions, her choices, had been carefully calculated to allow him a chance at survival, once he awoke from the sleep she'd induced. If she'd wished him dead, after all, what had stopped her from killing him when he'd dozed off? She could easily have run him through with his own sword, once he'd lost consciousness. and she certainly must have known that.

Nay, he acknowledged, continuing to sit and mull it all over in his still-dulled mind, the girl did not wish him dead. She was not like his people: stealing all they could lay hands upon and killing any who got in their way. She was Erse and a Christian, in both profession and practice. The poor, befooled wench!

In keeping with this conclusion, Storr's fingers moved onto the waterskin, and he, in his terribly parched state, began to seriously consider taking it up and drinking from it.

But, no! He stopped himself. All possible benevolence aside, this was precisely how he'd fallen prey to her in the first place. He'd been doltish enough to let himself believe that her sudden willingness to be helpful had been motivated by some sort of genuine conversion to serfdom on her part. He realized now that he would prove twice the fool, if he made such an assumption again.

On the other hand, was he really so very happy to have awakened? Now that he once again found himself among the living, and he was faced with such grueling tasks as hunting for food and finding his way back *on foot* to his cantankerous fellow raiders, was he truly so grateful to have been spared? Part of him, however ashamedly, had to admit that he was not. He had, in fact, longed for death ever since he'd lost Freyja to it. This was probably what accounted for his having taken an arrow for Sigurd's son several days before, and for his choosing to place himself in many other such suicidal straits in the past year.

He lifted the waterskin and began to uncap it. This was it, was it not? The previously undisclosed gift Odin had meant to bestow upon him via the girl? It was the death Storr had been secretly seeking for so long: peaceful, painless, and, most importantly, unwitnessed. With fortune's favor, the chit may have left some of her mysterious potion within the skin. With fortune's favor, he could swallow deeply now, even persuade his beloved pet to do so, and the two of them could find their way to Valhalla without their bodies ever being found. It would follow then, that when he didn't return to his camp, his countrymen would conclude that he'd been killed somehow while out scouting, and he would be credited with a hero's death. So, in every way, this course seemed ideal.

But, as Storr brought the bag to his lips with a brave swallow and began to drink rather tentatively of its contents, he could taste none of the poison's bitterness. And, after quenching his thirst, he dashed the skin to the ground and pushed up to his feet with great fury. *A plague upon her! To* Hel *and its nether regions with the pitiless vixen!*

He staggered over to the nearest tree and steadied his spinning senses against it. If the truth be told, she had done something even worse than attempting to murder him. She and her damnable potion had taken him to the very edge of death, the enticing, blissful perimeter of it, then jerked him back . . . back into this harsh and empty existence. He had no way of knowing where more of her magical liquid could be found, if, in fact it was naturally occurring; and any death he could devise for himself now was sure to be precarious and excruciating. She had, indeed, done him a far greater wrong than simply killing him — she'd actually proven heartless enough to let him *live!*

It was not until late on Alanna's second day of travelling that she really began to panic at the possibility of not being able to find her ring-fort once more. For two days she'd been desperately trying to undo what that despicable raider had done. It seemed she'd ridden a mile southeast for every one he'd stolen her towards the north and the west. And yet, to her great dismay, the terrain she was crossing even now did not look the slightest bit familiar.

She brought the stallion to a halt near a stream from which he could drink, and, for what seemed the fiftieth time since escaping her captor, she resolved to study the map he had created and try again to place herself on it. She dismounted and led both the horse and Faolan down to the water to quench their thirsts, as she filled her waterskin. Then she walked back up the bank and tied the stallion to an oak which stood nearby.

With a weary sigh, she again withdrew the parchment from the saddle-pack and sank down in the shade of the tree to have another look. But it was hopeless, she acknowledged, as she unfurled the map and began perusing it. She didn't understand the little squiggles he'd drawn in here and there. She wasn't sure if they were somehow meant to denote hilly areas, or were some sort of lettering used by his people. Nor did she comprehend his representation of distance from one point to the next. She, therefore, had no idea how far she and her companions had come or how much farther they had to go.

The sea. She knew she should be smelling, feeling the salty dampness of the sea by this time, if she were anywhere near her home. Unfortunately, however, what breeze there was had been blowing from the west for days, so this crucial bit of guidance was lost to her as well.

It was her own fault, she supposed, hers and that of her people. Perhaps, if it had been in their nature to travel well away from their forts from time to time, she would have been taught to recognize the land beyond her tribe's fields. But what could be done about such timidity, such inexperience now? What on earth could she do at this point, about the fact that she'd ridden for nearly two full days and had yet to see any sign of an

Erse settlement at which she and Faolan could take refuge?

Nevertheless, she knew she mustn't let herself become too discouraged. She might have been an utter failure at this alien art of map reading. She might even have been, as she suspected, hopelessly lost. But she sensed that she should give herself credit for what she'd accomplished. She had, since escaping the Norseman, kept herself and her companions fed and watered. She had somehow managed to steer clear of the paths of any other raiders or thieves. With the aid of some curative herbs, which she'd found along the way, she had helped Faolan's slash wound to heal more fully, and she had prevented her stallion from being injured or maimed over all the unknown terrain they'd had to cross. Most importantly, though, she had seen to it that her former captor couldn't follow and overtake her. Though she knew she wasn't out of harm's reach quite yet, she felt pretty safe in assuming that the cur, if he was alive, was still too incapacitated to attempt horse theft and pursuit.

And, lest she forget, she should also give herself credit for somehow surviving all the solitude, all the terrible loneliness she'd experienced since escaping. She'd simply never been alone before. Short of her occasional jaunts to the brook near her ring-fort on summer days, she had never been without human company, and she was forced to admit to herself now that even the broken Erse and surly looks of that Storr fellow had been preferable to finding herself completely on her own.

But she wasn't really alone, a voice within her assured. The stallion was proving quite helpful and obedient, knowing her Erse commands so readily that she was again forced to conclude that he was *twice* stolen, once she'd taken him. And, of course, there was always her dear harrier's company. He made her laugh with his antics and his comical foraging for rabbits. As always, he'd curled up next to her and kept her warm on the previous night. And, when they'd sat before the campfire she'd built, he had, indeed, appeared to be listening and understanding as she bared her soul to him and said her vespers.

Alanna looked up now, from this again-forsaken attempt at map reading, and scanned the grassy bank all about her for her pet. She wanted to call him to her, so she could hug and thank him for helping to sustain her as they journeyed. But, to her alarm, he was nowhere in sight.

She sprang to her feet and, from this heightened position, she began scouting more insistently for him. The daft animal! Where, in the name of Heaven, could he have gone? Didn't he know better than to wander off upon such unfamiliar ground?

She ran back down to the stream and looked over its splashing waters in both directions, fearing that he might have been somehow lost to the current while attempting to swim. But, alas, she was still unable to spot him.

"Faolan," she heard herself call out, though she knew it was far from the safest thing to be doing. She'd deduced, during her days of solitary traveling, that such a distressed voice, such a *female* voice might not only draw potential rescuers to her, but strangers equally intent on harming her. And up until now, she had done her best to go unheard and undetected.

"Faolan," she yelled again, beginning to seethe at the little wag for compelling her to do so.

After a few seconds more on the stream's edge, she ran back up onto its bank, and this time she was able to spot something, far to the south, that might have been the harrier. She shaded her eyes with her hand and squinted fiercely in an effort to make out whatever it was. It was clearly tan and white, undeniably the colors of Faolan's markings from behind. As she continued to study it, it did seem altogether possible that what she was seeing were his hind legs and upreared posterior, as he labored at some sort of digging or rooting about.

She dashed back over to where she'd left the map, rolled it up, and hurriedly returned it to the saddle-pack. Then she untied the stallion, mounted it once more, and reined off towards the south to have a closer look. The dotty beast had probably pinned another hare in its burrow, and was, doubtless, counting on her to come and help him make short work of it. And, realizing this, acknowledging that he might well be up to such a worthwhile task, she knew she couldn't stay cross with him for long—despite the scare he'd just given her.

But, as she neared the creature in question and could finally confirm for herself that it was, in fact, her harrier digging, she was also able to see that it wasn't, in the end, a rabbit that he withdrew from the depths of the hole. Rather, it was something far smaller and decidedly inanimate.

A *bone,* she realized, as she came within just a couple yards of the dog. It was some sort of bone which he carried off towards the west now and lay down to gnaw in the grass.

But how could he have smelt it there? she wondered. Something so little and buried so deeply? How could any hound have caught scent of such a thoroughly concealed object? . . . Unless, of course, it was he, *himself* who had put it there? And, in that same instant, recognizing the connotations of this, Alanna looked towards the east and saw that what was, just yards earlier, a fullfledged stream, had now narrowed to a brook. *Her* brook. The brook she had never before had occasion to cross and, consequently, to see from this strange, new perspective. But here, indeed, were all the landmarks before her: the very thicket in which she'd hidden from the Viking's view days before and the heavily wooded ground that lay beyond—the land whereon he'd knocked her unconscious.

Without another second of hesitation, she issued a joyous whoop and spurred the stallion
down, across the brook, and onto the opposite
embankment. Faolan followed, of course, his tail
wagging with triumph at having finally unearthed
one of the beef bones Alanna's aunt had, no
doubt, given him. The silly hound apparently had
no awareness of their far greater victory in all of
this. They were definitely headed home! The dear
Lord be praised, Alanna was just minutes away
from her tribe!

Eight

The trees and underbrush they passed were blurred with speed as the stallion carried Alanna towards her people's ring-fort. She knew this stretch of land so well that she felt completely confident in letting her horse cross it at a dead run.

As her unbound hair flew back, and she looked behind her to see that Faolan was traveling faster than it seemed he'd been able to in days, she knew that she would probably never again feel so exhilarated, so supremely proud and happy as she was now.

She slowed the horse a bit, as they finally reached the field that lay before the fort's circular wall. Her eyes darted up, and she saw, to her disappointment that there was no one standing guard on the rampart. There was nobody to herald her return; but, far more importantly, there was no one keeping a look out for the sort of Viking scout whom she could now testify had hovered dangerously near only a few days before.

Such carelessness would have to end, she acknowledged with an angry cluck; and she knew, even without being told by her loved ones, that she had matured to untold degrees during her relatively short absence. Fortunately, though, her great joy at this homecoming was not eroded by this. Her childlike glee and excitement still felt uncontainable, as she finally got down from the horse and walked over to open the stone ring-fort's wooden entrance gate.

The first to lay eyes upon her, as she did this, were the little children of one of her father's cousins. They gaped with amazement, apparently at seeing her alive and well. Alanna knew, without a word being spoken, that so much time had passed that her poor clan had simply been forced to conclude that she'd disappeared, never to return.

The youngsters, as though having seen a ghost, began screaming for their parents to come and witness this spectacle for themselves. The tribe did so, some abandoning their tasks within the fort's open spaces, others emerging from its four wattle and daub houses, to come rushing towards Alanna with a seemingly unified gasp.

There was nothing from them at first, neither salutations nor scolding. They were just a throng of paled faces staring at her with awe and questioning. Alanna truly had no way of determining whether she was about to be hailed for surviving her ordeal, or reproved for having, however unintentionally, caused them all such worry.

Then, from out of the hush, stepped Alanna's uncle, Scully, and his tear-filled eyes made her realize that it was a warm welcome she was about to receive.

"Where have you been, child? What, in God's Name, became of thee? It has been days," he exclaimed, striding over and hugging her to him as though he never wished to let go.

Alanna's eyes also welled up in those seconds, as she wrapped her arms about his stout form and reciprocated his rocking, weepy greeting. The next thing she knew, it wasn't just her uncle's arms that surrounded her, but her aunt's and those of their flock of adolescent offspring. Through a fog of tears, Alanna saw her female cousins, Ciarda and Torra, stepping in to take their turns at hugging her, and their worry-worn faces told her in a glance that they had, indeed, become as close as sisters to her through the years.

"What? Have you no answers to my questions? *Thrice* we did venture out in search of thee," her uncle chided, having finally stepped away from her.

Alanna shook her head and wiped her eyes with the sleeve of her tunic. "Oh, aye. Of course. Of course, I have answers. 'Tis just that 'tis so wonderful, so bracing to see you all once more, that I . . . I was abducted, Uncle," she concluded, her voice cracking at having finally heard herself acknowledge it, at having, blessedly, lived to explain it to her family.

168

"Abducted?" he echoed.

"Aye. Just as you said I would be, both you and Aunt Kyna, if I went on taking Faolan to the brook for swims," she said with a sob.

Her aunt stepped away from her as well and looked her over carefully, as if expecting to find some visible evidence of this claim. "Oh, you poor dear," she moaned, clutching Alanna once more. "Are you hurt?"

Alanna shook her head.

Her aunt knit her brows. "Abducted by whom, prithee?"

"By a Norseman. As God is my witness, by a *Viking!*" It was an incredible thing to be saying, Alanna realized, even as the words were leaving her lips. As far as she knew, none of her clansmen had had occasion to so much as catch a glimpse of a Northern raider, let alone get close enough to be abducted by one. And to have survived such a plight and come home to tell of it, was truly nothing short of phenomenal. It stood to reason, therefore, that she should expect at least some measure of disbelief from her people.

"Good Heavens! Are you certain that's what he was?" her aunt pursued, once the amazed murmurs of the crowd died down.

Alanna nodded and pointed back at the stallion she'd left before the gate. "Aye. Go and see. Go and see for yourselves. I took that stallion from him, along with many of his possessions."

Her surrogate parents, still looking astounded at her declaration, moved to take her up on this suggestion. They pushed their ways through the gathering and went at once to take stock of this latest addition to their croft.

"Looks to be an Erse horse, though," Alanna heard her uncle observe in an undertone, as she followed them over to the mount.

"Aye. But not the saddle. Not the spear and the pack," her aunt countered. "They are clearly of foreign crafting," she declared, reaching up and taking hold of them.

Kyna wasted no time in digging into the pack, once she had it down. Slipping it under one arm and swiping at the acquisitive hands of the curious children who had gathered about her, she managed to withdraw the Viking's map and unroll it a bit. "By troth, it appears Alanna is right, Scully," she affirmed, handing the parchment to her spouse after several seconds. "I have never seen its like. 'Tis some sort of map with outlandish script upon it."

Scully, now clutching the Norseman's spear, reached out with his free hand to receive the document. He studied it for a moment or two, then nodded rather reluctantly. "So it is," he replied, and it was clear to Alanna that part of him was simply too distressed by its implications to want to believe it.

"But the Norsemen have never raided this far

south," Alanna's oldest male cousin, Taidhg, pointed out.

"It appears they are about to," an elder retorted.

"Then we must away at once to the higher walls of the monastery," Scully's enfeebled, old mother exclaimed. " 'Tis no longer safe here with them ashore!"

Scully raised an allaying palm to her. *"Whisht,* Mother. Hold a moment. How many of them were there, Alanna?"

She shrugged. "Well, just the one. There was only the one who captured me."

"There were no others? You are quite sure, girl?" Great-uncle Padraig asked, leaning towards Alanna and narrowing a quizzical eye at her.

Since her childhood, she'd found gruff-looking old Padraig rather frightening; but, strangely, she felt unfazed by his intense regard now. After all she'd been through, having known real terror at the raider's hands, she found she could look the elder unflinchingly in the eye as she answered. "Just the one. I am certain of it, for he led me nearly three days to the northwest. And we were bound for his countrymen's camp."

Her clansmen seemed to take some comfort in this statement, but scarcely a second or two passed before another question was leveled at her. "So, how did you manage to escape him?" Scully inquired.

Alanna gave forth a weary laugh. "Well, 'tis a

171

long account, indeed. I—"

"*Whisht* with you, as well, Scully Mac Aille," Kyna suddenly interrupted. "Silence, the lot of us, with all our infernal questions! Can we not see that the girl is hungry and wayworn? Isn't that so, Alanna?"

Not wishing to add to the trouble she'd obviously caused by straying into the Viking's grasp, Alanna couldn't bring herself to complain much about her plight. Rather, she simply responded with a noncommittal shrug.

This, however, was all it took to make her aunt begin hastening her towards their house. "Come, hear more, if you must, the pack of you," Kyna called out as they progressed through the crowd. "But let us first get the girl and her sweet hound fed!"

Alanna and Faolan had no objection to this plan, of course. As they entered the horseshoe-shaped dwelling minutes later, Alanna's mouth immediately began watering at the smell of the food cooking within. She made a beeline for the hearth, where it stood in the center of the house, and there, to her delight, she found a boiled bacon hog in the great cauldron. She reached out to pull a bit of the pork from the carcass and devour it. Before she could do so, however, her aunt swept her away and sat her down at the dining table, where she could be properly served.

Within a couple minutes, a plate laden with

slabs of bacon, cheese, and freshly baked bread was set before her; and Faolan instantly abandoned his unearthed beef bone, as a dish containing much the same fare as Alanna's was placed upon the floor for him.

Alanna managed to get through most of her meal without being forced to relinquish chewing for talking. But, by the time she was on her second cup of sweet cider, and about to partake of a bowl of her aunt's coveted strawberries in honeyed clustering cream, the questioning from her kin began again in earnest.

They were on all sides of her, it seemed, dozens of them packed into a dwelling meant to house only a fourth their number. They were, youngsters and elders alike, sitting all about the clay floor and perched on every horizontal surface, from the rim of the long hearth to the straw-filled sacks that served as beds.

Under ordinary circumstances, Alanna might have felt rather intimidated by them, surrounded and suffocating for lack of fresh air. But, given all of the hours she'd just spent alone, given the fact that, only a short time earlier, she was beginning to abandon hope of ever seeing them again, she felt only warmed and guarded by their assembly now.

"So, tell us, pray, how you got away from the villain," an eager-eyed second cousin encouraged.

"Through the aid of Uncle Scully's vast knowledge of herbs," Alanna answered, smiling as she saw how her father's brother blushed at the compliment. "Nightshade it was. I just squeezed the juice of some of its berries into the Norseman's waterskin, when his back was turned."

This disclosure was greeted by a hearty round of cheering from Alanna's tribe, but, again, her ever-conscientious aunt called for silence. "Oh, mercy, Alanna," she exclaimed. "You didn't kill him, did you? We cannot allow such a deed to hang upon your soul!"

"But it was her life or his, wasn't it?" old Padraig contended. "You cannot, in faith, blame the girl, if the devil did chance to die of it."

"Most ingenious," Kyna's spinster sister praised, beaming. "I always said the Lord redressed in wit what the child lost in family."

Though this utterance was obviously well-intentioned, Alanna couldn't help noting how Kyna glared at her sister in those seconds. Kyna and Scully had never sanctioned much talk of the deaths of Alanna's parents. This was, in part, because the tragedies were, of course, upsetting to them, but also, it seemed, in the hopes that Alanna would better be made to feel a natural part of their immediate family, if she wasn't reminded of having been orphaned.

As if wishing to downplay the awkward silence that followed, Scully began asking about the specifics of the poisoning. He was interested in how large Alanna had judged the raider to be, and how much of the berry juice was needed to put him to sleep.

Alanna answered, as best she could, only to have Great-uncle Padraig bring the conversation back to a subject that was sure to be more favored by the tribe. "Prithee, describe this Norseman. Tell us what you saw when you first set eyes upon him."

Alanna felt her face warm with embarrassment, and she knew that her cheeks had just turned tellingly red. She quickly regained her composure, however, and resolved to give Padraig the description he so eagerly sought — at least from the Viking's *waist up*. "Well, he was very large, as I have just said. Very tall and muscular. His hair was long and blond. The color of wheat. And his eyes were as blue as the deepest waters of the sea . . . So 'tis all true, what we've heard from the tribes to the north. The Norsemen are fair of eyes and hair, but their skin browns, as does ours, in the summer sun."

"And what did he call himself, this Viking?" Cousin Ciarda queried with a blushful giggle.

Though Alanna knew she was probably trying to fight it, Ciarda's dark eyes positively sparkled with unseemly interest now. "Storr," she answered simply, and, as she should have expected, her clan roared with laughter.

"Storr?" one of her male cousins repeated in a disparaging tone. " 'Tis not a name, but a thing!"

To the Erse way of thinking, he was probably

right, Alanna realized. All about her were the things to which her people had assigned one-syllable terms. *Tech* for house, *tuath* for tribe, *liss* for the open spaces within a ring-fort. Erse names for people, on the other hand, were almost always longer.

"Well, I must take exception with you all, for Storr doth sound more frightening, than laughable to me," Cousin Torra offered after a moment. And her troubled expression did seem to have a sobering effect upon the crowd.

"Oh, indeed. Indeed he was frightening," Alanna confirmed, enjoying her family's levity, but knowing that some fear should again be instilled in them where such raiders were concerned.

"And so, did he harm thee?" Cousin Taidhg asked, squaring his broad shoulders in a big-brotherly way—as though half considering going after the Norse brute, if Alanna said yes.

She shook her head. "Nay. In truth, 'twas I who did the most harm," she confessed, and, though she wished to feel only pride in this, part of her was almost sorry about it now. "I gashed his wounded arm with my brooch, and I broke a couple of his toes. Then I poisoned him," she concluded in a wavering voice.

The wonder-struck silence that followed told her that her kin were both amazed at these feats, and dismayed by the level of fear and defensiveness that must have caused her to carry them out.

"But you are wrong on one count, Alanna," her other male cousin, Suidhne, suddenly declared. "For everyone knows that the Norsemen's hair is not worn long. 'Tis common knowledge that they crop it, as we do."

Alanna shook her head, happy for this rare opportunity to refute one of her haughty male cousin's claims. "Nay. He wore it well past his shoulders, I tell thee . . . And I have this to prove it," she added, remembering the comb the raider had trusted to her keeping.

As she withdrew the mysterious toothed object from beneath her belt, some of her clan rose from where they sat on the floor about the table, and they slipped forward for a closer look. " 'Tis called a comb," she explained, extending it well above her head for all to see. "And 'tis used thus." With a jaunty flick of her wrist, she brought it down and began running it through her mane, dazzling her kin with the implement's ability to make her windblown locks fall into a kind of order.

"But I have seen such a thing," Kyna tendered.

"Where?" her sister demanded skeptically.

"I have seen a taller and more narrow version of this, worn in the hair of some women from the Erse tribes to the north. Worn, as we do our bands, to keep our manes bound."

"Humph," one the elders joined in. "Worn? And not simply run through the hair as Alanna hath just shown?"

Kyna scowled at this continued incredulity on the part of her family. *"Worn,* I say! And, in truth, it looked to me so uncomfortable an adornment, that I chose not to barter for one and bring it home."

"Aye. The Vikings' way is better," one of the youngsters zealously agreed. "So, might you pass the comb 'round, Alanna, and let us all take a try with it?"

Though relieved to have her dear aunt's claim finally tabled by this interruption, Alanna was reluctant to meet the request. She'd seen, time and again, what a shambles the clan's children could make of things, and she knew this to be far too prized a possession to risk having any of its teeth broken out.

"We shall comb your hair for you, Ciarda and Torra and I," she declared after a moment, flashing both of her female cousins an entreating look.

Under ordinary circumstances, the girls might have refused such a troublesome task. But, given that Alanna had just returned from one of the most incredible adventures any of them would ever hear tell of, she sensed that they would, for a time at least, prove more compliant than usual. She, therefore, handed the comb to the eldest, Ciarda, and the children, tittering with delight, began queuing up for their turns at this completely new grooming experience.

"So this was a white Gall, was he?" old Padraig inquired, once Alanna was freed of the comb and all the demands it drew.

"White?" she echoed, never having heard this term before.

"White. You know." He clucked impatiently. "Truly from Thule . . . due north, and not from somewhere to the east of that, as the 'black' raiders are."

Alanna continued to look at him in perplexity.

"But, of course, he was white," Scully answered in his niece's stead. "No one has spoken of seeing a black Norseman of late. Besides, the girl could not have talked with him much. They speak an entirely different tongue, you know."

"Well, he did speak a bit of Erse," Alanna explained. "Far more than I would have supposed. I think he learned it from those of our people whom he has taken as slaves."

There was another apprehensive silence, one that seemed filled with dread at the realization that such fates had truly come to pass for some of their fellow countrymen, and were not simply the imaginings of idle Erse minds.

"And so what did he tell you of his land?" Uncle Scully asked.

Alanna searched her memory. So much had happened in the past several days, so many thought-muddling ups and downs, that she drew a blank at this question.

"Oh . . . he spoke to me of bears," she declared after a moment.

"Bears?" Scully asked, looking confounded.

"Aye. Great furry creatures who wander about Thule on all fours. He even drew one for me in the dirt," she said, with a note of pride in her voice. "He claimed they have fierce claws and teeth, and that they are many times larger than a man. And he told me that his people ofttimes call their sons by this name, bear, so that they might grow up to be brave warriors."

Scully, who was seated kitty-corner across from her at the dining table, leaned back in his chair and emitted a long, wonder-struck breath.

"This might account for the Vikings' cruelty then, living in a land that hath such savage creatures," Great-uncle Padraig noted, from where he sat, just to Scully's right.

"Oh, and he told me of letting his Erse slaves go free," Alanna added brightly.

Scully narrowed his eyes. "Why would he do that? Who takes slaves only to set them free?"

"The Norse do, apparently," Alanna answered evenly. "Storr said this is their practice, because . . . Now what were the reasons he gave?" She paused to recall. "Oh, aye. Because they believe that the hope of being set free makes a bondsmen work harder for his master, while still in his keeping."

Scully pursed his lips and scratched his balding head, giving this some thought. "Probably so," he replied after several seconds. "But, you must admit, 'tis not at all in keeping with what we have heard about the Norse. 'Tis far too just a custom for so ruthless a race."

"Aye. But 'tis what he told me, none the less."

Scully's eyes widened defensively. "Oh, I've no doubt of it, my dear. We have never known you to lie . . . Our tribe must expect discordant accounts, after all," he went on consolingly, "having no knowledge, at the first hand, of these barbarians."

Alanna bit her lip, not wanting to stir panic in her people, but finally realizing that now was the time, with all of them gathered, to broach the subject that had been gnawing at her since her return. "Well, I fear such knowledge will be ours soon enough, good Uncle, if . . . if we do not begin at once to make use of our rampart." No matter how high her station in Erse society as a whole, Alanna knew it wasn't her place to question the men of her clan about such masculine realms as sentineling. Nevertheless, her conscience would not let her remain silent. She knew full well, as they should have, that their very lives depended upon her speaking up.

She watched uneasily as her uncle's face began to redden. But with which? she wondered. Anger or chagrin?

She squeezed her eyes shut for an instant, silently praying that God would help her find just the right words to calm him, yet compel him to follow her hard-won counsel. "For, dear Uncle, I was only as far as the brook, when first I laid eyes upon him. Not more than three minute's ride from where we all sit so peacefully now! And there he stood, looking tall as a mast, bathing in its water . . ." Her words broke off, and her jaw dropped in horror at what she'd just heard herself say. "Oh, dear," she mumbled, blushing.

"Bathing?" he echoed in a low growl. *"Bathing,* you say?"

Alanna recoiled a bit at seeing how the cords in his neck were tightening. "Well, perhaps he was only wading. I was hidden in the thicket and may not have gotten a full enough view."

Scully was beginning to seethe. *"Bathing* out in the open? For any of our maidens to gaze upon?" he exclaimed. He was, generally, an even-tempered sort; but Alanna knew that, once he was moved to real anger, he could be most difficult to placate.

"Do not raise your voice to the girl so, husband," Kyna objected. " 'Tis not her fault the raiders are such heathens."

In those same seconds, as if knowing that his wife would succeed in gentling him, Scully locked eyes with Alanna, and she saw instantly, wordlessly, the greater question that would await her, once their kinsmen finally went off to their respective houses. *Did he violate you, little one? Were you raped in his keeping? Will we have a Norse bastard to contend with in several months' time?*

His wise, penetrating orbs searched hers with the

182

thoroughness that only a physician's could. And, though Alanna knew that neither of them truly wished to take up such a delicate subject in the presence of so many others, she found herself shaking her head in response.

"Alanna is right, Scully," Padraig interjected. We must begin at once to keep an unceasing watch from the ramparts. We would be fools not to with a Viking scout having been seen so near."

Alanna sighed with relief at hearing her recommendation endorsed by one of such stature in the tribe.

Scully mercifully transferred his incisive gaze to the elder. "Aye," he softly agreed.

Alanna again squeezed her eyes shut—this time in thanksgiving. Her abduction, her harrowing efforts to escape from the raider and make her way home, all of the suffering she'd done, seemed somehow worthwhile now. With this new resolution afoot, it was very likely that her four-day tribulation might serve the highest possible purpose: saving her clan from the Norsemen's murderous hands.

In the minutes that followed, the Viking's map was withdrawn from his saddle-pack once more, and the elders gathered around Scully and launched into a heated debate as to how the alien representation was meant to be read. Alanna, remaining at the dining table to finish her bowl of strawberries and cream, showed the men the point on the map that she believed indicated their ring-fort. Then, to her relief, her Aunt Kyna chose to ask that the tribe adjourn for the time being, so that her niece could retire to her bedstead for some much-needed rest.

Alanna's female cousins, Ciarda and Torra, seeming happy to be temporarily freed of the task of combing the youngsters' hair, immediately followed in Alanna's wake. They accompanied her and Faolan to the rear of the house; and there they all lay near the second hearth, upon the straw-filled sacks that served as their beds.

"Alanna needs her sleep now, mind," Kyna scolded her daughters, as they eagerly flanked their cousin with their reclining forms. "I've not sent the rest away, only to have the pair of you keeping her awake with your silly questions!"

"But we shall be quiet, mother," Ciarda promised. "We give thee our word."

Kyna waved her off wearily. "Ah, blather. You will not." The three maidens, so close in age, had always been inseparable, and Kyna must have known that any protests or threats from her now would ultimately prove useless. Ciarda and Torra had been Alanna's lifelong confidantes, after all, and it went without saying that they would risk almost any punishment in order to be the first two to converse with her in private. "But I had better not hear even whispers when I come back to cast an eye over you," the matriarch added nonetheless, before returning to the front of the house.

The minutes that followed reminded Alanna of their giggly childhoods. Ciarda pressed a fist to her mouth to fight back a mischievous laugh, where she lay to the left of Alanna and Faolan. Then Torra, finally able to relish the Viking's comb in relative privacy, sat up, shook her black hair free of its amber-colored band, and started running the prized implement through it.

"You must tell us everything," Ciarda began in a fervent undertone, once she was certain her mother was out of earshot.

"Aye. Everything," Torra urged, stopping her exuberant combing to look her cousin beseechingly in the eye.

Alanna bit her lip, half-amused at the aggravating coyness her cousins were sure to find in her response. "Everything about *what?*"

As she could have predicted, Ciarda greeted this by rapping her in the forehead with her wooden bolster. "About seeing the Viking bathing, of course, you wangler! About him. *All* of him!"

"Aye," Torra agreed. "With such fine, fair features, was he not the most comely man you have ever seen?"

Alanna gave this some thought, then nodded. All coyness aside, she had to confirm that he was.

At this, Torra flopped back on her bed with an impassioned sigh. Then she clapped her palm over her heart, as though just having been struck there

185

by Cupid's arrow. "Ah, faith and by God, I did fear you would answer thus. Forsooth, was it full-body bathing he was about?"

"Aye," Alanna admitted, again feeling the heat of embarrassment in her cheeks. "But you must not speak further of this with anyone. You both witnessed your father's ire at it."

"Oh, we shan't. Of course, we shan't," Ciarda assured. "So, please, do not continue to torment us with your silence." Then, with her usual flair for the dramatic, she emphasized this plea by seizing Alanna's left shoulder and leaning over to coax her out of her reluctance with an insistent gaze.

This compelled Alanna to offer a little more. "Well, he had great, broad shoulders and a fine, muscle-bound chest."

"Aye . . . *and*," Torra prompted when she fell silent for a second or two.

"And the rest I should not speak of. Nor, in keeping with the Church's teachings, should you be asking," she said pointedly.

In spite of this well-founded reproof, Ciarda pounced on Alanna's implicit admission in all of this. "So, you *did* see his sinful parts!"

"Well, aye . . . But I did not permit my gaze to linger upon them, mind."

The irritation reflected in Ciarda's next words warned that Alanna could expect an equal lack of cooperation from both of her cousins, when next she needed it. "So you have absolutely naught to

186

tell us?"

"Well, perhaps there is a bit more," Alanna conceded after several seconds, having weighed this tacit threat and decided she didn't wish to have it leveled against her. "But, lest I be considered sullied by the rest, you must both swear to secrecy."

The two maidens did not hesitate to do so, and, within the space of just an instant, it was again Alanna's turn to speak.

Her companions were completely still, as if with prurient anticipation; and Alanna could only thank God that the window-less dwelling was so dark as she began to say more. She was certain that she would simply have died of abashment, if she'd been called upon to do so in the exacting light of day.

"Well, what is it?" Torra asked impatiently.

"Only that I believe it . . . it changes form . . . This thing about which you ask."

In the space of a heartbeat, Ciarda's face was again over Alanna's, her swarthy features drawn together in total befuddlement. "But how is that possible?"

"For the sake of Heaven, keep your voice down," Torra hissed to her older sister, and another hush fell over the threesome.

"It just is," Alanna maintained in a whisper. "It looked to be small and limp as he bathed. Yet it was quite long and hard, when he lay next to me."

At this, Ciarda clapped a hand over her gaping

mouth and fell back down upon her bed.

Her sister, on the other hand, sat up with an aghast expression. "God forfend, Alanna! What did he do to you that you are now able to talk of such things so frankly?"

Alanna gave forth an indignant cluck. " 'Twas not his doing, but yours! 'Twas the pair of you who goaded me into speaking thus."

"Dear Lord, you mean to tell us he made you lie with him?" Ciarda choked.

"Nay. No *lie,* as you might think of it. He simply chose to sleep beside me, in the cold of the night. And naught came to pass between us. I swear it," she added firmly.

"Naught?" Ciarda fished, apparently sensing, at her advanced age of nineteen, that this wasn't entirely true.

"Well . . . only . . . only that he kissed the back of my neck," Alanna stammered after a moment.

"He kissed what?" Torra exclaimed, continuing to sound astounded.

"The back of my neck, Torra. Did you not hear me?" Alanna snapped, beginning, in her travel-weary state, to feel annoyed by this inquisition.

"Well, why . . . why would he do such a thing?" Torra faltered.

Alanna shrugged. "Because he was dreaming, I think. Dreaming of another. I am quite certain the kisses were not meant for me."

Torra sat up and shook her head in wonder.

188

"Two full days with the villain, and all he did was kiss your neck?"

"Aye."

" 'Tis unlike aught we've heard in tales of such raiders," Ciarda noted gingerly.

"Per chance that is because they were simply tales, good Cousin. While what *I* have imparted is God's Own Truth."

Ciarda gave Alanna's hand a reassuring pat. "Oh, I've no doubt of that. 'Tis simply too much for our minds to grasp, I fear . . . your being spirited off by a Viking. Just think of it! And, rather than raping or killing you, as we have always heard tell, he simply kissed you and gave you his comb!"

"He didn't give it to me. He merely consented to my holding it for him."

"Why?" Torra inquired, her brown eyes wide with continued marveling.

"Because I asked him if I might."

"And he said aye? As simple as that?"

Alanna nodded.

"Hmmm." Ciarda rolled onto her right side and propped herself up musefully on one elbow. "And was this pleasant, pray? This kissing at the back of your neck?"

Alanna didn't need to consider her answer for very long. The memory of it, as if to mock her, was still disquietingly fresh. "What do you think?" she retorted, raising a brow at her older cousin.

"Well, circumstances aside, I should think it

189

would be."

Alanna donned a faint smile. "It was," she confirmed. "In truth, I think, when I marry I shall ask my husband to do the same."

Torra began pressing her palm to the sticky clay flooring and pulling it back, producing a suctioning sound. Alanna, in turn, realized that, never before had she seen her cousins in such contemplative states. They were absolutely filled with the weight of wondering, and the burden of having to extract the information they sought. Never had she seen them resort to such ambages. "So you didn't dislike him, this raider? This Storr, as he was called?" Torra pursued.

"But, of course, I did! He knocked both Faolan and me senseless. Then he trussed my hands and carried me, against my will, so far from our fort that I truly thought I might never find my way home. Of course, I disliked him! Wouldn't you?"

"Of course," her cousins replied, in a repentant kind of unison.

"Even so, he could have been far worse to you," Torra remarked after a moment. "Indeed, judging from what you've said, it would seem he was almost civilized."

"Well, he was . . . in some measure," Alanna agreed. "Despite their killing and sacking, they seem to have their own sense of civility, the Norsemen. That is, if Storr was any example."

"Pity you had to poison him. I mean, considering he did not attempt to kill you," Ciarda said wistfully. To Alanna's surprise, she felt an even more profound twinge of regret at this now, than she had when she'd left the Viking lying in the woods two days before.

"But, if she hadn't, she would not have gotten free of him and found her way back to us," Torra reminded.

"Still, in all, I shall never know how you kept your wits about you in the company of so comely a man," Ciarda went on with an almost lovesick sigh.

"Ah, you would have done the same in my stead," Alanna assured, beginning to realize now that, no matter how many questions she answered for her cousins, the reality of her experience could never be brought into line with their maidenly musing.

On the contrary, it wasn't rapture she'd known in being swept off by the Viking, but terror. She had experienced untold apprehension and humility in his keeping, in being treated as a slave, after a lifetime of enjoying upper-class respect and privileges. And, rather than being seduced by his fine looks, his manliness—as her cousins seemed to feel she should have been—she had largely felt afraid of him, of the consequences he might have brought to bear upon her.

But, alas, there truly seemed no way to put such feelings into words for her companions, to make them see that finding one's self utterly alone with such a warrior could be fraught with just as much uneasiness as it could passion. They were probably just aroused by the fact that the raider was an outlander, a novelty. The very idea of his foreignness seemed to hold so much allure for them, that they simply didn't realize how threatening such a man could be.

On the other hand, as Torra had just pointed out, it was undeniably true that her captor could almost have been said to have been good to her, under the circumstances. He had seen to it that she was fed and watered. He'd let her ride with him, when he could have, just as easily, forced her to keep pace on foot. And, most importantly, no real harm had come to her in his keeping.

And, given this, Alanna did hope that, one day—with enough time to savor her return to safety, to sit near her clan's hearth and heal her spirit—her memories of the Viking might begin to have the heart-smittening effect upon her that her cousins obviously experienced from hearing of him. She might even come to terms with the jumble of emotions she felt each time she wondered whether or not he had survived the nightshade and found his way back to his countrymen.

For now, however, it was all still too real to her, too vividly fixed in her mind; and she prayed that, in the days to come, she could somehow persuade the men of her tribe to do more than simply keep watch about the fort. While their enclosure was tall enough to prevent cattle theft and foraging by wild animals, it would not, as it stood, bear up against the kind of concerted attack that she now knew vocational warriors, such as Storr, were capable of mounting.

There was no question that her people would have to arm themselves, as well. They would somehow have to become prepared for full-scale defense, and they would probably be given precious little time in which to do so.

Nine

Gunther was keeping watch from one of the sea-cliffs surrounding the Viking camp, when his older brother, Storr, finally came into view. He nearly reeled out of his footing atop the cliff at the sight of Storr. He'd begun to think that Storr was dead after so many days afield. But, alas, here the scoundrel was again, riding straight and tall upon a saddle-less Erse stallion, which Gunther did not recognize.

Through gritted teeth, he muttered a stream of obscenities. Then he peered out at the rider once more, hoping against hope that he'd simply been mistaken. Perhaps it was someone else who advanced upon the hidden encampment now, he told himself hearteningly.

But, no. It was Storr, sure as *Hel*. In a land of such dark-haired people, there was no mistaking his brother's blond mane, blowing out behind him as he rode. Then, too, there was his loathsome dog, Biorn, trotting after him. As if aware of Gunther's secret desire to kill its master, the hateful hound had bitten him more than once in the past couple years. And the very sight of the animal made Gunther grimace and seethe with painful memories.

Oh, to the blazes with Biorn! an anxious voice declared within Gunther. If he acted quickly enough now, he could chuck his spear down at his brother and probably manage to convince the others that it was simply a blunder—that he hadn't seen enough of the fast-approaching rider or his pet to realize he was a fellow Viking.

With this in mind, he scrambled to lay hands upon the weapon. Then he poised himself to throw it. To his dismay, however, Storr's freeman, Leif, who was standing watch on the cliffs to the east, chose that same second in which to call out his chieftain's name. He shouted this greeting in such a resounding voice, in fact, that Gunther instantly realized that yet another golden opportunity to off his brother had just slipped through his fingers. With Leif, and whoever his shout had just alerted, to serve as witnesses, there was no question that Gunther would be tried for murder at the next Viking assembly, if he followed through with this plan.

With a furious huff, he dashed the weapon to the ledge beneath him and began scrambling down to converse with his foster father, Earl Sigurd, about this unfortunate turn of events. Though three days late, Storr was not dead at some Erseman's hands, but returning now—in all his stolen glory. And Gunther again had to face the fact that his brother still held the position and wealth that should have gone to him upon their father's death.

Harkening to his freeman's call of welcome, Storr reined towards the east, the direction from which it had come. By the gods, he thought with a surge of gratitude, how good it was to hear another Norseman's voice, after so many days of conversing in nothing but Erse!

His elation was quickly dampened, however, as he again became mindful of all the questions he would have to face, once he reached the heart of the camp. His pack was gone, as were his knife and the horse upon which he'd departed. Far worse, however, his harpy of a captive had even seen fit to relieve him of his map—the very thing that he had journeyed out to create! His first task, therefore, would have to be finding some parchment upon which he could scribble out what he remembered of the raiding sites he'd spotted.

He would enter the camp from the south, he suddenly decided, prodding the horse to a run and signalling for Leif to end his echoing salutation. Once he reached the servant, they would make their way to his tent via the most roundabout route, so that his return might escape his fellow chieftain's notice for as long as possible.

Obedient freeman that he was, Leif's heralding came to an abrupt halt at Storr's gesture. The yeoman completed his hurried descent from his watch point in silence, while Biorn dashed forward to greet him. Storr couldn't help smiling as they closed upon one another in a spirited embrace seconds later. They were his most trusted beast and freeman — as constant and true a pair of companions as he was certain he would ever know. And, though the past year had taught him just how mortal such relationships could be, he found himself relishing the scene now.

"What ho, master?" Leif inquired uneasily, when Storr finally reached him. "Why the call for silence? Have you an Erse bowman on your tail?"

Storr continued to smile at his husky attendant. Born of both Erse and Nordic blood, Leif possessed the dark hair and complexion of his enslaved mother, and the height and brawn of his Norse sire — who was, most suspected, Storr's own dad. Still, Leif had never displayed an instant of dissatisfaction regarding his patrimonial entitlement. With three legitimate sons to his name, Storr's father had had ample heirs to assume his title and holdings; and Leif seemed quite content to have simply been made a freeman upon the family stead and to have been appointed Storr's right-hand man. And, though it wasn't a Viking's way to give voice to such sentimentality, Storr had come to regard Leif as the loyal sibling he had lost in Gunther.

"*Neinn.* 'Tis merely that I do not want Sigurd told too soon of my return."

"I understand," Leif assured, stepping down from the foot of the cliff to help Storr dismount his horse. Again, however, his efforts were met by his master's halting palm.

"*Neinn.* Let me ride in," Storr directed, remembering the trace of a limp that still hung with him due to the Erse girl's attack. " 'Tis for the best that . . . that I ride," he added, taking his eyes from his freeman's penetrating gaze. He hadn't yet devised an alibi, a tale that would serve to answer his fellow Vikings' inquiries about the suspicious details of his return; and he knew, with Sigurd and his sons so anxious for his demise, that he couldn't afford to show too much fallibility—even to his own entourage of servants and kin. He owed it to them to continue to appear invincible. "Round about these cliffs to the east, then straight to my tent," he added firmly.

"As you wish, master," Leif replied, taking hold of the horse's reins.

Storr did his best not to be fazed by the silence that ensued between them, as his freeman led him along. He knew that Leif burned to be told of his scouting, of the adventures he had missed by being ordered to stay behind and help Storr's paternal uncle oversee their half of the encampment. Yet there was so precious little that Storr could tell. He was painfully aware, however, that the fact that he was on an entirely different stallion, and without his saddle and virtually everything else he'd taken with him, must have told enough. It had to have been apparent to Leif that his revered master had somehow been assaulted and robbed during his curiously prolonged absence.

The truth had to remain unspoken, nonetheless, Storr decided once more. He fixed his jaw and sat up as erectly as possible on the horse, as he was ushered, like the nobleman that he was, to his residence within the camp. No one, not even his most steadfast companion, should be told of his utterly humiliating interaction with the girl. Had she been a man, perhaps so. Had she been at least Storr's physical match in some way, he might have broken down and confessed to being outwitted. But no, not given that she was a mere maiden! No one must ever learn that she had managed to escape him, and was probably, even now, busily warning her clan of this Viking presence.

Storr would find a way to steer his countrymen clear of Alanna's forearmed tribe during their raiding. He wasn't certain just yet how he could accomplish this, but he was sure that, given enough time, he would think of something. *Anything*—besides simply having to admit that, rather than going out and spotting Erse victims, he had proven fool enough to have been spotted by one of them!

He'd entertained the thought of going after Alanna, when she'd left him for dead in the forest. Once he'd recovered a bit from the poisoning and discovered that he had the strength to steal himself another horse from the nearest Erse settlement, he'd honestly considered pursuing the girl and finally killing her. He had, in the end, decided against it. She did, after all, have close to a two-day head start on him; and, given that he was already half a week late getting back to his encampment — and that alone would probably raise his fellow raiders' suspicions — he'd decided it was best to simply return to his countrymen as quickly as possible. What was more, he couldn't help feeling that anyone with as much spirit and cunning as she'd displayed in escaping him, probably deserved to be free.

He had, doubtless, been a fool to have taken her in the first place. Just as with the huge bird that had heralded her arrival in the woods, she had shown herself to be too wild and clever a creature to be suitable for capture. He knew now that he should either have killed her, as a true warrior would have upon her attack with her brooch, or simply have let her go and taken his chances with her warning her people.

It was finally clear to him that, whether blessed of Odin or her own perplexing god, Alanna was the wiliest of foxes disguised as a maiden. She had, very likely, been meant to succeed in offing him with her poison. But she'd ultimately failed, because his will had simply proven too strong for such a demise — no matter how much a part of him craved it.

So, Storr had become convinced that the only other divine purpose she could have been sent to serve was to simply bring him very close to dying, thereby furnishing him with a surefire reminder of all he still owed to his clan and forefathers. As the old Norse saying went—"Cattle die. Kinsmen die. But there is one thing that never dies: the reputation a man leaves behind at his death."

Storr now knew, once and for all, that, had Alanna succeeded in killing him, the reputation he'd have left behind would have been far from satisfactory. There was yet much work ahead, much earthly toiling and penance to be done, before he could hope to be given an honorable seat in Valhalla. And, having learned this, he would begin to take the roles and responsibilities, that his father had left him, much more to heart. Granted, he might have to carry them out with the mechanicalness of a grain grinder. He might even become an empty shell of a man in the process: passionless and utterly unfeeling in every realm of his life. But, by the gods, he knew he must live to see them through!

Storr's huge tent came into view, as he and Leif finally rounded the cliffs. But, just as Storr was beginning to believe that he could escape into it and try to revitalize himself before facing any more of his men, several of his newly acquired Erse slaves caught sight of him and came running in his direction. Within seconds, they encircled his horse, dropping to their knees with lauds and cries of welcome, and completely blocking the way to his quarters.

"Dreaded thunder," he groaned. "Get them up,

Leif! Get them up and back to their work, before the others hear!"

The freeman, looking equally annoyed with their captives, drew his sword and, with his expert command of the local tongue, began shooing them off in all directions.

"I do apologize, my lord," he said, turning back, red-faced, to Storr, as he resheathed his weapon. "I have told them that such groveling is not the Norse way. But they've yet to learn."

Storr shook his head sullenly. "More a reflection of their fear of Sigurd's cruelty, than any real affection for me, I warrant." Then he gestured for Leif to hasten their pace to his tent . . . His *tent*. How he thanked Odin for it now: the one mark of a chieftain, the one true luxury he'd allowed himself since becoming an earl. He might have, just as easily, slept out in the open with the rest of his men—as he had when raiding in his youth. Such comforts as shelter from the wind and rain weren't really necessary in a climate as mild as Erin's, and a skin bag for sleeping would certainly have been sufficient. But, with Sigurd along, so flagrantly flashing all the trappings of earldom, Storr had realized that it was best for his men's morale, if he did the same. And now, now when he could scarcely take a step without betraying the injuries he'd suffered on his trek, he was most grateful for the privacy the tent would afford him.

Nevertheless, he did have to endure the stares of many of his clansmen and serfs, as he finally reached the entrance of the dwelling. He did, in fact, probably lean too heavily upon Leif, as his servant helped him down from his horse and escorted him inside. But the gathering was quickly disbanded by Storr's assurances that he would soon call them all together with news of his scouting, and, once alone with his freeman, he was able to rely solely upon his own footing again. Biorn, meanwhile, wasted no time in crossing to lie down upon the fur rug beside his master's elaborately carved bed.

"Post two men to see to it that I am not disturbed," Storr ordered, trying to don a comfortable expression, as he steadied himself against the first thing he came upon: a metal oil lamp anchored into the dirt floor of the tent.

As Leif went back outside to do so, Storr seized the opportunity to make his way over to a nearby sea chest; and he was safely seated upon it by the time his freeman returned from carrying out his command.

"Have you need of aught else, earl?" Leif asked, as he reentered.

"*Ja*," Storr confirmed, knowing precisely what he required next and glad that it would once again cause his freeman to exit and take his exacting regard with him. "A quill, parchment, and ink. Prithee get them for me forthwith."

To his relief, his yeoman hurried out of the tent once more, and Storr was, at last, granted a couple of minutes in which to rise and withdraw the skin of mead that he kept in the chest. For days he'd been without such drink, and forced to endure both his physical and emotional pain. But, Odin be praised, it was not necessary for him to suffer any longer, and, after laying hold of the liquor, he settled back down upon the chest and sat drinking deeply of it. As he lowered the skin, however, he saw that he was, once again, not alone in the shelter. Leif had returned in those seconds, and was standing just inside the door with his arms crossed over his chest.

"Is it for your broken foot you drink now, master, or your oozing arrow wound?" he asked in a low voice.

Storr looked up at him as though completely unaware of what he was referring to, but Leif's unflinching expression said the ruse was over.

"Your cape and sleeve were sticky as I helped you inside," he explained.

" 'Tis neither," Storr growled, clenching his jaw against the pain, as he reached up to feel this alleged wetness for himself. "Just go and fetch that for which I asked."

"*Ja.* I have sent to your uncle's tent for the parchment," Leif declared, uncrossing his arms and striding over to Storr as though bent on having a look at his injuries.

Storr couldn't help flushing slightly in those seconds. He knew that his upper arm had been bleeding on and off, since Alanna had gouged it. He'd had no idea that it had seeped all the way through

204

to his cape, however; and he felt quite exposed now, as Leif's blue eyes, his *father's* azure glare, came into alignment with his. As the freeman, no doubt, hoped, it was proving more than ample scolding for Storr's attempting to hide so serious a condition.

"I sutured it well enough, did I not?" Leif asked, as he moved to Storr's side and knelt to examine the wound.

Storr braced himself upon the chest at feeling the servant push his cape aside and begin easing his torn tunic away from his punctured flesh.

"*Ja,* you did."

"Then what happened that it should be opened anew?"

" 'Tis a . . . a very long story, my friend. One I am certain Sigurd will not allow me to finish before he comes round demanding to see the map of my scouting."

"The map you plan to draw upon the parchment you just called for?" Leif inquired pointedly.

Storr nodded.

"Then I must see to your arm, as you render it, master," he declared, crossing to a roughhewn table and dragging it over to where Storr still sat upon the chest. He then proceeded to another of the chieftain's trunks, withdrew the implements he would need to treat the wound, and placed them all on the table.

"But the ink and parchment," Storr protested. "*Anyone* might enter with them."

"*Nein*. I bade the men I posted to call out upon their arrival, and I will carry them in to you myself . . . It festers terribly, Earl," he added, as he returned his attentions to Storr's arm. He began cutting away at the blood-hardened tunic with a pair of scissors. "Did you not feel the peccant humor in it?" he asked with an incredulous rise to his voice. " 'Tis as though 'twas a poisoned weapon that pierced you this time!"

Storr shut his eyes and moaned, as Leif started drawing out what suturing remained. It was half pain, half itch, part anguish, part relief, to finally be freed of the stitching and feel the festering begin to drain at the pressure of his freeman's ready rag.

"Poisoned, indeed," he replied with a bitter laugh. Struck twice in the *same* place by Erse natives in the course of just a fortnight, he was starting to view them as far less easy prey than he ever had in his shortsighted youth. He'd been poisoned rightly enough. Leif was correct in assuming that it was a toxin that had left his arm in such a precarious state. It was just that it hadn't entered through his blood, but via his own damnable mouth! He'd been utterly beguiled; and, even now, two or three days' journey away from her, that accursed maiden's actions were causing him agony! "These people know of potions that you and I can scarcely imagine," he concluded, wincing.

"Pray, tell me where I might find the Erseman who did this to you, and I will away at once to slay him," Leif vowed through gritted teeth, as he began restitching the wound.

His left hand trembling with pain, Storr lifted the skin to his lips once more. Then he took another long swallow of the liquor. "Never," he replied. "For, I swear upon my father's grave, there is no such man." *This was the truth, at least,* he thought with marked relief. The sorry fact of the matter was that his servant had been wrong in assuming the gender of his attacker, and this again gave him the means of evasion he seemed to keep seeking.

With Leif's continued assistance, Storr managed to map out as much as he could remember on the parchment, and he was completely sutured and redressed in clean raiment by the time Earl Sigurd — or "Sigurd the Serpent-eyed," as he'd come to be called — sent for him. Storr, however, knowing that he would not hold up under his antagonistic neighbor's scrutiny, if he tried to leave his quarters in his injured state, declined the elder chieftain's summoning. With the sort of posturing that had become rather frequent between the two earls of late, Storr sent back word that, being that he had journeyed for so many days to obtain the information that the "good chief" now sought, it seemed only just that Sigurd should deign to travel the short distance that separated their tents.

As Storr hoped, the gruff old Norseman did

deign to do so. Unfortunately, however, he also saw fit to bring his entire entourage of kin and key freemen with him. This, in turn, obliged Storr to call all of his clansmen into the meeting, as well. Within minutes, his tent was as crowded as his stead's feasting hall upon their return from a long summer's raiding!

Leif, fully aware now of the injuries his master was striving to conceal, did the footwork of assembling Storr's cortege and kinsmen; and Storr was able to remain behind the table upon which he displayed his hurriedly prepared map. He sat there quite imperiously, in fact, as his noble counterpart was forced to simply continue standing in the crowded quarters. And this was precisely the upper hand that Storr had hoped to gain.

Admittedly, however, Storr's head was spinning. The pain of having Leif digging about in his abscessed wound was lingering with surprising acuteness; and all the mead he'd drunk in response, coupled with the general lack of air in the congested tent, were definitely taking their toll on him. Nevertheless, he knew that, if he could just keep from losing consciousness, he would probably be able to convince Sigurd that the map spread out before him was actually the one he'd created while out scouting, and that it contained *all* of the raiding sites he'd discovered.

As Sigurd and his kinsmen bent to peruse the rendering, Storr's eyes came to rest upon his brother Gunther's downturned features. He didn't see his sibling much during their stays in Erin. For the past several years, Gunther had preferred to dwell with his foster family, Sigurd's clan, while they were out raiding, and he was careful not to converse too much with those of his own stead. But, for the first time in months, it seemed, Storr was able to study him at this close range, and he wasn't surprised to find that it was as though he beheld a total stranger.

Gunther was as fair-haired as Storr, and, in their boyhoods, they had ofttimes been mistaken for one another. But, as the years had passed, Gunther's build had remained slight, while Storr had filled out considerably. Seeming to take more after their mother's side of the family, Gunther had never attained his older brother's brawniness, and, after being fostered for many years by Sigurd's family, he had returned to his own clan with what struck Storr as the mean, wiry traits of a weasel. What measure of this had been in his blood from the start and what portion could be blamed upon Sigurd's influence was difficult to say. The one sad certainty in it all, however, was that this clan-to-clan practice of fostering one another's sons had not only failed to forge the peace-keeping bonds intended, but had actually contributed greatly to the growing rift between the neighboring families. Rather than wishing to return home from his years of being fostered and take his rightful place as second in line to an earldom, Gunther had come back quite reluctantly. It seemed he had not only forsaken all allegiance to his kinsmen, but now held Sigurd's sinister bidding foremost in his mind.

Sigurd and Storr's late father, Ivar, had, in truth, never had much of a rapport. It was apparent to Storr that their cooperative efforts in such undertakings as raiding expeditions had been nothing more than a matter of convenience for them both. They had, under the surface, always been rivals of the sort that no amount of fostering could really ally; and, upon Ivar's death Storr had inherited his father's role in this rancorous relationship.

Though Storr's father had done his best to win Sigurd's second-eldest son, Rutland, over to his point of view during his years of being fostered at their stead, he had not succeeded in this. Being far more honorable than old Serpent-eyed, Ivar hadn't believed in manipulating those of free birth, and Rutland had managed to remain impervious to any persuasion. The same could not be said for their own, slender Gunther, though. Sigurd had, therefore, succeeded where Storr's father had failed, and Storr was, consequently, also saddled with the mutinous aftermath of this outdoing.

As nearly as Storr could determine, Sigurd's ultimate aim in all of it was to add Ivar's ponderously large farmstead to his own impressive holdings. He had already managed to convince Gunther that he was somehow more entitled to have been named chieftain, upon Ivar's death, than Storr was. And thus this tacit, but, nonetheless, baneful contention had begun between the two brothers.

Suddenly, to Storr's horror, he came out of all of this reflection and saw that Gunther, apparently feeling his sibling's eyes upon him, had lifted his gaze from the map reading.

Storr swallowed dryly at his regard, but did not take his eyes away. It was such a rarity for Gunther to even acknowledge him, that he found himself silently screaming all of the things he'd so long repressed. You are my *brother*. My own *brother*, a voice within him exclaimed. *How is it possible for us to be such strangers? Such enemies? How can you be so certain you wish to fill Father's shoes? Can't you see that you are not equal to being, at once, a hunter, farmer, warrior, and chief? Don't you realize that even I, who was groomed for such roles, feel incapable of fulfilling them much of the time? Don't you understand that you are naught but a pawn in Sigurd's greedy game?*

This was to no avail, of course. Before Storr could even detect a glimmer of pregnability in them, Gunther's steely eyes narrowed to the same accusatory squint he'd been flashing him since their father's untimely death the year before. Then he abruptly returned his gaze to the map.

He would, most assuredly, blame Storr for Ivar's death for the rest of their days. Nothing would ever convince him that Storr hadn't killed their father off for the purposes of hastening his ascent to the position of earl.

Their country was a harsh and mountainous one. In all probability, there had never been a time

211

when there was enough land to go around for all of a chieftain's male heirs. Storr had been told since childhood that, for every eldest son who inherited his father's title and farmhold, there were several younger ones who were destined to become malcontents. He'd known this for as long as he could remember; he had just never dreamt that such an adversarious relationship could develop between him and his old playmate, Gunther.

They'd been together constantly in their childhoods. They had slept side by side each night, and worked in the fields or trained for warring by day. Their minds and souls were supposed to have been linked by the common purpose of furthering the family's holdings. Their hearts were, incontestably, joined by virtue of the fact that they pumped the same familial blood. Yet, the slash scar on Gunther's palm attested to the fact that he had sworn blood brotherhood only to the men of Sigurd's clan. Sigurd's sons, Eric and Rutland, bore corresponding marks that told that the threesome had definitely formed bonds that equaled or even surpassed those of kinship. All of their actions confirmed that they'd each become enslaved by the Serpent-eyed's mesmeric gaze.

"Gunther says the horse you just rode in on was not the same as that upon which you left," Sigurd suddenly declared, again breaking Storr's woeful train of thought. "He also claims you were without your saddle and pack as you returned."

A breath-stopping silence ensued, and Storr was

well aware that every eye was upon him, as the warriors awaited his response to the senior chieftain's accusations.

"My stallion was startled by a storm one evening, before I had pause to tether him. Thus he fled at a dead run, *Sigurd,* and I did lose all that my brother claims," Storr replied, amazed at his ability to think so quickly, given his dubious physical state.

As usual, the aged earl flinched a bit at Storr's omission of title before speaking his name. In truth, however, Storr was the only man among them with enough rank to bring off such impudence, and, in the interest of maintaining this equality, he showed as much familiarity as possible.

"So, you did not amply break the horse," Gunther interjected with a critical sniff.

"Evidently not," Storr retorted in a monotone, reasoning that this was far preferable to some of the other charges that could be leveled against him at this point.

"And no one caught sight of you as you scouted? You are quite sure of it?" Sigurd demanded, seeming to ignore the brothers' derisive exchange.

Storr returned his gaze to the chieftain. " 'Tis as many of my men as yours who will go raiding to the south. And, forsooth, I have no will to lead my men into any sort of ambush."

Sigurd continued to glower at him. It was a vexing regard that, coupled with the bad breath caused by his rotting teeth, made Storr want to shove aside the table between them and tear the tyrant limb from limb. He kept his head, nevertheless. Such a show of anger with a fellow Viking not only went against Norse law, but would, ultimately, only serve to jeopardize Storr's men as well.

Fortunately, Sigurd returned his gaze to the map in those seconds and he brought a finger down upon the northernmost site Storr had denoted along the coast. "So this is the first of the places we are to raid, son of Ivar?"

Storr nodded, irked by this derogatory epithet, but too anxious to be rid of these unwelcomed guests to risk starting any further debate with them. "*Ja*. 'Tis a monastery. Filled, beyond doubt, with a multitude of gold and silver offerings to their god."

This wasn't the truth, of course. It was Alanna's fort they would come upon first, while sailing that stretch of shore; and Sigurd, seeing the cove where it should have been indicated, must have sensed that it was an ideal location for such a settlement.

Storr remained firm in his answer, nonetheless. If, in fact, it was later revealed that Alanna's tribe was not sufficiently hidden from their passing vessels by the hook of seacliffs that stretched out before it, he would think up some tale to prevent his fellow raiders from adding it to their list of targets. For now, however, he would continue to act as if it simply didn't exist.

Sigurd and his men were hungry for a raid. In

the many weeks since their arrival in Erin, the provisions they'd brought from home had been all but depleted, and they were most anxious for their next opportunity to procure more food and wine. Though Alanna's fort would obviously provide this opportunity, Storr would have to steer them away from it. He would have to persuade their crews that the spoils would be much better farther down the coast at the monastery he'd just told of; and, given the general lack of cooperation he'd come to expect from his fellow chieftain, he realized that this wouldn't be easy.

Ten

In the days that followed Alanna's return, virtually every member of her tribe cornered her and asked his or her own particular question about the Norseman who'd captured her and what she'd learned from him. Each evening, as her family gathered about the hearth before retiring, it was Alanna who was called upon to share the folktales that had, prior to her kidnapping, always been told by the man of the house, her Uncle Scully. So, just as she'd mused, when secretly watching Storr at the brook weeks before, she had, indeed, become the center of her tribe's attention. She was the one with whom a private word was the most coveted; and she was learning, to her dismay, that such a status was not only an honor, but a burden.

In truth, she simply wanted to forget it all now: the abduction, the captivity, the poisoning, and her frightening journey home. Her memories of these were fraught with almost as much anguish, as they were heroism, and she sensed that finally being allowed to put them out of her mind was the only way she would come to know peace once more.

She did, however, never cease chiding her tribesmen regarding the importance of taking a more offensive stand in the protection of their fort. She had carped at Scully and her Great-uncle Padraig so mercilessly, in fact, that they had not only begun posting a watchman in the rampart night and day, but had actually engaged some bowmen from a noble's fort to the north to come and teach the men and boys of the tribe all they could about archery and self-defense.

Even now, as Alanna sat playing her lyre-sized harp near the entrance of her family's house, she could hear her male cousins shooting arrows at the straw targets they'd erected for such practice. Unfortunately, however, these sounds were accompanied by an equal measure of imbecilic laughter. It was the sort of merriment that said that archery had become more horseplay to them, than the serious mode of combat it was intended to be. And each day that passed, without the attack that Alanna had so emphatically predicted, seemed to wear down her kinsmen's resolve to become better prepared for it.

As was true for most of Erin's tribes, Alanna's people depended almost solely upon the cattle they kept for the meat they needed. So the men of her clan didn't hunt often and, consequently, hadn't developed the keen eye and steady hand with a weapon that stalkers like the Vikings had. What was more, such murderous skills were generally frowned upon by the local clergy. The Church taught that prowess at warring was not only dishonorable, but downright sinful.

It was common knowledge, on the other hand that the Norse raiders were trained from earliest childhood to become both precise and swift with sword, spear, and battle axe; and to match such agility would clearly take years of preparation. Far more time than the southern tribes were likely to be given. So Alanna knew in her heart, as her uncle and the other elders must have, that their best defense now was simply to pray that their ring-fort would go unseen by any passing raiding ships.

There was, fortunately, a hook of cliffs that blocked the fort from all but the most skewed views of the sea, and it was very likely such long-ships would be well past the tribe before it could come to the notice of their crews . . . Unless, of course, the fort had already been spotted by land, and, much as Alanna wished she could deny it, her encounter with Storr had revealed to her that, indeed, it had.

Acknowledging this once more, she stopped her playing and set her harp down with an uneasy sigh. She looked about at her companions. Her cousin Ciarda was busy weaving in the far corner. Torra, wearing the put-upon frown she always donned when doing her share of the domestic work, was sitting near the hearth, churning butter with Faolan curled up at her feet.

"Keep playing," Ciarda urged, as the silence in the room finally seemed to come to her notice.

"Aye. It makes the churning easier," Torra agreed, flashing Alanna an entreating look.

Alanna rose and walked to the door to watch her male cousins, as they went on with their half-hearted attempts at archery. "I will, anon. I am restless is all . . . I wonder if I should have gone with your father this morning."

Just before dawn, her Uncle Scully had been summoned to treat an ailing man at a nearby fort; and, though he'd roused Alanna and asked that she accompany and assist him on the call, she had declined. It was the first time since her abduction that she'd been given reason to leave the ring-fort, and, in spite of the benumbing hour, she had recognized that she was still too frayed by her ordeal to agree to go with the physician.

Scully had scowled at her. Even in the foredawn blackness, she was able to see how his brow furrowed at having his usually eager assistant—a girl enthralled with the study of healing herbs—refusing to rise from her hard little bed.

"Very well," he had answered, drawing away from her, and the drop in his tone had told Alanna that he was somehow aware that it was the memory of her kidnapping, rather than any sudden disinterest in his work, that was preventing her from agreeing to go along.

In the minutes that followed, Alanna heard her drowsy Aunt Kyna offer to accompany Scully in her stead. Then the couple went off, along with the runner who had been sent from the other fort, whispering behind them the promise that they would return by nightfall without fail. Alanna knew that she was the only one of their brood to have heard this pledge, and to know of the circumstances which had called them from slumber. The rest of their children were still fast asleep, snoring on their floor mats and bolsters, happily oblivious to their parents' departure into the dangerous darkness.

"There will be another time, surely," Ciarda consoled, interrupting Alanna's recollection of it. "Father thinks you most aidful at bedside, and he will ask for your help again, have no fear."

Alanna shrugged, taking her gaze from her male cousins' foolery to offer Ciarda a grateful smile. "Aye. But I should have gone this time. 'Tis not right, having both of them out there, out where anything might become of them. Where there are so many . . ." *Raiders and thieves,* was what she wanted to add. Not wishing to scare her female companions unnecessarily, however, she let her words break off, and she simply stood with her arms wrapped about her in the morning's chill. She couldn't bear the thought of both her aunt and uncle being at risk. She knew she could not live with herself, if her cousins were now orphaned—as she had been, at such an early age. That, to her, was the greatest tragedy imaginable, and she wished, for all the world, that she had somehow summoned the courage to go along with her uncle, rather than causing her aunt to do so.

But she was just wrought up, she told herself, blinking back a tear or two in the drafty doorway. It was simply her encounter with the Viking that had her so upset, so gloomy, and convinced that just because she'd been orphaned, just because she'd happened into a raider's hands, those fates were destined to befall her remaining loved ones.

"You worry for naught," Torra declared, rising from her chair. Then she crossed to Alanna and wrapped a comforting arm about her.

"Ah . . . any excuse to free you from your churning," Alanna said teasingly, reaching up to blot her eyes with her tunic sleeve, before her younger cousin spotted her weepiness.

Torra pulled away from her slightly. "And what of *your* chars?" she countered.

"I did them just after your parents set forth. I found I could not fall back to sleep after that."

"So, what is it by the sun, Alanna? Nearly noon?" Ciarda asked, still busied at her loom.

Alanna squinted up at the overcast sky, trying to catch sight of its brightest point, and thinking it was high time she bound her hair and got on with the rest of her day. "Aye. Nearly that, I fancy."

"Then, by God's own Grace, we've not more than seven hours to pass before they return," Ciarda noted brightly.

"Aye. Not more than that, I pray," Alanna replied, catching a glimpse of the whitecaps that were rolling into the cove just to the east of them. This was precisely the sort of thing her mother had told her when her father had disappeared at sea in her childhood. "He shall return to us. By God's own Grace, he *shall,*" she'd been told, over and over again. Until, months later, word had finally come from the north that the good jurist, sent to rule in a cattle dispute between two warring tribes, had been lost aboard a returning ship in the midst of a late-summer storm.

Alanna bit her lip and clutched her torso all the harder at the memory of it, of how she and her mother had walked the shore of that bay day in day out, searching the sea beyond . . . until they were nearly blinded by the sun's silvery glare. Her mother's ghostly sobs at the news of her husband's death still pierced Alanna's ears from time to time, again reminding her of how forlorn she'd felt at being unable to assuage her sorrow. But, then again, *no one,* nothing could have assuaged it, for the woman had simply proven inconsolable. She had, in fact, taken her own life a short time later— secretly consuming poison, then swimming out, in the dark of night, to drown in the very sea that had claimed her spouse.

There was that same sort of summer storm brewing today, Alanna realized. And she somehow knew that it would be as baneful as the one that had taken her father. She sensed this down to the marrow of her bones, and she was suddenly filled with inexplicable foreboding.

But she had no loved ones at sea at present, she told herself, trying to quiet the growing panic within her. Her aunt and uncle had gone by land, not water. So how was it possible for her to be feeling such impending doom emanating from that direction? With a frightened swallow, she left the threshold and returned to her chair to resume her harping.

She should take nothing but comfort in the approach of a storm, a voice within her counseled, for, while it might delay Scully and Kyna's return, it would also bring virtual assurance that no Viking raid was soon to come. It was widely known, after all, that the Norsemen never chose to travel on storm-tossed waters. "Violent seas promise peace upon the land," as the old Erse saying went.

Storr's grip tightened upon the tiller, as he and Leif continued to man the helm of his lead ship. The waters were becoming a bit choppy for some reason, but the sailing still looked smooth ahead.

Repairs to the damaged hull of one of Sigurd's longships had prevented Storr and his countrymen from departing for their raids on the Southern tribes until now—a full two weeks after Storr's return to the camp. But this had, fortunately, given both of Storr's injuries sufficient time to heal, and, with Leif's steadfast aid, he had taken command of his family's two warships and was now leading them into the upcoming forays with renewed stamina.

Storr kept telling himself that he was as hungry as Sigurd and the rest for a raid. He was hungry for the fresh food and stupefying wines they would find in the forts they were about to attack. Nevertheless, he dreaded the carnage, the terrible tragedies he and his men would be called upon to bring to pass in procuring these goods.

Up until a year before, the raiding hadn't bothered Storr much. He could charge a fort without an instant of pause, his ready sword impaling anyone who dared to cross his path. He could tear through human flesh with the same indifference he'd always felt when stabbing the straw-filled thrusting bag his father had strung up for such practice. And, by the time he was just paces into an Erse settlement, his weapon was crimson to its hilt with the blood of several of its residents.

Yet it wasn't remorse he'd felt through it all, but a sense of pride. Unlike those of Sigurd's clan, Storr had striven to make his victims' deaths as swift and painless as possible. As with the wise wolf of the Norse woods, he aimed for throats and the crucial organs up under a man's ribs, and, nine out of ten times, those were the points his weapon hit. He'd been quick, precise, and unfaltering, and he believed, in his heart, that his god, Odin, was greatly pleased by such proficiency.

When obliged to ravish a woman with the rest of his cohorts, Storr had taken his turn as duteously as any, not wasting time with forcing kisses upon the poor wench, not even stopping to fondle her, but thrusting into her with the same speed he would exhibit in devouring a long-awaited meal. She was, in that instance, no different to him than the bolted gate of her people's fort. He'd simply joined in the act of ramming, until the innermost reaches of her gave way to him. She was merely part of his booty in all of it, a brief reward for a raid well carried through; and he'd known no compunction at such deeds.

But something had come over him since Freyja's death. The howls of pain he heard, as Sigurd's men blinded or maimed their more recalcitrant prisoners, were actually starting to affect him. They sickened him and wrenched his stomach into knots, and he knew that he'd somehow lost his appetite for conquest.

In the past few months he'd even begun meeting his victims' eyes as he fought, inadvertently catching sight of the souls that shone within them and feeling their bodily warmth as he withdrew his sword from their torsos. And he knew that these were the sorts of missteps that could debilitate even the best of warriors. For reasons that eluded him, he was now forced to raid without his most potent weapons: the gifts of single-mindedness and insensitivity. Without those, he knew he was, in the truest sense, disarmed.

He wished, with all his heart, that he could give up raiding entirely. He simply wanted to return home and finish out his days in the more pastoral, chiefly pursuit of farming. But every Norseman knew that an earl's willingness to raid was a measure of his courage and ambition. It was what kept his name from tarnishing with the passage of years, and, given all of that, most chieftains were obliged to engage in the sorry business until the end of their lives.

Though Storr would never admit to it, a secret part of him continued to pray that he might chance to find his end at some lucky Erseman's hands this time out. And, while he knew that this fortunate native was most likely to be found among the people of Alanna's forewarned tribe—the tribe that was now a short way behind them—he continued to hold out hope that he might yet meet his match at one of the settlements that lay ahead. It would, at least, be a hero's death, one that wouldn't expose the rest of his raiding party to any greater-than-usual risks. And he had long since decided that he couldn't settle for anything less.

He knew he wasn't likely to find such a demise on their first raid of this trip, however. He was sure to have to wait at least a few days beyond that to encounter any real resistance, for Erin's monasteries were invariably filled with rabbity men, who wouldn't so much as raise a finger in their own defense.

From one vicinage to the next, they were always the same: those strange little monks with their partially shaven heads. They did not fight to defend

226

their holdings or even themselves. They simply fled into their churches, like packs of trembling mice, and knelt, praying to their invisible god for salvation.

It was most perplexing. Indeed, it was even disappointing at times, for Storr had come to believe that some of them, a few of the thicker-set ones, might have made quite adequate warriors with any sort of training. So, it did seem rather a waste.

In any case, monasteries were among the easiest of sites to raid, and always wonderfully well stocked with the region's best wine. And Storr realized that, as weakened as his countrymen had become with their depleted rations, it was probably for the best that they begin with the most passive prey . . . But then he'd seen to this, hadn't he, when he'd chosen to omit the first southern site, Alanna's settlement, from his map.

Just as he'd hoped, the girl's ring-fort had been hidden from view when they'd passed it minutes earlier. The hook of cliffs that stood before it had done a sufficient job of blocking it from their line of sight. If Storr hadn't known it was there, he was certain it would have escaped his notice, just as it obviously had Sigurd's. Nevertheless, he hadn't been able to resist trying to spot it, once they got beyond the mouth of the cove. He'd shot a surreptitious glance down the sheath-shaped inlet, and he had, indeed, spied the fort, just to the west of the little bay.

It had scarcely been more than a dot, a brownish

splotch from that angle, that distance; and, after directing a gaze back at Sigurd's following ships and acknowledging that the settlement truly would go unseen by the surly chieftain and his men, Storr had squeezed his eyes shut with a prayer of thanks to Odin. He was deeply grateful for their blessed lack of attentiveness; and he was sorrily aware that he would probably be needing many more of such blessings in the days and weeks to come.

He realized, however, that not even the mighty Odin could help him through every strait. Even now, as he stood at the stern of his lead ship, he could see schools of dark fish darting outward, past his vessel and on to greater depths. And the usually crystalline waters near shore were suddenly clouding up with what appeared to be a churning mixture of silt and sand. A quick look skyward confirmed that the sea gulls were headed inland and away from the threat of an approaching storm.

Storr winced as the first of the thunderclaps came from behind him several seconds later. It had been a gray and windy day from the first, cooler than most mornings in this almost tropical clime; but neither he nor his companions could have predicted the coming of the black canopy of clouds that was, all at once, threatening to overtake them. Forsooth, the fish and fowl were only now racing for cover, so how could humans have foreseen it any sooner?

As a chilling rain began to fall, Storr released his hold on the ship's steering oar, leaving it, for the time being, to Leif's able hands. Then he moved forward as quickly as possible, rocking and swaying all the while upon the roughening waters. Twenty-eight oarsmen, half starboard, half port, were rowing with their capes aloft in the growing northerly wind. Nevertheless, each tried to muster a smile for their chieftain, as he made his way to the serpent-headed stem, where he would be afforded the widest view of the three ships that followed.

The driving rain stung his face, and it was difficult to keep his eyes open, as he finally reached the bow and turned to see how his second ship was faring in the sudden turbulence . . . Just as he'd feared, it was becoming dark as night behind them, and he knew that the sky and sea would soon be one, huge whirl of clouds and waves at the Thunder God's angry hands.

Though he didn't want to accept it, he could see that Sigurd was signalling for his crews to head to land. But the old earl was right, of course. The storm was just about to envelop his ships, and he had no choice but to order his sails dropped, before they were torn by the wind. Indeed, there was sure to be nothing but ruin ahead for them all, if they didn't put to shore soon and bail what water had already collected in their hulls.

With an aggravated growl, Storr ordered his men to take down his ships' sails as well, and to begin rowing landward. No matter how anxious they were for more provisions, no matter how needy, there was no fighting Thor. Storr had come to know at least that much through the years. Why, even the stronger war god, Odin, was ofttimes forced to delay his sacred battles when Thor's wrath willed it so; and it appeared that that was his will again now.

Storr headed back to the stern, stopping to help with the lowering of the enormous mast. Then he ducked and dodged to stay out of the way, as his men took down the sail and began tying it, in festoon fashion, to the spar.

Leif clearly needed help with the steerage in the pitching waters. His face was already contorted with the effort as Storr reached him. With so many of the rowers busied with the sail, it was going to take tremendous strength to turn the ship inland and begin moving to safety.

"So you and the Serpent-eyed are in agreement for once," Leif shouted in greeting, having to fight to make himself heard over the now-roaring wind.

Storr smiled at the teasing remark. The grin was quickly replaced with a grimace, however, as he took hold of the tiller and began doing his share of the steering once more.

Though it seemed an eternity, the oarsmen finally returned to their posts minutes later, and they added their might to the effort of rowing the huge ship to shore. It was much easier with all hands, Storr acknowledged. Yet it was still amply miserable. In spite of the fact that the rain had only just begun, it was so heavy, so driving, that Storr's hair

230

was sopping now. He could feel icy trickles of water snaking all the way down to the crotch of his breeches, and he had to lock every muscle in his thighs, it seemed, in order to keep the wet soles of his shoes from slipping out from under him on the slippery deck.

He shut his eyes with the strain of continuing to tear through the towering waves, and he reminded himself that he was still in temperate, gentle Erin. Nevertheless, this seemed as cold and cruel a storm as any he'd weathered in his native land.

The sound of his men chanting, that was all he heard above the storm in the harrowing minutes that followed. Even the fierce wind couldn't seem to drown out the counting of their strokes, as their unified shouts issued forth. And, all at once, Storr was inexplicably caught up in it, filled with wonder at having so many men, so many oars, answering to his orders. This was, he realized, the first time, since he'd assumed the role of earl, that he'd felt anything quite like it. The power of it, the awesomeness. It seemed to invigorate him, suddenly making him forget how drenched and troubled he was.

With each drag backward on the huge oar, with each push to the fore, he felt merged with his beloved freeman, inextricably linked to his kin and crew, and he was amazed that this exaltation could be found amidst such wretched conditions. No matter what he'd believed since his father's tragic death, no matter how low his spirits had sunk, he realized now that he was not alone with the terrible yoke of command. Rather, there were scores of men engaged in the very same effort, dreaming the same dreams for the prosperity of the stead they jointly occupied.

Just as Storr was beginning to bask in this realization, however — just as he was starting to feel unstoppable at the surging of the vessel as they continued to propel it through the torrential weather — he heard one of his men calling out for him to have a look behind him.

He did so, and, to his horror, he saw that Sigurd's ships — as if imprisoned by the eye of the storm — had fallen a surprising distance behind his. Far worse, however, they were no longer headed for the adjacent shore, but had turned about and appeared to be bound for the sheltering point of land that was now several ship lengths back.

Alanna's hook of cliffs, Storr inwardly exclaimed. *By the gods,* it was that accursed Ersewoman's cove into which Sigurd was retreating!

"*What* is he doing?" he hollered to Leif.

The freeman looked over his shoulder as well. "It appears his ships have been swept backward, master. So he is seeking the cover of that inlet . . . as I am sure you would in his stead."

"Fie, he cannot! He *must not!* The people of that tribe are armed against raids!"

"What tribe?"

"The one inside that cove."

Leif donned a perplexed expression, as they both

continued to struggle with the tiller. "But you drew no such site on your map."

Storr clenched his teeth, though he realized how senseless it was to take his anger out on his confidant. "Because I knew that fort was prepared for such attacks!"

Leif glanced back against the driving rain once more. "But it appears he seeks only the shelter of the hook, master," he concluded, flashing Storr a look that beseeched him to show not only wisdom now, but *mercy*. And, though Storr felt an almost overwhelming urge to somehow battle his way back to Sigurd and Gunther and warn them of the danger that lay just behind them, he knew the most merciful course for his own men was to keep heading to shore. They simply had to make their way to safety, before the storm battered his two ships to pieces!

"*Ja*. To shore," he finally replied, seeing, as always, the twinkle of sweet reason in Leif's regard.

They would simply have to get the vessels to land for the time being. Then, once the squall passed, Sigurd's crews could start sailing southward once more and catch up with them . . . With any luck, the storm's mistiness would linger, and Alanna's tribe would again escape their notice.

This was possible, Storr supposed, doing his best to calm himself. It was possible, but, given how drenched and ravenous the old earl probably was by this point, it wasn't particularly likely. And, if Sigurd did, indeed, decide to descend upon the fort, there was no question that Storr and his men would have to join him. Without Storr's warriors to back him, he probably wouldn't succeed with such a raid; and Storr already had too much of his kinsmen's blood upon his hands to risk being responsible for Gunther's demise as well.

Eleven

Alanna sat bolt upright at one of the storm's explosive thunderclaps. Drowsy from having been roused so early that morning by her uncle, she had retired to her bedstead for a nap an hour before, and she'd sat playing her harp, until she'd drifted to sleep.

She was sorrily awake again now, though, and she couldn't help grumbling some curses at the interminable storm for having wrenched her from such a peaceful state. How cruel it seemed to have been awakened, only to be returned to the business of fretting about her aunt and uncle.

But, perhaps, they had already come back, she thought hopefully, listening for indications of this in the dimly lit dwelling, and finally calling out for Ciarda or Torra to come and tell her of any news. No one answered, however. All she heard was Faolan barking quite insistently all of a sudden, and she rose from her bed and began heading to the front of the house to see what was upsetting him.

Screaming, she realized, getting as far as the front hearth, then stopping with a horrified gulp. It wasn't any sort of play or merriment she was hearing beyond her pet's shrill barks, but rather, cries of distress!

Her aunt and uncle, she thought. Someone had just arrived with tragic tidings about them. Something terrible must surely have happened, for why else would there be such woeful sounds filling the air?

She rushed to the threshold of the dwelling, half anxious to learn what was causing the hubbub and half dreading it. Nothing she could have imagined, however, would have prepared her for what she saw . . . It was chaos! Hell upon the earth! The people of her tribe were running in all directions, and dozens of Vikings, bearing drawn swords and striped shields, were chasing them!

Alanna's eyes focused for an instant upon the fort's entrance. Its huge double doors, kept bolted with a sizable log, were now rended asunder and half-unhinged . . . The *thunderclap*. Of course. It wasn't the storm that had roused her, for it appeared that the weather was finally clearing. Rather, it was the booming sound of those doors giving way. But that hadn't been more than a minute or two before, and yet so much damage had been done by the raiders!

Several of her kinsmen and women were already cornered by them. They were being held at spearpoint in the far right corner of the fort. Many more, unfortunately, had been run through. Their bloodied bodies were scattered about the footpaths of the settlement.

Unable to bear such sights, Alanna's regard fled towards the back of the fort. There she saw three of the tribe's elders hurriedly helping some of the women and children to escape over the stone fence. Then something radiant caught the corner of her eye, and her gaze sped forward once more to see that the raiders were setting fire to the first of the settlement's houses. It was old Uncle Padraig's hut, and its rain-drenched thatched roof was sending off a black smoke against the still-gray sky.

To her continued horror, Alanna looked back over to the right and saw that her cousin Ciarda had just been added to those being held by the spear-bearing Norsemen . . . But where was Torra? she wondered, her mind racing, along with her eyes. The two girls were never far apart, so she had to be somewhere nearby.

Oh, *Sweet Jesus,* there she was, darting about the fort's graveyard with a gray-bearded heathen snatching at her tunic all the while!

Alanna beheld all of this in the instant she stood in the doorway. Then, scarcely taking the time to gasp at the catastrophe, she dashed back into the house and went to the chest where her aunt kept their butchering knives. Her hands were trembling so that she cut one of her fingers, as she fumbled about in search of the right weapon. But, too smitten with shock to even feel the pain of it, she stowed one of the larger knives in the back of her belt and headed for the door once more.

If Torra was still free, there was yet some hope of coming to her rescue, she concluded, fixing her jaw determinedly. She would do what she could to distract the Viking on her younger cousin's tail, so that Torra could break away and run to the elders to be boosted to safety.

Ciarda, on the other hand, was probably beyond such aid. Surrounded, as she was, by spear- and sword-wielding barbarians, there seemed no way to liberate her.

She could still help Torra, however, she told herself again. She had been just a few yards from the house when Alanna had spotted her, and Alanna knew she wouldn't be able to live with herself, if she didn't try to rescue at least one of her beloved cousins now.

But where were the boys? Where were Suidhne and Taidhg? She hadn't seen them as she'd peeked outside. They weren't among the cornered prisoners, nor, thank Heavens, those who had already fallen. The only sign of them, in fact, had been the arrows that were speeding down from the rampart on the southern side of the fort. She'd even seen a raider or two being struck by the randomly fired shafts. It had, nevertheless, been more than apparent that such efforts were doing precious little to deter the intruders.

"Faolan, run to Padraig and the rest," Alanna ordered, as they reached the threshold. She doubted whether the Vikings would bother with her pet. She had seen several of the tribe's animals running about in the uproar, and none of them seemed even to have been noticed by the Norsemen. But, on the off chance that some sadistic warrior should seek to lay hold of the harrier, she wanted him hoisted over the wall to safety.

"God save us," she whispered, raising her crucifix to her lips for a prayerful kiss, as she moved to step out into the havoc. Then she reached back reflexively, wanting to assure herself that the knife was still hidden in her belt. To her relief, she found that it was.

She had never killed a man, of course . . . but she certainly could now, she realized. After seeing how these devils were slaying her kinsmen, she knew she would not hesitate to murder a dozen times over in defense of them and herself. What was more, she was aware that it wasn't any sort of valor that was making her heart pound so deafeningly now. Rather, it was *rage*. Insane, reasonless fury!

She scanned the frantic scene once more, trying to catch sight of Torra again. But, just as she was stepping outside, just as she determined in which direction she should run, someone grabbed her from the left and pushed her back into the house! She lost her balance; but, before she reached the floor, the huge, helmeted brute caught hold of her tunic and returned her to her feet.

Filled with renewed panic and rage, she heard herself let out a banshee's screech. Then, seemingly without her mind's command, her hand reached back, withdrew the knife, and jabbed it forward, into the slanting gap between his wooden shield and his torso. Before the long blade could hit his chest, however, he jumped away, out of its path—and, all at once, she was free of him! He'd relinquished his hold upon her, and she seized that instant to retreat to the darkened back of the house.

He was on her heels, of course. She could hear him coming after her, even before she reached the second hearth and squatted to hide behind it. He had to be just a few paces from her. Yet, as she continued to crouch behind the masking oblong structure, she heard no further footfall.

She pursed her lips, fighting the urge to gasp for breath and doing her best to quell her windedness through the quieter route of her nose. With so few places to hide within the hutlike dwelling, he would find her soon enough even without such noise betraying her.

She was tempted to stir, as the silence continued, to turn and make certain he hadn't found some way to creep up behind her. But she fought this urge as well. Now that she'd been still for a second or two, her deafening heartbeat was beginning to quiet down, and she thought she heard him breathing somewhere—just on the other side of the hearth.

The Publishers of Zebra Books
Make This Special Offer
to Zebra Romance Readers...

AFTER YOU HAVE READ THIS
BOOK WE'D LIKE TO SEND YOU
4 MORE FOR *FREE*
AN $18.00 VALUE

No Obligation!

ONLY ZEBRA HISTORICAL ROMANCES
"BURN WITH THE FIRE OF HISTORY"
(SEE INSIDE FOR MONEY SAVING DETAILS.)

MORE PASSION AND ADVENTURE AWAIT... YOUR TRIP TO A BIG ADVENTUROUS WORLD BEGINS WHEN YOU ACCEPT YOUR FIRST 4 NOVELS ABSOLUTELY *FREE* (AN $18.00 VALUE)

Accept your Free gift and start to experience more of the passion and adventure you like in a historical romance novel. Each Zebra novel is filled with proud men, spirited women and tempestuous love that you'll remember long after you turn the last page.

Zebra Historical Romances are the finest novels of their kind. They are written by authors who really know how to weave tales of romance and adventure in the historical settings you love. You'll feel like you've actually gone back in time with the thrilling stories that each Zebra novel offers.

GET YOUR FREE GIFT WITH THE START OF YOUR HOME SUBSCRIPTION

Our readers tell us that these books sell out very fast in book stores and often they miss the newest titles. So Zebra has made arrangements for you to receive the four newest novels published each month.

You'll be guaranteed that you'll never miss a title, and home delivery is so convenient. And to show you just how easy it is to get Zebra Historical Romances, we'll send you your first 4 books absolutely FREE! Our gift to you just for trying our home subscription service.

BIG SAVINGS AND FREE HOME DELIVERY

Each month, you'll receive the four newest titles as soon as they are published. You'll probably receive them even before the bookstores do. What's more, you may preview these exciting novels free for 10 days. If you like them as much as we think you will, just pay the low preferred subscriber's price of just $3.75 each. *You'll save $3.00 each month off the publisher's price.* AND, your savings are even greater because there are never any shipping, handling or other hidden charges—FREE Home Delivery. Of course you can return any shipment within 10 days for full credit, no questions asked. There is no minimum number of books you must buy.

4 FREE BOOKS

TO GET YOUR 4 FREE BOOKS WORTH $18.00 — MAIL IN THE FREE BOOK CERTIFICATE T O D A Y

Fill in the Free Book Certificate below, and we'll send your FREE BOOKS to you as soon as we receive it.

If the certificate is missing below, write to: Zebra Home Subscription Service, Inc., P.O. Box 5214, 120 Brighton Road, Clifton, New Jersey 07015-5214.

FREE BOOK CERTIFICATE

4 FREE BOOKS

ZEBRA HOME SUBSCRIPTION SERVICE, INC.

YES! Please start my subscription to Zebra Historical Romances and send me my first 4 books absolutely FREE. I understand that each month I may preview four new Zebra Historical Romances free for 10 days. If I'm not satisfied with them, I may return the four books within 10 days and owe nothing. Otherwise, I will pay the low preferred subscriber's price of just $3.75 each; a total of $15.00, *a savings off the publisher's price of $3.00.* I may return any shipment and I may cancel this subscription at any time. There is no obligation to buy any shipment and there are no shipping, handling or other hidden charges. Regardless of what I decide, the four free books are mine to keep.

NAME _____

ADDRESS _____ APT _____

CITY _____ STATE ZIP _____

TELEPHONE (_____) _____

SIGNATURE _____
(if under 18, parent or guardian must sign)

Terms, offer and prices subject to change without notice. Subscription subject to acceptance by Zebra Books. Zebra Books reserves the right to reject any order or cancel any subscription.

GET
FOUR
FREE
BOOKS
(AN $18.00 VALUE)

ZEBRA HOME SUBSCRIPTION
SERVICE, INC.
P.O. Box 5214
120 BRIGHTON ROAD
CLIFTON, NEW JERSEY 07015-5214

AFFIX
STAMP
HERE

"Alanna?" someone called out in a low, male voice.

She became dead-still in those seconds, stunned at hearing her name. Was it the raider who had said it?

Had those words come from the same place as his heavy respiration? Or was the tumult outside muddling her perception and just making her think so?

She went on listening. It wasn't one of her male cousins she'd heard; she was certain of that. The voice had been too deep, too mature, to have come from one of them. But she supposed it was possible that it was her returning uncle or one of the elders coming in search of her.

Go away! she thought. *Don't come hither to help me, or he'll kill you as well!* . . . But there was no scuffling, she realized, no sounds to indicate that the raider had turned back and was battling anyone who might have entered behind him. So there was only one other possibility.

Dear Lord! It was *Storr!* The great, towering beast, who'd just laid hold of her, was Storr, and she simply hadn't recognized him because of his enshrouding helmet. She'd been in such a state of shock since waking, she was so consumed with the desire to save herself and Torra, that it hadn't even occurred to her that her previous captor might be among this party of warriors. But now, now that she was being given pause to think on it, it did seem possible that the eyes she'd just seen—shadowed as they'd been by the Viking's nose-guarded headgear—could well have been Storr's.

"Alanna," she heard again, and, just as before, it sounded as clear and well-pronounced as if it had come from the lips of an Erseman.

"Alanna, throw down your knife."

She bit her lip, scarcely breathing now. It *was* Storr! Heaven help her, it truly was! She hadn't been certain seconds earlier; but now, with this longer utterance, his guttural accent was apparent, and her heart felt as if it was sinking to her feet.

He wanted her to put down her weapon, her only means of defense. He was commanding her to obey him, as he had so many times before, and to return herself to his mercy.

Her mind flew back to the last time she'd seen him. He'd been lying, poisoned at her hand, in a distant wood; and, suddenly, this acquaintance, this potential rescuer from the mayhem all around her, seemed absolutely the last person to whom she should consider surrendering. There was just something about leaving a man for dead in the forest that made her believe he'd be less than lenient with her now.

She, therefore, chose to simply go on crouching where she was. In spite of the fact that she could hear him moving once more, slowly making his way in her direction in his soft-soled shoes, she continued to clutch the knife. Her throat was a swell of apprehension. She'd tried to kill him once, a voice within her wanted to cry out in warning. So

242

why didn't he have the good sense to just leave her alone? Why didn't he realize that she would try to fell him again, if given half a chance?

He drew even nearer, and she readied herself to spring up with her weapon the instant she saw him.

"Throw down the knife . . . before one of the others comes to claim you in my stead," she heard him growl in his broken Erse.

For a second or two, Alanna actually saw some sense in this monitor. In spite of everything she'd done to him, he had, on the whole, been fairly merciful to her in his keeping, so perhaps she could rely upon that same forbearance now . . . Perhaps. *Perhaps* . . . But, with his footsteps growing closer and closer still, she knew she *must* decide.

Finally, to her horror, he stood at the end of the hearth, and, before she could get to her feet and either stab him or cede her weapon, he pivoted out in front of her, and her eyes were level with the hem of his mail coat.

He'd vowed to kill her once, she suddenly recalled. When she'd stomped his foot that first night, he'd threatened to dispatch her, if ever she tried escaping him again. And, indeed, she had. What was more she'd succeeded, and, realizing this, she brought her weapon down now in a last-ditch effort to save herself.

Once again, however, he proved too quick for her. He'd apparently freed his left hand by setting his shield down somewhere along the way, and, as

243

she moved to plunge her knife into one of his legs, he caught her wrist en route.

"Stop that now," he bellowed, but she really didn't have any choice in the matter. His grasp was so blood-stoppingly tight that her hold quickly gave way, and the weapon fell to the floor.

She was too proud to acknowledge defeat, however. She loathed the idea of looking up at him, of seeming like a cowering minikin. Nevertheless, her eyes shot up to meet his in those seconds—to determine whether or not he would finish her right then and there.

His teeth were bared and gritted. His eyes were dark with anger, and, though she finally did recognize him, she couldn't believe this was the same face she'd known out in the wilderness. It was simply too cold, too fierce a countenance, to have ever been brightened by the rare smiles and laughter she remembered.

But would he kill her? That was the question. Was it murder she was seeing in those sapphire orbs? Or would he choose to take his wrath out on her in some other way?

She didn't know. Even as he switched his grip to the neckline of her tunic and raised her to look him straight in the eye, she just couldn't make out the intent behind his frosty glower.

Time seemed to stand still for Storr, as he yanked the girl up and stood holding her face to his. He couldn't believe his ill fortune in finding himself burdened with her once more! There were scores of Norsemen with him and dozens more Erse victims; yet here he was again, face to face with the one human being who had come closest to killing him in his long, sorry life. And, as before, he was saddled with the awful task of having to decide her fate.

He had tried to submit with a good grace when Sigurd's stubbornness had dragged him into this clutch. He had recognized his duty and obligations, and had led his men after the elder earl on their charge upon this damnable fort. Even once inside, he hadn't slackened in his role as commander. He had forged ahead into each of the dwellings, braving ambush in his search for spoils. But such forging had, unfortunately, made him subject to this disturbing encounter; and he truly didn't know how he should proceed.

It had, of course, occurred to him that he would come upon Alanna, one way or another. But that had seemed, at the time of their charge, to be the least of his concerns. And, with the wishful thinking that made all sanity possible for him these days, he had simply assumed that Sigurd, being the first to enter the fort, would be the one to acquire both the finest of its riches and the most nettling of its occupants.

He'd been wrong, though. That much was clear as he continued to hold the plaguing wench out before him.

But she was nothing now, he told himself, as he studied her. She was neither poisoner, nor assailant;

so why should he continue to find her so galling? Why did her unwillingness to accept her defeat bother him to such a degree?

He should just run her through and have done with it, he told himself. She'd been naught but trouble to him, from the first time he'd set eyes on her. Why, she would even have stabbed him just seconds before, if he hadn't managed to stop her. So, what was the point in attempting to take her captive a second time?

"Why are you yet inside here?" he suddenly heard himself growl. "Why are you not fleeing with the others over the back wall?"

"Because I . . . I was abed as you battered the gate. I was sleeping until a few moments ago," Alanna stammered, clearly taken aback by this inquiry. She'd expected anger from him, of course—but certainly not for *failing to escape!*

By thunder, he should kill her, the voice within Storr urged again. He needed to get back to his men and see how they were faring in the midst of this wrack. His leadership was required out in the thick of things, so he knew he should just impale the dotty maiden and have one less matter with which to deal.

But no . . . He stopped himself before he could raise his sword. As foolish as it seemed, he wanted some sort of repentance from her first. He wanted something—even just a flicker in her doelike gaze— to tell him that she was, at the very least, truly afraid of him now. He wished to see some recognition from her that he was indeed, a master. *Her* master, and not just a sire, as she'd always insisted upon calling him.

Though she'd escaped him once, he wasn't going to be foiled by her again; and he wanted to make damned good and certain that she understood that!

Unfortunately, however, there was nothing from her now. Not a sound or gesture to indicate remorse. The insufferable girl was hanging from his hand, unable to get even a toe to the floor in an effort to flee. Yet her gaze was completely unexpressive — as impervious to his as a moss-covered wall.

She expected him to kill her. *That* was what her eyes said. As with the others he'd just slain in their precipitous charge upon this settlement, she expected him to run her through — like the monstrous, unsaveable soul that she clearly saw him as being. And, because she expected it, because she was pompous enough to believe she had him completely puzzled out, he would do something else. He would think of something that would hurt her far more than a swift death.

He would violate her. *That was it*. Though he would never be fool enough to attempt a rape while the combat phase of a raid was still afoot, he'd pretend that he was about to now, and have her thinking she would be dispatched to her ridiculous god in a sinfully sullied state!

He heard the turmoil outside growing closer to the house's entrance, and, realizing there wasn't much more time to spare, he let go of his sword, took off his helmet, and flung it to the floor. Then he set her down, replaced his hold upon her tunic by encircling her waist, and he pressed his lips to hers with an urgent firmness.

She struggled, of course. Just as he'd hoped, her eyes finally filled with horror as his face closed down upon hers, and she began wriggling about in a fierce effort to break free. It was, as a result, not much of a kiss. It was rather more like being pummeled in the mouth by an enraged sibling, as his lips continued to muffle her squeals of protest. Nevertheless, he was hell-bent on seeing it through.

He'd been right! He'd been absolutely correct in concluding that he would get much more of a rise out of her with this sort of advance, than with a lethal one.

It didn't make any sense to him, really. But, for once, he had been able to fathom this mystifying maiden, to offend her as surely as she had him, and he took a great deal of pleasure in it.

She continued to fight against his kiss. Reaching up past his clinching arms, she tore at his chest. But, in spite of the pain she was inflicting, in spite of her agitation, there was still a surprising degree of enjoyment in it for him. He just hadn't realized before how diminutive she was, how fragile to the touch. And only now, with her tiny shoulder blades moving about beneath his fingers like two delicate whalebone dishes, did he feel her slenderness—the willowy build that he had loved so much in Freyja.

She was clearly trying to hurt him. Her she-cat claws were fully extended and catching in the metal scales of his flexible armor, as she went on tearing at his torso. But try as she might to stop him, try as she was to make herself into a writhing tigress, parts of her—her breasts, her thighs, and squirming posterior—were soft as could be to his touch. And, for an instant, for a fleeting second or two, he half entertained the thought of taking the time to force her down and ravish her. Still wet and cold from the storm, the toasty fireside seemed the perfect place to shed his clothes and sink into her, as he might the welcoming mattress of his now-distant bed.

But, no matter how much he wished to make her believe he was about to do so, no matter how he liked the feel of her silky, unbound hair, where it was pinned back, beneath his spanning palms, there truly wasn't the time for such indulgence; and he knew that he must decide her fate or risk letting Sigurd and the others do it for him.

His comb. Had she used his comb in her hair that morning? he wondered, continuing to be aware of the soft tresses that rested under his fingers. As his ships had been tossed about in the cruel, cold sea to the south, had she sat like a princess in this warm little hut, combing her waist-length hair?

But *Odin help him!* What was he doing? Feeling her bodily warmth, seeing her spirit shining in her eyes . . . What, for the love of *Valholl,* was he doing? It was she who was supposed to be most affected by this kiss, this advance. It was she who was meant to be smitten and vanquished by it, not *him!*

With an iron will, he pushed away, continuing to hold her fast, but removing himself enough to see the expression on her whisker-chafed face. To his surprise, it wasn't one of anger or righteous repulsion. Rather, it reflected continued horror—mingled now with an odd sort of astonishment.

Storr suddenly realized that it wasn't him her wide eyes were fixed upon, but some elusive point beyond where he stood. She was looking at something over his shoulder. And now, with her mouth finally freed of his, it was not a curse she screamed, not an Erse wish that he be struck down and rot to worm's meat. Instead, it was his *name!*

"*Storr,*" she blurted, poking a hand under one of his arms and trying to push him to the right. "*Move! Save yourself!*"

It was some sort of trick. Another of her ploys, meant to distract him, so she could knee his groin or stomp his toes once more and break away. But, as he searched her eyes, he did, indeed, detect genuine warning in them; and he turned around to see a man about to swipe with a sword. It wasn't, however, an Erseman, as he expected. It was *Gunther.* Gunther was primed to behead him!

Storr sprang aside, but he did not release Alanna. "Gunther," he gasped. "Gunther! *The gods forfend,* 'tis only I!"

His brother, looking almost equally astounded,

stepped away from him. "So . . . so, it is," he stammered, lowering his weapon. "I did . . . did not recognize you without your helmet," he added weakly; and Storr realized, in that instant, in that heartbeat, that it wasn't the sudden revelation of his identity that had kept his brother from striking, but Alanna. Gunther had meant to kill him well enough, there seemed no ignoring that. But when Alanna, an *Erse* maiden whom Storr had, supposedly, only just encountered, had called him by name—indeed, when she'd found reason to warn him against another Viking's attack—that had been what had given Gunther pause. That, and that alone, was what had prevented him from following through with the deathblow.

The three of them stood in silence for several seconds, each obviously stunned and puzzled by the actions of the others. Then, keeping his eyes locked upon his sibling's, Storr bent down and retrieved his helmet from the floor.

"So, is there not an Erseman or two left for you to slay in lieu of me?" he asked, as he rose to his full height again and slipped the heavy headgear back on.

"*Ja*. And one or two for you to slay, as well, good earl. That is, if you have finished in here," Gunther retorted, clearly disapproving of his choice to stand kissing this curious young woman in the midst of a raid. Then, not showing a jot of remorse at being caught attempting murder, he turned and strode out of the filthy hut and back into the surrounding upheaval.

"Who was that?" Alanna whispered in his wake. "Not one of your men, surely."

Storr looked down at her sternly and pressed a finger to her lips. "Not a word of it, do you understand? Not a word of what you witnessed to anyone!"

Alanna nodded, just grateful to hear that he might let her *live* to tell of it.

"And no more trouble from you, either, wench, or I shall allow you to fall into the hands of men such as he. The sort who will blind and slash you. And, if that happens, you shall wish, with all your heart, that I *had* chosen to kill you."

Again Alanna nodded, offering no further resistance to his hold upon her. Seeing the venomous glare of his would-be murderer was all it had taken to convince her that Storr was, in truth, the lesser of the foes she now faced. And she knew that continuing to fight him would be most foolish.

Storr reached down in those seconds, and, to her dismay, began undoing her belt. *Heaven help her,* she thought, shutting her eyes and suddenly feeling near tears. He was going to rape her, anyway. In spite of the wrenching interruption they'd just been through—regardless of the fact that he had, only seconds before, been reminded of the need to return to the fighting—the stubborn barbarian intended to proceed with violating her!

But it wasn't his carnal touch she felt, as he finally slipped the belt out from around her waist.

Far from it, in fact, he was turning her away from him, not drawing her closer. And, as she opened her eyes again, she felt him pulling her arms back and tying her wrists behind her.

"Have you aught you wish to bring with you?" he asked, still keeping his voice low, as he hurriedly turned her back to face him.

She knew she should speak, should open her mouth and tell him of anything she valued. Part of her realized that this was it—the last she would see of her home, her fort—and she should take whatever she could of it now. But it had all happened so suddenly, and she just couldn't seem to think clearly.

"My harp . . . and Faolan and my cousins, of course," she quickly added. "If you could find and save them, good sire, I would be forever in your debt."

"*Verily?*" he asked, raising an aroused brow at her.

She drew back a bit at this blatant solicitation, then averted her eyes. "Aye."

He resumed his usual dutiful tone, as he bent down to take up his sword. "I will do what I can . . . And where is this harp you speak of?"

She nodded toward it. "Over there, upon that center bed."

As if still not trusting her fully, he looped an arm into hers and led her to the mat she'd specified. Then he scooped up the instrument and

253

placed it in her bound hands. "Have you a good enough hold upon it?"

"Aye."

"Then I shall lead you to one of my freemen, and he will see you to my ship . . . For whatever your reasons, woman, you did save my life just now, and, provided you obey me in all things and swear not to speak of the first time we met, I shall try to see you spared as well."

Twelve

Storr's freeman, a dark-haired warrior who looked very much like Alanna's people, spoke Erse with surprising fluency. He was far more proficient at it than his master; and this, at least, was making it easier for Alanna to communicate now, to tell him everything she could about the cousins whom Storr had ordered him to seek.

Though Alanna knew she must look for Faolan and her next of kin, as she was led to Storr's ship, her first impulse was to keep her gaze directed downward. She'd known enough tragedy in her short life to realize that the sights she saw, the writhing, run-through bodies of the tribesmen she passed, would stay with her for a lifetime. And she was fully aware that the fact that she was so powerless to come to the aid of any of them would only make such memories all the more indelible.

She did, however, force herself to look off towards the right in search of Ciarda, as they headed for the fort's gate. But all of the prisoners she'd seen gathered there were now gone for some reason. *Already led off,* she told herself hearteningly. There were no bodies in that area, so it stood to reason that her older cousin was still alive.

She did find the strength to look up fully, once the freeman took her past the ruptured wooden doors. Off towards the south, she saw a few of those who'd been fortunate enough to escape, running in the direction of the nearest monastery. They were obviously hoping to find refuge there, behind the monks' taller walls. Then, turning towards the north, she saw one of her clan's herdsmen feverishly driving his sheep onward, out of the range of the pillagers.

She couldn't help gasping as she looked out before her. It was the most formidable display she had ever seen! Just paces ahead were no fewer than twenty Vikings. They were standing abreast with their shields raised to form a seemingly impenetrable barrier, and she realized that they'd been posted to protect the four huge longships that were beached behind them. With their usual shrewdness, the Norse raiders were not running the risk of having any Ersemen make off with their only means for a quick retreat.

In spite of the freeman's hastening hold on her, Alanna locked her feet in the sand at the sight of this. He was leading her right into the center of the line of spear-bearing pagans, and the prospect of passing through them had far too much of a gauntlet feel for her.

"Come along, girl. They won't harm you," her

escort assured, turning back to her with a scowl. Then he continued to pull her forward.

"They've no helmets," she noted, still dragging her feet.

"Of course not. They are not chieftains like our master."

Alanna's mind raced back to the moment when she'd seen Torra earlier. The old man who had been chasing her had been helmeted, and this somehow seemed significant; so she told the freeman as much.

He led her on with an unmistakable note of sympathy in his voice. "She is Sigurd's then."

They both fell silent once more, and Alanna's breath caught in her throat, as they finally stood before the wall of warriors. One of them stepped aside to let her and the freeman through to the ships. Still dressed as she was for napping, with no cloak, sandals, or hair ribbons, she fully expected to be derided or pawed by the heathen rabble as she passed. To her surprise, however, she and her escort slipped through without incident.

"And what doth that mean, pray?" she pursued, as they got farther away from the warriors. "I do not know this word—Sigurd's. Do say, good sire, that 'tis not your term for dead," she choked, recalling his strangely condolent tone as he'd uttered it.

The freeman, obviously eager to get her aboard one of the vessels and return to the more pressing business behind them, spoke very hurriedly now.

"Nay. He is the second chief among us. And, if he truly is the man who claimed your cousin, she will be found aboard one of the other ships."

Alanna leaned back heavily against his endless tugging. "Then we must fetch her."

He'd evidently had his fill of trying to pull her along; and, with a great huff, he turned back and swept her up into his arms. "We cannot. If she is, indeed, Sigurd's prisoner, then only our master may seek her. Per chance by making a trade for her, when we reach our camp."

"But it may be too late by then," Alanna objected, beginning to struggle in his arms. "The great brute was lecherous after her, even as I saw her!"

The freeman looked down at her, as he carried her the remaining steps to the third ship in the formation. "She shall be raped in Sigurd's keeping," he declared, and Alanna felt her cheeks flush a bit at his matter-of-factness. " 'Tis inevitable, for the Serpent-eyed rapes all of the women he takes."

"But Storr doth not?"

He gave forth a dry laugh, one Alanna knew she couldn't hope to understand. "Nay, wench. He doth not."

She was, of course, most relieved to hear this. But then she realized that the answer to it should have been evident to her, after all the time she'd spent as Storr's captive, and she quickly returned her concern to her family's plight.

"And what of my other cousin? What of Ciarda,

who was, as I've told you, among the prisoners gathered at the front of the fort?"

The freeman gave his head a sorry shake. "Sigurd's as well, I fear."

"Then put me on this Sigurd's ship," she suddenly ordered. "I wish to be with my cousins, no matter what the cost."

"You do not," he snarled, as they finally reached the vessel, and he heaved her over its sloping starboard side.

Though she landed on her feet, she couldn't help but fight for her balance in her still-bound state. Once she'd gained her footing however, she felt ready to oppose him once more. "Aye. I *do*," she maintained, glaring down at him.

Without warning, the freeman jumped up and caught hold of the ship's gunnel. Then he swung his legs up into the vessel. Lighting upon the deck, he turned to Alanna with a glower that seemed to say he was about to strike her. Instead, however, he reached behind her and snatched the harp from her grip. He set it down upon the far side of an adjacent sea chest. Then, grabbing Alanna's shoulders, he forced her down upon the other half of that same trunk.

"You should be threshed for clamoring for another master," he hissed, reaching down to a coil of rope that lay near his feet and plucking it upward. "You would surely be beaten or maimed as the Serpent-eyed's slave and, far from protesting, you should be thanking your god 'twas Earl Storr who chose to take you." With that, he stepped behind her and used the rope to link her trussed hands to the chest with an admonishing roughness.

Alanna fell silent at his scolding. For whatever his reasons, he seemed to believe all that he was saying, and she felt, even if just for a second or two, every bit the ingrate he was accusing her of being.

Before she could say anything more to him, however, before she could ask any additional questions about her cousins' probable fates, he took himself away. Perching on the gunnel once more, he jumped down to the beach. Then he drew his sword, and headed back to the ring-fort at a dead run.

Alanna bit her lip and let out a whimper in the seconds that followed. Save for the pair of fair-haired boys, who were busily stowing booty in the back of the ship, she was the only one aboard; and she knew that she was in for a torturously long wait — one filled with the horrible sight of her ancestral home being plundered and burnt.

As before, she directed her gaze off to the side — avoiding the atrocities that lay in front of her. One of the longships to her right, the one that had obviously entered the cove first on this raid, held several of her people, and she couldn't help craning her neck now, in an effort to see if any of her cousins were aboard it.

She squinted against the newly breaking sunlight to the north, and she moved her head about as she tried to see past the trestled masts and riggings that stood between her vessel and theirs.

But aye, she suddenly acknowledged with an exhilarated chill running through her. If she rose a bit on the chest, if she strained against the rope that anchored her, she could seem to see the profile of a woman who looked very much like Ciarda.

It was difficult to tell for certain, though. She was many yards away from the ship in question, and Ciarda did resemble a few of Alanna's other kinswomen, so it was possible that she was confusing her eldest cousin with someone else.

Nevertheless, she continued to study the maiden in the hopes of getting a fuller view of her. Anything: a front-on look or the spotting of a characteristic gesture—*anything* might confirm for her that at least one of her cousins had survived.

For the longest time, however, there was nothing more to tell. The black-haired female simply sat there, apparently upon a chest like the one Alanna occupied. She just sat there with a dazed sort of rigidness, supporting the blanketed form that was propped up against her.

Then, all at once, something of a bright yellow hue slipped out from beneath the leaning bundle, and Alanna finally had her answer. It was *Torra!* Torra was the only one of their tribe to possess such vividly colored ribbons, and Alanna now recalled that her younger cousin had, indeed, donned them that very morning.

Without giving thought to the consequences of

261

such an action, Alanna rose up as much as possible and began calling out to her cousins. Ciarda turned and looked in her direction . . . slowly, searchingly, as though still too stupefied by the raid to respond with any more speed.

" 'Tis I," Alanna shouted. "Are you and Torra all right?"

With her hands obviously tied behind her as well, Ciarda could do little more than nod in answer to this. The half-dozen surly-looking Vikings standing watch all about her, clearly seemed to be preventing her from calling back.

Alanna had her answer, nonetheless. They were both alive, at least. Perhaps already violated, maybe even wounded amidst the hubbub. But they were, by troth, still drawing breath, and she wouldn't find herself bereft of their companionship at whatever destination lay ahead.

What of the boys and Faolan, though? she wondered, finally daring to look back up at the settlement. Would they all emerge from that smoke-crowned enclosure and find themselves captured, too? Or had they already perished? Had her aunt and uncle chanced to come back and be slain while she was still asleep? Or were they yet at the other fort?

The time left to wait for the answers would become an eternity. That was the one thing she knew she could be certain of now.

* * *

In the hour that followed, all manner of prize was loaded upon the ship Alanna occupied. A large load of honey and bread was the first of these to arrive; and what Norsemen were on deck by that time immediately closed in upon it. All but drooling with anticipation, they set the treasures down at the front of the vessel and began tearing at the loaves with great haste. Then they dipped their wads of bread into the crocks of nectar, and devoured them as though they hadn't partaken of such fare in ages.

Alanna would have thought that a race as resourceful as theirs would have cultivated plenty of such delicacies. Yet, listening to their foreign, but obviously delighted chat now, watching them exchange bready smiles like overgrown children, she had to conclude that, if they had such foods in their diets, they had failed to bring any of them along to Erin.

The next booty to arrive was several casks of her people's wine, and, as the raiders carried these to the vessel, it was apparent that they had already consumed large amounts of the intoxicating juice. Some of them even seemed hard-pressed to stand up, once they struggled onto the deck; and it was obvious that such spirits were far more recreational to them, than to Alanna's people—who had always viewed wine as a beverage meant principally to accompany a meal. Alanna had, therefore, never had occasion to see such blatant drunkenness, and it was, naturally, with growing uneasiness that she continued to sit, bound near the front of the ship.

To her relief, however, the warriors went on ignoring her, as they passed the casks about and stood drinking heartily from them. It was as though they somehow already knew that it was their chieftain who had claimed her, and that he, alone, had the right to interact with her.

She was safe, she kept trying to tell herself. She was every bit as unharmed as she'd been in Storr's keeping the first time around. Yet part of her—the stunned, devastated part that seemed yet too new to speak for itself—knew that losing one's home, one's way of life, and so many of one's clansmen constituted anything *but* well-being.

The third of the loads was the carcasses of what sheep and cows the raiders had been able to drive together and slaughter. These, too, were stowed at the bow of the ship—hopefully to be eaten or dried fairly soon, before they began to rot.

What arrived after that were jumbles of spoils, which the Vikings had piled into several of her people's wooden chests. They seemed to contain objects made chiefly of gold and silver, and it was apparent that these outlanders were not interested in trifles—such as hair ornaments and spindles—which were said to attract Erse raiders. Far from it, in fact, the Norsemen seemed to have chosen those things that Alanna and her relatives held most dear, like religious icons and jewelry. But, obviously prizing these for far different reasons, the outlanders had simply tossed them, helter-skelter, into the chests. The arms of little crosses were poking out in all directions, and several carvings of the Virgin and the Saints were stuffed, upside-down, into the heaps.

Though she would never have thought it possible, the fifth bit of "cargo" brought a smile to Alanna's face. It was *Faolan,* her beloved harrier. He was being carried, nipping and squealing all the while, by the freeman who had brought her to that same ship.

In spite of not wanting to attract the crew's attention, she couldn't help trying to rise and call out to her pet, as she spotted him. She wanted him to stop fighting Storr's poor servant, and she knew that, if she could make it clear to the hound that he was simply being returned to her, he might curb his snappishness. This was to no avail, however. By the time the freeman reached the vessel, he had clearly been bitten in two or three places. Quite understandably, he hiked the animal up and heaved it at Alanna as though ridding himself of a hive of stinging bees.

Faolan landed on her lap with such force that he instantly rolled onto the deck before her. Then, snarling fiercely, he righted himself and scrambled to his feet. It took a second or two for him to grasp the fact that the infuriating raider had actually reunited him with Alanna. But, once he saw this, his tail began wagging with great rapidity, and he wet her face quite thoroughly with an exuberant round of dog kisses.

"The little wretch," the freeman exclaimed. His eyes seemed to spit daggers, as he reached up to dab the blood from his bite wounds with his tunic sleeve. "I would have speared him from the first, had my chief not insisted that he be brought to you."

"And well he should have, for the dog is mine," Alanna confirmed.

"Well, I cannot imagine why our master would want him along! Good-for-naught little cur," he grumbled, continuing to blot his wounds and inspect his cuff each time for what measure of blood was being drawn from them. "I hope, by Thunder, that he is not diseased!"

"He's not. You have my word. And you also have my home-felt thanks for finding him for me. I shall never forget it."

He scowled. "I didn't find him, chit. *He* found me! I was merely scouting about one of your huts for any stray treasure, and he sprang from the shadows at me, as though from the mouth of Hell!"

Alanna bit her lip, fighting back a laugh at this. She wasn't, in truth, of any sort of humor at present to be easily amused; but the sight of such a strapping man being outdone by her two-stone harrier struck her as most comical. "He hath slept upon my bed and eaten from my hand since his weaning, sire, and I tell thee again that he is not, in any way, ill."

"Well, just you see to it he keeps to himself

266

henceforth, girl. Or, whether I have our master's leave or not, I shall dispatch him!" With that, the freeman was off again, muttering in annoyance as he headed back up to the fort.

Alanna wanted to call after him, to ask if her male cousins or aunt and uncle had been found, but she stopped herself. He had obviously been close to flying into a rage, and she was afraid that any further requests might cause him to come back and carry through on his threat to finish Faolan.

She returned her gaze to her pet in the seconds that followed, staring down lovingly, as he rolled onto his back and lay wriggling, as though craving her touch.

"I cannot, Little Wolf," she whispered, silently admiring the courageous stand he'd just taken against the heathen. "My hands are bound, but, God willing, I shall have the chance to pet you yet today."

The last of the lading arrived roughly half an hour later. It was comprised of several of Alanna's captured and bound clansmen and women, and, at last, she had the opportunity to inquire about her still-missing kin. None of them had seen her aunt or uncle; but two, sorrily, did report that her cousins, Suidhne and Taidhg, had been slain.

Alanna, though half expecting such news by this time, greeted it with a choked gasp. Then, in her usual stoical manner, she turned her face away from the new arrivals and let the welled-up tears stream down her cheeks. She remembered how

Taidig, the oldest of the two, had blustered weeks earlier at hearing of her abduction. She recalled how zealous both boys had been when the bowmen from the North had come to teach them more about how to fight.

Just hours before, they had been vibrant, laughing lads at play with their arrows and target; and it was almost unimaginable that their bodies now lay cold and still upon that rise that once had been their homestead. But then, Alanna told herself, lifting a shoulder to dry her tear-dampened face, it would be a very long time before she could bring herself to believe that such a decimation had truly taken place.

Storr suffered nothing more than a flesh wound and lost only two of his men in the attack, so it was with a sense of relief that he finally headed back to his lead ship. Given how forewarned he knew this tribe to be, he'd expected to lose far more during the raid. He could, therefore, only conclude that Alanna's people hadn't anticipated such an assault in the wake of a storm, and had simply been caught by surprise.

Not all of Storr's concerns were behind him yet, however. He knew he would still have to ponder his brother's attempt to murder him and try to decide what action should be taken—if any. And, then, of course, Alanna was back in his keeping, and he'd learned, from sorry experience, that she was not one who would be easily enslaved.

Leif walked at his side along the bay now, and,

as fatigued by the brief combat as they'd be from a long day's work in the fields, they both moved with heavy-legged strides.

"What betided your face?" Storr inquired, looking up and noticing, for the first time, the scattering of tiny punctures on his freeman's neck and cheeks.

" 'Twas that accursed harrier you had me take to the girl, master. He did break the skin in several places."

To Leif's surprise, his chief's only response to this was to fight a laugh, as the harrier's owner had. He scowled. "You are the second to find this amusing, Earl. Do I truly appear so comical?" he asked testily.

Now mindful of his part in all of it, Storr wiped the smirk from his face. *"Neinn.* Of course not. 'Tis only that he was such a little hound . . . I would have thought him more governable." Storr took his gaze away in that instant, fearful that his eyes might somehow tell his companion that this was not the first encounter he'd had with the harrier.

"Why did you ask that I bring the animal along?" the freeman pursued in his usual, straightforward way. "It has never mattered to you before that our prisoners are torn from their kin and pets."

"This one is different," Storr answered after a moment, seeing no other way but to speak plainly with his confidant.

269

"Why?"

"Because. Because I fancy her," he replied, picking up his pace so that Leif had to run a bit to catch up with him. What better reason could he give? What other excuse could be offered for sequestering Alanna the way he knew he would have to, in order to prevent her from divulging all the secrets she held? He could hardly come right out and admit that the damnable girl had just saved him from death *at his own brother's hand!* Such a confession, even just shared with one as trusted as Leif, was sure to leak out eventually and bring untold shame upon the entire clan.

"Fancy her?" Leif repeated, his voice cracking a bit with surprise. "But you have never given a second glance to a bondswoman."

"Then 'tis fully time I did. Don't you think? Why, you, yourself, were likely sired of such a joining, so what possible shame can be seen in it?"

"None, I suppose," Leif answered.

But what of your dead wife, Earl? What of the abstinence you swore to observe in her memory? Storr knew those were the questions Leif's next pause contained. He wouldn't be fool enough to voice them, however. None of Storr's men ever were. They just hovered there: *When, if ever, would Ivar's son take another bride? What was to become of their stead, if he didn't beget an heir?*

Storr had come to recognize all of their silences, all of the concerns behind their questioning gazes. He heard them in his sleep, as well as in his daylight hours. And, if nothing else, perhaps starting such talk about his alleged attraction to an Erse maiden would help to keep their nagging expectations at bay.

Thirteen

A hush came over the crew. Then they instantly abandoned their eating and drinking and rallied as though to prepare the longship for relaunching. Alanna, her eyes having been directed downward at Faolan, looked up at their scattering and spied its apparent cause. It was Storr's helmeted form approaching the ship, along with his dark-haired freeman.

Far from being relieved at seeing him—her one hope for mercy in all of this—Alanna felt an inexplicable lump forming in her throat. She knew him, had dwelt with him, had even saved his life an hour or so earlier. Yet now, beholding him at a distance in his awesome warrior's raiment, seeing how his dozens of men scrambled at the very sight of him, she felt quite unnerved. She was suddenly fearful. But not for her life, she realized. For something deeper . . . For her soul, perhaps.

She kept her eyes locked upon him. She tried to recall him as he'd been at the brook: alone, unarmed, and naked. Seeing his masterful stride, however, the unfazed manner with which he was walking away from her ravaged village, she sensed that she hadn't come to know him in the slightest. The man she'd encountered in the woodland seemed someone entirely apart from this clearly renowned chieftain.

She swallowed dryly and took her eyes from him. But, as the minutes raced past and she saw his men rushing about to lower chests to the shore and facilitate his boarding, she couldn't help looking his way once more.

He didn't see her. He seemed oblivious, in fact, to the sea of eyes, both Erse and Nordic, that were fixed upon him, as he moved to the bow and began issuing orders in his ugly mother tongue. Then, once he'd finished his commanding, he was surrounded by several of his men, each apparently asking for his direction in the matters of storing their cargo and launching the ship.

He was let alone finally, as most of his crew began unbinding the sail and erecting the ship's enormous mast; and, only then, did his eyes deign to scan the faces of the dozen or so slaves before him. Only then did those icy blue orbs light upon Alanna's.

She met and held his gaze for several seconds. Then her eyes shifted to the frightful, serpent-headed bowsprit behind where he stood. She thought of Thule, the monster-ridden land from which her people claimed the Norsemen hailed, and something snapped within her. Suddenly, the prospect of being spirited there, of having to leave her homeland for such a fierce new world was overwhelming; and she heard herself give forth an earsplitting wail.

Storr's face froze agape in those seconds. This was obviously the last thing he'd expected from her. And, as her mouth opened anew, caught in the soundless sort of emission that precedes a frightened child's crying, his expression betrayed both panic and confusion. It was as though he had never seen such a reaction from one of his prisoners. He had probably heard keens of mourning and anger from them, but never one of such unabashed terror; and he seemed lost for a response.

Through a blur of hysterical tears, Alanna saw him hurry down from his perch at front of ship and come rushing towards her. "Leif," he called to his freeman as he moved. He gestured for the servant, now on the starboard side of the ship, to head towards Alanna as well.

"What? *What* is it?" Storr asked, taking hold of one of her shoulders and leaning over her, as he reached her. She had saved his life the last time her face had registered such distress, and it was clear that he again placed a great deal of import upon discovering what was upsetting her.

Seeing his genuine concern, Alanna did her best to explain. Unfortunately, however, her words came rushing out in a soo-garbled mass.

"*What?* I cannot understand you," he whispered.

Leif was bent over her as well now, and some distant, still-rational part of Alanna couldn't help but feel, a bit embarrassed at the scene she was obviously causing.

"I think she said she fears the sea, master," the freeman offered.

The furrow in Storr's brow deepened. "The sea?"

"*Ja*. She says her parents died in these waters, and she seems to think she will do the same if we reembark."

"But that is madness. The storm has passed." He elbowed Leif. "For the sake of *Valholl*, tell her it has!"

The freeman obeyed, repeating his master's broken Erse slowly and deliberately; but Alanna found she could only respond with continued rambling and sobs.

Leif did his best to keep deciphering her words, nonetheless. "It . . . it seems she fears our prow as well, Earl. She evidently believes the serpent's head is . . . is real."

Storr looked confounded. "But how is that possible? 'Tis part of the ship. 'Tis made of wood, like the rest."

Alanna's utterances had become little more than hiccupping gasps, but she felt compelled to go on explaining.

"*Neinn*. 'Tis not our snake she fears, after all, master, but real ones. The ones she has been told lurk in our northern waters."

Under any other circumstances, Storr would have

laughed at such an infantile concern. Given that the girl held so many of his confidences, however, he knew better than to offer anything but solemn reassurance. This, after all, had been the response his forefathers had wanted to evoke from their victims, when they'd begun creating such teratic bowsprits decades before. They wanted the outlanders they attacked to be afraid of putting to sea in search of the booty and kin that were stolen from them. They wanted the rest of the world to believe that monsters were hidden in their waters, guarding them from the same forays they so often made upon others.

"That is daft, Alanna," he said softly, dropping to one knee before her and letting his hand slide down to her elbow. "I have sailed my waters and yours since I was a boy, and I have never once seen any sort of serpent."

"Then how . . . how do your people know how to carve one?" she choked. "Where have they seen such creatures, so they might fashion them?"

Though Storr was finally beginning to make out her words without his freeman's aid, this question took him aback. "Well . . . we've serpents upon the land. *Little* ones," he added, not wanting to frighten her afresh. "Haven't you such *harmless* creatures here?"

"Nay! And I've no wish to go to any land that doth!"

"Odin help us," Storr growled. What could he possibly say in answer to this? Except that he was her master henceforward. She was his to keep or to trade at will, and she was bound to go wherever he wished to take her.

He knew that such harshness wouldn't do, however. In her wrought-up state, she would only make matters worse, if threatened.

"And what of the bears in your land?" she suddenly demanded. "Will you also try to tell me now that they are harmless?"

Storr could feel Leif shift his gaze and glare down at him in those seconds; but he did not acknowledge the silent inquisition. "Tell her, freeman, that I am the earl of my stead, the most powerful man in my region." He got back to his feet. "Tell her that, save that I will it, no harm can possibly befall her."

Leif narrowed his eyes discerningly, as Storr met them with this request. It was possible that the Erse girl could have learned of bears from a Christian missionary. It didn't seem very likely, however, and he clearly suspected that something was afoot between his master and this cloakless little waif. Something beyond Storr's simply having taken a fancy to her during the raid. Leif did as he was told, nevertheless.

Alanna listened to a second or two of his reiteration of Storr's claim. Then, with a surge of anger, she jerked her way up to almost a standing position and called after their retreating commander.

He wasn't so invincible! Why, just a short time earlier, she'd seen him nearly beheaded by one of his own countrymen, and she simply wouldn't abide such a lie!

"Two of my cousins are dead," she exclaimed. "Your men have killed two of my next of kin, and I want them buried, you horrible pagan! I am sure animals, such as yourself, do not believe in proper burials, but my people do. And I want *all* of my fallen clansmen given Christian graves before we away!"

Storr stopped dead at hearing this outrageous demand. Only seconds before, the girl had been nothing more than a blubbering maiden. But now, unfortunately, she seemed to have returned to her former self; and he knew, as he turned back to face her, that it was a very thin line he walked. He had hoped that she wouldn't prove fool enough to defy him in the presence of his men and captives, but she had; and he would be forced to silence her.

"We *do* bury our dead, wench," he hissed. "And in far grander graves than your people can even imagine! But I shall not place my warriors in further peril to do as much now. Those of your people who fled could be returning with an army of bowmen, and it is Earl Sigurd's will, and mine, that we leave forthwith . . . Two of your cousins may have been slain, but I am told that two yet live. And, if you wish for them to continue to do so, you will never again speak to me in such a manner!"

Alanna, seeing how the rest of the captives and crew were cowering at his outburst, bit her lip and sank back down upon the chest. Storr, in his ire, had just spoken in the most eloquent Erse she had ever heard from him, and she required absolutely no translation.

It was one thing to risk her own neck by continuing to challenge this haughty earl. It was quite another to put Ciarda and Torra in more danger by doing so; and she knew that she must bite her tongue from here on, no matter how enraged she became.

Just as on the first night she'd been in Storr's keeping, she was realizing that a forthright method was not the best choice with him. She would need to begin reining in her temper. She would require something subtler with which to counter him and start gaining some advantage.

It couldn't be anything as life-threatening as poison this time, of course; for, if he was, indeed, the more merciful of the two chieftains, it was to her advantage that he remain alive. *Something subtler still,* she thought, fixing her eyes upon his back, where he stood at the bow once more. She had already learned two of his secrets: that he hadn't told his cohorts of being foiled by her while out scouting, and that at least one of his fellow Norsemen sought to kill him. What more, then, might she learn, if she genuinely attempted to win his confidence?

She was not, and never would be, his physical equal. Open confrontations were, therefore, futile for her, and she knew she should have learned as much by this time. Rather, her strength lay in her spirit, her God. She had sensed, from the first, that both of these could rival his, no matter what the circumstances. He was, despite his rank and prowess as a warrior, a strangely tortured soul, and he left her no choice but to begin taking advantage of that fact.

Once the mast had been raised and the sail unfurled, Alanna and her clansmen were removed from the rows of chests at the sides of the ship, and shoved into an uncomfortable huddle at the center of the deck. Then, as the vessel was pushed back into the water, their seats upon the sea trunks were taken by the Norse oarsmen and the rowing got under way.

Alanna had fought the urge to look back at her people's fort, as the longship had moved out of the bay. She knew that doing so, seeing the only home she'd ever known engulfed in smoke and flames, would only cause her to start weeping once more, and she was determined to never again give her captor that sort of satisfaction.

Instead she strove to remember the settlement as it had been before the attack: sandy white against the verdant, Erse countryside. She mentally encased this pastoral image for later recollection. Then she put all of her energy and emotion into praying for the souls of those who had fallen.

As if in answer to her supplication, it was not

280

up the coast that they had sailed, once they were out of the cove, but down. This seemed to indicate that the Vikings were not headed home to Thule just yet; and Alanna took great comfort in the realization that there might still be some hope of escaping them. But it was not to their hidden camp that they were traveling either, she'd suddenly realized, for Storr had said that this was located in the north, and that was clearly the direction in which he had spirited her weeks earlier.

It was possible, she supposed, that the Norsemen had moved their encampment in the time that had passed since her return home. But, short of coming right out and asking Storr or his Erse-speaking freeman where they were bound, she knew she would find no answers; and she was simply too proud to make such a vulnerable inquiry.

This information came soon enough, however. Within half an hour of being put to sea, the ships were brought to shore before the nearest monastery, and the unimaginable took place. The Vikings attacked the unarmed clergymen, decimating the ring-fort with what seemed even more speed than they had Alanna's; and, in just a matter of minutes, Alanna found herself surrounded by bound monks.

This was it! she silently raged. Slaying and capturing clergy was absolutely unforgivable, and she knew that she would have all she could do to contain her seething, once Storr returned to the vessel.

As with the attack upon her people, Storr and

his freeman were the last to come back. They sauntered out of the burning monastery as though having just carried out nothing more strenuous than swatting at flies; and, once again, Alanna felt something snap within her.

"Kindly pray for me, friar," she suddenly said to the monk who sat closest to her. She had never addressed a man of the cloth through clenched teeth before, but she was, sorrily, doing so now.

The clergyman, still looking dazed by the raid, knit his brow. "In truth, not only for you, daughter, but for us all," he whispered back.

"Nay. For me especially, friar, for I must not lose my temper when the chieftain reboards."

"For you then, especially," he replied, and he nodded his head towards her as though in lieu of being able to raise one of his trussed hands in benediction.

However tentative its delivery, Alanna did find strength in this blessing, and she managed to address the earl in an admirably calm and steady voice, as he and his freeman made their jocular ascent to the deck minutes later.

"A word with you, sire, prithee?" she asked, flashing Storr one of her most endearing looks, as he turned to head to the helm.

He sobered and crossed to her, raising a curious, yet warning brow, as he made his way through the mass of bound prisoners.

"Aye?" he queried, bending low once he reached her.

282

Alanna strove to keep her voice hushed and un-accusing. "Do you know who it is you have just taken?"

"The abbot?" he asked after several seconds, as though just having been invited to play some sort of riddle game with her.

"Aye. The abbot, sire, and all of his men. *God's* men," she added, lowering her voice all the more and donning a somber expression.

"So?"

"So God shall smite you for it. You cannot go about enslaving clergy and expect to be saved."

"Saved from what?"

Alanna was beginning to realize just how differ-ent their two faiths were. "From damnation, of course," she replied, her patience starting to slip a little. "Do you truly wish to find your soul in Hell? For, verily, good sire, I would hate to see that fate befall you."

He looked pleasantly surprised by this. "You would?"

"Of course. Would I have warned you earlier against the sword of your attacker, if I wished to see you perish?"

The chieftain pulled away slightly and pursed his lips, as though considering this question. Neverthe-less, an aggravating trace of his previous jocularity remained in his blue eyes. "Nay. I suppose not . . . In that case, what would you have me do with these men?"

"You must set them free, of course. And the

283

sooner the better . . . before God sees what you
have done! You simply cannot go about enslaving
those of the cloth!"

"Will your god strike me down with a lightning
bolt for it?" he pursued in an even voice.

"He might."

"But my warriors and I have been taking monks
for many years now, and never once have we been
attacked by this god of yours. Why, he doth not
even see fit to give his men the strength and will
with which to fight back. So, why, prithee, should
I fear him today?"

Alanna, beginning to lose all hope of keeping
her temper, drew in a deep, prayerful breath. She
could see, in the Norseman's expression, that part
of him was indeed, toying with her, as she suspected. Yet, she detected another, more hidden aspect of him, as well. A part that was genuinely
intrigued by her religious beliefs and wished to
learn more of them. "You simply *must*, Storr. For,
just as my God allowed me to save you back in my
uncle's house. He is directing me to save you again
now."

"And I shall be saved, if I let the holy men go?"

"It will certainly help to insure it."

Storr pressed a finger to his lips and narrowed
his eyes, as though giving this full consideration.
"Very well, then," he said after a moment. "As
soon as one of the nearby tribes comes forth with
a ransom for them, they shall be set free."

Alanna, though most grateful to hear this, knew

that the promise still held an unsettling contingency. "Nay, sire," she said gently. "Not for a ransom. 'Tis best if you simply release them out of the goodness of your heart."

He scowled. "But I hold no goodness for those who are not my countrymen."

"Oh, but you *must,* if your soul is to be saved. You must learn to love *all* men. Prithee, do trust me in this!"

Again he fell silent, as though considering her counsel. Then he shook his head. "Nay. Only for ransom," he concluded, rising and striding away before she could offer any further objection.

In the minutes that followed, Storr pulled one of the captured monks up to his feet and untied his hands. Then, with the help of his blue-eyed freeman, the chieftain dictated the message that he wanted the clergyman to carry to the nearest ringfort to the south. It was, quite simply, a description of the ransom which he and his fellow raiders required in exchange for the monks. They wanted a large gold casket for the release of the abbot, and two bags of silver for the rest of the clergy.

The ruffled friar nodded his understanding, thanking the two men profusely for this opportunity to save his brethren. Then, with Storr's help, he made his way over the side of the ship and back down to the beach and took off running southward like the most fleet-footed message-bearer.

The Norse crews, in turn, proceeded to relaunch the ships and row them a short way out to sea.

There they stayed anchored for what seemed to Alanna an eternity. It was two days and two nights in the damp, chill ocean air, with hardly enough room to even recline on the crowded vessel at eventide.

From time to time, amidst this suffering, Alanna did entertain the idea of giving in to her urge to cry once more. Her resolution to remain stoic in her captor's presence proved surprisingly strong, however, and she seemed to keep summoning enough strength to fight back her emotions.

As if spurred by this stoicism, Storr deigned to address her again, on the morning of the third day. She and the other female captives aboard had just been taken to the stern to use the Norsemen's makeshift privy; and, before she could be returned to her place in the huddle at the middle of the ship, Storr came and blocked her passage with his towering form.

Not wishing to let him see the misery in her eyes, she declined to look up at him.

"I do not give you greater portions at meals, only to have you render them to the others," he scolded sotto voce, as the rest of the women were herded back to the center of the vessel.

"What is given to me, sire, I assume is mine to do with as I please," she answered, keeping her voice equally low.

He reached out and lifted her chin, so that he could look down into her face. "What I give to you is meant only for you."

"But they are mothers and children, Earl. They've more need than I. Would you not, in my place, do the same for the young of your clan?" she asked, hearing, to her annoyance, an emotional quaver in her voice.

He withdrew his hand from her. "Probably . . . But, doubtless, 'tis more your monks' will than your own."

"Perhaps," she conceded.

"I simply wish to make certain, 'tis *me* you obey henceforward, Alanna. Not them."

"I shall try to prove obedient, sire," she said under her breath after several seconds, remembering how her cousins' fates rested upon her actions as well. Then she turned to the right a bit, as though to make her way around him. "May I be allowed to pass now?"

He caught her shoulder, obviously wishing to keep her there. "Why did you warn me of the danger back in that hut?"

Storr did his best to maintain an even voice as he asked this. While he would gladly have perished at another man's hand on the raid, he, sure as *Hel*, did not wish for it to be his *brother's;* and he knew he must strive to keep his tone and expression from betraying to the girl the jumble of emotions he was still feeling over the incident.

"I did not want you killed," she replied, tossing her hair back in the morning wind and looking him squarely in the eye.

"Why? Because my attacker seemed to you an

even worse foe?"

Alanna considered this question, searching her memory for what she might have been thinking during those harrowing seconds near the hearth. "In truth, sire, I don't believe that was in my mind at that moment . . . Perhaps you'll have need of your freeman to translate for you my reasons."

"Nay," he said firmly. "This shall be kept between you and me."

She was silent for several seconds, again scanning her mind for all she might have been thinking at the time in question.

"Was it simply your Christian loathing for killing?" he asked finally.

"Aye. Maybe."

"And nothing more?"

She looked up at him defiantly, annoyed at his continuing to hold her there in the brisk, morning wind. "What more would you have it be, my lord? Some untold fondness for Norse raiders?"

He looked, for just an instant, wounded by this retort. "Nay. Rather, I had hoped some fondness for a man you had ere then come to know out in the wilderness. One who could scarcely be called a stranger to you . . . And do not pretend such gentility with me! Many of your countrymen are raiders as well!"

"Aye, but not with your people's taste for murdering and enslaving!"

" 'Twas not my intent to raid your fort, in any case," he suddenly offered.

She looked at first surprised, then mocking. "Not your 'intent,' *chieftain?*"

His hold began to give way to an open, stroking palm upon her shoulder, and Alanna found his touch distractingly warm. "Nay. I did my best to steer my men clear of it. 'Twas the storm that took us from our course. And, with Earl Sigurd's ships suddenly turned back towards your bay, I could do naught else but follow."

Alanna continued to look skeptical. "Then let us go with the monks, good sire, if it was truly not your will to take us."

She saw something in his eyes at this retort, something between a flinch and a flicker, and she knew that she had once again touched upon an area that was not wholly under his command.

"I cannot," he whispered. " 'Tis not the Norse way. 'Twould shame me before my fellow chieftain, and my men would suffer accordingly."

Alanna pulled away from him, fixing her jaw angrily. "Well, my people suffer now, too, sire, so do not feed me more than my due, if you do not wish it shared with some of them."

With that she strode back towards where her tribesmen were gathered, and he made no effort to call after her. She had gone without adequate rest and nourishment for so long now, that she simply had no will to continue sparring with him. They were, despite the days they had passed alone together, of two very dissimilar cultures, and there was beginning to seem less and less possibility of bridging their differences.

On the afternoon of that third day, the monk Storr had sent as a messenger returned on a horse-drawn cart carrying the specified ransom, and his fellow clergy were released as promised. Though Alanna was again greatly saddened at the fact that her people weren't being freed as well, she was most grateful to Storr for having liberated the monks, and, in her enthusiasm, she chanced to tell his freeman as much.

Leif offered her a befuddled look and explained that it had never been their intent to enslave those of the clergy who had survived the raid. He claimed, in fact, that such men were exchanged for ransoms *almost without exception.*

Alanna responded to this by flashing Storr a scathing look at her next opportunity. He, in turn, launched into an angry discussion with Leif—obviously having deduced that he was the one responsible for Alanna's renewed displeasure.

Neither of the men spoke to her of the inadvertent disclosure, however. Her fuming was simply met with the presentation of a large woolen blanket from the earl at nightfall. It was, apparently, another of his attempts at contrition—clearly meant to pacify the girl who had saved his life and who held more than one of his darkest secrets.

Alanna looked about the crowded warship for him, as his freeman came and spread the bulky cover over her legs. She finally caught Storr's eye seconds later, where he stood conversing with another of his crewmen at the bow. Even in that shadowy, evening light, she was able to detect the beginnings of an ingratiating smile upon his lips.

She continued to glower at him, nevertheless. Her eyes said that she wouldn't be so easily allayed. Then she began to writhe about in her bound condition, kicking free of the blanket and shoving it, with her feet, into a balled mass. It would, in such a state, serve as the perfect bolster for the heads of the Erse children who always slept just a few feet before her on the vessel.

Storr's smile faded at this; and Alanna lay down and turned her face away from his view. She could rest satisfied in the knowledge that she had once again succeeded in rebuffing him.

Fourteen

In the days that followed, the Vikings proved even more daring navigators than Alanna had imagined them to be. While her own people made it a rule never to let their vessels slip out of sight of land, the Norsemen did so without hesitation, avoiding the notice of any Erse settlements they might pass while heading north once more, and thereby denying Alanna one last glimpse of her people's burnt-out fort.

She recalled her resolution, however. She truly did not wish to remember the settlement as these monsters had left it, but as it had been for so many lifetimes before such barbarians had begun coming to shore.

Her pride kept her from speaking to Storr during this time. She sensed, nonetheless, that it was not Thule for which they were bound, but the encampment he'd attempted to steal her to weeks earlier. What was more, the living conditions upon the cramped longship had become so unbearable, that she had begun to realize that she really didn't care where they put to shore, just as long as they eventually did so and thereby ended the misery she and her tribesmen had been forced to endure from the start. They were cold, exhausted, queasy, and in desperate need of decent rations, and a death at sea was starting to seem almost preferable to having to go on this way.

On the third morning after leaving the monastery, the Norse ships finally began heading back towards shore. Even in the mist of that cool, gray day, the chalky white of Erin's beaches, the green of her coastal meadows began to come into view, and Alanna and her fellow captives couldn't help moving towards the bow, in an effort to get a better look at what lay ahead.

Alanna could see two huge tents upon the beach, each at opposite ends of the camp, and in between was a long scattering of what looked to be bedding, cook fires, and the people who were making use of them. She couldn't tell from that distance whether or not these inhabitants were Norsemen or Erse prisoners, but she knew, as they drew closer, that the nature of the population into which she was about to be inducted would soon become painfully clear to her.

But it was land, in any case. No matter what might come to pass upon it, it was solid, unswaying, predictable beach and grassland. And she knew that, no matter how strange it might seem to her, when compared to the terrain in her native southern region, she was still in Erin and some hope remained of breaking away from these heathens and finding her way back to her aunt and uncle.

It would, of course, be much more difficult this time, than it had been with Storr in the woods. She no longer had just one abductor with which to deal, but an army of them. And it was not just herself she would have to try to free in the dark of night, but her two cousins and any of the rest of her clan who seemed capable of such a stealthy escape.

Still, in all, there remained some hope of finding herself a free woman once more, and she did her best now to try to ignore all of the obvious obstacles to this, and just concentrate on any opportunities God might set before her.

As she could have predicted, however, such chances were not to be immediately afforded. As they finally reached shore, the Vikings were so methodical in herding them off of the ships, that there was no possibility for slipping out of formation and attempting a getaway.

Alanna had thought, at first, that she and her people were simply to be added to the groups of Erse slaves who had already been made part of the camp and who were presently milling about the beach. To her horror, however, she peered far ahead in the line and saw that they were being kept separate from the rest, so that they could be systematically stripped and *bathed* by their captors!

What she had assumed to be cook fires, were, in fact, heating cauldrons of water, which were, in turn, being emptied into some huge wooden tubs on the tideland at the center of the camp. And, as the prisoners, from the first of the vessels to put to shore, were hurriedly disrobed and led to this fate by their male captors, she was filled with genuine panic once more.

She had never engaged in such a sinful act, let alone at the hands of the opposite sex; and, in spite of any resolutions she'd made regarding throwing herself upon Storr's mercy, she found herself calling out his name in desperation now.

To her dismay, however, it wasn't Storr who finally came and ended her outcries by plucking her from the line, but the very man who had tried to slay him back in her uncle's house. She recognized him instantly, as he took hold of her tunic sleeve and jerked her off to the side. His eyes bore the same, sadistic gleam they had as he'd raised his sword to murder Storr, and she found herself almost mute with terror.

"Silence, wench," he said through gritted teeth, his Erse even more foreign-sounding than Storr's had seemed to her at first. "You are plainly prized by our earl, and I shall see that you are not bathed with the rest of this cattle."

Alanna, failing to find any comfort in this pledge, couldn't help struggling a bit in his grip.

His expression became even more fierce in response, and she turned her face away with a wince, as he lifted his hand to strike her. To her surprise, though, no blow came. Instead, she felt herself being tugged from behind, out of his reach, and she nearly fell backwards, as Storr stepped out from beside her and took hold of the younger Viking's tunic.

Storr growled a sentence or two in his mother tongue. Then he released the man with an angry shove, causing him to stagger back a few steps before regaining his balance. Once he had his footing, however, his eyes narrowed to vengeful slits, and, though he didn't say a word, it was clear that he would have again attempted to murder Storr, if not for all the potential witnesses.

With a huff, he brushed his tunic off a bit, as though to rid himself of the chieftain's touch. Then he turned and stalked away.

Alanna breathed a sigh of relief at seeing him go. Before she could thank Storr for coming to her rescue, however, he swept her up in his arms with a put-upon sigh and began heading for one of the huge tents she had spotted earlier.

She called for Faolan to follow, and, as she looked back over Storr's shoulder seconds later, she saw that the harrier was doing so—happily wagging his tail as he made his way along in the shifting sand.

"Who is he, sire? Who *is* this man who again

comes to thwart you?" Alanna whispered, as Storr continued to stride towards the shelter. She was, of course, unnerved at his having gathered her up in such a manner. But, given the other two fates with which she'd just been threatened, she knew better than to offer any protest.

"One who opposes me, clearly," he replied, obviously winded by the confrontation.

"But he called you *our* earl, as though he were of your stead."

"He was once. But we shall speak of it no more," he said sternly.

Alanna fell silent, finally having learned not to press him too far. Any further inquiries she might have made were pushed out of her mind in any case, as they reached the tent, and he carried her inside.

Her mouth dropped open in awe at what she saw within. The interior was even larger than she could have imagined, and its walls were lined with yards of insulating fur. This lining had obviously been taken from beasts far larger than any that walked upon Erin's soil, and she wondered if it could have come from the bears of which Storr had spoken.

There were exotic-looking lamps of shimmering gold hanging from the ceiling here and there. And, in the midst of the shelter, was a huge oblong wooden structure with two horse-head-like carvings upon the posts at the taller of its ends. It was spread, from side to side, with yet more fur, and she could only assume that it was some sort of bed.

"This is yours, my lord? You slee—sleep in here?" she stammered, as he set her back on her feet.

He gave forth a soft laugh at her awe. "Aye. 'Tis my right as chieftain to bring a tent with me," he replied, pulling a knife from his belt-strap and stepping behind her to cut the binding from her wrists.

Alanna, responding to this with a thankful sigh, instantly brought her freed hands forward and stood rubbing the abrasion left by the tight rope. For days she'd been allowed the use of her hands only at mealtime, and words couldn't express how grateful she was to have them permanently unbound now.

In those same seconds, Faolan, having been several paces behind them, entered the tent as well. On his heels came Storr's dog, Biorn, evidently returning from having just greeted his master's ships on the shore.

The two dogs hailed each other by issuing low, precautionary growls. Then, after engaging in a mutual sniffing of one another's privates, they sank down in panting unison upon the floor next to what was, apparently, Storr's bed.

" 'Tis good we are alone," Storr noted under his breath. "My men would wonder at the dogs being so quickly friends."

"Aye," Alanna agreed, crossing to the wooden monstrosity and running a hand over its plush cover. "This is a Norse bed, is it?" she asked, cocking her head with curiosity.

"Aye," he replied, continuing to sound amused by her marveling.

"But it is so large. How many people is it meant to hold?"

He raised a brow, evidently surprised at this query. "Why, two, of course."

She eyed it once more. "Aye. Two or three, I fancy . . . But you said you were no longer wed?" she added, facing him with a questioning rise to her voice.

His amusement seemed suddenly dampened. "Aye, I did. And, as you must also remember, Alanna, I forbade you to speak of it again."

She bit her lip and let her gaze drop, doing her best to look penitent. "I am sorry, sire. 'Twas just that I simply couldn't fathom why it should be so large, or why you would carry it across the seas to what is merely to serve as a camp."

He walked to a nearby sea chest and withdrew a waterskin from it. Then he closed the box, sank down upon it, and took several swallows of the beverage. " 'Tis *my* bed. 'Tis where I find my best respite, and I wished to take it with me."

Alanna shrugged and turned to perch upon its mattress. "To each his own, I suppose. But I feel I must warn you that 'tis dangerously soft. And, here

299

in Erin, we believe that 'soft beds make for soft warriors.' "

His eyes darted up to meet hers once more, as though he was taken aback by this disclosure. "Verily? And here, all this time I thought your people just too lazy and dull of mind to fashion aught more comfortable than a mat . . . Hmm," he concluded, pressing a fist to his lips and stifling a belch. "You could be more interesting to have about, than I had at first thought, my dear. Some mead?" he offered, raising the skin in her direction.

She shook her head. "Nay. My people drink spirits only with meals."

A smile tugged at the corner of his lips. "Not unto drunkenness, as mine do?" he said mockingly, as though completing her thought for her.

She blushed a bit at his astuteness. "Aye. I suppose that was my meaning."

"So, my men offended you on the ship, my little Christson virgin? Swilling too much wine?"

She shrugged, still not sure of his moods or his intentions towards her. " 'Twas not so much offense I felt, as fear."

"Why? They would not have touched you, in any case, for I did tell my freeman that you were to be mine alone."

"*Yours?*" she echoed, her voice cracking with uneasiness.

Again a faint smile danced upon his lips. "Aye.

Of course. You know too much for me to chance you sleeping in the arms of any of my men or Sigurd's."

She swallowed bravely and squared her shoulders. "I have no intention of finding myself in *anyone's* arms, good sire. So, you needn't fear that."

He laughed under his breath. "And neither do you. For, as I've said, you are mine alone and certainly no stranger to me."

Suddenly feeling apprehensive upon the carved bed, she lifted herself from it and went over to sit upon one of his other chests.

It was a successful retreat. She'd managed not to get cornered upon the bedstead. But her new resting place had the distinct disadvantage of bringing her several feet closer to where her captor sat.

"Thank you, my lord, for saving me from the bathing," she said suddenly, hoping this praise of his chivalry might encourage him to go on conducting himself in a gentlemanly manner. "I just knew it could not be your will to have me disrobed by your countrymen."

Again he raised a brow at her, as though continuing to find her entertaining. "Indeed not," he concurred. "But, make no mistake, you shall bathe, none the less."

This revelation made Alanna feel as though her heart had just ascended to her throat. "But *why?*"

"Because of filth, of course. Because of pesti-

301

lence! Have your people no knowledge of how plagues begin?"

She hugged herself, suddenly feeling chilled at the thought of such a purging. "But we've God to keep such things from us."

"Be that as it may," he declared, setting his skin aside and rising, "you shall now have soap and hot water, too."

"But, nay, my lord," she replied, rising as well with a pleading tone to her voice. "You cannot mean to take me back out before all those others . . . all those *men!*"

He laughed. "Nay. You shall bathe in here with me." He crossed to the door, stuck his head outside, and called for someone in his native Norse.

Alanna couldn't seem to take in much more of what he said or did after that. The prospect of having to undress before him and share whatever tub he had brought into the tent was simply too overwhelming for her to do anything but slip into a daze of sorts. And, all at once, she felt as though it might actually be more merciful of him to simply rape her, as he had seemed about to do back at her fort. That—by all accounts she'd heard at least—would probably not have entailed full nudity and would surely have been over with more quickly than aught as torturous as having to sit in a vessel of hot water with him.

"You have ordered the bath?" she inquired

302

numbly, as he returned to his seat and took up the skin of mead once more.

He nodded.

"But what of my . . . my cousins, sire?"

He looked at her blankly. "What of them?"

"You cannot let them be stripped by the others either. They should not be thus shamed, any more than I."

"What is all this care about cousins? You speak out for them as though they were your sisters."

"Oh, but they are, my lord. I did lose my mother and father, as your freeman told you on the ship. So my cousins and their parents are virtually all the family I have ever known."

"Well, perhaps you do not understand. They were captured by Sigurd's men, not mine. So I have no say in what becomes of them. I will try to see that they are not killed or maimed. Alas, I can do little else."

"But your freeman said you might be able to make a trade with this Sigurd for them."

Storr lowered his chin and raised his brows. *"Did* he?" he asked in a steely tone.

"Aye."

"Do remind me to thrash him at my next opportunity," he grumbled. Then he spoke up again, locking eyes with her intently. "In truth, Alanna, Sigurd is more enemy than ally to me. And you would have to please me *very* greatly before I would stoop to barter thus with him."

303

"But what of my cousins' virtue?" she implored, feeling that continuing to focus upon them would somehow keep her from dwelling too much on the mortifying experience that lay just ahead for her. Even now, Storr's blue-eyed freeman and another of his servants were entering the tent with the requested tub; and two more Vikings came in soon after with a couple cauldrons of steaming hot water to fill it.

Storr shifted upon his sea chest in an effort to keep her in view amid the bustling. "Their virtue?" he repeated, knitting his brow. "Very likely, my dear, Sigurd and the others took it from them before they even reached his ships. So I doubt they will find a bath any more shaming . . . Surely not as troubling as you seem to," he added in the brief solitude between the deliveries of bathwater.

"So a woman's virtue is of no import to your people?"

"Of what woman do you speak? Is she bride or slave?"

As he surely must have intended, this retort simply served to make Alanna all the more nervous. She swallowed dryly and let her gaze drop to her feet. Only the sound of one of Storr's servants pulling the door flap shut and securing it seconds later let her know that all preparations had been made, and the time for bathing had finally arrived.

She continued to keep her eyes focussed downward, nonetheless, as she heard Storr rise and, with the clinking of mail and rustle of fabric, begin to disrobe.

"My freemen have gone, and they will not return, unless I call for them. So, you needn't fear their seeing you," he explained in a low voice.

"Thank you, sire. Your words do comfort me," she replied; but she still declined to look up and acknowledge what he was doing.

"What? No desire to watch me this time? You seemed interested enough back at that brook."

She could again hear gibing in his tone, the sportiveness of one who'd had a great deal of experience with the opposite sex; and a hot swelling seemed to fill her throat. "You . . . you startled me was all. I did not expect to see anyone there, and I simply stood, frozen with fear."

"Nay. A moment or two of watching. That is, as you say, startled. But we both know you looked for much longer . . . You and that silly hound of yours," he added, smiling and nodding towards Faolan. "So, no interest in seeing me now in full view? Free of the cloak of thicket and bush? Per chance you will like what you see."

She shook her head emphatically, her eyes still locked upon the fur-covered floor.

"Ah, pity. For I would gladly feast my eyes upon you, were you to make the same offer."

"You may be sure, my lord, that I shall not."

She heard him laugh under his breath: "Not even if I order it?"

A brief silence ensued as she searched her mind for something, *anything* to say that might prove a further deterrent to him. "But then . . . then, sire, 'twould not be an offer from me, would it?"

She heard the water slosh as he apparently climbed into the tub and sat down, and some tiny portion of her sighed with relief at this. While she knew she was far from out of the meshes yet, she had at least managed to avoid being caught again in the sin of beholding his nakedness.

"Ah, but then you assume that I care what is given and what is taken, when, forsooth, I may not."

At this, she cast her gaze heavenward and issued an anguished sound. "Oh, do not torment me further with bandying," she beseeched. She finally met his eyes where he now sat with the lower half of him safely hidden from view. "Am I or am I not to be allowed to bathe alone when you have finished?"

He ran a cake of soap over his chest and under his arms, and his eyes narrowed as though he was pondering this. Finally he shook his head. "I think not. For the longer you wait, the less warm this water will be, and I would hate to see you take ill with cold, my dear . . . Aye, I do think it best that you join me forthwith," he concluded, giving the side of the tub a gamesome slap.

She bit her lip, recalling what he'd just said about her having to please him in order to see her

306

cousins traded, and she pushed up to her feet. "Very well, then," she replied, beginning to walk towards him. "I shall bathe in my tunic, if 'tis all the same to you. I am sure it needs cleaning at least as much as I."

"Oh, don't be daft," he snapped, all of his former amusement seeming to have disappeared. "You cannot get clean with that flea-ridden frock hanging about you. Take it off at once, before I am moved to come and do so for you!"

His sudden impatience took her by surprise, and she found her fingers trembling as she started pulling up the garment seconds later. He was *serious,* she realized. This was not just some carnal game to him, some exercise in harrying innocent slave girls. Rather, his tone was more like a father's now, a man who genuinely feared this "pestilence" of which he'd spoken; and she knew better than to offer any more argument.

"Besides," she heard him add, as she turned her back to him and finally brought the tunic up, over her head. " 'Tis pleasant, this bathing. 'Tis one of our most treasured pastimes in my land. We build houses for it where great hearths are kept burning and one can bathe in comfort, even on the coldest of days. Do come and give it a try," he invited, extending a hand, as she turned back to face him with her tunic clamped to the front of her. "Come, little lamb. I'll not look as you let your frock fall."

He appeared sincere enough in those seconds.

307

His eyes shone with some sort of compassion for her, and his expression was as benign as she'd ever seen it. So she moved towards him. One tentative, shaky step and then another, until she stood at the opposite end of the huge tub.

She kept her eyes fixed upon his all the while. Whatever shyness she'd hitherto felt at meeting his aqua gaze was gone now in her desperate desire to keep it engaged. To keep it from slipping down-ward—to her bared shoulders, her naked legs.

"Drop it," he whispered, continuing to keep his eyes upon hers. "You've my word I will not look down."

She let a second or two pass, and his stare remained steady, unflickering, as she continued to test his resolve. Then, not able to bring herself to risk having him see her, she turned away, let go of the tunic, and lowered herself into the deep tub in a blur of motion. She came to rest in its hot, chest-deep water with her back still turned to him.

To her relief, he greeted this sudden change of heart with nothing more than a surprised laugh.

"*Alanna*," he said.

"Aye?"

"Why did you do that? Is my word not enough for you?"

"Aye."

"Then why did you turn away?"

"I am sorry, but 'tis my God's Word I must honor above all others, my lord."

"And this is in the sagas of your god? That you must not bare yourself to a man?"

"I believe it is, sire, for 'tis what the Church teaches us."

"A wife cannot even be bared before her husband?" he asked in amazement.

"Not even then."

"Then how do you . . . I mean, how do your people . . ." His words broke off as though he could find no suitable way to phrase his question.

"How do they what?" she asked, sinking farther down in the tub in an effort to stay warm.

"How do they beget children?"

She felt her face flush at this, and she was all the more grateful that she'd chosen to turn her back to him. "I am sure I couldn't say, for I have never heard tell of such things."

"Nay. I don't suppose you have," he replied with obvious disgust; and, to Alanna's dismay in those seconds, he suddenly unfolded his long legs and let them come to rest on either side of her.

She looked down, into the depths of the soap-clouded water and studied his foot—the foot she'd stomped so many weeks before. She couldn't help wondering just how much of her posterior was visible to him at present, and she hoped he was finding the bath equally murky.

He was right, though, she realized, continuing to try to calm herself. Bathing *was* pleasant when the water was hot enough. She'd never felt anything

309

quite like it, in fact. There had been warmish tides in her people's bay, of course. She'd enjoyed the sun-heated currents in the shallower waters near the shore, when she had swum there as a child. And of course the brook was always temperate when she'd gone wading in summer. But those experiences had never been aught like this. They had never proven so enveloping.

This Viking type of bathing was warmer than any blanket or familial embrace she'd ever known. And again, as with the huge, plumped mattress on Storr's bed, she found herself wondering at this strange, warring race, and their ironic penchant for things soft and calid.

Her thoughts were interrupted, however, as she felt him wrap his arms about her waist and slide her farther back — into the vee created by his legs.

"Don't," she exclaimed, the utterance bordering on a screech.

"Why not? I thought your god only forbade my seeing, not my touch."

"That is forbidden, as well!"

"But I have touched you many times hitherto, have I not? As I slept at your side in the woods, as I kissed you in your uncle's hut. Why, even as I carried you here, to my tent. And what harm has come of it?"

"But this is different."

"Why?"

"Because we wear no raiment, sire."

310

"I am seeing you bathed. Not bedded," he declared, letting his irritation with her deity's endless edicts show. "When it is my intent to claim you, believe me, you will know it. There shall be no question in your mind! Now, use this," he commanded, dipping his hand into the water at her side and bringing it back to the surface with the cake of soap in his palm.

She was hesitant to accept it from him. "But this is for clothing."

" 'Tis for skin, as well. 'Tis just that your people are too laggard to know it."

She reluctantly took it from him. "But it burns, does it not?"

"Parts of you, maybe. Your eyes . . . and down here," he continued, plunging his free hand into the water and, to her horror, letting it come to rest for an instant near the recess between her legs.

She gasped and slid away from his fingers.

"Well, would you have me fail to warn you?" he asked defensively. "And, as I am sure you can understand, I do not know your people's words for such parts."

Though his hands were both accounted for once more, hovering at the level of her waist again, she remained stunned, sitting bolt upright at this unspeakable action.

"Oh, be at ease, will you," he murmured, bringing his lips down to her right ear and pressing a soft kiss just below it. "I've had many women and

311

even a wife, and a man is bound to hear of such things . . . 'Tis not, in any case, a part of you that you wish to have hurt, is it?"

Alanna, still abashed by it all, simply shook her head in response.

"I thought not," he whispered, kissing the nape of her neck. "I have always favored pleasure over pain, myself. That, I suppose, is why I thought it so mean-spirited of you to stomp my toes and poison me. Tell me, were you obeying your god then?"

" 'Twas not my intent to kill you with the poison. Only to put you to sleep. Besides, I was fighting for my very freedom, and you know it as well as I," she snarled, giving the soap a cursory run over her arms and chest and then thrusting it back at him. "You would have done the same in my stead!"

"Indeed I would have. But then I do not profess to be a Christson."

"Christian," she corrected, fighting a smile at his mispronunciation. She quickly sobered, however, at his lingering implication that she wasn't, in fact, as holy-minded as she claimed. "And, aye, you are right, my lord," she confessed after several seconds. "I do contest when cornered. 'Tis one of my failings, I'm afraid."

"Nay. 'Tis your strength. 'Tis what sets you apart from your cowardly people, your craven monks. It is just that I want you to understand, Alanna, that there is no longer any need to contest against *me*.

312

For I take you into my tent, my bath, not for cruelty, but for kindness. You must *give* such, you know, if you wish to get it back," he concluded, letting his fingers come to rest upon her shoulders.

A shower of tingles ran through her at his touch, and she sank farther down into the water, continuing to crave its warmth and concealment. "But I saved you, my lord. You know that I saved your life back in my uncle's house."

"And I am saving you as well now, am I not? Saving your life, your virtue, here in my private bath?"

"Aye," she choked. "But many's the sin you've committed against me as well."

"Such as?"

"Such as lying to me about freeing the abbot and his monks."

"I did not lie. They were freed. You saw them rowed back to shore."

"But you led me to believe 'twas a favor you did at my request alone. When, in truth, 'twas what you intended to do all along."

"Oh, what does it matter at whose behest, so long as your precious holy men were released?"

"It matters to me, Storr . . . for I wish to come to trust you."

"You do?" he asked and before she could answer, his fingers began to knead the tense region at the base of her neck with an adeptness that made her feel limp all over.

313

"What are you doing?"

"We call it massage. You do not do it here?"

"Nay," she sighed. "I have never heard of it."

"Do you like it?"

"Aye. But how do you know just where and how to touch?"

" 'Tis simply something my people do. One learns from where one hurts. And I sense you aching *here*," he said, his fingers tightening upon her shoulders. "So tense. So afraid of the one Norseman in this camp who has absolutely no will to harm you. It makes no sense to me, forsooth. Does it to you?"

She shut her eyes and let her tired, ship-racked muscles roll about in his deft grasps. "Nay," she answered, feeling almost too transported to go on conversing. "This is not . . . not part of bedding a woman, is it?" she stammered after a moment.

He gave forth a soft laugh. "Nay. Men do it to one another and women to women in my land. 'Tis safe enough, little lamb."

Her voice remained dreamy and low as his fingers continued to rub away the days and nights of bondage upon the rocking ship. "Why do you call me that?"

"What?"

"Little lamb?"

"But is that not what your god calls you? His lambs?"

Alanna laughed under her breath. "Nay. His

314

sheep. We are the sheep of Christ's flock, you see."

"He is a shepherd by trade?"

"Nay. He was a carpenter."

"Was?"

"When He lived upon the earth. He was a carpenter."

"You mean he lived among you once?"

"Oh, aye. As a man. Some eight centuries ago."

"And where is he now?"

"In Heaven, of course."

Storr nodded. "Oh, *ja*. Heaven. My slaves have spoken of it. 'Tis like our *Valholl*. Odin's hall of the slain . . . But then, if he is dead, this god, why is he said to be sheepherding now?"

Alanna was again tempted to laugh at his curious line of questioning. She kept herself from doing so, however. She was painfully aware now that she would have a great deal to learn of his people as well, if she was to dwell here for any length of time; and she knew she wouldn't want him to laugh at her queries. "Well, Christ keeps watch over us from on high, you see. And, in this way, we are as His flock."

"So he saw you and your people as Sigurd led the attack upon your fort?"

"Oh, aye. He and His Father see all things."

"Then, why did he not protect you? Why did he not give you the will to warn your tribe of seeing me at the brook?"

"But I *did* warn them. I warned them most urgently! How can you think I wouldn't?" she asked, turning her face back to flash him an incensed look.

He shushed her, and his massaging gave way to a set of placating pats. " 'Twas just that they were so unready for us, and—"

"But how could we have known?" she interrupted. "You came in the midst of a storm, when, 'tis said, no Viking sails. And so much time had passed, how were we to know you would yet come?"

"Shhh," he said again, this time closer to her ear. Then he leaned forward and pressed his lips to the crown of her head. "Let us speak of it no more. I have had enough of warring to last me for ten lifetimes," he admitted, in a tone that sounded almost as plaintive as hers.

Alanna, though surprised by this admission, could not let the subject drop. He had to understand. She had to make him see that it was not cowardice that kept her people from defending themselves. "But you must not judge my tribesmen, my clergy, as craven, sire. At least let me explain that 'tis our beliefs that keep us from fighting back. Our God forbids it, you see. Surely, with all the Erse slaves you have taken, you must understand that."

"Then you must understand that 'tis not merely greed that makes my people raid; for it is much colder where we come from and there is far less land to farm. And, after a hard summer's rowing and a winter so long no grapes can be grown, my men should not be blamed for partaking too well of your wine. They are good and loyal warriors, serving our god, Odin, as surely as your race serves yours, and they are entitled to much of what they claim."

Alanna let a brief deferential silence pass. Then she spoke again. "Well, be that as it may, I was simply trying to point out that your weariness of warring is shared by my God. He hath had his fill of it as well . . . You've that in common with Him," she added softly.

At this Storr leaned away slightly and took hold of the silver chain that was clasped about her neck. "So he is wise, this god of yours?" he asked, reaching forward and sliding her crucifix back to where he could again examine it.

"Oh, aye. Very wise. And kindly disposed. You would like Him, I think."

Storr fingered the odd little pendant. "Perhaps. But I would never wish to be in danger beneath his watch."

"Even if He could save you from death?"

"But he cannot, Alanna. Many of your people died back there. Many, many more than I would have had fall," he ruefully admitted.

"But they are not truly dead, sire, for their souls live on in Heaven."

"And what did they do? What bravery did they

317

show to have earned a seat there?"

"Why, none, my lord. One does not have to be brave to be saved. One simply must believe."

"Believe in what?"

"In God's Power, His Promise to save us, as He saved His Son from that cross you hold."

"So 'tis not a letter?"

She gave forth a soft laugh. "Nay. 'Tis a crucifix, upon which a man is nailed and dies for his crimes."

Storr grimaced and returned the pendant to the front of her. "Oh, how dreadful. Such a slow death."

" 'Twas a Roman death. The Romans were our ancestors. They were, perhaps, even more cruel than your people in that way."

"Aye," he agreed, swallowing dryly. Then he brought the soap to the surface once more and began scrubbing her back for her. "So your god somehow freed his son from this cross, did he?"

"Nay. Christ died on it."

Storr gave forth an exasperated breath. "But I thought you said he could save people from death. Why would he let his own son die in such a horrible way?"

"So that He could rise again and save the rest of us."

"How?" he asked, his growing impatience continuing to be evident.

Alanna shrugged. "I am not sure. I only know 'tis true."

"Hmmm. 'Tis most odd, this faith of yours, girl. I do grow dizzy trying to reason it out. Have you, yourself, actually seen this Christ, your shepherd, among the quick again?"

"Well . . . nay. I have not seen Him. But I have surely felt Him with me. I have surely felt His Spirit inside me."

"*Inside* you?" Storr repeated in amazement. "A man inside you, you say? But I thought that a sin to your people."

Alanna turned her face back and glowered at him, only to see that he appeared not the least bit teasing. He looked utterly serious, in fact — as though he was truly trying to grasp the nature of her Deity. "It is! I did not mean it in *that* way!"

Storr was taken aback by the sudden sharpness of her tone. She looked as though he had just made the most unforgivable of blunders, when, in fact, the question had seemed quite legitimate to him. Their god of fertility, the Norse god, Frey — depicted with his male organ erect — was ofttimes said to visit the wombs of women who wished for fruitfulness, to bless them with the ability to bear children. So it seemed altogether possible that this Erse god might sometimes do the same. "Well, in what way did you mean it, wench?" he barked in return. "Can you not make your meaning more plain?"

319

She gave forth a weary sigh. "I shall try, my lord." Then, to Storr's surprise, she reached back, drew his scrubbing hand forward, and pressed it to her midriff.

Storr's breath caught in his throat in those seconds. She, *she* was holding his fingers there, just over the beating of her heart, just beneath the soft hang of her left breast, and, after the great disapproval she'd just shown at his carnal inquiry, he couldn't imagine what trickery she was up to. "I meant *here*. In my heart. In my soul," she explained. "I simply meant that I sometimes feel Christ here. And I am filled with His Word and His Will for me."

To Alanna's amazement, her captor seemed completely unmoved by this poignancy and the emotion in her voice. Rather, he pulled his hand away quite abruptly and returned to the business of washing her back.

"Well, were I you, I would tell him to find his own body in which to dwell," he retorted critically. "What right hath he to claim yours?"

Alanna bit her lip, trying not to show her amusement at this response. They were no fools, these Vikings. She'd come to know this well enough in all the time she'd now spent with them. They seemed, however, rather inflexible in their thinking. Strangely single-minded. "But 'twas I who invited Him to dwell in me, sire. For 'tis the only way to salvation."

"But I thought you said believing was the only way! Do you try to confuse me?"

"Nay, nay. Forsooth, I believe you would find great peace in knowing more of my God. 'Tis just that it is difficult to explain, when you know so little of my language ... Maybe we should try speaking of it through your freeman sometime. Perhaps that will aid your understanding."

"Perhaps," Storr agreed after a moment. "Mayhap tonight the three of us could speak of it further. Now close your eyes, so I can wet your hair," he ordered, suddenly wishing to have the bathing over with, so he could move on to business he would find less disconcerting.

It was one thing to take pleasure with a slave girl, to share a hot bath with her and see to it she didn't spread her deadly filth to his living quarters. It was one thing to extend such favors as calming her with kisses and touch, and to toy with the idea of asking her to do the same for him. But, when she suddenly, inexplicably, took the helm, when she began speaking of such weighty subjects as loyalty and what a person holds in his or her heart—when her words and gestures made the depths of him give way to an unplanned arousal, a hasty disengagement seemed most advisable.

He had thought, back in her uncle's hut, that his deepest wish was to bury himself inside her. To escape into the warmth of her land, her body, and leave all of his pain and responsibility behind. But

321

he was discovering that, upon the brink of things, he couldn't bring himself to follow through. He just couldn't bear to throw himself upon her, with her wailing for him to stop all the while. He desperately needed to have his lovemaking requited, not repulsed. And he knew, in his still-mourning state, that he couldn't endure the rejection implicit in any resistance she might offer.

He was not, and never could be, as brazen and heartless as chieftains like Sigurd. He'd learned too much compassion in the past year, and the memories of his beloved Freyja were yet too fresh for him to risk defiling them in such a way.

"Oh, we must wash our hair as well?" Alanna groaned, interrupting his thoughts.

"We must. Now shut your eyes or you'll find soap in them, as I pour this water over you," he warned again, reaching outside of the tub and taking up the ladle one of his freeman had left for such purposes.

Alanna did as she was told, giving forth an uncontainable moan, as the showers of warm liquid started rushing over her. She gasped a bit, when the pouring finally subsided and she was able to catch her breath. Then, as she reached up and wiped the remaining water from her face and eyes, she felt him rub the cake of soap over the crown of her head and draw the rest of her mane up into the resultant lather.

"Will you wash your hair too, my lord? Or is it

only long hair that must be cleaned?"

" 'Tis all hair," he said coldly. "For, if your people passed as much time intent upon *this* world, as they do upon this place you call Heaven, you would know that hair is where fleas and lice most like to dwell."

"Have I offended thee in some way?" she asked, wondering now at his chilliness, when it seemed he'd done so much to mull the mood between them.

"Nay," he denied. "Close your eyes once more."

Alanna did so, and again the warm showers came, obviously meant to rinse the soap from her hair.

"You are bathed now," he announced, hoping she could be persuaded to get out of the bath before him—before he emerged and she saw the lingering effect her apparently innocent gesture had had upon him. "You may dry yourself and dress to take your leave. Wear any of the tunics you find in my chests, and pass your own on to my freeman for laundering."

"But it shall be cold as I rise, shall it not?"

He clucked with annoyance. "For a moment or two, perhaps. But the towel my servants left for you is right at hand. Just hanging there, upon that bench." He pointed to the seat where it stood, only a couple feet away. "And you have my word I will not look at you . . . Make haste now, will you, girl, for I need the room in this damnable vessel to bend forward and wash my hair as well!"

Alanna couldn't help turning back to face him again in those seconds, to search his eyes for the answer to the question she'd asked. What had she done? What had she said to make him suddenly so distant, so cross with her? She had tried to be obedient, to humor him in the interests of saving her cousins from the other chieftain, but something had caused her captor to shut her out.

She searched his sky blue orbs for any answer, any sign of his former warmth and kindness. She entreated him, as best she could, with her own doe brown eyes. But to no avail. He seemed, in fact, as icy as his homeland had always been rumored to be.

"As you wish," she replied, in a wavering voice. Then she began to rise.

He wouldn't look, she told herself, doing her best to keep her back towards him. He surely would not stoop to leering at her, after having just given his word on it.

But, to her horror as she rose, his gaze was the least of her problems. Her feet suddenly gave way on the bath's slippery bottom, and she found herself reeling backward.

She tried to break the fall, to extend a hand and catch hold of the right side of the tub. This effort proved futile, however. Instead, she landed upon him, and, in the instant that followed, she realized that she was turned so that he could see her profile, her breasts and rounded posterior. Worse still, her hand had come down in the most ineffable of places. Between his legs! Dear God! Cruel fate! Her fingers were upon the very part of him she had most wanted to avoid!

Those seconds seemed to freeze for them both. He was as he had been when he'd awakened with her that morning in the woods: enlarged to a size she could never have imagined and inexplicably hard to the touch. And, as her eyes shot up to again engage his, she saw that he looked every bit as ill-humored as he had back then.

It *hurt,* she realized. This state, this malady, that kept befalling this male portion of him, must have hurt as surely as any injured and swollen part of her ever had. And, drawing a chagrined breath in through her teeth, she jerked her hand away as though she had just set it down upon a bed of live coals.

"Sorry, my lord," she croaked. "I did slip was all."

As she could have predicted, his tone was a distinctly pained one as he answered. "Aye. I am aware of that."

"Did I hurt thee?"

He rolled his eyes wearily. "My dear, I was a fool to think you capable of doing aught else."

She shielded her chest with her forearms and knelt down to let the water cover the lower half of her once more. "I shall stay and wash your hair for you, in turn," she offered amenably.

"Nay, girl. Just dress yourself and go."

"But I did not mean to anger you. I did not mean to fall. 'Tis not like the first time you stole me. I understand that your taking me now was, verily, an act of mercy. For it was either that or death for me. Or falling into that wicked Sigurd's hands, as my cousins did. And I truly have no designs to harm you, Storr. I do too much appreciate the kindnesses you've shown," she concluded, sounding tearful in spite of her efforts to avoid it.

Seeing how her eyes glistened with emotion, he swallowed dryly. " 'Tis not you, Alanna. 'Tis not your fault this time, but mine. Pray, be assured I am not really angry with you."

"Then with whom?" she pursued, beginning to shiver in the chilling air as she continued to kneel.

"With . . . with everyone . . . and no one," he faltered, as though lost for the Erse words he sought. He caught sight of his bed, *Freyja's* dowered bed, which he'd shared with her after their wedding—and every long, lonely night since her death. And suddenly, sitting so near it, naked with a bungling slave girl, seemed almost vulgar to him.

But Alanna was no ordinary chattel, another part of him acknowledged. She had spirit and a defiant pride; and when she'd pressed his hand to her heart and spoken of her god earlier, her voice had exhibited the same reverence and love that Freyja had always shown him. Somewhere, in the festering depths of him, Storr realized that it was not the brush with Alanna's bared breast that had so aroused him, but the sound of fondness and devotion in her words. How he longed to have that same worshipfulness directed at *him* once more!

"With . . . with not understanding your gods or mine," he continued, his voice barely audible now. "With your hair feeling so like my wife's, and yet being so dark—" His words broke off as though he feared he had just slit his throat with his own tongue.

"Well, perhaps you wish her back, sire. Perhaps you wish this wife you once had to return to you," Alanna said sympathetically after a moment.

A sad smile came slowly to his lips, and he shook his head. "Oh, my dear, you couldn't know how much."

Fifteen

Gunther brushed off his tunic and squared his shoulders, as he stood before the draped door of the chieftain's tent, preparing for his audience with Sigurd. He had sought to delay this discussion with the earl for as long as possible. An admission of failure was not something that a race as proud as his handled well. But, now that all of the ships had been brought in and he could no longer avoid his foster father by reason of being called to man the second of his war vessels, he knew the time of reckoning had come. And, after that enraging, and rather humiliating, clash with Storr in the bath line on the beach, Gunther was of a mind to get all of his confrontations behind him forthwith.

As he finally stepped inside, the conversation between Sigurd and his two sons came to a halt, and the chieftain clapped his hands to dismiss his attendant freemen.

"The second of my ships is being unladed?" he asked frostily, fixing his eyes firmly upon his foster son's, as he stood on the threshold.

328

"It is, Earl," Gunther answered with equal detachment.

"Pray, see that no one tarries outside and that my door is secured, so that we might speak further," Sigurd ordered.

Gunther made haste to oblige him, having even more stake than the earl in their not being overheard. Then he returned to his place, just inside the tent.

Seeing this, the chieftain donned as gracious an expression as he seemed capable of, and motioned for Gunther to come and be seated upon the sea chest that was situated across from him.

Gunther did so, uneasily arranging his cape behind him as he sat.

"Wine?" Sigurd's younger son, Rutland, suggested, rising from his place upon the chest to his father's left.

Sigurd waved him off. *"Neinn.* We shall keep our minds clear until we have finished our talk."

Rutland sat back down.

"Tell me, now, Gunther, of what did betide you in your effort to do as we had planned," the earl continued.

Gunther cleared his throat, grateful for the discretion shown in his foster father's vague wording.

"I was . . . was interrupted, my lord. My sword was poised for the swipe, when an Erse woman did warn my prey. He was kissing her. About to rape her, I think. And then, to my astonishment, she did look over his shoulder in this act and warn him of me. 'Twas most odd. I'd have thought she would have wanted his advances stopped."

Sigurd sat back and pondered this, scratching his bearded chin. "Maybe you frightened her more than he."

"But she called him by name, as she told him of me."

Sigurd did finally look suspicious. "By his name?"

"*Ja.* I heard her say it, as clear and well-pronounced as if 'twere a Norseman speaking it."

"Well, perhaps she heard him called it by one of his men before he cornered her. But 'tis odd, none the less," he agreed. "For he has not raped since the death of his wife. Indeed, I am told he has sworn not to."

Gunther nodded. This was what he'd heard as well.

"What did he say to you, as he turned and saw you poised?"

"Well, not much, my chief, for I simply claimed to have mistaken him for someone else. For an Erse warrior."

Sigurd knit his furry brow at the preposterousness of this claim. "In his mail coat and helmet? Did he not call you a liar?"

"*Neinn.* Forsooth, he appeared too surprised to do aught but growl at me, and tell me to go back out into the fray and find someone else at whom to swipe."

Sigurd looked relieved to hear this, but Gunther

knew that a problem yet remained. The maiden had seen him. She'd seen him try to kill his own brother. And, while her testimony might not stand alone at the Viking assembly, she could, indeed, serve as a witness to the murder attempt, should Storr decide to press charges against him.

"I tried to seize that same girl just now, out of one of the lines for the baths, but Storr stopped me in a rage and scooped her up to take her to his tent."

A dissatisfied rumble came from somewhere low in Sigurd's throat, and he reached up to pick at his teeth with his thumbnail. "Perhaps 'tis better made a task for Eric or Rutland. Maybe one of my own will prove more able to stop simply *trying,* and finally succeed with this."

Gunther, though wounded by the remark, straightened his back and lifted his chin. "But 'tis not my will to fail, Sigurd. You, of all men, must know how much I want him slain! Besides, as we have agreed many times, I truly am the best man for the deed, for I am the only one the earl would hesitate to take to trial. 'Tis his own blood money that would be spent, if he admits before so many chieftains that his brother is given to murder."

"Maybe, if we simply do away with this Erse witness, our problem will be solved," Sigurd's eldest son interjected.

The earl shook his head. *"Neinn.* We all know that 'twill not be solved by the killing of this woman, but this man . . . this man who blocks his brother's path to greatness."

The dwelling was silent at this piercing truth, and, after several seconds, Gunther rose to take his leave. "So am I to be allowed another try?" he asked in a voice that he somehow managed to keep rock-steady.

Sigurd nodded. *"Ja.* On our next raid, one more try will be given you. But you must succeed, my son. 'Twill probably be the last foray of the season," he added, his eyes narrowing to the exacting, "serpent's" expression that had so entranced Gunther in his youth. This man, this blessed earl, above even Gunther's own father, had been the only one who had ever cared enough to plant the dream of chieftainship in his heart and mind. Sigurd had made Gunther see that he was fated to rule vast spreads of land one day, to own not just scores of slaves, but hundreds. To press on towards the acquisition of a veritable kingdom, in spite of the fact that his own blind clan had always tried to keep him down—to keep him second in their simpleminded scheme of things.

Gunther was clearly more the warrior than his older brother had ever been. And if only his true father, Ivar, had lived to see how Storr had faltered and softened in the past year, Gunther felt that even he would have been forced to agree.

"Thank you, Earl," he said, dropping to one knee and bowing his head to the chieftain before leaving.

Sigurd reached out and patted his hand as he rose again. "You were right to yield back at that fort and not risk fighting him to the death. You know that we cannot afford to have you killed in any of this. And we must, I regret, have one of your foster brothers see it through on next summer's raids, should you prove unsuccessful again."

"I shall not," Gunther vowed, clenching his jaw. He could hardly refrain from beginning to tremble with rage at the very thought of Storr, and how he had killed their father the year before. "For your sake, as well as Ivar's, you can rest assured of that!"

With that he left the tent, and his foster family waited until they were certain he was out of earshot to say anything more. Then Eric leaned over to Sigurd with a resentful whisper. "You should let me do it, Father. I would not fail. I would never make the bungle of it that he has. Is it not enough that you bid him pilot the ship that should be commanded by me?"

Sigurd responded by giving him a stinging pat on the back. "Shhh! Rein yourself, boy," he returned in an equally low voice. "Let us not rush the carving. If 'tis well done by him this time, then the only killing we'll have before us is Gunther, himself. After that, all that will stand between us and dead Ivar's plentiful stead is a widow and her little brats. And they will be as blades of grass beneath our feet."

In the days that followed, Storr remained distant

with Alanna. She continued to be fed more than she felt was her share, however; and, short of having to abide by a few rather puzzling rules, she was free to move about the camp as she pleased. The main restraint was that she wasn't to go too near the other tent on the beach. That shelter was Earl Sigurd's, apparently, and, after the incident in the bathing line, it didn't take much for Storr to persuade her that she could easily fall back into the wrong hands, if she wandered too far from his side of the encampment.

This, of course, prevented her from having much contact with her cousins. She was able to speak with them briefly one morning. To ask if they were both unharmed and inform them, in a very hushed voice, that Storr was, in fact, the raider who had captured her weeks earlier. She told them that she felt she had won some favor with him—some goodwill that might eventually work to save them from Sigurd. But, short of such hurried discourse, short of asking if they had gone unviolated by their captors and having the inquiry greeted with a painfully telling drop of their gazes, there wasn't much time for conversing; and Alanna knew that any plans for a coordinated escape of the camp would have to wait until they could steal more time together. They would have at least another month in which to get away, in any case. Alanna had asked Storr when he and his countrymen planned to return to Thule, and he had claimed it would not be 'til summer's end.

The lesser of Storr's restraints was that, while Alanna was expected to sleep within his tent, she was not to dress or undress in it when he was present. Nor was she allowed to occupy his bed at any time. And, given that he'd required her to strip and bathe with him on the day of their arrival, she found these last two edicts surprising.

It was possible, she supposed, that he had, for some reason, decided to begin respecting her Christian wishes. His interests had definitely shifted from kissing her to such cerebral pursuits as challenging her to board games and having her regale him with her harp. Nevertheless, he continued to seem cynical about her faith, as he questioned her on it each evening through his freeman; and she rather doubted that religious conversion could be the cause of his sudden morality.

From time to time, she entertained the idea of just coming out and asking him what had happened to him back in the woods as they'd slept and then, again, in the tub as they'd bathed. She truly wished to know what she might have done to cause such a vexing change in his form and in his manner. But, as with his warning her of the soap, she found herself lost for the words necessary to engage in such a conversation, and she refrained from making mention of it.

The malady was, in any case, hitherto unknown to her. She had not seen or heard tell of it in all the years she'd attended patients with her uncle. So it was altogether possible that it was something that afflicted the Norse alone, that only their men suffered from it, and only their physicians knew how it should be treated.

Their medicine certainly seemed advanced enough. For days Alanna had watched the Viking women in the camp treat those hurt in the raiding, and she was most impressed with their skills at surgery and the dressing of wounds. They'd even devised an ingenious test for determining the seriousness of stomach lacerations. They fed the patient a porridge of onions, then waited for the smell of same to seep from the site of his injury. If it did, death was said to be inevitable. But, fortunately, in the case which Alanna was allowed to observe, no such smell could be detected.

She offered to help the women in their efforts, knowing that, given her experience, this was where her talents could best be put to use. She found them unwilling to let her do anything but watch, however, and it was later explained to her—rather gingerly by Storr's freeman, Leif—that they thought her too dirty to risk having her touch their charges. Given their fixation with cleaning not only themselves, but every instrument they used, in steaming hot water, Alanna found this neither offensive nor surprising.

They seemed utterly obsessed with cleanliness, in fact. As if it wasn't bad enough that all of the slaves and warriors had been required to bathe upon their arrival at the camp, Alanna had later learned that they'd be expected to continue doing so *every* Saturday for the rest of their natural lives! She truly did not know whether to laugh or cry at this revelation. While she hadn't found bathing entirely disagreeable, all that boiling and hauling of water struck her as a great deal of work for such short-lived results; and she couldn't help voicing as much to Storr and his freeman.

As she should have guessed, however, the earl greeted this observation with the same sternness he'd shown when she'd tried to avoid removing her tunic a few days earlier. Pestilence was their enemy, he maintained, and it was the duty of every man, woman, and child in the camp to fight it.

He had even begun to snap at her of late about such petty matters as tossing the occasional bread crust or half-eaten game-bird limb on the floor of his tent. He told her that these scraps should either be fed to their dogs, or thrown into one of the camp fires for the flames' consumption. What was more, he threatened to banish her from his dwelling at mealtime, if he caught her committing such a mindless act again.

"You shall not turn my tent into one of your filthy huts," he snarled, as if repulsed by her ways.

Though hurt by this, Alanna did her best not to let it show. She would not respond to the chiding by slinking out, onto the beach — as she had recently begun doing in order to accommodate his moodiness. Rather, she remained where she was, eating supper with him now, at the makeshift table his freeman set up nightly for such privately taken meals.

"They are not filthy, my lord," she countered evenly, careful to dab her fingers and mouth with the serviette with which she'd been provided. "Our floors are spread almost yearly with a new layer of clay."

Storr donned a snide smile and nodded knowingly over at Leif, who had chosen to join them at this particular meal. "More to smooth a path for walking, than to cover the rot and stench, no doubt."

At this Alanna closed her hands about her wooden plate and cup and rose from the table. "Well, I could go and join the rest of my people on the beach, if you find my kind so revolting," she suggested, knowing how he disapproved of her consorting with her fellow prisoners.

Storr sobered at this, and his freeman looked almost equally disturbed by the threat. "Nay," the earl said, catching hold of her arm and pressing her back into her seat. "You know that I wish you to eat in here with me."

Her voice wavered as she spoke again. "But why? You have done naught but growl at me for nearly a week now. Nothing I do seems to please you."

He grew even more serious, and his voice dropped to an ominous murmur that seemed to warn her of challenging him further in Leif's presence. "You please me well enough. I ask you of your god each night, and play board games with you, do I not?"

"Aye. But all this talk of pestilence! First it is our bodies we must keep bathed, and then our *floors?* So much worry about filth and disease. Why, the way you carry on, sire, one would think your dearest friend had died of such things," she exclaimed, feeling no longer able to restrain herself at his ceaseless criticism.

The dwelling was silent for several seconds, and, to Alanna's amazement, the earl looked as though she had just hit him in the forehead with a rock. Then he bolted from the table, inadvertently breaking his own rule about not letting food fall to the floor, and he stormed out of the tent without another word.

Alanna and the freeman sat staring dumbfoundedly after him.

"Why did he do that?" she asked Leif under her breath.

The freeman was red-faced, but she couldn't seem to tell if this was due to anger or discomfiture.

"He has not told you?"

"Told me what?"

"Of the deaths?"

"Nay. What deaths?"

"Well, if he hasn't spoken of them with you, my lady, 'tis certainly not my place to do so," he concluded firmly.

"But do, prithee. How can I hope to go on

dwelling with him, when I cannot understand his moods from one moment to the next?"

Leif must have seen some sense in this appeal, because he looked suddenly more accessible. "Well, let it serve for me to say that our master *has* had some nearest to him die of pestilence, and you would do well to oblige him in fighting it."

"Aye. But 'tis not just my habits he disdains. 'Tis me, *myself*. I have truly tried to be obedient and to appease him, but he is so withdrawn, so aloof."

"Aye. *Lifs ne dauoa*," he mumbled, nodding in agreement.

"What?"

" 'Tis Norse for 'neither in life nor in death.' He is caught somewhere in between, I fear."

Alanna shook her head thoughtfully. "Nay. 'Tis something simpler, I think. 'Tis his love for this wife who left him. Freyja, is she called?"

Leif nodded, gesturing for her to continue to keep her voice down.

"I have heard him cry out for her as he sleeps, and I know he misses her terribly. Pray, is she here in this camp? Or must he wait until the return to Thule to see her again?"

The freeman's face went strangely pale at this question; but Alanna couldn't imagine why.

"Why, she's . . . she's dead, my lady. Has he not told you that much?" he asked, his words barely audible.

Alanna felt her heart sink a bit, and her eyes widened with concern. *"Dead?* Dead, you say? But he has never once made mention of being a widow-man. Even out in the wilderness, he never—" Her words broke off as she acknowledged the secret she'd just betrayed.

"In the wilderness?" Leif repeated, looking suddenly enlightened. "So you *had* met before we took your fort. I suspected as much when our master said he fancied you, for he has never been one to take swiftly to a woman. Especially a slave."

Though stunned to hear that the chieftain had professed to fancy her, Alanna knew she must first address the more pressing of these subjects. The freeman slid off his seat and dropped to his knees to begin cleaning up the mess Storr's outburst had created; and she quickly followed suit, slipping down beside him and coming to his assistance, where he could continue to hear her whispers.

"But you must not let the earl know that I told you of having met him while he scouted, for he swore me to secrecy, on pain of death."

Leif smiled slightly and shook his head. "So many secrets for just one man. I cannot believe he seeks to keep us *both* in the dark . . . But have no fear," he assured. "I'll not speak of it, if you keep my confidences as well. I cannot, you see, have him railing at me again, as he did when you asked me about the monks we held for ransom."

"I shall be more cautious henceforth," she promised. "But what of this fancying me, Leif? How can that be? At his request, I neither share his bed nor change my raiment before him."

The freeman sat back on his heels and frowned. "Alas. I had so hoped he'd let you close to him. Me thinks 'tis the only way he might begin to heal, and learn to forgive himself for Freyja's death."

"He killed her?" Alanna asked, her voice rising with alarm.

"I suppose it could be said he did. His brother would certainly say so. And that he killed their father as well."

Alanna felt a frightened chill run through her. "His brother?"

"Aye. The man who seized you in the bath line, of course. Were you not told who he was?"

She tried to hide her astoundment, fearing she might reveal yet another secret to him and further endanger herself and her cousins. "That man was his brother?" What madness! It had not only been another Norseman, but Storr's very *brother* who had tried to kill him! "But . . . but he dwells with Sigurd's warriors, does he not?"

"Aye. Sigurd fostered Gunther in his youth, and 'twas, sorrily, a bond that grew even stronger than the one he shared with his own blood clan."

"But why would Storr kill his wife? He seems, even now, so smitten with her. I can find no reason in it," she continued, starting to feel fearful for her own safety.

"Well, 'twas not done by design, I don't think."

"By accident then?"

Leif drew away from her, setting the fallen objects he'd gathered upon the adjacent sea chest and

342

getting to his feet. "Aye. More or less," he answered sotto voce. "But we must speak of it no more, my lady. 'Tis a topic that is forbidden." He reached out and helped her back up.

"But what of his father? Did he die at the same time as Freyja?"

"Nay. I think a day or two thereafter," he answered, with what struck her as almost brazen matter-of-factness—given that the subject was that of murder.

She hurried back to the bench she had been sitting upon and tried to steady herself at all this news. However inadvertently, Storr had *killed* his wife and father! Leif had just said as much.

She knew the Vikings to be murderers, certainly. She had, only days before, witnessed many of her own tribe being slain. But she had always thought them civilized enough to balk at killing their own kin! . . . Until, of course, she had seen Storr nearly beheaded by a man who was now revealed to be his brother. Then, she realized, *then* she should have known that they fought amongst themselves with the same violence they directed towards outlanders.

Who was this man, this stranger she'd come to dwell with in such intimate quarters? Alone. She slept *alone* with him each night, and never once had she guessed that he might chance to do her in as well.

"What is the matter? You suddenly look so pale. What is it that troubles you, my lady?" the freeman asked, bending down to study her face.

"Do you think our master crazed enough to . . . to kill me, too?"

Leif drew his chin back in surprise. Then he smiled slightly. "Nay. Of course not. He fancies you, remember? He told me so himself."

"But he loved his wife, I am sure. And look what became of her!"

"Aye. But, as I told you, 'twas not his intent. And every man deserves a second chance, does he not? Surely your Christian faith must have taught you as much."

Drink, Alanna realized in that instant. Perhaps these unintentional killings were somehow linked to the Norsemen's lust for spirited drink. It was possible, she supposed, that Storr might have, on more than one occasion, become possessed with demon mead, and flown into a Viking rage of sorts.

Aye. That would explain his freeman's evasive impartation of it all. More importantly, however, it explained why Alanna needed to be all the more obedient with the earl henceforward.

"What exactly doth this mean, 'fancies'? I am not sure I understand what it is he feels for me."

Again Leif looked uneasy; but this expression seemed of a lighter, more ticklish variety than his previous one. "Well, I do many things for the earl, my lady. But 'tis truly not my place to do his wooing. Has he not spoken to you of desire? Of love?"

She shook her head, continuing to look at him blankly.

344

"You mean, he hasn't . . . hasn't *taken* you? Not even once?"

"Taken me where?"

He looked, for some reason, amused by this question, and Alanna couldn't help feeling a bit annoyed.

"Ah, forget that I asked," he replied. "We must let our master teach you of it in his own good time . . . But," he continued, stooping to gaze into her face once more, "be not afraid, Alanna. Just do whatever he requests, and he or I shall see that you are not shamed, and that you and any children you might bear of this are well fed . . . Befriend him," he beseeched, taking one of her hands in his. "Win his confidence and his love. For whatever sin you might see in lying with him, there is far greater sin, I promise you, in letting such a man cut himself off from the living and die."

"He is dying?" she asked, thinking now that her mind couldn't accommodate yet another piece of shocking news.

"He is thinking of it. And far too often. I can see it in nearly all he says and does."

Her breath caught in her throat; and, for an instant there was a flash in her mind—a sight she scarcely recalled having seen until now. It was of her mother's drowned body washing up to shore. "Of killing himself, you mean?" she asked in a tremulous voice.

Leif nodded and pressed a finger to her lips. "But you mustn't speak of it. Not to anyone! Simply keep it in mind. Keep in mind what a fine and gentle master we might lose, if he is not soon given more reason to live. Gunther would surely claim the earl's holdings upon his death, for their only other brother is still just a child," he added pointedly.

"But what am I to do? I know nothing of the ways of the flesh. Naught of how to win a man's heart."

"You might already have. It could just be that he doesn't yet know it. So, don't strive to be a lover, my lady. Just, as I said, a friend. Touch him and encourage him to talk to you. For a Norseman will always confide in a woman, before he will another man."

"An *Erse* woman? A *bonds*woman?" she asked, her tone betraying her simmering anger at her present situation.

"Oh, aye. Forsooth, his father confided thus in my mother, and I am told she was stolen from a ring-fort not far from here."

"Your mother was Erse?"

He laughed. 'How do you think I came to know so much of your tongue?"

"Then Storr's father . . ." She fell silent at the scandalousness of it.

"Was also mine?" he finished for her with a soft smile. "Aye. He may well have been."

"Oh, but that is disgraceful," she gasped. "The Lord God hath decreed that a man should have only one mate!"

346

"Your Erse god, perhaps. But that is not what the Norse believe. However that may be, *our* earl no longer has a mate of any kind. You are very likely the only woman he's touched since his wife's death. It appears *you* are the one he has chosen, Alanna," he declared, rising once more. "And, be you wise, you will make the most of it."

Sixteen

Storr's fingers wavered over one of his walrus-ivory chessmen. Then he withdrew his hand and glared up at Alanna, where she sat across from him at the gaming board. "So your god's son was born to a *virgin,* you say?" he asked, making no effort to hide his skepticism. "Pray, tell me how this was possible."

Alanna did her best not to let his exacting gaze vex her, as Leif repeated his master's question for her in her native language. Storr's Erse had become so much less rusty in the past couple weeks that it hardly seemed necessary to have the freeman continue to translate for them. But his presence seemed to prevent any carnal advances by Storr, so Alanna went on acting as though his services were needed.

She shrugged and returned her eyes to the playing pieces on the *taflbord*. "As I have stated, my lord. The blessed Mother Mary was visited by the angel of the Lord, and he did cause her to come with child."

Storr squinted with further perplexity. "Visited? What doth this mean? For, in my tongue, it is simply to pay a call upon, and you and I both know that more than that is needed for siring a child."

Alanna sighed with exasperation. Storr had seemed to accept the story of Christ's resurrection easily enough—the miraculous triumph over death itself. Yet, when it came to the Savior's birth, an experience all men had in common, he just couldn't seem to reason it out. "Well, perhaps angels do not sire children as mortals do," she suggested after a moment. "Don't you think that could be the cause of such phrasing?"

She glanced up to see, however, that the chieftain continued to appear dubious.

"Fetch the gospel book," he said, snapping his fingers at his freeman. "I wish to have Alanna read to me of this afresh."

Leif went and withdrew the bound writings from his master's sea chest. The volume had been acquired during their raid upon the monastery south of Alanna's fort; and, though few of the Norse knew how to read their own tongue, let alone that of the Erse, such elaborately lettered books could be counted upon to bring a very good price in their trading towns.

Alanna gave forth another weary sigh as the Bible was placed in her lap for what seemed the twentieth time that week alone. "Then you want to hear of the Nativity once more, sire?"

Storr leaned back upon the bench he occupied

and nodded. Then he gestured for Leif to be seated again and stay quiet, so that he might try to decipher Alanna's reading for himself.

"Aye. Make haste," he pressed, as she paged through the book in search of the passages he'd requested.

She clucked at his impatience, then glared up at him, as her fingers finally came upon the gospel of Saint Matthew. " 'Now the birth of Jesus Christ was on this wise: When as his mother Mary was espoused to Joseph, before they came together, she was found with child of the Holy Ghost. Then Joseph her husband, being a just man, and not willing to make her a publick example, was minded to put her away privily—' "

"That is it," Storr interrupted, jabbing a finger at her. "That is the line I seek. So, this Joseph learned that his bride was with child, even before he lay with her?"

"Aye, my lord."

"And he pondered sealing her away somewhere for this?"

"Aye."

"Well, he should have. He surely should have!" He folded his arms over his chest. "I would have, in his stead!"

"But this was before the dream, Earl."

"What dream?"

"Do you not remember? The dream in which the angel of the Lord told Joseph that the child his wife was carrying was Christ. 'And she shall bring forth a son, and thou shalt call his name Jesus.' Do you not recall that part?"

"And this 'Jesus' is also 'Christ'?"

She nodded.

"But 'tis confusing for him to have so many names. Do you not also call him Emmanuel, Savior, and Messiah?"

"Well, aye. But He is principally known as Christ. Jesus Christ, you see."

"So Christ was, verily, his father's name?"

"Nay," Alanna replied, thinking she might go mad at his endless quibbling. For nearly a fortnight he'd spent two or three hours of each evening quizzing her about every aspect of the Holy Trinity, and her forbearance was wearing sorrily thin. "His father is God, sire, and we simply call Him 'God' or 'Our Heavenly Lord.' "

"Then should Christ not have been called by his earthly father's name? Joseph's son?"

Alanna shook her head and groaned under her breath. "I don't know. I suppose 'twas possible in the language of His day."

"Ja, well, call him simply 'Christ,' whenever another name for him should appear in the writings, for it doth grow addling to me."

"As you wish. Now, where were we? . . . Oh, aye. 'And she shall bring forth a son, and thou shalt call his name Jesus'—*Christ,"* Alanna interposed. " 'For he shall save his people from their sins. Now all this was done, that—' "

"Stop," Storr broke in again.

"Aye?" Alanna growled, hoping that, if she could get a long enough stretch of reading done, there might be some chance of his simply nodding off, as he had on preceding evenings.

"How can a man be saved from his own sins? I thought it was *Hel* from which your god saves men."

"Well, perhaps, in God's eyes, sins and Hell are one and the same, my lord."

"Hmmm." Storr leaned forward, placing an elbow on the gaming table and resting his chin in his hand. "What if a man does not seek such salvation? What if he already has it?"

"But he cannot. Only through Christ can any man have such."

"But the bravest of Norsemen have it. We are saved from *Hel* and given a seat in *Valholl* by the great god Odin. Who is, by the way, wise enough to have chosen only one name for himself!"

"If that is how you feel in your deepest heart, sire, then there seems no purpose in my going on with this instruction," she declared, poised to close the book.

"*Neinn* Keep it open," he urged amenably. "Just read to me of something other than salvation. For 'tis not what I seek and I grow tired of discussing it."

"Well, just what *do* you seek, prithee?" Alanna snapped, wishing she held something she felt was suitable for hurling at him. Her head ached, and she was exhausted from a long day of hauling firewood to the beach and helping her fellow slaves with the camp's laundering.

Storr was silent for several seconds. Then he spoke again, in a voice so low Alanna felt certain he meant for her alone to hear it. "Peace. Love . . . Do your god's *skalds* never write of such cheering things?" he asked with a note of disparagement.

He had, for so many nights, taken such pleasure in simply scoffing at her faith, that Alanna couldn't help feeling taken aback now at this apparently earnest appeal.

"Aye, my lord. Of course," she replied defensively. "Our apostles are said to have written about peace and love in many of their letters." Then, suddenly fearing that she might not be able to find any passages to substantiate this claim, her fingers began to fumble in her search for them.

The Twenty-third Psalm, she thought. Surely this Norse chieftain and his sin-laden soul would find some comfort in that. Unfortunately, however, she couldn't seem to locate it among the ornately penned headings of the volume, and, all at once, she found her heart racing with chagrin amidst her companions' anticipatory silence.

I am the rose of Erin, a voice within her echoed, and, whispering up a prayer of thanks for this divine intervention, she quickly turned to "The Song Of Solomon," wherein, the Erse clergy alleged, some of the Bible's most beautiful verse could be found. She had never heard or read it. Save for the line about Erin—which, it was rumored, had originally been: "I am the rose of Sharon"—she knew nothing of this book. She was content to trust in the monks' endorsement, however, and she dove into reading it without further hesitation.

" 'The song of songs, which is Solomon's. Let him kiss me with the kisses of his mouth: for thy love is better than wine—' " She gasped, as her mind seemed to catch up with her utterances, and she looked blushingly over at her captor.

"I'm sorry, my lord! I had no idea the Scriptures contained such things! Surely this is not the sort of love you were asking about," she said, moving to turn to some other book in the volume. She was inwardly aghast that the clergy could have commended such passages.

"*Neinn*. Leave it open there," the chieftain ordered with an approving expression. " 'Twill do just fine. Keep reading."

She looked to Leif for some intercession, some rescue in those seconds. To her dismay, however, he appeared even more pleased by this choice than his master. He raised a brow at her and smiled broadly, surreptitiously urging her on with a flick of his fingers. It was clear that he saw this as a means to the rather unseemly end he had advocated just a couple evenings before.

Alanna gulped and let her eyes drop back down to the text. Her voice was aquiver as she began to read again. " 'Because . . . because of the savour of thy good ointments thy name is as ointment

354

poured forth, therefore do the vir—virgins love thee—' Oh, please, sire, must I go on with this?" she asked, her tone unavoidably pleading.

"*Ja, ja.* I insist," Storr replied, and the imperative glint in his eye in those seconds made it very apparent that he did.

" 'Draw . . . draw me, we will run after thee: the king hath brought me into his . . . his chambers—' " *Oh, dear God, where were the earl's infernal interruptions now?* she wondered in desperation. " 'We will be glad and rejoice in thee, we will remember thy love more than wine: the upright love thee. I am black, but comely, O ye daughters of Jerusalem, as the tents of Kedar, as the curtains of Solomon. Look not upon me, because I am black, because the sun hath looked upon me: my mother's children were angry with me; they made me the keeper of the vineyards; but mine own vineyard have I not kept. Tell me, O thou whom my soul loveth, where thou feedest, where thou makest thy flock to rest at noon: for why should I be as one that turneth aside by the flocks of thy companions? If thou know not, O thou fairest among women, go thy way forth by the footsteps of the flock, and feed thy kids beside the shepherds' tents. I have compared thee, O my love, to a company of horses in Pharaoh's chariots. Thy cheeks are comely with rows of jewels, thy neck with chains of gold. We will make thee borders of gold with studs of silver.' "

Christ be praised, the verses did seem to be rein-

ing in now. They spoke of nothing more titillative than chariots and gold, and she breathed a relieved sigh, beginning to relax a bit as she continued to read. " 'While the king sitteth at his table, my spikenard sendeth forth the smell thereof. A bundle of myrrh is my wellbeloved unto me; he shall lie all night betwixt my breasts—' " That was it! She clapped the volume shut, and, trying to hide her irritation, informed the chieftain that the book ended there. With that very line.

Looking skeptical about this, he leaned toward her. "Are you certain?"

She nodded, pressing the gospel heavily into her lap.

Storr's expression changed from doubting to one of blatant disappointment. "Give it to Leif, that he might judge this for himself," he said sternly after a moment.

"But, master, I do not read Erse. I . . . I only speak it," the freeman countered feebly.

" 'Tis in Latin, in any case," Alanna explained.

Storr returned his gaze to her. "What is Latin?"

" 'Tis the language of the Church."

"So 'tis different from Erse?"

"Aye."

"Hmm. Have a look, none the less," he told his freeman.

Alanna, feeling certain Leif could not hope to find or decipher the particular book from which she'd been reading, reached across the gaming board and handed it to him.

They sat in tense silence, as he paged through it. He was squinting terribly in the dim lamplight, and it was evident that he was simply attempting to judge the thickness of the pages on both left and right in order to reopen the text at roughly the same place she had.

"Oh, take it forth from here and continue looking beside the cook fire," Storr said finally. "I wish a word alone with Alanna."

Leif, giving her a stealthy wink, pressed the gospel to his chest and rose. He obviously felt that she'd done an admirable job of setting the mood, and he did not hesitate to take his leave.

"That was nice. Very nice, indeed," Storr praised softly, once they were alone. "I did not realize your godly sagas told of such things."

"Neither did I, my lord. You may believe me," she replied, rolling her eyes in continued abashment.

"But it was nice, my dear. You must not apologize for it," he continued, reaching down to where he'd left his mead skin on the bench to his right. He grabbed it up, uncapped it, and took a long swallow of its contents.

Alanna tensed a bit at seeing this. The skin looked as though he'd nearly emptied it since supper, and she feared he'd already had too much of the intoxicant to keep a peaceable head about him.

"It made me think there might be something worthy in your faith, after all," he continued, wiping his lips with the back of his sleeve. "Such a joy for life this Solomon possessed. Who was it he was describing?"

"His bride, I believe. As I've said, I know very little of that particular book."

"So it wasn't sinful, you see, if 'twas his bride he was describing."

"Nay. I suppose not," Alanna conceded, looking down at the gaming board. "Was it your move next or mine, sire?" she asked, hoping to draw his attention back to their previous activity. Despite Leif's monitions, she just couldn't seem to bring herself to encourage any real advances from the chieftain. In the short time she'd known him, she'd come to feel that the freeman was a good and honest soul, and she believed his claim that he or Storr would take adequate care of her and any children she might beget with the earl. Nevertheless, her plan remained to escape the camp with her cousins at their earliest convenience; and she was painfully aware of how such defilement would shame her and her family, if she did succeed in making her way back to her clan's region.

" 'Twas yours, I believe. But I do not wish to play any longer, for, as I told Leif, I've something I wish to discuss with you. Something of importance. And something that should be spoken of by me and you alone," he concluded, motioning for her to come and join him on the bench.

Alanna hesitated, not at all certain what this mysterious matter might be. Even without further explanation from him, however, she spied an odd

358

sort of resolution in his eyes, something that seemed to warn that the time for intimacy between them had finally arrived, and that he might have chosen this very evening in which to "take" her, as his freeman had phrased it.

"Well, come along, girl," he pressed again with a laugh. " 'Tis safe enough, for you must know that I am not some angel of your Lord who can get you with child with no more than a visit."

She rose and crossed to him, half craving such closeness, after so many days of having been separated from her cousins, and half fearing where it might lead.

"Oh, do be at ease," he coaxed, as she finally sat down beside him and he put an arm around her shoulders. "I simply wish to hold you for a time and take in the scent of your newly washed hair." He bent down and pressed his face to the crown of her head. " 'Tis much softer and more shiny when you wash it, you know," he whispered.

She nodded, continuing to feel apprehensive. "Aye. There is more color, more lightness to it now, I think. Though, 'twill never be the gold of your wife's," she noted gingerly. She wasn't sure in that instant what had made her say this. To hurt him, perhaps, or, more specifically, to dissuade him from taking things too far. It had, nevertheless, slipped out, and she knew she would have to bear the consequences.

He drew his face away from the top of her head. "Who told you of her hair?"

Alanna looked up into his eyes. "Why, you did, of course, my lord. Don't your remember saying, as we bathed that first day, how disappointed you were that my hair was so much darker than hers?"

"So I did," he replied after several seconds, again hugging her to him.

A silence fell between them, and Alanna did her best to keep her racing heartbeat from betraying just how nervous she was. The rhythm in his chest, by contrast, seemed as unhurried as a lazy river current. She could feel it now at her side, and she was awed once more at how nonchalant he was with her, how obviously accustomed to such interactions with females.

As he continued to hold her, he again rested his chin upon her crown, and, to her surprise, he began to hum. It was one of the tunes she'd rendered for him the night before upon her harp. He remembered it now, note for note, yet she was certain she'd only played that particular melody for him twice since they'd come to the camp.

" 'Tis like your Solomon, taking pleasure in his bride's form, her fairness."

"Ay—Aye," she agreed, not sure where any of this was leading. She only knew that it felt good, after so much rejection from him. It felt good to know that he finally approved of her grooming, her cleanliness—of *her*.

"What is it you wish to speak of, my lord?" she asked, thinking it best to get it over with, to determine just how "pleasing" she would be expected to become with him before the night's end.

"Well . . . it is not easy for me, Alanna, you understand. I am not a man who is wont to ask *favors* of others, particularly of my serfs."

Dear God, she thought with a dry swallow, was he about to propose marriage to her? Did they do such things, the Vikings? Or did they, as she had come to suspect, simply steal their mates, as they did their chattels?

"But you may ask, my lord, for whatever you wish," she choked. "I thought that was understood by the chieftains of your people."

He gave forth a soft, sad laugh. "Aye, I suppose it is. We may *take* what we want, in any case. But what I wish from you must be freely given. It is certainly within your power to refuse . . . though, I pray you will not."

She turned and looked up into his face, willing to risk his kissing her now. Willing, perhaps, for him to take matters even further, if only he would tell her what it was he wanted. Her curiosity was piqued, as he must surely have hoped it would be. And, finally able to study him at this close range again, she couldn't help melting a bit at the color of his eyes. They were the enveloping blue of a full moon's light upon a seascape.

"What is it, sire? Prithee tell me."

"I . . . I wish to have you . . ."

Oh, Mother Mary, she thought in the pause between his words, why was she encouraging him? Forsooth, he could want anything. *Anything!* Including some unspeakable servicing that only the most seasoned of concubines knew how to provide!

"I wish to have you find . . . find me more of that poison you used on me in the woods."

A chill ran through her, and her heart seemed to sink to her feet. Sweet Jesus, it was precisely as Leif had told her. Storr *did* wish to kill himself, and now he was attempting to draw her into the iniquitous scheme as well!

"For my warriors, of course," he quickly added. "To ease the pain of their wounds when we go to raid again."

This was what his lips said. But, as Alanna pulled away from him, she could see that his eyes were saying something else. There was more to Leif's claim that Storr longed for death, than she could have imagined. He was desperate, aching, *empty*. It was all there in those blue orbs, and she wondered why she hadn't been able to recognize it before.

She broke free of his encircling arm and rose from the bench, anxious to get away from him before he read her thoughts in turn and all the spirits he'd imbibed caused him to become violent. The truth, however, was that it was she who wanted to strike out at him. She wanted to slap him for his amorous preface to *this!* For leading her to believe that she had finally won her way into his confidence, his affection, only to make such an abhorrent request of her.

"You should be ashamed," she heard herself hiss.

"*Ashamed* for asking for such a thing, when all around you are those who care so much for you!"

He looked almost as surprised at her words as she must have at his, but she went on ranting, undeterred.

"I know you've lost your father and your wife to death, and I am most sincerely sorry. But don't you think I was heart-stricken, burying both my parents at so young an age? Don't you think I crave the love of my aunt and uncle from whom you and your men have torn me? Why, your father was lost to your trusted man, Leif, too. And I wager you have never once thought of the grieving he must do as well. Because you are selfish. *Selfish,*" she exclaimed. "Do tell me you know this Erse word!"

He nodded, continuing to look stunned by this outburst. He was forlorn. He hurt more deeply inside than she could ever have guessed, and she seemed, somehow, to have surmised as much. Yet, rather than taking pity upon him, rather than simply letting him have the poison and its promise of a painless death, she was choosing to rail at him!

"Well, that is what you are, Earl! Trifling with killing yourself. 'Neither in life nor in death,' as your freeman says . . . when you have a mother and little siblings whom you must protect from the likes of Sigurd and his clan!"

He continued to look dumbfounded, shocked not only at all she'd discovered about him, but at her deep-seated anger. "But you do not understand,

Alanna. You have never pined, never wed. You do not know what it is to lose so cherished a companion as a . . . a spouse."

"Nay, perhaps I do not," she agreed, beginning to simmer down. "I only know that you've yet a freeman, a confidant . . . indeed, quite likely, a half-brother who would die for you, sire. And you have *me*. Me here with you each evening, trying so hard to please you with the reading of our gospel and the playing of my harp. And all you do is stave us off. Dwelling upon details that we all know make little matter . . . Trust in me, Storr! Take me into your heart and then your bed, if you must. But do not shut us out from you, as though we were nothing more than mute pets gathered about your feet! Learn to love more truly those whom God hath left in your life and brought new to you. Do this or else poison yourself completely with that mead you swill each night! For, on pain of death . . . even if tortured, I will *not* tell you where more of that deadly plant can be found! I will not describe it, nor give you its name!"

With that, she turned and ran out of the tent, out onto the torchlit beach, where Leif was propped up against some dunes several yards away, continuing to page through the stolen gospel book.

Alas! She had done it again! She had, in her rage at Storr, betrayed the secrets Leif had told her of him . . . But it was time, she rationalized, continuing to seethe. She and the earl had outgrown their need for the freeman to act as their go-be-

364

tween. They had reached the point where no translating nor message-bearing was required between them, and she would no longer pretend that it was.

She turned towards the north, the opposite direction from where Leif sat, and began striding angrily along the shore. She knew she shouldn't wander far, and she didn't wish to have this flight awaken any of the slaves or warriors who were sleeping upon the long stretch of sand between the chieftains' tents. Nevertheless, she just couldn't bring herself to return to Storr. She was too afraid of both his ire and her own, to risk seeing him again until she was fully calm.

It was her pernicious pride at work once more! Whenever she clashed with others, she soon discovered that her damnable ego was in large part to blame, and she kept praying for God to quell it.

But it was different this time. It wasn't just a sense of rejection, of having what beauty, what charms she did possess be so blatantly rejected by him. It was something more.

Her *mother*. Her mother, in her grief at her husband's death, had taken a fatal dose of the very same poison the earl sought. Her mother, as if not caring what became of her only child, had chosen to die and leave Alanna to fend for herself in this cruel life. And now Storr was threatening to do the same! He was actually willing to let her, his freemen, and the rest of his family fall into his murderous brother's hands!

She was suddenly aware of the tears that were

welling in her eyes and beginning to stream down her cheeks. This mourning Norse "master" of hers had stirred up some memories, some pain that she had thought fairly well buried; and she wouldn't soon forgive him for it!

She kept walking, silently weeping as her feet sank into the shifting sands. Her soles were being poked by the rocks and sharp bits of shell she was treading upon in the darkness, and she wished that she had thought to leave her sandals on. It did, however, seem a fitting sort of penance for one who had again allowed her blasted temper to get the best of her.

How could she hope to go back to him after the scathing things she'd just said? She had not only left him no way to save face with her, but she'd used Leif's secrets, his very confidences with which to do it! And she realized now that she shouldn't blame either of them, if they simply chose to strangle her upon her return.

But, perhaps, they would not be kept waiting that long. To her dismay in those seconds, she began to hear footfall behind her, and she picked up her pace, wiping her angry tears away with her tunic sleeve.

"Prithee, let me be, Leif," she whispered over her shoulder, not stopping. "The earl and I will settle our differences anon. You needn't trouble yourself over it!"

He caught her by the arm, and she swung back to face him with a scowl. She was tired of his efforts to make her into a suitable concubine for his chief. Sick unto death at both men's attempts to keep her caged in that tent!

Amazingly, though, it was not Leif, but Storr who had come after her and now held her by the arm. He had actually deigned to pursue her, to risk being seen in such pursuit by any of those who were still awake on the beach; and she stood staring agape at him in the moonlight.

"Will we?" he asked under his breath.

"Will we what?" she croaked.

"Settle our differences anon, as you would have just told my freeman?"

Her throat ached at his sudden sportiveness, at all they were both doing to mask their old wounds. She'd longed for this show of affection from him and, yet, half dreaded it; and the jumble of emotions she felt made her eyes well up anew. "Oh, I don't know . . . Just unhand me and let me walk awhile longer on my own."

"*Neinn*. Come back with me now, Alanna," he urged softly. "I swear I will not speak of the poison again."

She bristled as his hand tightened upon her arm, and she jerked free of him. "Nay. Let me go before I find myself as disgusted by you and your ways as you have so obviously become by mine. You reek of mead, and I wish to be away from you at present!" This was a lie, she realized. In truth, she couldn't remember when she'd felt so drawn to him. The moonlight was lending a princely shadowing to his chiseled features. And, as his long hair blew back in the sea breeze, it looked to be accentuated with strands of silver and gold.

On the contrary, it wasn't repulsion she felt, but fear. Fear that he would ravish her, if she returned with him—and an even greater fear that she'd simply permit him to do so.

She was touched to her core at his willingness to come after her and try to set matters right. She felt hungry to be naked with him once more, and have his huge warm hands upon her. But she sensed that he was probably too drunk now to even remember such an act in the morning, and she knew that she'd definitely be alone with her remorse.

"Nay, nay. Just let me be, pray," she implored, waving him off with both hands and beginning to run away.

She thought surely his Norse pride would finally be spurred by this, that he would show the good sense to do as she'd asked and simply let her come back when she was ready.

He didn't, however. Even over her own windedness, she could hear him close upon her heels. And, as she entered Sigurd's side of the camp and moved to hide behind a grass-covered ridge that jutted out onto the beach, she was astounded to feel him catch hold of her tunic and push her down to the ground with a terrible roughness.

The wind was knocked out of her upon impact. But she managed to suck in more breath and turn back to struggle against his pinioning.

To her horror, however, it wasn't Storr who knelt atop her, but another warrior, a man she hadn't yet seen in the camp. One of *Sigurd's* clan, she deduced; and, as she continued to fight against his crushing weight, she felt the cold sharp edge of his knife come to rest across the hollow of her throat!

Seventeen

"Let her go, Eric," Storr growled in his native Norse, as he came upon the scene and saw Alanna being held at the blade of Sigurd's oldest son. He had not anticipated such an encounter and was, consequently, without his sword. His knife was still sheathed at his waist, however, and he quickly withdrew it.

"Let her go," he said again, not giving his opponent the time to slit her throat, as he leapt down upon him.

Eric, seeming well aware that he might be stabbed in the back in that instant, relinquished his hold on Alanna and rolled over to face his attacker with his weapon still raised.

"Run, Alanna," Storr urged, grabbing Eric with his free hand and pushing them both off to one side, so that she could fully free herself from beneath their combined weights. "Get ye back to our half of the camp!"

Once unpinned, Alanna struggled up to her

feet. She knew she should turn and run southward as Storr commanded, but it seemed she could hardly stand for the pain in her left leg. That was where her assailant had first impacted her, and she wondered if he'd managed to break one of her bones. She wanted to stoop to rub the bruised tissue in those seconds, but Storr's greater need instantly called her to action.

"Nay," she screeched, dropping to the ground again and reaching out to aid the earl in his effort to get the knife away from Sigurd's man. Gritting her teeth, she managed to catch hold of the stranger's wrist and, thereby, draw his blade away from Storr for several seconds. This, fortunately, gave the chieftain the clearance he needed to bring his own weapon down, across their attacker's neck.

The advantage didn't last long, however. There was a thunderous footfall from just a few yards up the beach, and Alanna lifted her gaze to see that they were about to be surrounded by several of Sigurd's spear-bearing men.

They'd apparently been awakened by the struggle, because they were all barefooted and wearing nothing more than their thigh-length tunics as they closed in.

One of them, the man who had snatched Alanna from the bath line days before and whom Leif had claimed was Storr's brother, stepped forward from the group and ordered Storr to drop his weapon.

But, before Storr could respond to this, a

bearded old man came rushing onto the scene. Even without his helmet, Alanna knew he was Earl Sigurd: the brute she'd seen chasing Torra about their tribe's graveyard. He said Storr's name, then proceeded to address him in an angry stream of Norse which Alanna had no hope of deciphering.

Storr answered him in his native tongue, finally climbing off of their assailant and rising. Then a tense silence fell between them, and Storr made a show of resheathing his knife, as if it were an offer of parley.

This seemed to have no effect, however. Within seconds the two chieftains were again snapping at one another, and it was sorely apparent that they were reaching some sort of deadlock.

Alanna wrapped her arms about herself in the night wind and fought back a whimper. It was now painfully clear to her that she and her heedless emotions had led her and her lord into what was essentially enemy territory, and they would probably be lucky to escape with their lives.

As if to bear out this conclusion, Storr's brother took hold of her tunic and jerked her towards him with an air of acquisition. To her relief, however, Storr was just as quick to turn and pull her back to where he stood. Then he put an arm about her and clutched her to him, as though to confirm for all concerned that she was his and he would tolerate no other arrangement.

She wanted to take greater comfort in this

action, but the sadistic gleam in Sigurd's eye, where he stood with his torch upraised, told her that her fate was still up to him; and she finally began to realize that it was *she* whom the two men were discussing. It wasn't just that Storr was trying to explain how she had unthinkingly led him onto what was, essentially, Sigurd's territory. It was more. They seemed, in truth, to be haggling over her!

"She is not for sale or trade, Sigurd," Storr said again in Norse, doing his best to keep his temper.

"But we've her two cousins . . . who nightly cry for her as though she were their sister. So it doth seem a circle of kinship that we, in our raiding, should not have rendered asunder. Hence, let the girl come unto me, Earl, that I might lay proper claim to her and reunite her with her loved ones," the old man concluded, extending his free hand to Alanna.

"Neinn," Storr objected. "Rather, let her cousins come to me, that I might pay you well for them."

Sigurd threw back his head and let a dry laugh issue up towards the starry sky. *"Neinn*. For they are not for sale or trade either."

Still winded from his struggle with Eric, Storr heaved a weary sigh and stared downward. "What, then, will satisfy you?" he demanded, meeting the tyrant's eyes once more. "For my freeman is never long behind me, and he will bring many of my men with him. And I am quite certain you do not wish to have this grow into a true battle. We do

373

not sail as far as Erin, after all, to attack *one another.*"

Sigurd drew his head back a bit, as though trying to arrive at his terms. As he did so, he exhibited a telltale wobble where he stood, and Storr finally realized that he was intoxicated — probably dangerously so. Storr had thought at first that he was merely sleep-muddled. Irascible and uncoordinated at having been roused at this late hour. But, no, he was *drunk,* and it was widely known that he was capable of great violence in such states.

"*Nein.* We do not want a battle," Sigurd concurred, and Storr was markedly relieved to hear this. "I think, rather, that you should come up to my tent and speak of this further in private. Do you not agree, young Earl, that, in such, we stand our best chance of settling this . . . this transgression?"

Though still quite wary, Storr saw this as being the best of his present alternatives, and he decided to humor the old sot.

"Very well. But I am keeping my knife."

Sigurd laughed again. "Oh, do. If 'twill help you to rest easier."

With that, the elder chieftain turned and began heading back to his well-lit tent with a somewhat faltering gait. Storr followed, moving Alanna along under his arm; and Sigurd's men brought up the rear.

He wished to save face, for some reason, Storr

realized, as they trudged after him. He obviously recognized the stalemate they had just reached, and he was about to propose a secret exchange that would simply make him appear to be the victor in all of it.

Alanna shivered with both cold and misgiving, as they continued to make their way over the rocky terrain. "What does he want? Why are we following him?" she whispered up to Storr.

"He wishes to speak to me in private. So he must see some ground for letting us go."

"But you can't leave me alone outside with all the rest," she said in a barely audible voice. "Please, sire, you mustn't!"

He shushed her and tried to smile. "Nay. Do not fear. You will go where I go."

Sigurd paused before the threshold of his tent seconds later, and turned to raise a halting palm to Storr and the rest. Then he went inside, his rotund figure silhouetted against the tan wall of the dwelling, and, after he bellowed an order or two, the occupants came darting out of the tent like frightened birds fleeing a nest.

There were four of them in all, one for Sigurd and each of his sons, Alanna surmised; and, to her dismay, she saw enough of their shadowy forms to realize that two of them were her cousins. She wanted to call out to them, to try to steal a word with them before they dashed away; but Storr again silenced her and drew her forward.

"The girl comes in with us," he said to Sigurd,

his tone indicating that this point was not negotiable.

"Oh, but of course," the older earl declared, waving them in with a broad smile. "Forsooth, I would have it no other way."

Storr escorted Alanna inside and stood scanning the disheveled bedding that lay all about them.

Sigurd, meanwhile, turned back to the doorway to issue a final order for his men to stay where they were. He then bent to secure his door flap before facing his callers once more.

"Something to drink, Storr?" he offered, crossing to what clearly served as his supper table.

"*Neinr.* I think we have both had enough."

The Serpent-eyed cocked his head rather teasingly. "What? You and the girl?"

"*Neinr.* I meant *you* and I, Sigurd. We should simply end this nonsense and both get to bed in the hopes of sleeping it off. Don't you think?"

Sigurd nodded. "*Ja.* All in good time, my friend." Then, obviously choosing to ignore this suggestion, he took up a wineskin and drank heartily from it.

"Come now, Earl. What is it you want from me? Pray, do be brief."

He wiped his lips with his sleeve and leaned back upon his bench. "The girl, as I've told you."

"You can't have her," Storr said again, this time through clenched teeth.

"But why not?"

"Because she is mine."

"Yours?" he asked quizzically. "What do you mean? Have you made her your concubine? Your bedmate in Freyja's stead?"

Storr wanted to swing at him for this, but he managed to keep himself in check. "What I do with my slaves is my business!"

The old man slammed his skin down upon the table. "Not when you let them stray into my camp!"

"And for that I apologize. What more can you ask? The girl caused no harm, after all. She simply forgot herself and wandered too far, and we are both most sincerely sorry."

"And she is yours? You are certain that she wasn't one of ours whom you were trying to lure over to you?"

"She is *mine*. You said yourself you hold her cousins, so you must know she's been in my keeping since our last raid."

"Prove it," he challenged, again donning the villainous smile that Storr had always found unsettling. "Are you willing to prove it? For, if you are, you may leave with her at once."

Storr furrowed his brow. "But how . . . how am I to attest this? A man doth not brand his slaves like cattle!"

"*Neinn,* but he will not hesitate to lay claim to a woman . . . that is, if she truly is his."

Storr's jaw dropped open in disbelief. Before he could offer any protest, however, the old man rose from the table with a sword in hand. He'd obviously had it hidden there, propped up against one of the divergent legs of the structure, and he lunged forward now to block the door with its long blade.

"I am not like you, chieftain. I do not defile my bondswomen, but simply choose to put them to the work for which they seem best suited."

Sigurd stepped before the door, blocking it with his body now, as he stood with his legs spread and his sword down at the level of his waist. "Then it is time you began conducting yourself more like an earl, don't you think? Pray allow me, at least, to hold my head up when I tell the rest of our region that I raid with you. Let me be able to say that you are as much of a man as your father before you."

"But she is a virgin, Sigurd . . . and should not be taken in such a manner."

"What manner is that?"

Storr brayed at his obtuseness. "In this way. With others watching."

"What others? There is only I with you. And you have joined my men and me in raping many times on our raids. So why no stomach for it now, Earl? Have the burdens of chieftainship weighed you down so that no part of you might be raised once more?"

Storr continued to address him through gritted teeth. "Were it that the girl spoke Norse, I would not deign to answer this. But, as she doth not, I will tell you that I've no trouble a'tall in that

378

realm. I am nightly hard for her."

"Then take her now. By all means," he insisted again, lifting his blade with a grand spread of his arms. "That I might know you to be my equal and the girl to be rightfully yours. For, if you do not, I swear I will! I have tasted of this wench's sweet cousins, and she doth begin to look better and better to me with each second we pass . . . *Take her,* damn it, Storr! Or she shall not leave my ground alive, and you know full well that no Norse assembly will listen to your testimony that such an *unclaimed* prisoner was stolen from you and murdered by another chief!"

Storr took a step backward, moving Alanna with him. For someone who was as inebriated as Sigurd seemed to be, he certainly still possessed a persuasive enough tongue.

"Hath it come to this, old man? That you must simply settle for watching others in the act of love?" he sneered, in a last-ditch effort to dissuade the Serpent-eyed from this demand.

Sigurd, in a fit of anger, jumped forward and attempted to snatch Alanna from him. Storr managed to move her out of his reach, however; and the chieftain stumbled and took an instant or two to regain his footing.

"Blast! Take her, you coward, or I swear to you that I shall," he threatened again.

Alanna gasped at this show of force, and Storr gave her a reassuring squeeze with his encircling arm. "Very well," he said finally in a low voice.

"Never quarrel with a fool," as the Old Norse saying went. And, given that he had so little hope of getting both Alanna and himself out of the dwelling alive, if he did choose to fight, he thought this proverb even more sagacious than usual. "But only under the linens of your bed," he added. "I will not strip her before you!" *If it was games the old voyeur was after, that was sure as* Hel *what he'd get!*

"Go and climb beneath the covers," he whispered to Alanna, turning her towards the chieftain's bed.

She looked up at him in shock, and her arms closed around him with a heart-wrenching tightness. "You are giving me to him then?" she asked in horror.

"Nay. You are to remain with me, and I must now prove that that is my intent."

Her brown eyes grew wide with befuddlement.

"Just do as I say, girl, lest greater harm befall thee!"

Alanna eased away from him and began backing up towards the bed as he'd instructed. It was her foolhardy emotions that had gotten them into this strait, and she knew that she could do nothing less than obey now.

She trembled, as her calves came into contact with the bed's frame a second or two later. The villain Sigurd's four-poster. It made her stomach churn to feel its mattress beneath her, as she came to a sitting position upon it; and she looked up to see the devil's grin where he stood, just yards away. Would *both* of them violate her? she wondered, sliding her legs up after her and hurrying in under the fur cover. Or would she be tied there, to its carved posts, and beaten for her trespassing? . . . She couldn't be certain, and for the seconds that would pass until the answer was revealed to her, she turned and buried her face in one of the pillows, wanting to sob at the mess she'd obviously made of things.

The men conversed in their language for a moment more. Then, finally, one of them walked over and sat down beside her.

"Alanna?" she heard Storr say, and she breathed a sigh of relief at feeling his hand upon her back, his fingers stroking her hair.

She rolled over to answer him, but, before she could do so, his face was bent down to meet hers, his body seeming to purposely shield her from the other chieftain's view. He moved to kiss her, closing his eyes and pressing his mouth to her left ear. But, rather than kissing, his lips addressed her in a faint voice. "He wishes me to lay claim to you, but I would not shame either of us in such a way. So we must simply pretend. Do you understand?"

She nodded. "But how?" she asked, drawing away from him slightly.

He hugged her to him once more, again putting his mouth to her ear. "Nay. Make as if to kiss me, if you've a question," he murmured, "for I know not how much Erse he hath troubled to learn through the years."

She did as she was told, reaching up and pressing her mouth to his right cheek. "But *how?* I know nothing of such things, my lord. How can I hope to deceive him?"

"Just do precisely as I say," he replied, arching over her and letting his hand descend to his waist.

Against her better judgement, Alanna glanced down between their bodies in those seconds. To her dismay, she saw that he was opening his trousers—and, again, the male part of him was in that strangely swollen state.

"Cry out," he continued sotto voce, lowering his face to hers once more. "Cry out, once I slip in under there with you."

Alanna again kissed his cheek to mask her question. "As in pain?"

"Aye."

She wanted to ask just how much pain he meant exactly. But, before she had the opportunity, he slid himself in over her, shoving her tunic up to her midriff; and the very shock of it caused her to gasp quite audibly.

"Good. Excellent," he praised, his kisses starting to become real, as his lips progressed from her ear down to her neck.

"Alas," she exclaimed, feeling his warmth, that turgid male part of him pressing up against her stomach. He'd said he would only simulate this act, but she wasn't so certain of it now. And, as his trail of kisses began to move clear down to the neckline of her frock, she wondered if she should offer some genuine protestation.

Her attention was immediately drawn to a much lower point, however, as she felt one of his hands slide up between her legs and come to rest, palm up, upon her maidenly vee.

This third utterance from her was surely the most convincing, she realized, even as it issued from her. But, before she could respond any further, before she could try to draw away, he started whispering to her once more. He was telling her sensation-addled brain how to proceed with this unnerving sham.

"Slide upward upon the pillow each time I push you here," he instructed, and she couldn't, for the life of her, imagine how he was finding the presence of mind to continue directing this act.

She, by contrast, felt utterly numb. She was too enraptured by his kisses and his touch to do anything more than lie there limply.

"Alanna," he said again, this time in an undertone that bordered upon a growl. *"Slide up,* as I pretend to thrust into you or you may not get out of here alive!"

His hand was still where he'd put it, politely cupped over her most private parts; but, as he began to push upward upon her, she could feel his palm's heat and moistness meeting her own. It was flesh upon flesh, and she just couldn't seem to make herself believe that it was nothing more than some inert object, meant to help them both feign this indescribable commerce.

"Alarna, *please*," he whispered urgently; and, somehow, at this imploration, she did find herself able to join into the rhythm of it.

It was better if she did, she told herself. His fervent nudging was causing the most sensitive parts of her to rub up against the ridge of bone above them, and, in the hope of ending this stupefyingly pleasurable sensation, she knew it was best to move with, rather than resist him.

Part of her, some wicked, bestial part, longed to have him actually thrust into her, but her more rational self knew that he was right. This was not the time or place for such a consummation. When he took her, *if ever* he chose to take her, he obviously wished for it to be a private exchange.

A chill ran through her at realizing how wise and strong-willed this chieftain was to restrain himself now. If she, who had never lain with a man, could be craving such a joining, she could hardly fancy how he was able to stay as clear-headed as he evidently was.

It went on and on: his body gliding over hers, inflaming her nipples with the friction created between their chests. She felt tortured by it, aching with the desire for it to either end or become more — become real.

Then, at last, he picked up his pace, his head and shoulders arching over her with breathless intensity, and she sensed that it was nearing some sort of end.

For just an instant, amidst this heightened movement, his fingers seemed to slip upon the wetness of her welcoming recesses, and they entered her with a dry, stabbing sort of roughness.

She gasped again. This time in actual pain. And, obviously realizing that she'd been hurt, he drew an apologetic breath in through his teeth and eased his fingers out of her.

He flattened his palm all the more, resuming the movement so that Sigurd wouldn't become suspicious. " 'Twill be over soon," he promised in an undertone.

It was, thankfully. In the seconds that followed, he closed down upon her, in a frenzy of motion. Then, taking his weight from off of his propping left hand, he slipped it under the blanket as well and made a distressed sound that seemed to somehow signal an end, a climax to it all.

Alanna heard it in his voice in that instant: the sudden inhalation near her ear. And, if she hadn't known that nothing had truly happened between them, she would have sworn that he was experiencing something genuine. Some true pleasure or pain that men were supposed to know at such times.

The next thing she felt was him pulling down on her tunic, apparently trying to cover her with it. Then, still holding her, he drew her off towards the left and threw back the fur blanket.

" 'Tis done, you lecher," he declared, lifting his

head and growling over his shoulder at Sigurd. "Now, let us go!"

To Alanna's amazement in those seconds, she looked over to see a bright smudge of fresh blood upon the spot where they had just lain.

Eighteen

Leif and a band of Storr's men were waiting outside the tent, as Storr and Alanna emerged from it minutes later.

"Are you unharmed, master?" the freeman asked, his sword drawn as though he would run Sigurd through right there, if his chieftain said no to this.

Storr nodded. "But carry Alanna back, will you? It seems Eric hurt her leg."

Without another word, Storr strode away, towards his side of the camp; and Leif, resheathing his weapon, hurriedly gathered Alanna up in his arms. Then he signalled for the rest of their clansmen to follow, and they began walking, several yards behind their earl.

"What on earth happened?" Leif whispered down to Alanna as they proceeded.

" 'Twas my baneful temper," she confessed, keeping her voice equally low. "I quarreled with Storr, and, when he came after me, I fled onto Sigurd's side of the camp. One of Sigurd's men knocked me to the ground, and, when the old earl came upon us, he insisted on taking us up to his tent."

"For what reason?"

"To punish Storr, I think. To shame him . . . for Sigurd demanded that our lord bed me before him."

Leif was clearly aghast at this. "Rape you?"

"Nay. Not rape precisely. Just 'claim' me, was all."

The freeman continued to look taken aback by this. "And did he?"

"Did he what?"

"Claim you?"

"Nay. I don't think so."

He knit his brow. "You don't *think* so? Alanna, believe me, you would *know* if he had."

"Well, he didn't then," she replied, a bit surprised in that instant at the blatant disappointment on Leif's face. "He told me his intent was merely to pretend."

"Damnable lecher, that Sigurd," the freeman muttered.

"Aye. That is what our earl called him as well."

Leif's tone was suddenly scolding. "Don't you know better than to wander that far, my lady?"

"Of course. 'Twas just that I was troubled by the argument I'd had with the earl, and I forgot myself."

"Well, you were fortunate, indeed, to have gotten away from there with naught but an injured leg!"

She winced at the limb's continued throbbing,

where it dangled from his cradling hold. "Oh, I am very aware of that."

"Is it broken, do you think?"

"I don't know."

"We must have a look at it when we reach the tent, then." With that, he hiked her farther up in his arms and quickened his pace after their chieftain.

Storr was sprawled face down upon his bed, as they entered the dwelling minutes later.

"She thinks her leg might have been broken, master," Leif announced, carrying Alanna over to one of the dining benches.

"I would not be surprised," he replied in a monotone, his words muffled by the pillow into which he'd buried his face.

"She will need some mead for the pain as I examine it. Would you like some as well, my lord?"

"Jaaa," he drawled, nodding his head, and it was apparent that he not only wished it, but needed it.

The freeman poured some of the brew into a wooden cup and handed it to Alanna. Then he crossed to the bed and gave what was left in the skin to his master.

Storr reached back and accepted it from him, issuing a groan that seemed to bespeak both weariness and relief.

"Just how does one feign a defloweiring, Earl?" Leif asked in Norse, and it was apparent that he was fighting a perplexed laugh.

"Oh, she told you about that, did she?"

"She did."

"By stabbing one's finger with one's own accursed knife," Storr replied, lifting the still-bleeding digit.

The freeman grimaced at seeing the jagged cut. "By Thunder, let it never be said that you are not a gentle man!"

Storr turned over and propped himself up against his headboard. Then he uncapped the skin and took a long drink from it. "Well, something had to be done to allay him. You know the worth in quarreling with fools."

"With that fool, anyway, my chief," Leif replied. Then he returned to Alanna and asked her to put her leg up on the bench for his perusal. "Have you drunk the spirits?" he asked, gesturing towards the cup she'd set on the table.

She wrinkled her nose with disgust. " 'Tis too strong for me."

Storr was moved to laugh at the childish face she made in those seconds, but he bit the inside of his cheek to stop himself. Leif was as imperious as a mother bear when it came to treating injuries, and, after what they'd just been through, he didn't wish to make the freeman angry and get stuck tending to the girl himself.

"Drink it down," Leif ordered, forcing it back into her hand "I won't have you yelping with pain at such an hour!"

Apparently hearing the determined tone in his voice, she raised the cup to her lips and, plugging her nose, consumed the mead in two gulps. Then, drawing her face back with another wry expression, she returned the cup to the adjacent table with an annoyed thump.

Seeing this done, Leif pulled a nearby soapstone oil lamp over to their side of the table, in order to better examine her leg by its light.

" 'Tis here that it hurts?" he asked, straddling the bench and running a hand over the knee of Alanna's outstretched limb.

"Nay. Lower," she answered charily. Though the freeman's touch was amazingly light, she knew, from her own experience at treating such impairments, that the worse was definitely yet to come.

He placed a hand on either side of her shin and let his fingers run slowly, probingly down it. "There?" he asked, as she drew in a distressed breath.

She nodded.

"Prithee, get up and try walking, my lady."

Alanna, feeling too spent by their ordeal to offer any more argument, pushed up from the bench, and, under the freeman's close watch, limped a couple paces towards the door and back.

"Can you put your full weight upon it?"

She tried, biting her lip at the pain of it, and she succeeded—more or less. "Aye. It seems so."

Leif threw up his hands. "Well, there then. 'Tis not broken. 'Twill probably just color and swell ... The big bully," he added in a snarl, obviously referring to the man who had pinned her.

"That he was," Alanna agreed, hobbling back to the bench.

The freeman rose and turned to Storr. "Have you aught else you wish from me, my lord?"

The earl, looking close to losing consciousness, shook his head.

"My lady?" Leif inquired, returning his gaze to Alanna.

"Nay. Thank you, just the same," she answered, settling on the bench and elevating her aching limb upon it once more.

"I shall retire to my bag then . . . with the hope that the two of you can manage to stay out of Sigurd's reach through the night," he concluded, shooting a parting glare at Alanna.

"Leif," Storr called after him, as he reached the door.

The freeman turned back. *"Ja?"*

"Thank you."

"For what, master?"

"For coming after us. For carrying Alanna back."

Leif cocked his head at this rare show of gratitude, then smiled. "You are most welcome, Earl." With that he took his leave, shutting the tent's door flap behind him.

"There. Was that better, my dear?" Storr asked Alanna, when he was certain the freeman was well away. "Or did I yet treat him as a 'mute pet at my feet'?"

A smile tugged at one corner of her lips, and she

dropped her gaze. "Much better. And my homefelt thanks to you, as well, for not scolding him for all he told me . . . of your dead wife and little siblings and such. His only aim in it was to bring me closer to you," she explained in a wavering voice.

He gave forth a cynical laugh and leaned back more heavily against the headboard. "I know all about his aims. You needn't echo them. The damnable man won't be satisfied until I've a wife and *twelve* children swarming about me!"

"A fate that is not possible, if you poison yourself, you know."

"I won't," he said firmly. "I told you on the beach that I will speak of it no more with you, and I will not."

"I pray you don't, my lord, for 'twould be a terrible loss for your people."

A chill ran through Storr at this unexpected praise. Then he silently chided himself for being affected by it. She and that crazed freeman of his would probably say or do anything to keep him alive — or, more rightly, to prevent themselves from falling into Gunther's hands.

"And you, Alanna," he suddenly intoned. "Would it really be such a loss for you? Wouldn't you, forsooth, rather be with your cousins?"

"Oh, nay," she declared, and, to his surprise in those seconds, her quavery words were punctuated by her rising and making her unsteady way towards him. "I would not for the world that _you died. In truth, my only hope now is that you might, one day, buy my cousins away from Sigurd."

His expression grew somber. "But they are not for sale or trade. He just told me as much . . . So, knowing this," he continued, bracing himself for her response. "Do you still wish to stay with me? For we cannot hazard your sneaking back there to speak to your kin after what came to pass tonight." He knew he should warn her further, should make sure she understood that the true danger lay not so much in falling into Sigurd's hands, but Gunther's. He reasoned, however, that she must have realized this much, after what she'd witnessed back in her family's hut. What was more, he did not wish to scare her out of making the decision that was truly her own.

She was silent for several more seconds, and Storr hated himself for the great uneasiness it brought him. He felt like a vulnerable youth again: his heart hanging upon nothing more than a maiden's whim. He tried to tell himself that this situation was much graver than that, however. The girl was clearly being asked to choose between him — the lesser of two Norse evils — and what remained of her family. And that was no easy decision to make.

"I would stay with you, then, of course, my lord. Of course," she answered at last, still teetering on her good leg near the bed.

He was warmed to his very soul by this seemingly sincere response, but he tried not to let it show. She would attempt to escape the camp before they departed for his homeland. That was simply a given with a woman as ungovernable as she; and he didn't wish for her to know how much her succeeding with such a scheme would ultimately hurt him.

But she was his for now, he told himself, gesturing for her to come and sit beside him. For the present, anyway, she was here to goad him back into life and amuse him with her ingenuous ways, and he knew he should make the most of it. "Oh, come take the weight from your leg," he said, his brusque tone meant to mask the mix of emotions he'd just traversed. "I'd have ravished you back in Sigurd's tent, if 'twas my will."

Though somewhat wary, after what they'd just been through, Alanna made her way to him and sidled onto his mattress.

"Aye. Thank you for not . . . not harming me back there," she said, lost for a delicate term for the act they'd just simulated.

He laughed to himself. Then, wrapping an arm about her waist, he drew her up next to him.

"In truth, I fear I might have harmed you, when my fingers slipped. But I did not spoil you. You may rest assured of that."

"I am *so* sorry for falling into Sigurd's hands. Why would he make such a depraved request of us, my lord?"

"Oh, 'twas more to hurt me, than you. You may be sure of that." He fell silent and sat running his hand over the tendrils of hair that flowed down her right shoulder. " 'Twas because he learned that I vowed chastity to my wife upon her death. 'Twas a demand he knew would wound me."

"But it didn't, did it," she noted brightly. "Because we tricked him."

He let her hair slip in between his fingers. Then his hand closed about her mane and he gently pulled her to him and pressed a kiss to her left temple. *"Ja."*

"That blood upon his linens, it came from you then?"

Again he laughed softly and showed her his lacerated finger. "But of course. It wasn't yours, was it?"

"Nay. 'Tisn't . . ." She wanted to tell him that it wasn't her time of the month for such a thing, but she stopped herself. It was improper to speak of such matters with a male—particularly an outlander. And, on the chance that Norse women did not experience such cycles, she thought it best not to put herself in a position where she'd have to teach him of them.

"But how did you do that?" she pursued.

"I still had my knife, remember?"

"Oh, aye. So you did. And this . . . this is your custom, then? For a man to cut his finger, when he beds a maiden?"

His chuckle was low now, muffled against her hair as he continued to bend his face close to hers. "Nay, silly girl. The blood was supposed to have come from *you.*"

There was a surprised rise to her voice. "Me?"

"*Ja.* 'Twas supposed to be virgin's blood. You know, the sort that comes when first a maiden is entered by a man . . . I thought, with your uncle being a physician, you'd surely know this much."

She shook her head, grateful for how dimly lit the tent was, as a hot blush came over her.

"Your elders should teach you of such things, you know. So you won't be frightened when the time comes."

"Forsooth, I was not so very frightened," she confessed.

"Of course not, because I told you we would only feign the act. But I meant afeard when you do finally submit to a man. "

"I think that the Church believes it is a *husband's* duty to teach his bride of such things."

Storr gave this some thought. Who was he, after all, to criticize her people's ways, when Norse children were often told such rubbish as storks being responsible for delivering babies? "Perhaps," he conceded.

"Anyway, I should count myself fortunate, I suppose. For tonight hath taught me all I will need to know."

"All of deflowering, maybe," he agreed, bringing an open palm up and rubbing it over her slender shoulder. "But not much of love, I'm afraid."

"Of love, too," she maintained, bringing his wounded finger up to her lips and giving it a soft kiss. "For you would not have shed your own blood in place of mine, if not for true caring."

His heart seemed to rise to his throat at this. Oh, by the gods, *don't,* Alanna, a voice within him exclaimed. *Don't* kiss my finger or press my hand to your heart, as though you could actually love me, when we both know 'tis your god and your cousins you seek above all else! Fortunately, however, he did not say any of this. Only the word "don't" escaped his lips, as he slipped his finger out of her grasp.

"Don't what?" she asked, clearly offended.

"Don't . . . don't do *that.*"

She pulled away from him. "Why? Because you think me too unclean to touch your broken skin?"

"Oh, nay. 'Tis not that at all," he assured, worried now that she might fly into another rage and run off as she did earlier. "You are clean enough."

"Well, what is it then?"

He shushed her raised voice. "Just don't . . . don't touch me in that way."

"In what way?"

"As you do your harp and the gospel book. Tenderly. As if you cared."

"But I *do,*" she insisted, turning and looking fully into his eyes.

"You couldn't."

"Why not?"

"Because I stole you from your people. Not just once, but twice. Because so many of your tribesmen died at our hands. Because you were brought to this camp unwillingly. In bounds."

"But you did not mean to raid my fort. I understand that it was by cause of the storm."

He nodded and dropped his gaze.

She swallowed bravely and reached out to him again, lifting his chin with her hand. She knew he didn't like her touching him, that he alone wished to be in control of any caressing that occurred between them. Nevertheless, she felt compelled to violate that unspoken decree. The act they'd affected in Sigurd's bed had allowed her to touch him without fear of rejection, and, in that alone, the Serpent-eyed's demand had proven an odd sort of blessing to her. She'd learned that she liked the feel, the scent of Storr. She liked being the pursuer and hearing the almost pained sighs he gave forth when she was so near; and she wouldn't let him push her away again.

"Oh, sweet thunder, Alanna, *don't,*" he murmured once more. "Because, when you do, you tempt me to distraction. To a point where I would lay claim to you against your god's law. And I fear that, if I break it, he will never allow me to know the peace that seems to fill you and your people."

It was more than a request from him now, it was a plea. Recognizing this, she took her hand from his chin and eased away. "Peace?"

"Aye. You know, the way that you have endured through all of this. Giving to your people and even to mine, when you think you can help with their injuries and illnesses. You are right. You are strong in all things, and I sense that you could die this very moment, in slavery, with so many of your people slain, and still feel that you had triumphed somehow. That any fate is bearable, because you're so filled with your god's peace . . . Let me not take the promise of it from either of us by straying into temptation with you . . . You were right when you railed at me earlier. I am selfish to go on mourning my wife's death above all else. But 'tis not just mourning, Alanna. 'Tis worse. Over time it hath become despair. A malaise that makes one long to sleep and never wake . . . But, when you stood scolding me here, it was like being slapped back to life, wrested from the hands of the grave itself. And, far from apologizing to me for wandering into Sigurd's hands, 'tis I who should be thanking you. It made me *care* again, you see. Freeing you from the earl made me care about something, for the first time in what has seemed an eternity."

There were actually tears in his eyes now. She caught a glimpse of them, shimmering in the lamplight, and she instantly looked away. Seeing this nobleman in so accessible a state would only cause her to reach out and comfort him; and she knew that he did not want such contact made.

She drew her arms in close to her sides and moved farther away from him. She'd had no idea there was so much in his mind, in his heart, and she didn't want to do anything that might add to his anguish. "I should go then and sleep in my place upon the rug."

To her surprise, he reached out to stop her. "Nay.

Sleep ye here please. That I might 'lie all night betwixt your breasts.' Do you think your god would permit this, if I vow to do naught else?"

She pondered it for several seconds. "Since 'tis written in the gospel, I think it permissible."

He looked both grateful and relieved, as she settled upon the mattress once more. Then, blotting his eyes with his sleeve, he slid down and slowly, gently, let his head come to rest upon her chest—his right ear pressed to the level of her heart.

He dreamt of Freyja again. So vulnerable and bloated with child. He saw her waist-length golden hair fly out behind her, as she turned and began to run from him. And he felt himself start to give chase.

In his mind's eye, he could already see the grave: as long and deep as half a warship's hull. Cold, dark, and filled with the earthworms that squirmed out of its newly dug sides.

By the gods, how Freyja had feared such things: all creatures that wriggled like snakes. And how it had wrenched him to see her buried there to be forced, by custom, to commit her to rest in *Hel's* own doss beneath the earth, when he needed her—would *always* need her—so desperately in his own sadly spacious bed.

He chased her now. Because that was always what happened. It seemed he could no more change the dream, than he could the past itself.

He chased her, and she ran . . . across the verdant meadow, which, nine months of each year, lay dormant beneath the snow. But it was green once more, greener than in any summer he could remember before or since. And he prayed to Odin that he'd fall in it. That the billowing grasses would reach out and catch his trousers with such force that he might never again rise. Then it would finally be possible that *he* would die by cause of the gift he held for her. That *he* could suffer that horrible death in her stead.

He kept running, nonetheless. Undeterred by the tall grasses and the faint premonition in his head. He outcoursed her in no time, and finally stood before her with his damnable silken offering still hidden at his back.

But, this time, as he brought it forward, as she reached out to receive it, she did not fall. She did not topple back, in seeming alarm, and break her neck on the floor of the huge grave that suddenly opened behind her.

This time, by some miracle he would never understand, he actually had the presence of mind to catch her! Odin be praised, he *grabbed* her and stood clutching her to him, thereby preventing the fatal fall.

He'd caught her! *Saved* her! He wanted to shout it a thousand times over for his entire clan to hear. In the name of *Valholl* and all that was sacred, he had rescued her, and she was yet alive! Alive!

He could feel her warmth, the beating of her heart against him as distinctly as any rhythm he'd ever experienced; and he knew that the next step would be to try to learn whether or not he was awake.

But how could he be dreaming? It was all so true, so real to his senses. Such a magical mix of matter and thought.

Her hair. It was soft as always beneath his hands, as he reached back and caught her . . . as he cradled her now from out of the grasp of death.

Her breath. He could even feel her hot respiration at his ear, as he bent to draw her farther into his curving form. Sweet and musical . . . *Freyja.* "Frey—ja," rising soft and melodic, as though from a panpipe at a Viking feast.

Dear Heaven, Freyja, you're back! I can kiss you and feel you kissing me!

His eyes fell open to darkness, a space no longer lit by the used-up oil of surrounding lamps. A darkness merciful in its denial of sight.

It was a state bereft of everything but the sense of touch. It was a wash of inky blackness that made one woman's name sound very much like another's. And it no longer mattered which one of them he held—only that he'd saved her . . . *saved* her this time, instead of causing her death.

Nineteen

Storr woke with Alanna in his arms. She still lay beneath him, sound asleep at this early hour, and he didn't, for the world, want to disturb her.

He slipped his arms out from under her waist with a whisper-light stealth. Then he eased onto his right side and lay studying her for several seconds.

She was at peace, of course. When she wasn't raging at him or furrowing her brow with concern over some sick elder or orphaned child in the camp, she was always at peace. He was, in fact, the *only* person with whom he had ever seen her angry, and he wasn't sure whether to think this a compliment or an insult.

She was, when one reflected upon it, awfully small and pregnable to be standing her ground with such outlander warriors as he. But her often fearless actions, the sense that she was somehow unvanquishable, doubtless sprang from that perplexing faith of hers.

Her lips worked a bit now. They exhibited what looked to be the faintest smacks of contentment, as she shifted about in her continued slumber. She cast one of her arms upward, and her thin, fragile wrist came to rest upon her flood of reddish-brown hair.

The infernal minikin! How dare she raise her voice to him as she had the night before? His drink-addled brain seemed to recall it all now. Not once, but *twice* she had become confrontational with him. She had, with her little tongue, threatened to cut him to his quick, seeming to know him better than he would ever know himself. And he acknowledged that she had at least that much in common with Freyja.

Norse women — aware that the law allowed them to receive fully half their husband's holdings, should they grow angry and leave them — almost always stood their ground. Freyja had been no exception, of course. There were times — though it seemed he hadn't recalled them until just this moment — when her eyes had shone with a dagger's sharpness. When she had been so angry with him over some inconsiderate action that he thought she would actually strike him. And, most of those times, he remembered with the whisper of a smile, he would probably have deserved it.

But this Erse girl was different. Her anger was quicker, keener, and crueler in its own way. Capable of slicing to his very core and, oddly — as a lancet to a peccant wound — just as capable of healing him.

In this alone, her claims that she had often assisted her physician uncle seemed substantiated. For how else could one account for her knowledge of poisonous herbs and her uncanny ability to determine just where a man hurt?

He reached out and carefully lifted her left hand upward. Up to meet his lips, as he bent to kiss it.

Alanna. "Al . . . anna." It did have a musicality of its own, this strange, foreign name. This appellation that she'd said meant, "Bright one. Fair. Beautiful." This name that, like the Norse "Freyja," denoted beauty and love.

The gods help him, he could grow to adore this woman. Odin save him, he thought, setting her lily-white hand back down beside her and again feeling the nagging swelling in his groin, he probably already *had*.

He must rise and get away from her. He must bury himself in the demands of the day. They were preparing for another raid. There were weapons to be mended, ships to be bailed, and men to be drilled. There were scores of tasks to fill the hours ahead of him, hundreds of details to be seen to. But none, he was sorrily aware, could come near being as gratifying as simply doing what his body longed to now.

She probably wouldn't fight him, the voice of temptation whispered inside his head. If his mead-clouded memory served, she'd seemed almost willing the night before.

But no. Not here. Not now. Not in his dear, dead Freyja's bed. 'Twould be an offense that even his own liberal faith would not abide. And, again realizing this, he somehow found the strength to pull away from her and take himself off of the mattress, by slipping around to the carved footboard.

He managed to change into clean raiment and comb his hair without waking her. Then, trying to forget what Sigurd had made them do, trying to deny how it had probably changed his relationship with her forever, he slipped out into the fresh air of that hazy morning. The golden light of sunrise seemed to promise another precious, hot, summer day.

The camp was already noisy with early-morning hubbub as Alanna finally awoke. She looked about for Storr, but found the tent empty, as she sat up with a yawn.

Dear God, he'd pretended to make love to her the night before! It all came flooding back to her now, causing a sheepish blush to warm her cheeks. Pushing the covers aside, she studied her bruised left leg, and the foolheaded actions she'd indulged in several hours earlier returned in a painful flash.

How could she have spoken to Storr in such a way? How could she have bared her fangs with so little compunction? With so little regard for the secrets Leif had told her?

Part of her wanted to feel hurt, wounded that the earl had already risen and simply left her sleeping there, after what they'd been through together. But another part, a wiser, more reserved part, understood totally and was actually grateful for it.

All things considered, it was probably best that they give one another a wider berth henceforward. The fool would probably go off and finally get himself killed at the hands of an Erse bowmen one of these days. And she, herself, still had plans, however unconfirmed, of escaping before their decampment. So it wasn't very stable ground for an amorous alliance to take root in; that much was certain.

But, God, how she ached when she thought of him—of the tender, touching things he'd done the night before and for as long as she'd known him. Of his cutting his own finger, before he'd see her harmed in any way. Of his shielding her nakedness from Sigurd's view. Of how he'd kissed her, when he'd lain over her in the other chieftain's camp.

But it was only an act, she told herself. Not a reflection of his true feelings, but simply an obliging of the other earl's disgraceful demands. Demands she herself had brought to bear upon them.

In truth, Storr didn't want her to touch him. Even to take his hand. In very sooth, he sought something far grander and more important than she could ever hope to provide: God's Own peace. The gifts of a Lord who might not be willing to dwell with him, if he continued to indulge in the iniquitous pleasures of the flesh . . . And she, she who had sat for hours on end, trying to teach him of the Christian faith, she, of all people, must know better than to lead him into temptation!

She would sleep on the floor again tonight, she decided, rising from the bed. No matter what he said, no matter what appeal he made to convince her that she should lie with him once more, she would say him nay. Her will would have to be strong enough for them both, she told herself, wincing at the pain as she put her weight upon her battered leg once more. She had endured many rending things in her short lifetime, and she could certainly bear this!

Just as she resolved as much, however, just as she was beginning to make her way to the mirror that hung from the front wall of the dwelling in order to comb her hair, the very man she was trying to swear off appeared in the doorway.

"Ah, you are up," Storr greeted softly.

She looked over at him, at his astute blue eyes in the morning light, and she instantly dropped her gaze to her bruised leg. "Aye, my lord. In some measure. But not in much better form than you were when I stomped your foot."

She stole another glance at his face. Enough to see that he appeared grateful for this acknowledgment of her own, injurious actions. Then she averted her eyes again, and, limping to an adjacent sea chest, sank down upon it.

"That is why I've come back in. Leif . . . well, nay . . . I, *I* think it best that you stay off that leg for a time. You needn't work with the rest of us today."

"But Great-uncle Padraig hath taken ill—"

He raised a silencing palm to her. "He'll be seen to by our own women. They are quite good with such maladies as well, have no fear."

"As you wish," she replied after a moment, her voice wavering with the sudden awareness that this wasn't really about her leg, but about him. About *them*. He didn't want her out where he could see her all day on the beach, out where she might distract him from his work and his talks with his men. He wanted her out of sight and out of mind, and this seemed as valid an excuse as any.

"Oh, pray, don't look so hurt," he said, obviously trying to sound far more jocular than he felt. " 'Tis for your own good that I order it."

She nodded. "I know."

He should have taken his leave in those seconds. She looked up at him, offering a compliant, if shaky, smile; and he should have gone again. But he remained there, frozen by something . . . perhaps by her own tremulous expression. And, in that instant, she knew they were both done for. What was more, she could see he knew it, too.

He stepped farther inside, letting the cloth door fall closed behind him, and his continuing regard seemed to fetter her where she sat.

She wanted to ask "What?" What more did he want to say? But his eyes seemed to hold all the answers she needed. She recoiled slightly, reflexively at the intensity of his stare. Then she slid back a bit on the rounded chest top; and, in a heartbeat, he crossed to where she sat and dropped to one knee before her.

His hands were upon her injured calf, his fingers drawing it forward, as though for further perusal by the light of day. And she thought, for a fleeting second or two, that there might still be some hope for preventing the ruin that had seemed so inevitable just an instant earlier.

Her eyes locked upon his hands, as they framed the swollen part of her leg. And, when they did not stop there, but glided upward, up to her knees and under her tunic, she gave forth a wistful sigh and felt her arms fall forward and begin to close around him.

He rose a bit, actually seeming to welcome her embrace, and he pressed his face to her breasts with a worshipful moan. "Please, God help me, I can't bear this any longer!" he whispered, taking a firmer hold upon her and sliding her off of the trunk.

"Nor can I," she admitted, as she came to rest on the fur rug beneath him.

His jewel-like eyes were over her, speaking his next words before his lips could. "Don't fight me. Don't struggle. Please let this be what you want, too."

She nodded, not willing to allow all of the sin of it to be upon him. She couldn't have answered any other way, however. The heat of his passion was absolutely encompassing her in those seconds, and no other response was possible.

His stream of fevered utterances moved up from

her breasts, from the neckline of her tunic, to her lips, and, for the first time since he'd come upon her at her ring-fort, he kissed her mouth.

But it was different now. It was not forced and crushing, but gentle, enticing. Beginning just at the corner of her lips, then easing over towards the middle, as though beckoning her to join in.

As she did so, tentative, unsure of herself, he seemed finally too impatient, too aroused to wait. Like the practiced lover that he obviously was, he took her face in her hands, tilted it to one side, and kissed her so fully that she had no other choice but to let her mouth open to his, to his probing tongue and hot breath.

Storr let his right hand slide down to her thigh in those seconds. It had been over twelve months since he'd lain with a woman, and he longed to just take her now and gratify his own needs as quickly as possible. He stopped himself, however. He was determined not to let this be anything like what she'd had to endure the previous night. She was far too precious to him to be taken in the same, heartless fashion he had so many Erse maidens before her. She should be wooed, gentled, led with the utmost care into the act, and he would not allow his own passion-starved body to rush either of them.

He slowly withdrew his lips from hers and pressed a trail of kisses down her throat to the neckline of her tunic. Then, slipping his hands under her, supporting her head and shoulders with his hold, he slid the sleeves of the garment down her arms, baring her breasts as he lowered his mouth to pleasure them.

He expected her to gasp, to offer some complaint at being thus exposed in the starkness of daylight; but, instead she was almost limp in his arms. Her head was flung back, and her long reddish hair flowed across the rug like a waterfall.

"Dear lamb," he murmured, hugging her to his own massive chest. Then, melting once more at how she seemed to trust him, seemed even to care in return, he let his lips make their way to her cleavage.

Alanna felt paralyzed, too weak to offer any protest, even if she'd wanted to. Her eyes were closed, unwilling to witness what she was allowing—nay, in truth, *inviting* to happen below. They were more than just kisses now. His lips had parted over the peak of one of her breasts, and she could actually feel his tongue flickering across it, teasing it to a hardness that caused hot waves of sensation to run all the way down to her loins.

Clearly knowing her body's responses better than she, he brought his left hand forward and fondled her other breast with much the same effect. It was torture, exquisite distress; and, when she couldn't bear it any longer, she gave forth a small anguished cry and reached down to bring his face up to hers for another kiss.

He seemed to understand. For once, neither of them had to fumble about in the other's strange tongue in order to communicate. He simply seemed to sense that she couldn't bear any more of what he'd been doing, and he mercifully moved on to the next step.

As he kissed her lips, his hand slid down to her right hip. Then it descended to her thigh and drew up her tunic, baring her as he had under Sigurd's covers. But it was different now. It was just the two of them, and she sighed with relief at knowing that only he would see what lay beneath.

To her surprise, it wasn't she who gasped at his intimate touch this time, but he. Letting his face come to rest next to her right ear, he gave forth a whisper of a moan, like that of a way-weary farer, at long last finding a place to sleep.

But his fingers wouldn't simply rest there now, she realized. They couldn't possibly just cup her as they had the night before. They would enter her. Not by painful mistake, as when he'd slipped in their feigning, but slowly, purposefully. Not stabbing, but gently, kindly . . . as they presently were, as though parting the petals of a rose. Then, in the minutes that followed, they curved upward, reaching to points of pleasure she'd scarcely known she possessed.

"Will you tell me when to cry out?" she heard herself inquire near his ear, as his fingers continued their caressing.

As she'd hoped, he laughed at this. A low, relieved chuckle that seemed to dispel any discomfiture that remained between them.

"Let us hope you'll feel no need to," he whispered back, sobering. And, as his hand moved farther into her, up to heights that took her breath away, she began to realize just how serious, how invasive this act would be.

But it wouldn't be his fingers that would finally claim her, she acknowledged, trying not to tense up on him. Even without being told, she had finally deduced that it would be that huge, swollen part of him which had mystified her for so long. The part that, even now, was pressing up against her right thigh with an undeniable urgency.

She knew she would bleed, and, in so delicate a place as this, quite probably suffer a sting at least as fiery as the one he had inflicted upon the finger he'd lanced for Sigurd's benefit. She knew this, and yet she arched up towards him, wanting him to continue pleasing the lower levels of her.

" 'Tis all right, Alanna," he murmured, as though again able to read her thoughts. "You will find more pleasure than pain in it. I promise thee."

She trusted him. After all he had done for her, she knew her confidence could rest in him, and she whispered back a stoic, "I know."

Then, as though unable to bear this prelude to their joining any longer, he withdrew his fingers from her, and they were slowly replaced with that other part of him.

Alanna felt strangely detached in those seconds, oddly mournful at having it finally come to pass. Nevertheless, she welcomed it. Having already received his soul, his deepest secrets into her heart, it was only natural to welcome his body now as well.

It was overpowering, however. Too large and satisfying for her to do anything more than slump back upon the rug and groan. She had wanted not to feel all of it, to remain removed from the deed somehow and thereby be able to deny to herself later that she had actually permitted it to happen. But it was just such an enveloping experience. The pain, the pleasure of it, summoned all of her senses, all of her awareness to that portion of her, to the place where the two of them were finally merged — finally one.

She groaned again, and, even without her will, she could feel the depths of her secreting a warm wetness in their own poor defense.

She had no control. She had seemingly surrendered completely to him, and, as he began moving in and out of her seconds later, she turned and muffled her ecstatic cries against the back of her up-flung hand.

But this wasn't the mechanical rhythm of the night before, she realized. This was his most private flesh meeting hers. Meeting, stroking, pushing her to her very limits. Then withdrawing, only to return an instant later and make the same rapturous contact all over again.

Again and again, until he no longer seemed to possess the mindfulness to issue his words of love to her in Erse. Rather, he began speaking in his own language, one she had yet to master. But then she sensed that she didn't need to understand each word. If he was feeling even half of the bliss he was bringing to her in those seconds, she knew full well what his hot utterances expressed.

Twenty

Storr lay over her in a shuddering, helpless mass minutes later—painfully aware that he had just known the most transporting experience of his life. It was magical! The chills were still running up and down his back, and he scarcely had the strength to go on holding himself up, to keep from crushing her with his weight.

He cursed under his breath. A Norse exclamation or two, which he was fairly certain she hadn't yet learned from life in the camp. Then, finding himself able to put her needs above his once more, he lowered his lips to her right ear and told her he loved her in her own tongue.

She didn't respond. Her eyes were still closed, and her brow was furrowed a bit. This was, he assumed, either at the pain of deflowering, or at feeling him moving to uncouple from her now. He couldn't be sure which. As her arms closed around him an instant later, however, the answer was apparent.

"Are you all right?" he asked, letting her pull him down upon her once more.

Her eyes fell open, and she looked up at him with a couple disoriented blinks. "I . . . I'm not sure."

"Have I used the wrong word? This Erse word 'love,' doth it not mean what I thought?"

A faint smile came to her lips. "You can confirm it with Leif later. But I think it was what you meant to say. I surely hope so, in any case," she added with a shy laugh.

The sudden color in her cheeks made Storr feel like losing himself to her all over again. He sensed that it was time to either withdraw or fall to the temptation of spending the whole day indoors with her, and he knew that the latter would not go unfrowned-upon by his clansmen.

But, as he drew back, trying once again to extricate himself from it all, she issued a ghost of a whimper, the tiniest appeal. It sounded like a stranded kitten's mew in a blustery wind, and down he sank again . . . weak and unnerved by the entreaty.

Oh, by the gods, *don't*, Alanna, he thought, as he had the night before. *Don't* draw me into you a second time. Let me save some shred of belief that I'm still in control of my life, my actions! Even as he thought it, however, he knew that it was simply too late for any more don'ts with her. Hearing them would only make her angry, and, after knowing her this way, after having possessed her sweetest, softest recesses, he simply couldn't bear to have the biting side of her turned against him once more.

He, therefore, did as she wished, halting all efforts to get up and just giving in to his urge to lie clutching her to him.

The *bed*. That vexing bed he had vowed not to sully with another woman's vestal blood, came into focus for him in those seconds. Its huge horse-head posts loomed over him and his new lover with their usual formidable expressions, and, for the first time, he thought them the cruelest of carvings.

Everything had changed for him in the past twelve hours. He had been rescued from both his hellish nightmare and the prison of his own chastity. Yet, there it sat, as imposing as always: the four-poster, that reminder of all his obligations to this generation and the one it was still incumbent upon him to produce.

There would be no dowered beds from Alanna's family. No noble Viking lineage shared, nor feuds settled by their pairing. Her people's riches were already in Storr's keeping, stolen, along with the virginity of her tribe's maidens; and, no matter how great the spoils they'd acquired from her clan, he knew there would definitely be disapproval at his choosing to love her.

Chattels were fine for the occasional diversion or to give a Norse wife reprieve from childbearing. But as permanent additions to a chieftain's dwelling . . . Well, an earl would have to be more powerful than most to get by with that!

Storr shut his eyes, and, tangling his hands in Alanna's long hair, pressed his right cheek up against hers with a pensive sigh.

"What is it, my lord?"

" 'Tis nothing," he assured. "And pray do stop calling me that when we are alone. 'Tis hardly fitting now, do you think?"

"Then what should I call you?"

"By my name, of course. I've heard you use it more than once . . . Or, if you wish," he continued, drawing away enough to smile softly down at her, "something more fond."

She reached up and brushed some strands of hair from his face, her sudden forwardness throwing him off balance a bit. She was like that. She had been from the beginning. Timorous as a child one moment, then cutting to his vital center with her uncanny savvy the next. "What have we done, Storr?" she asked, her dark eyes exacting an answer.

He wanted to respond with some pleasantry, some waggish reply that would downplay the seriousness of the step they'd just taken. Unfortunately, however, he could only seem to swallow and shake his head. "As you said earlier, I'm not sure."

"Will we know in a day or two? Will this bewitched feeling begin to leave us?"

She sensed it, too, he realized, experiencing an ironic mix of relief and even greater concern. She now knew, as he had seemed to from the moment that ravenlike bird had appeared with her in the woods that they were fated to come together. That it had, from the first, been simply inevitable. But were they meant to save one another? Or, rather, to prove each other's undoing? That was the question that yet remained.

He only knew that he couldn't reveal how frightened he was of wanting her, how he'd sworn never to love or need again—and had viewed such commerce strictly as a means to sire children when that duty could no longer be postponed. He couldn't let her know that she possessed the power to take what was left of his heart and crush it to dust in her hands. And, above all else, *no one* must ever find out that what had just happened between them had actually surpassed anything he'd experienced with Freyja!

But it was simply that he'd been so starved for it, he tried to tell himself. Going over a year without making love was bound to cause a man to believe that he was knowing paradise itself, when he finally did succumb.

Ja, that was the reason for it, the only possible cause. But, just as he was repeating this rationalization to himself. Just as it was beginning to settle into a solid, credible sequence upon his mind—something he was sure he could tell himself over and over again—there came a rustling from somewhere behind him, and his stomach seemed to leap to his throat.

It was Leif Obviously not expecting to come

upon such a scene at this hour, he'd stepped mindlessly inside and was now standing, agape, before the door. *"Fie,* my lord! I am sorry," he said; and, before his master could utter a word in response, he made a brisk exit.

"The day beckons, love," Storr whispered down to Alanna. Unwilling to listen to any further objection, he lifted himself from her. Then he gathered her in his arms and set her up on the bed. If he just kept moving, a voice within him counseled, his legs might be counted upon not to give out from beneath him. If he fought hard enough to regather his wits about him, he might actually get out of the tent without surrendering to the urge to join her on the mattress once more.

But he couldn't leave her like this, he realized. Not with her huge brown eyes staring up at him — so filled with bewilderment and dejection. She was still so innocent. Far too new to this fleshly realm of men and women to have any real idea what he was thinking. And he knew that he had to do something to assure her that his sudden withdrawal, the misgivings he was trying so hard to hide were not, in truth, her fault.

In his disconcerted state, the only gesture that occurred to him was, it seemed, the most practical one. He reached up and unbrooched his cape. Then, feeling an irrepressible flush come to his cheeks, he slipped it up between her thighs, and pressed it softly to the wetness he'd left with her.

She looked, for an instant, surprised — then a trifle embarrassed at this unspoken acknowledgement of what had passed between them.

He felt, on some level, compelled to apologize. But that didn't seem quite right either. He'd meant, with all his soul, to lay claim to her, and he didn't want her thinking otherwise.

"Stay . . . stay off that leg," he blurted in desperation, and not wishing to run the risk of bending to kiss her a final time, he turned and made a hurried retreat.

Leif was waiting for him outside. He was leaning up against the front wall of the tent with his hands folded over his chest, and a knowing smile threatening to erupt across his face at any moment.

"Not a word," Storr warned, "or I swear I shall run you through!"

"But what could I possibly have to say, my lord?" he asked with a shrug. "Only that you must now regret having waited so long?"

"I don't regret anything," he said from behind clenched teeth. "Now, what did you want?"

"The storm left your second ship's sails in worse shape than we had at first thought. You probably ought to come and have a look."

Storr did so, deeply grateful for this call to duty. He hadn't welcomed his tasks this sincerely in ages, it seemed. But then he hadn't ever needed so desperately to be saved from himself — from the outrageous urge to go back inside and beg an *Erse prisoner* never, *never* to leave him.

* * *

To Alanna's disappointment, it was not Storr, but his freeman who returned to the tent a few hours later. She had, fortunately, covered herself to her waist with Storr's cape before drifting off to sleep; and, as her eyes fell open now, she saw Leif quietly rummaging through one of his master's chests.

"Leif?" she greeted drowsily.

He gave a start and turned about to face her with a slightly flustered expression. "Aye?"

"Where is Storr?"

"Out on one of the ships. We'll be repairing the storm's damage for a couple more days yet, I'm afraid. So you shouldn't look for him until dusk, my lady."

"I fear I failed to please him."

The freeman was polite enough to look as though he didn't have any idea what she was referring to.

"You know," she went on evenly, "when you chanced to walk in on us earlier . . . Please don't make me say more."

"*Oh,*" he replied, mercifully choosing to appear suddenly enlightened. "Well . . . but I'm sure you did."

"How?"

"How what?"

"How are you sure?"

"Well, you must remember, I have known the earl all of my life, so I am good at judging his moods."

"And what . . . what is his mood, pray?" she asked gingerly, stiffening herself for his response. Though she had brought up this subject, she wasn't sure now if she could bear to hear that her first assumption was right.

"He is . . . ruffled, my lady."

"Ruffled?"

"Aye. You know, unable to keep his mind set upon the work at hand. Given to staring off at naught."

She couldn't hide her hurt. "Then I did not please him."

Leif drew his brows together apologetically. "Oh, nay, nay. That is precisely my point, you see. 'Tis because you did that he behaves this way."

"Forsooth?" she asked dubiously.

"Oh, aye. Do trust me. I have seen this in him before."

"When?"

"Why, when he wooed his wife, of course."

Alanna felt something in the very center of her begin to soar at this revelation. While Storr had said he loved her, he had been so quick to leave after their amorous union, that she could only conclude that she had said or done something wrong. "Will it pass?"

"His dreaminess you mean?"

She nodded.

"With time, of course. No man can stay in such a state for very long . . . I fancy he will have to . . . to take you a few more times before his feet

426

return to the earth though," he added somewhat sheepishly.

Alanna did her best not to reveal her reaction to this. It was, after all, the sin of fornication they were speaking of here. In spite of herself, however, she was delighted to hear that there was very likely much more of it to come. "When will you raid again?" she asked, summoning what solemnity she could to switch over to this distressing topic.

"In a day or two."

"And will it be your last for the summer?"

Leif hesitated before answering, wondering why she was asking this of him, rather than their master. The last raid was usually the one during which their Erse prisoners were most apt to attempt any escapes from the camp. And, though he didn't want to think as much, he imagined it was possible that *this* prisoner could be so inclined. "Aye, my lady. I believe so."

"Then you must be careful not to leave Storr's side," she warned, suddenly lowering her voice.

The freeman was clearly taken aback. "Why?"

Alanna bit her lip before speaking, knowing there was yet this one last confidence to be divulged. But it was for Storr's own good, she reasoned. "Because his brother will try to kill him again."

Leif's face paled. *"Again?"*

"Aye. He tried when Storr came upon me in my uncle's house, and, save that I warned him, the earl would have died at his brother's hand."

"Are you quite certain of this, my lady?"

"Aye. 'Twas the very same man who tried to take me from the bath line just a few days later. I shall never forget his face."

"Why didn't you tell me this before?"

"Storr swore me to secrecy, for some reason . . . But I have told you so much hitherto, it seems this one last confidence cannot really matter. And, verily, I do speak of it in the hope of seeing Storr return here alive."

"Dear God," the freeman exclaimed in a low voice. "It truly is murder then that Gunther is about."

"Aye. Murder. Prithee, tell me that such an act is seen by you Vikings as the great offense it is here in Erin. Or can it possibly be simply 'slaying' to you, as it is against the Erse on your raids?"

Leif heaved a heavy, worried breath, and, closing the lid, sank down upon the sea chest through which he'd been rummaging. "Oh, nay. 'Tis grave enough. Why, based on what you've just told, our master could have Gunther adjudged guilty by Norse law, and either executed or banished from our land for the rest of his days."

"Then why would Storr ask me never to speak of it?"

The freeman shook his head. "I'm not sure . . . Because he doth not wish to hazard seeing any more of his clansmen killed, perhaps."

"But Gunther hath taken his allegiance away to Sigurd's clan, has he not?"

"Aye. He has. However, I fear our lord is simply still too aggrieved at having lost his father and wife to accept that truth just yet . . . But, of course, Gunther would attempt such a crime on a raid, where he could later claim 'twas a defending Erseman who slew his brother," he continued, as though thinking aloud.

"Well, that is why you must make certain Storr is never alone this time," Alanna cautioned again.

He rose, emitting another perturbed breath. "Aye. Thank you *very much*, my lady, for telling me this. And you can be sure I will not leave his side. Now, I must return to the ships, I'm afraid." He walked as far as the door, then turned to face her once more. "I will, of course, do all I can to insure that our master comes back unharmed from this raid, but . . . 'tis . . ."

"What?" Alanna coaxed at his faltering.

"Well . . . 'tis your own efforts, you see, that might most serve to save him."

She couldn't imagine what he meant. "What efforts would those be?"

"You could . . . mayhap, promise him that you will yet be here when we return."

His penetrating regard in those seconds made Alanna draw away a bit. It was as though he could read her mind, as if he somehow knew of the plans she and her cousins had discussed; and she felt suddenly entrusted with more than just one man's love. There were people's fates, both Erse and Norse, hanging in the balance here. Storr was so high-ranking, that the future of an entire clan and its servantry rode upon his ability to act cautiously and well. And *she,* in turn, had apparently gained a measure of influence over that.

She didn't answer the freeman. She couldn't. She simply sank down and turned away from him on the bed, until she heard him take his leave. Then she squeezed her eyes shut and tried to pray—to beg guidance from a God whose law she had just so impetuously broken.

It was after dark when Storr finally returned to the tent. And, to Alanna's surprise, he looked at her, when entering the shelter, as if she were a lioness about to be loosed upon him. He was guarded, suspicious, as though somehow believing she possessed the ability to overcome him, if given half a chance.

Leif served them supper, but left them soon thereafter. Again, as on every night before, his parting was accompanied by a motioning with his eyes that urged Alanna to move closer to the earl and comfort him in any way possible. On previous evenings, she had simply glared at his meddling in this area; but she was careful to nod compliance to him this time. She was now aware that she would definitely be needing his continued counsel and aid.

"How is your leg?" Storr asked stiffly, once they were alone.

"Better now, I think. Less swollen."

"Good."

"How are your sails?"

"Oh, Leif told you about them?"

She nodded. "Aye, torn beyond repair in the storm, were they?"

"Nay. Not quite that badly, thank the gods."

"But I would that they were, Storr," she declared, her tone piercingly earnest.

Though she wasn't sure why, his look verged on a glare in those seconds. "Of course. Because you do not wish to leave Erin."

"Nay. Because I do not wish to have you leave for raiding," she replied, with a hint of scolding in her voice.

He nodded wearily. "I know. 'Tis a sin against your god."

She reached out and placed a hand over one of his. "That it is. But what I fear most is losing you to one of my countrymen or *yours*."

He eased his fingers out from under hers and took another swallow of his wine. "I have been raiding since boyhood, woman, and I've yet to be killed at it. So why should I be this time?"

"Because your brother wants you dead. And, if I hadn't been there to warn you—"

"Alanna," he interrupted, "I asked you never to speak of that! So, prithee, do be good enough not to turn the wife on me."

"Why not? From what I've heard, you have been in sorry need of one for quite some time."

This brought a full glower from him; and he rose from the table and crossed to lie down upon the

431

bed with a roiled air. "I *must* lead my men in raiding. 'Tis my duty."

"And there is no way to free yourself of it? Say, if you had become ill with that arrow wound you had in your arm when I met you? Who then would have led your men?"

"My Uncle Olaf, most likely. With Leif commanding the second ship. But, if a chieftain is well enough to stand up, he is expected to go, my dear; so let us please stop speaking of it!"

She fell silent. Then a final appeal came to mind, and she got up and made her way over to the bed. "And, if I were to tell you that I fear your finding another Erse maiden on that raid . . . one you might consider more pleasing?" she asked coyly.

After an instant or two of surprise, he shook his head and laughed. *"Neinn.* There will be no others. I find you quite enough to manage," he replied, extending a hand to her.

She took it and let him pull her over to where he lay. "I would sin again with thee a million times over, my lord," she said softly, raising his hand to her lips for a kiss. "I believe now that aught as Heavenly as what we did simply cannot be so great a transgression in God's Eyes. But this raiding, this killing . . . don't you see it must stop?"

He tried to pull his hand away once more, but she held it fast, stilling him with the determined look in her eyes.

"Alanna." It was a low growl, escaping from

somewhere deep in his throat.

She would not be silenced again, however. "Don't you understand? If you go, I may not be here when you return. There are those of my clan who would seize your absence in order to try escaping here, and, with you gone, they will see no reason why I should not flee with them."

Storr's breath caught in his throat. He hadn't expected such candor from her, and he was momentarily lost for a response. "Do . . . do you wish to stay?"

She bit her lip and nodded. She knew that it was, at once, a shameful and a touching confession.

He tried to hide the great relief and elation this brought him. "Then just stay. Simply tell them you are staying."

"But they will not understand, Storr. They will think me every bit the turncoat that your men would at your not leading the raid."

He jerked his hand free of hers and rolled away, onto his left side. "Flee then, if you must. There is naught I will do to stop you. But, for the sake of *Valholl,* do not fail at it, for any warriors Sigurd leaves behind will surely come after you!"

"But 'tis not my will to leave," she said again in a barely audible voice.

He'd heard her nonetheless. "Then don't. Please don't."

She was silent for several seconds, staring at his back, watching as his shoulders slowly rose and fell

433

with his breathing. Suddenly she felt as she had at her mother's inconsolable state after her husband's death, and she was lost for words in either of their languages. As inarticulate as the child she'd been at the time of her mother's suicide.

Yet, somehow, through what could only have been divine guidance, she had the wisdom now to stop trying to speak. She realized that they would only continue to argue if they went on conversing. And, sensing this, she dared to reach out to him again. This time she put her hands upon his shoulders and started to massage them, as he had taught her in the bath the day they'd arrived at the camp.

He gave forth a relieved groan, and it was obvious that this was more due to his gratefulness at having her still trying to come to terms with him, than to her fledgling ability to rub away his tension or pain.

After a moment, he reached back and caught her right hand in his.

"You do not wish to have me touch you?" she choked.

"Neinn," he replied, rolling over to face her, his eyes twinkling with sincerity. "I do not wish you ever to stop."

She didn't need any direction from him this time. She knew, as he cupped his palm to the back of her head and drew her mouth down to his, precisely what to do. His face, his hands were so much bigger than hers . . . the rest of him so foreign. And, yet, as she lay kissing him, as they fi-

434

nally disrobed and slipped in beneath the bed's linens together, it seemed the most natural match in all the world.

Could this be a Viking? Taking her, devouring her—aye, as they did Erse honey and bread. But so gently, so savouringly, as though knowing every move, every breath-stopping whisper that set lovemaking so far apart from rape. For, if this was rape, *he* wanted it, too. As he moved her hand down to his throbbing, yet silky hardness, she understood that this veined appendage was the most vincible part of him, and that he wanted it touched and kissed with the same tenderness he was now directing to her breasts.

She moved to do so, letting her fingers stroke its velvety tip, until he groaned and became too distracted to continue his attentions to her.

"*Neinn*. No more," he said in an urgent whisper, catching her hand in his once more. "Let me save it for inside you."

As he lay over her, he again pressed his huge, warm hand to her lower lips. Lightly, lovingly, as if feeling for fever upon a forehead. "Unless you are yet sore from this morning, poor lamb."

She was, but not enough to deny him or herself the satisfaction of their joining again. "Nay. 'Tis all right."

His fingers parted her. Slowly, carefully, guiding his shaft over the chafed tissue within. And, as he surged her to abandon minutes later, he breathlessly explained that it wasn't only he who had claimed her stead, her worldly holdings amidst this summer's raiding—but she his. For, if she stayed, if she would just find it in her heart not to try fleeing with the others, he would marry her by Norse law, and Viking wives indisputably owned at least half their husband's holdings from the day of such wedding.

Alanna was, however, too enraptured to care about such things in those seconds. Her senses were simply too charged to take it all in. She heard his words, but did not fully understand them. She only knew that she would not mind becoming the wife of an earl, would not object to regaining her status as an aristocrat—would dearly love to let this man lie with her for the rest of her days.

Twenty-one

Alanna was able to steal a few words with her cousins on the day before the raid. They huddled amidst the hubbub of the midday meal, near Sigurd's side of the camp, and spoke for only a moment or two.

Ciarda had arranged the plan with some of their tribe's elders, who had also fallen into the Serpent-eyed's possession. Those participating in the escape would flee their respective sides of the camp at nightfall, immediately following the supper cleanup on the evening after the warships' departure. They would meet in the wooded area that was just west of there.

Alanna took careful note of this, committing it to memory. Then she reached out to squeeze each of her cousin's hands before heading back towards Storr's tent. "God bless, then. Let us hope we can all away unscathed."

Lord, how good it was to see their faces up close once again. To actually be able to touch and speak to these cousins turned sisters. She saw them now as they'd been as children: Ciarda, the taller, and Torra, the lighter-haired and more playful of the two. She had always known them, had always sensed that their future would be a tragic, fateful one, and that there would someday be a moment like this—stolen, desperate upon an enemy beach. They were like seeing her own reflection in a pond, so simple to read, so easy to be with. And she knew that, if all of their plans went as intended, she would miss them more than words could ever tell.

"But why the tears, cousin?" Ciarda asked, seeing them even before Alanna was aware of them herself.

Alanna reached up and hurriedly blotted them with her sleeve. She wanted to answer, but found herself too weepy to do so. Aught that slipped from her lips would be a lie in any case, she realized; and she certainly didn't want her parting words to her cousins to be false.

" 'Tis just that the Norsemen *expect* this," she said finally. "Don't you understand? They have been raiding Erin every summer for years, and they have come to expect such attempts to flee so near their leaving for Thule."

Torra looked vexed at this. "What are you saying then? You haven't the daring for it? Our fiery Alanna? Punished at every turn for her mischief as a child? I cannot believe it!"

"I am only saying they will likely kill us, if we fail. Storr hath told me as much."

"Fie! 'Twill be better than having to go on lying under that sot, Eric, night after night," Torra hissed.

Ciarda looked about them cautiously, making sure their little rendezvous was continuing to go unnoticed by the nearby Vikings. Then her eyes narrowed quizzically as she returned them to Alanna. *"What* has this man done to you, that you should suddenly be so timid? 'Tis not that you fear you're with child, is it? For you must know that Torra and I bear the same risk now."

Alanna shook her head. "Nay," she answered, swallowing dryly. *'Tis worse, Ciarda. Don't you see? He's made me love him, made me know how much he needs me and that is far, far worse than any violation, any pregnancy!* a voice within her screamed. But she couldn't tell them this. They would never understand. In the keeping of a Norseman as cold and cruel as Sigurd, they simply would not be able to conceive of any greater trap.

"Unless I am stopped somehow, I shall meet you in the woods," she replied, taking each of their hands and pressing them in turn to her still tear-dampened cheek.

She feared for them greatly; but she sensed that nothing she could say or do would stop them now. And, forsooth, what further reason could she give them to stay? Storr had just told her, only a few nights before, that there seemed no hope of his buying either of them away from Sigurd.

Their paths were probably parting, once and for

all, and she couldn't even bid them a proper farewell. This was the saddest part of all, she realized, as she finally let go of Torra's hand and began backing away. It was likely that she would never see them again, and they truly didn't seem to perceive this.

She kept her eyes upon them, until her blind, backward motion caused her to bump into a tall scowling freeman. Then, facing Storr's tent once more, she continued her slow course, glancing back off and on, searing the sight of them — their ragged cloaks and tunics, their windblown hair and sweet, familiar faces — upon her brain.

"Walk with me awhile on the beach," Alanna said to Storr after supper that evening.

He gave forth a weary sigh and shook his head. *"Neinn.* We must rise at dawn, my dear, and I am very tired from the day's work."

It had, in fact, been a terribly long day. He had woken well before sunrise and toiled to ready his ships, men, and weaponry, so as to be primed to depart with Sigurd's forces the following morning.

"But I wish to walk with you by the sea that will take you from me. Don't you understand?" Alanna continued, lowering her voice and leaning towards him so that Leif could not overhear. "If I must lose you to her . . . if she is to be your lover in my stead in the coming days, I would take you to her reach and let her fingers wash up and touch me as well."

He looked, for a moment, dumbstruck at this strangely poetic explanation — then *melted* by it, as Alanna had hoped. He remembered that both of her parents had drowned in those waters, and he knew he couldn't deny her this last request before his departure.

"All . . . all right. But just for a short while," he added, clearly wishing to maintain some semblance of control over the situation.

"Aye. I think it a very good idea, my chief," Leif chimed in, raising a teasing brow at Storr, as he began gathering up the supper dishes for cleaning.

Storr, scowling with wonder at what had gotten into his two companions, rose resignedly from the table. "But not far, Alanna, prithee," he declared, as she took hold of his hand and hastened him out of the tent.

They strolled towards the south, away from the camp and the threat of encountering any of Sigurd's men. And, at Alanna's insistence, though the evening breeze was a bit chilly, they walked on the tideland, where the waters could splash over their feet.

" 'Twill be a clear day again tomorrow," Storr predicted, looking up at the cloudless evening sky. "The sunset was very red, so we shouldn't have stormy weather to contend with."

Alanna gazed upward as well. "Are they very different in Thule?"

"What?"

"The stars."

He squinted, studying them more closely. *"Neinn*. Not really. Constant enough to navigate by them from there to here, naturally. But it doth seem there are more of them this far south . . . Of course, my people cannot really see the stars in the first half of summer."

Alanna found herself both disquieted and perplexed by this. "Why not?"

He smiled, almost roguishly. "Because the sun does not set."

She stopped walking. "What?"

"The sun does not set for the first six weeks of our summer, my dear. It just lingers on the edge of the earth the whole night through."

" 'Tis cruel of you to tease me in this way! Especially when you know how I fear going there!"

He stopped as well, turning around to face her. Then he walked back to her and gave her an affectionate hug. "But I'm not teasing, love. 'Tis the truth. Ours is the 'land of the midnight sun.' Didn't you know?"

She looked as though she was beginning to believe him. 'But with light throughout the night, how do your people sleep?"

He smirked, the knowing kind of expression that she would not have understood before she had lain with him. "We *don't*," he replied, bending down to nibble her neck with a softly wicked laugh.

She felt herself blush to her very toes. She realized in that instant that she would always be Erse: hopelessly sheepish about the pleasures of the

442

flesh, and never, never so at ease with them that she could engage in such sportive banter.

"Oh, come now, Alanna," he purred. " 'Tis only I out here with you, and I won't think any the less of you, if you smile at such things."

"But I can't. I *mustn't*," she declared, biting her lip to stifle an embarrassed laugh.

"Your god is wrong in this, you know," he said, stepping back beside her and wrapping an arm about her shoulders as they continued to walk. "I know you revere him, and I agree that he is very wise, indeed. But love between a man and woman is simply too precious a thing to be so quelled by one's faith. Even I, in my great love for Freyja, now feel some regret at all the time I've spent mourning, when I could have been with someone new . . . like you. Life is very short, you know."

A chill ran through her, as it often did when he spoke this way.

He stopped walking again. Then, catching hold of her hand, he drew her back to him with it. "And he is wrong about something else."

She dropped her gaze and smiled to herself at how dear he was, for obviously dedicating so much thought to her Christian teachings. "What is that?"

Storr was silent for several seconds, allowing her to take in the sound of the lapping waves and the feel of the evening breeze in their hair. "The world was not made in only six or seven days. *Neinn*. Anyone can see that it took much, much longer to create all of this," he concluded, letting one of his

443

arms sweep up to the twinkling heavens.

"Well, perhaps a day to God is not the same length as it is to us."

He laughed under his breath. "You will defend him to the death, won't you."

"Why not? He surely will me."

"Even though we've sinned together?"

"Even so," she answered unwaveringly.

He wrapped an arm about her once more, and they resumed their languorous gait. "I am simply jealous is all," he confessed.

"Of what?"

"Of the fact that you love him so."

"Do you not love your Norse gods?"

He hesitated, giving the question some thought. He'd never actually considered this before. *"Neinn.* 'Tis not love we are taught to feel for them, but respect. One must be in a god's good graces, if one is to call upon him or her in troubled times."

"So you simply fear them?"

"Nay. Fear and honor them, both."

"Hmmm. Seems too cold to me somehow."

"It would. For your people have only known a world of warmth. Mild winters and tepid seas."

"And how then, do you suppose *your* gods created the world?"

"Slowly," he answered without pause. "By mixing light and darkness. Fire and ice. Evil and good. Link by link, as one forges a chain. Opposites, you see, Alanna . . . like you and I were when we met. Fighting, hurting. Then loving and tenderness . . .

the kind that gives rise, in turn, to more life," he added, pressing this murmur to her ear.

She thought she would swoon right there in his hold, but she managed to keep walking. "Don't go tomorrow," she softly implored. "If it truly is serenity you seek from my God, you must come to understand that you cannot be at peace with yourself, when you are forever warring with others!"

"Alanna." His tone was edged with annoyance, as it had been when she'd made the same appeal the night before. She could tell, however, that he was doing his best not to become angry with her, not to spoil the winsome mood they'd just established.

"Alanna, I *must* go, as I've told you. But I give you my word that I will try to bow out of such forays in the future, if you . . . if you will only promise me that you will yet be here when I return."

"*If* you return."

"*When* I return," he said firmly, looking her squarely in the eye.

"For God's Sake, don't let Gunther kill you. Don't let him get close enough to run you through! I know you feel the deaths of Freyja and your father heavy upon you, but you mustn't go on thinking that way. You must not allow your brother to overcome you with your own remorse. If you truly were guilty of murder, don't you think your Viking assembly would have tried you for it?"

He was silent for several seconds, as though letting her words wash over him. Then he donned a subtle, discerning smile. "What I think is that I've been letting you spend too much time alone with Leif."

"Ah, but he means well, my lord. I think he loves you almost as much as I do. If that be possible."

Storr froze at this, feeling the words shoot through him like lightning. This was the first time she had said she loved him, and his legs felt almost too weak now to carry him back to the tent.

"What did you say?" he asked, narrowing his eyes. He'd become far more proficient at understanding Erse in the last few weeks than he had ever thought likely; but he knew it was possible that his wishful thinking could have caused him to misinterpret this.

"I said I think he loves you almost as much as I."

"*Ja*. That is what I thought you said," he replied, lowering his voice in the hopes of hiding the unavoidable shakiness in it. Then, without an instant more thought, he led her away from the water's edge. In the event that he didn't manage to suppress the urge to sink to the sand with her in those seconds, he didn't want them to get splashed.

He bent down and kissed her, and she was, as on the night before, soft and compliant. Her silken lips parted to his like a fragile, defenseless bloom that was capable of turning his heart to mush.

"Angan," he whispered against her cheek as he finally ended their kiss.

"What?" The question was more amorous sigh from her, than utterance.

"Angan, Alanna. 'Tis the Norse word for 'beloved one,' and I would very much like to hear you say it to me tonight. 'Twill be days, weeks, perhaps, before I'm likely to hear it again."

"An . . . Angan," she said, tittering at how inept she still was at pronouncing their strange, guttural words. "Did I speak it well enough?"

He hugged her to him so powerfully that she knew he didn't wish to let her go. "I've never heard it sound better!"

They were tellingly long in getting back to the tent, and Storr braced himself for his freeman's inevitable smirk. The damnable man! He was as pleased with himself for his success at facilitating his master's romance with Alanna, as a preening house cat! Storr had all he could do to keep from coming right out and *slapping* him these days, in fact.

Leif meant well, though. Alanna was right to keep reminding him of this; and, to Storr's relief, it was not teasing looks he returned to, as they entered the dwelling, but an inexplicable sort of solemnity from the freeman.

Even more surprising was the fact that Storr's paternal uncle Olaf was now there as well. Next in command of Storr's warriors, Olaf would captain their second longship in the morning. He greeted his nephew with a broad smile and an upraised cup, where he was seated with Leif at the makeshift dining table.

"I've come to drink to our success on the raid," he declared, picking up another cup of wine and rising with it. He quickly crossed to press it into his nephew's hand. " 'Tis the last of the summer, after all, and we must pray that Odin will be with us, and the seas will stay calm this time."

Storr, scowling at this uncharacteristic effusiveness from his father's brother, accepted the drink and followed him back to the table with it. "How is the second ship? Were your satisfied when you left her?"

Olaf nodded. "*Ja*. I just rowed back from her a few minutes ago. And you can rest assured that, unless our friend Sigurd tampers with her as we sleep, she will again prove seaworthy."

"But some of your crew does sleep aboard her tonight, sire, against the possibility of such tampering?" Storr pursued.

Again his uncle nodded. "Now *skoal,* chief. 'Tis unlucky not to drink what is poured for thee," he reminded, raising his glass to toast with him and then Leif.

"*Skoal,*" Storr replied, taking a long swallow of the wine. He paused before drinking any more of it, however. It really didn't taste very good to him, and he wondered if it had been amongst the cargo that had been unloaded from his second ship on their last raid. It was definitely of a different vintage than the sweet, fruity variety his ship had carried back with it. "Bitter," he noted with a frown. "Don't you think this a trifle bitter, Uncle?"

Olaf shrugged. "A trifle, perhaps. I don't know. 'Tis what my crew and I have been drinking since we left that monastery, so I suppose we've grown accustomed to it."

Storr scowled again, not really wanting to finish off the serving, but knowing, as every superstitious mariner seemed to, that bad fortune might be brought upon them if he did not.

The taste. He couldn't quite put his finger upon it; yet it seemed strangely familiar. He took another sip and let the liquid rest upon his tongue for several seconds. Chalky, he thought.

He finally swallowed. "And what of the shortage of shields your warriors spoke of?" he asked Olaf.

"*Ja.* Seven lost in the storm. Two split by Erse spears. And, of course, the one Burnaby chanced to catch aflame."

Storr donned a stern expression. "Tell Burnaby, from me, that he is not to set *anything* afire, once the drinking has begun."

Olaf managed to fight a smile. Burnaby, another of his nephews, was among the youngest in their raiding party this summer, and he was clearly exhibiting the bungling zeal of a newcomer to such adventures. "*Ja.* I shall, Earl. 'Twill not happen

449

again. And I am pleased to report that we managed to acquire enough hard wood to replace all of the lost shields."

Storr did find a measure of comfort in this, and he again raised his glass to his lips. He took another sip. Then, greeted with the beverage's odd taste once more, he surreptitiously eyed what remained in his cup. It appeared to be roughly the same color as most of the other Erse wines he'd consumed, and yet it was heavier somehow. Thicker. As though mixed with just a hint of some sort of syrup.

Bitter, he thought again, starting to feel as though he might not be able to choke down any more of it. And, all at once, the memory of this flavor came back to him in a frightening flash, and his eyes shot over to where Alanna still stood near the door.

The poison, he realized, filling with panic. Though the wine had masked it better than water, this was, unmistakably, the same taste he'd experienced with her in the woods! His heart began to race with fear and confusion.

"Alanna?" he queried, furrowing his brow.

She tried to smile, to look as though nothing was wrong. Yet there was, in that instant, the faintest telltale flicker in her eye; and he was sure he was right.

He lowered his voice as he spoke again, not wanting the others to hear. "But I thought you understood that I don't want this now."

She walked over to him and put a hand upon his shoulder, hoping to ease his apprehension with her touch. "I do understand. 'Tis only enough to make you sleep, my lord. I measured well. I swear it. So drink the wine off. Your good uncle doth know what is best."

Storr's eyes flew up to Olaf now. He had risen from the table in the past couple seconds and was crossing to where Leif presently stood, sentrylike, in front of the door.

As his uncle reached the freeman and turned back with his arms crossed resolutely over his chest, it was clear to Storr that they had no intentions of letting him leave. They were *all* in on it, and they would not hazard his going off to rid himself of the poison, to regurgitate it out on the beach, before it could take its effect.

"Finish it, nephew," Olaf insisted. "I have, after all, been captaining ships far longer than you. They will be in good hands, between Leif and me, and you know it."

"But *why?*" Storr demanded, refusing to drink any more until they gave him their reasons. It was, however, probably too late, in any case, he realized. He could already feel his eyes growing sensitive to the light of the lamp that rested on the table before him, and his vision was beginning to blur, as it had that night with Alanna in the forest.

For a sorry instant or two, it actually occurred to him that his uncle and Leif may have become displeased with the way in which he had managed

451

the clan since his father's death. Perhaps they thought it best to simply eliminate him before he somehow fell to Sigurd.

But, *neinn,* he told himself, as he squinted at them, trying to study their shadowed expressions. They were his dearest kin and companions. If he couldn't trust them, there was no one on earth he could trust. They would never do such a thing without, at least, having forewarned him of their fears and dissatisfaction.

"Because you and the girl belong together," his uncle answered evenly. "Because you must have reason to stay behind, and she must have reason not to flee. Because we have decided that more harm could befall thee at Gunther's hand than at the drinking of this lady's potion . . . So, do rise. While you still *can,* man, and make your way to your bed," he added with a smile in his voice. "Leif and I wish to be spared the task of having to carry you."

"But this is not fair," Storr countered. "I would that you had come to me with this scheme before simply effecting it!"

Olaf gave forth a cynical laugh. "Oh? And would you have agreed to play sick before both our warriors and Sigurd's?"

Storr hesitated, feeling the blasted syrup beginning to numb his lips. "Well . . . *neinn.*"

His uncle laughed again. "So, there it is. Our reason for making this choice. Now, up with you and to the bed," he ordered, gesturing for Leif to cross with him and help walk the earl to the four-poster.

Storr did his best to anchor himself to his seat, as they flanked him and took hold of his arms seconds later.

"Come along, master," Leif urged. "A bench is surely no place for a long sleep."

Though Storr was compelled to agree with this, he continued to fight them as they finally wrested him to his feet and began hauling him towards the bedstead. "But I'll be helpless like this. What . . . what if Sigurd leaves men behind to come and finish me?"

"Your tent shall be guarded night and day," Olaf assured. "Now lie down and let the lovely lady sing you to sleep. Or I swear we shall fetter you!"

"You always were such a kindly sort," Storr snarled up at him, as they pinned him to the mattress seconds later. "I used to fear you so as a boy, and now I know I was right to!"

Again his uncle responded by laughing dryly. "But I have never failed you, have I, son of my brother, and I surely shall not now. Nor, you know in your heart, will your good freeman."

Though Storr wanted desperately to believe this, he continued to fight his kinsmen in the minutes that followed. Gritting his teeth, he pushed upward against their holds, until he was so weak and winded that he fell back limply.

He'd asked for this poison once. No, more rightly, almost *pleaded* for it, when he'd thought

453

his heart and will too shattered for him to go on living. He had actually longed to have this distilled death envelop him and paralyze his limbs as it was now. And he realized, as it overtook him like a constricting snake that had dropped from a tree—making each breath shorter and more shallow, sucking him into sleep like a tiny vessel down an ocean whirlpool—what a fool he'd been to long for passage into a state that would deny him his senses. For he'd learned, in the past several days, that there was not, in any world, aught fairer than the sight, the scent, the feel of his Alanna; and he could not bear the thought of being torn thus from her—even if only for a couple day's sleep.

But the poison had a hold of him finally, dragging him down into the depths of slumber like a plummeting rock; and his companions seemed to know it. They were, at last, letting go of him, stepping away from the bed and allowing Alanna to take their place.

Storr couldn't be sure, for the dullness in his limbs, but he thought she was squeezing his hand. And he was certain that was her face over his, terribly out of focus, but luminous as a fairy's in the dim lamplight.

"Good night," she whispered. "Leif, quickly, before I lose him, what are the Norse words for good night?"

"Goda nott."

She smiled down at her lord. *"Goda nott . . . angan,"* she said in a soft, yet confident voice.

Twenty-two

Olaf and Leif were careful not to let word of Storr's precipitant "illness" reach Sigurd until just minutes before they were to set sail the next morning. As they could have predicted, the Serpent-eyed greeted the news with far more concern than seemed appropriate. It was a thin mask, indeed, for the rage he must truly have felt at again having his murderous plans foiled.

As Olaf informed him of the situation, the old earl stepped out of the rowboat, which he'd boarded to transport him to his anchored lead ship, and he insisted upon being taken to see the ailing chieftain at once. His sons and Gunther followed, of course, exchanging agitated whispers as they walked.

Gunther pushed ahead to Sigurd's side, as they entered his brother's tent minutes later. He was, after all, next in line for his father's earldom, should Storr become sick unto death, and he was not about to fall behind the elder chieftain's sons on such an occasion.

His suddenly self-important air was deflated, however, as he was greeted at the tent door by Biorn. While seeming unthreatened by Sigurd's entry, the huge hound immediately bared his fangs and poised to spring at Gunther's. His ferocious growl seemed to indicate an urge to tear the very privates from his master's brother; it took both Olaf and Leif to hold him back so that Gunther might come in.

Gunther hated himself for cringing in that instant, for showing fear of anything as insignificant as a dog. But it had simply been reflexive, he told himself—as inevitable as recoiling at the sight of an onrushing bear. It was a perfectly natural response. It was just that the circumstances were so embarrassing: his own sibling's pet wishing to tear him limb from limb every time he set eyes upon him.

Gunther had, of course, done his best to make sure that such encounters were kept to a minimum in the past few years. He was faced with one of them again now, though; and, to his abashment, the only thing that ultimately seemed to stand between him and a tearing dismemberment was a wad of bread.

His Uncle Olaf was good enough to throw the table scrap out of the tent for the beast to go after in those seconds. And, as the bread hurled past him, Biorn's snarling ceased. He shot out of the dwelling, with the girl's Erse harrier close at his heels. Leif, in turn, clapped the tent door shut be-

456

hind the animals, and Gunther was greatly relieved to see him take the time to secure its ties so they couldn't reenter.

"Your brother's dog doesn't seem to like you," Olaf observed pointedly. "I wonder why that is."

Unwilling to dignify this insinuation with a response, Gunther made his way to Storr's bed and stood staring down at him, alongside Sigurd.

"By the gods, what hath betided him?" the Serpent-eyed queried, reaching down and running a hand over one of Storr's forearms. "He looks to be *dead,* and he's almost as cold to the touch."

Alanna drew closer to the bed's footboard, nervous at letting these unspoken adversaries come so near her beloved lord.

"We do not know, Earl," Olaf replied. "He simply did not wake from last night's sleep, and we fear he has been poisoned somehow."

The chieftain continued to look perplexed. "But 'tis not like any poison we have in Norway. A man doth writhe and suffer at our feral herbs. Yet Storr appears merely to be dead asleep. Breathing without toil."

"*Ja,*" Olaf agreed.

Sigurd raised a suspicious brow at him. "*Most* curious."

"But, more to the point, Earl, 'tis most troublous for us. For, even if he lives, he will surely not be well enough to raid with us for days, and, as I'm certain you know, the winds already grow chill with the approach of fall."

There was nothing, in all of a Viking's experience, more threatening than having to weather an autumn squall at sea, and Olaf had to trust that Sigurd was duly aware of this—of the need for them to conclude their season's raiding and head back to their homeland, before conditions became too dangerous for them to do so. What was more, the time for harvesting was rapidly approaching at their respective farmsteads; and Olaf knew that even a man as unfeeling as Sigurd couldn't really wish to have his wife saddled with overseeing such a demanding season alone.

A tense silence ensued. Alanna's eyes shot over to Olaf's, then to Leif's, stealthily searching their faces for more indication of where their Norse conversation was leading. Then, finally, mercifully, Sigurd gave a resigned nod.

"*Ja. Ja.* This is true," he said, backing away from the bed a bit.

Gunther, however, was not so quick to relinquish his position "But he is my brother, for Heaven's sake! I am next in the line of ascendancy, should he die. So why was I not told of this . . . this illness until now?" he brayed.

Olaf raised an allaying palm to him. "I came to you and the Earl as soon as I learned of it myself," he lied. He was, by nature, an honest man; but this untruth did seem unavoidable.

Gunther snorted. Then his eyes fixed venomously upon Alanna. "*She* is behind this somehow! You may be sure!"

"Oh, don't talk nonsense, nephew," Olaf countered. "In the name of Odin, the girl is Storr's lover. So why would she want him dead?"

"Perhaps she doesn't. Per chance she merely wants him too ill to raid."

Olaf looked at Gunther as though thinking him quite insane. Then he lowered his voice to a patronizing softness, as though suddenly addressing a child. "But that makes no sense, boy. Don't you think it best to bite your tongue before your crazed accusations lead Earl Sigurd to forbid your captaining his second ship?"

" 'Tis not Sigurd's second ship I should be commanding, but my brother's *first*," he spat, his face reddening with indignation.

Olaf laughed to himself. "Oh, but, Gunther, you have not shown interest in such a task in ages. You have, forsooth, made it clear to all of us that your loyalty lies with your foster father."

Gunther's voice was nothing less than a serpent's hiss as he spoke again. "If Storr dies, 'tis all *mine* by law, Olaf. The stead, the ships, the warriors! And you'd do well not to forget it!"

"*Ja*. But he is not dead yet, is he? You can see for yourself that his chest still rises and falls."

"I want you at the tiller of my second ship, in any case," Sigurd interjected. Then, inclining his face to Gunther's right ear, he continued in an admonishing whisper. "Don't you see? 'Tis not safe for you to be surrounded by a crew of his men,

459

while he yet lives. There will surely be another time for our design."

Gunther's anger cooled a bit at this, and, pressing his fists to his sides, he turned and left the tent—not caring now if Storr's horrible hound waited just outside for him.

The dog was nowhere in sight, fortunately . . . But, damn it all, *just let him be,* Gunther inwardly exclaimed. Just let him come within reach, and, witnesses or no, it would be the last thing the infernal cur would ever do!

In the hours that followed the raiders' departure, Alanna remained steadfastly close to Storr's sleeping form. Olaf had posted four men outside the tent, as promised, and she, of course, found a great deal of comfort in this. They were not only sure to protect Storr from the threat of attack by the few men Sigurd had left behind, but they would serve to convince her cousins and the rest of her fleeing kinsmen that taking part in the escape would now be impossible for her.

At suppertime, one of the sentries was good enough to bring her a plate of hot food. He seemed to speak Erse fairly well, and, when he offered to keep her company with a game of chess, she quickly took him up on it. Her loved ones would attempt their getaway at anytime, and she knew that the fewer Norsemen there were out on the beach to detect the surreptitious flight, the better. Moreover, she was sorely aware that she would be needing all the diversions she could get in order to continue to resist the urge to join them—in order to quell her deep concern for them at so desperate a time.

The sentry, a youngish man who told her his name was Cort, was wonderfully polite through it all. He must have assumed that her careless moves upon the *taflbord* were due to her growing concern over the fate of their still-sleeping master, for he neither teased her about them nor took unsporting advantage of her in the game.

Roughly half an hour later, word that some of the Erse prisoners were missing must finally have spread about the camp. A second sentry entered the tent and began to speak to Cort in the worried, winded Norse of a man who feared that his rank as a freeman was now in jeopardy for some reason.

"What is it?" Alanna inquired when the second guard finally took his leave.

"He thinks a few of the prisoners may have gotten away from us, my lady. I will be allowed to stay behind with you, but the other sentries must go after them, I'm afraid. We cannot have your kinsmen telling any of the nearby tribes of our camp, you see."

Alanna bit her lip and nodded, understanding *both* sides in the dilemma and secretly hating herself for it. "Tell . . . tell me. If there has been such an escape, what will happen to those you recapture?"

"Nothing, until Sigurd and Olaf return. Or until

461

Earl Storr recovers. Only chieftains may decide the penalties for such offenses."

"And what is the usual penalty for this?"

He shrugged. "Death. Sometimes maiming. Or, if a master is of a kindly nature or hath come to be fond of the serf in question, naught worse than a beating." He suddenly lowered his voice and looked cautiously over at the bed, as though fearing Storr could somehow hear him in his insensible state. "That is all our master has ever ordered, if 'tis any comfort to you, my lady. Though I would thank thee not to tell any of your people as much."

"I won't," she promised, turning her gaze to the Earl as well in those seconds. Though she wouldn't be indiscreet enough to tell this companion as much, she simply couldn't imagine how a lover as tender and compassionate as Storr could ever have proven harsh enough to order even the least of these punishments. She could only conclude that he somehow managed to absent himself when such sentences were being carried out. *Aye,* she decided, that was precisely what the man she had come to know would do, given those circumstances.

Roughly two hours after sunset, word finally reached Alanna and Cort that some of the Erse prisoners had, indeed, escaped. A complete head count was difficult to obtain in the blackness of night, of course; but Alanna took some comfort in the fact that, when morning finally came, she would, at last, know more about the fates of her cousins.

She had only to wait, now, sit and *wait*—for any further news, for any more signs of life from Storr; and she was beginning to realize, like never before, just how torturous a thing waiting could be.

She mended clothing as she passed the hours. She paged through the gospel book again, and sat playing her harp off and on. And when it seemed that sleep would finally be merciful enough to overtake her, as it had her lover, she crossed to the bed and lay down beside him.

There was little comfort in it, however. He was so motionless and cold to the touch. And only resting her palm upon his chest, only the feel of it rising and falling faintly beneath her fingers, let her know he was still alive.

. . . *Soil.* That moist, rich scent, which had seemed so much stronger to him in childhood, was what filled Storr's senses now. Though it was not expected of him, he dug with the rest of his men. First his father's grave, then Freyja's. His father's was the bigger of the two, of course. Viking law dictated that it contain his mammoth lead warship, which would, in turn, house not only his dead body but those of his favorite horses and dog. They, too, poor creatures, had, by custom, become victims of Storr's perilous actions.

It took four days to complete the excavating.

463

Four days of that incessant sound: half a dozen spades cutting into the hard earth and tossing their loads onto the surrounding, grassy ground with such unceremonious thuds. It was, Storr thought, the most final and sorrowful of sounds. Yet he found a strange sort of comfort in the digging, in having so exhausting and endless a task to fulfill, in feeling the punitive stinging of his blistered hands at nightfall.

His men marveled at his ability to stay among them and keep doing so much more than his share of the work. Indeed, it wasn't until a heavy rain began to fall, on the afternoon of the third day, that his fellow gravediggers realized that it was not simply dutifulness and devotion that kept their new chief toiling so, but a kind of crazed desperation.

It was a torrential rain, one that was sure to change the upturned soil to mud, and the open graves into flooded trenches. But Storr kept spading. As his men threw their shovels aside and began climbing out of Freyja's deep resting place, he continued to dig, and not even Leif could convince him to stop.

The gods knew, Leif *did* try, however. Kneeling upon the soaking rim of the grave, he extended a hand to Storr and repeatedly urged him to retreat, like the rest, to the longhouse, where he could shed his wet clothes and dry himself by the hearth . . . But to no avail. With an aching lump in his throat and each shovelful now becoming as much water as dirt, Storr persisted.

He did, of course, force himself to look up at Leif as he made this final refusal. He knew he owed his most loyal freeman at least that much courtesy, and he felt fairly confident that the trickles of rain upon his face would hide the tears no Norse chieftain was ever supposed to show. What was more, he knew that Leif was capable of seeing all explanation in his eyes. He would not have to speak a word now about how stricken he was at losing two such pillars in his life: his wife and father gone, before the local physician could even be fetched to help them.

Fortunately, Leif did seem to read all of this in his face in those seconds, and he turned away and trudged back to the farmhouse, with his short cloak pulled over his head against the downfall.

He should have been running, Storr had thought, his eyes following the freeman. He should have raced to seek shelter from the miserable stuff, instead of plodding through it. But, perhaps, he felt he had failed Storr somehow, in not persuading him to repair to cover. Or, too, it was altogether possible that his leaden gait was due to the fact that he mourned Storr's father every bit as much as his legitimate sons did.

Storr just couldn't be certain, however. Leif was difficult to see into at times . . . as deep and motionless as the dark waters of a well.

When the freeman was far enough away, and Storr was fairly certain he would not return, he finally gave in to the urge he'd been suppressing for so many days. He sank to his knees in the accursed mud and sobbed like a child.

It seemed he hadn't had a moment alone since the deaths had occurred. On a farmstead buzzing with kinsmen and slaves—each seeking direction from their new master—a distant grassland in a heavy rain were just about the only circumstances in which such solitude could be found; and Storr seized them now.

Closing his own, empty arms about himself, he began to rock amidst the wretched wetness. *Cry, damn it! Free yourself of every last tear! Sob until your throat and chest ache. For, when the rain clears, there will be no more chance, no more private time for it.*

There wasn't. In the days that followed, he was besieged by all the friends and relatives, who came from far and near for the funerals. And, even as the last shovelful of dirt was being cast over his dear Freyja and the dead baby that still rested inside her, he was not given a moment to himself.

Life went on, as the old adage said, and, ready for it or not, the rigors and responsibilities of an entire earldom—of hunting, raiding, farming, and having to provide for scores of clansmen and serfs—now rested upon him. Seemingly with all of the crushing weight of a boulder.

Alanna's eyes fell open, as Storr finally shifted in his sleep.

466

"Storr?" she whispered. "Dost thou wake?"

There was no answer from him, but she did notice that more color rose to his flesh now, as she pressed a finger to his cheek, then quickly withdrew it. He was saying something. Something too faint, too Norse for her to understand. Then he said "Freyja." But not with longing, not woefully, as he had in nightmares past. Just softly, blithely, as though the very letters of the name were dandelion wisps to be blown into the wind.

Alanna got up from the bed and hurried to the door. "Cort?" she bid in a low voice.

The dear man, little more than a black shape on that moonless night, was roused at her first call. He crawled out of his sleeping bag and made his way soundlessly to the entrance of the shelter. "Aye, my lady?"

Alanna kept her voice to a whisper. "The Earl doth begin to wake, and I need your help with him."

"Of course," he replied. Then, covering a yawn, he followed her inside.

She led him to the bed, and they both stared down at the semiconscious chief for several seconds.

"He speaks, but I cannot understand him," she explained. "Pray, can you?" Nightshade was the "discoverer of secrets" her physician uncle had once told her. Men were known to "reveal their deepest souls" under the poison's influence; and, after so many lonely hours without Storr's company, she wished with all her heart to know what it was he was saying.

Cort listened for a minute or two. Then, donning an uneasy look, he reached up and ran a hand pensively through his disheveled hair. "Well . . . he speaks of the forbidden, my lady. Of the deaths of his father and wife, and I daren't repeat it to you. I am sorry."

His eyes shone with genuine fear in what remained of the lamplight, and he turned to leave.

Alanna, however, caught him by the arm and pulled him back to face her. "*Please* tell me what he's saying. 'Tis just you and me here, and I assure you, from many years of treating the ill, that our lord will not hear or remember that you translated his words. That is all you would be doing, you know. Simply repeating his utterances to me. And that doth seem harmless enough, does it not?"

He lifted a hand to his mouth and began nervously chewing his thumbnail. "And you will tell *no one* of it, my lady? You swear it?"

Alanna nodded and drew him back to the bed. "I swear upon my very life," she answered, giving his hand an earnest squeeze.

"He . . . he speaks of the gifts," the sentry faltered, bending his head low as if to hear what more he could glean.

Wanting to continue to seem as trustworthy and unthreatening as possible to him, Alanna did her best to mirror his posture and manner in those seconds. "What gifts?" she asked gingerly.

"The . . . the pillows."

"Pillows?"

"Aye. The pair of silken pillows he bought in a Norse trading town. Adorned with gold thread they were. And said to have been brought all the way from the Orient . . . They must have cost our master a small fortune," he said, as an obvious aside.

Alanna narrowed her eyes, unable to figure out what this bit of information might have to do with Freyja's death.

But, perhaps, Storr had flown into some sort of rage and *smothered* her with one of them, she thought with a horrified chill rushing through her.

"When . . . when did he buy these pillows? Do you know?"

"Over a year ago, I guess. I'm sorry, but I cannot recall exactly when. None of us paid much mind to them when he brought them home, you understand. Such noblemen are always returning to their farms with treasures. I remember only that they had golden threads woven all about their edges, and they glistened so in the light. I also remember feeling covetous of them," he confessed with a boyish blush. "But such are the trappings of an earl. Or, in this case, the gifts an earl is wealthy enough to present."

"So he gave them away?"

"Aye."

"To whom?"

"Well, to his wife and father, of course. And 'twas not long after that they were afflicted," he added, lowering both his voice and gaze.

"With what?"

"With a pestilence of sorts. Verily, 'twas not like any our people have seen before or since. It took them almost overnight, making them writhe, first with fever, then chills. Then besetting their lungs until they could no longer breathe. 'Twas something from the mouth of *Hel,* that." He grimaced. "And, since no one else was stricken with it, we could only conclude that 'twas sleeping on those pillows that brought it upon them. The bolsters were, as I've said, resplendent on the outside. But, 'twas later discovered, there were fleas burrowed in them!"

Alanna pressed a hand to her mouth and shook her head drawing in an incredulous breath. Then her eyes began to fill with tears. "And this . . . *this* is the way in which our earl supposedly killed his bride and father?"

Cort nodded, again dropping his gaze at her sudden show of emotion.

"Oh, Sweet Jesus, Storr . . . Storr," she whimpered, reaching out and taking hold of one of his hands. Then, kneeling down beside the bed, she laced her fingers into his and drew the link to her tear-streaked face. "You dear, sweet man and your fear of pestilence. Why, why did you not tell me it was something as innocent, as *blameless* as that?"

"May I go now, my lady?" the sentry inquired, obviously sensing he'd accomplished what she'd asked for and not wanting her sudden understanding of the tragedy attributed to him.

She nodded, unwilling to take her eyes from her lord in those seconds. Her master, her chieftain— her husband-to-be. He was stirring so much now that she was certain he would awake with the dawn; and, with her last breath, she would see to it that there would never again be poison in his body—or his soul.

Epilogue

Morning brought both good news and bad. Storr recovered fully from the nightshade, but not all of Alanna's kin succeeded in fleeing. It was later revealed that, while Ciarda had gotten away safely, Torra had been overtaken by some of the men Sigurd had left behind. She was brought back, along with a few of her fellow escapees, to stand sentencing upon her master's return from the raiding.

In the end, the only thing that Storr could offer the elder chieftain—in order to buy Torra away from him and, thereby, spare her the penalty of death—was his lead warship. It was, by Viking standards, a steep price, indeed, to be paid for the life of a single slave.

Storr was, however, quite unable to resist Alanna and her requests. Upon their return to Norway, in fact, he not only married her according to Norse law, but in keeping with her own. A Christian missionary, who they contacted in the trading town of Hedeby, was good enough to wed the couple in a secret ceremony.

Perhaps because his people felt that Storr had already known enough suffering for his years, his decision to take an Erse prisoner to wife was never publicly questioned. Nor were the six children the couple subsequently produced ever viewed as less than rightful heirs to his earldom.

Author's Note

I hope you liked this story of Storr the Viking and his Erse maiden, Alanna. After doing an adoption search three years ago, I was finally able to confirm my half-Swedish, half-Norwegian lineage. And, as Viking historicals started to become popular with readers, I finally decided to write one. The only problem was, I knew very little about ancient history of any kind. The earliest date in which I'd set a book was 1707 (my last novel, a Zebra Heartfire entitled *Wild Irish Heather*), and, after having to grapple with all of the eighteenth-century language and research for that story, I swore I would never set a book any earlier in time . . . I was wrong! "Never say never," as the old adage goes!

Fool that I was, I had also sworn off any interest in my Scandinavian heritage. While I knew that the

Norsemen were a proud race, I was equally aware that they were uncommonly predatory and brutal; and, for many years, I honestly didn't wish to know any more about them. The truth of the matter, however, was that the Vikings were astoundingly civilized when not raiding. They were generally loving husbands and fathers, and they went to great lengths to make certain that they did not clash with one another. Also surprising was their liberated attitude towards their wives. As this novel notes, Norsewomen were not only allowed to divorce, if unhappy with the union, but entitled to a generous split of their husbands' holdings.

Equally amazing to me was the Vikings' advanced knowledge of medicine. Whether aware of it or not their practice of placing all of their surgical instruments in boiling water before use, was probably responsible for saving many of their people from the deaths by infection which would go on to plague the rest of humankind until the time of Doctor Lister in the mid-1800's.

What was more, these ancient Scandinavians are credited with devising a test for possible peritonitis: the trial meal of onion porridge served to the warrior with the stomach wound in Chapter 15. That is much the same procedure that's followed in hospitals *today!*

So, I once again stood corrected. I learned that dismissing the Vikings simply as loutish barbarians was close-minded, indeed! And, while I'm still on the subject of medicine, it should be noted that the pestilence that claimed Storr's family members was the pneumonic form of the bubonic plague. This is a swiftly fatal strain of the disease, which was believed to have originated in the Orient — from where the gift pillows reputedly came.

Finally, there is much debate as to whether or not our own continent of North America was discovered by the Vikings some five centuries before Columbus claimed to have done so. Again, most of the historical guides I consulted indicated that it was very likely that these brave and remarkably skilled mariners did just that. Why then, you may ask, didn't the Norsemen make such a discovery better known to the rest of the world? My personal theory on this is that, given how short of farmland they found themselves in their small and mountainous countries, they weren't in any hurry to advertise the real estate they managed to find to the west. They were, above all else, an acquisitive people, and certainly shrewd enough to keep their mouths shut when it seemed in their best interests to do so.

Well, enough for now about all of the surprises my research of my Norse heritage unearthed. On a more personal note, I would like to thank my beloved dogs, "Bear" and "Dodger," who are much the same breeds as Storr and Alanna's hounds, respectively. Were it not for a certain Friday afternoon a couple years back, when my "harrier"-mix, Dodger, impaled himself on a branch or some such thing, while chasing a rabbit in the woods, my hero and heroine in this tender tale might never have had cause to meet!

With all best wishes to you, my readers,
   Ashland Price (née Janice Carlson)

P.S. You will see Storr, Alanna, and their children in my next Viking historical, due out in October, 1993.

DISCOVER DEANA JAMES!

CAPTIVE ANGEL   (2524, $4.50/$5.50)
Abandoned, penniless, and suddenly responsible for the biggest
tobacco plantation in Colleton County, distraught Caroline Gillard had no time to dissolve into tears. By day the willowy redhead labored to exhaustion beside her slaves . . . but each night
left her restless with longing for her wayward husband. She'd
make the sea captain regret his betrayal until he begged her to
take him back!

MASQUE OF SAPPHIRE   (2885, $4.50/$5.50)
Judith Talbot-Harrow left England with a heavy heart. She was
going to America to join a father she despised and a sister she
distrusted. She was certainly in no mood to put up with the insulting actions of the arrogant Yankee privateer who boarded her
ship, ransacked her things, then "apologized" with an indecent,
brazen kiss! She vowed that someday he'd pay dearly for the liberties he had taken and the desires he had awakened.

SPEAK ONLY LOVE   (3439, $4.95/$5.95)
Long ago, the shock of her mother's death had robbed Vivian
Marleigh of the power of speech. Now she was being forced to
marry a bitter man with brandy on his breath. But she could not
say what was in her heart. It was up to the viscount to spark the
fires that would melt her icy reserve.

WILD TEXAS HEART   (3205, $4.95/$5.95)
Fan Breckenridge was terrified when the stranger found her near-naked and shivering beneath the Texas stars. Unable to remember
who she was or what had happened, all she had in the world was
the deed to a patch of land that might yield oil . . . and the fierce
loving of this wildcatter who called himself Irons.

*Available wherever paperbacks are sold, or order direct from the
Publisher. Send cover price plus 50¢ per copy for mailing and
handling to Zebra Books, Dept. 4030, 475 Park Avenue South,
New York, N.Y. 10016. Residents of New York and Tennessee
must include sales tax. DO NOT SEND CASH. For a free Zebra/
Pinnacle catalog please write to the above address.*

**WAITING FOR A WONDERFUL ROMANCE?
READ ZEBRA'S**

WANDA OWEN!

DECEPTIVE DESIRES   (2887, $4.50/$5.50)
Exquisite Tiffany Renaud loved her life as the only daughter of a
wealthy Parisian industrialist. The last thing she wanted was to
cross the ocean on a cramped and stuffy ship just to visit the un-
civilized wilds of America. Then she shared a kiss with shipping
magnate Chad Morrow that made the sails billow and the deck
spin. . .

KISS OF FIRE   (3091, $4.50/$5.50)
Born and raised in backwoods Virginia, Tawny Blair knew that
her dream of being swept off her feet by a handsome nobleman
would never come true. But when she met Lord Bart, Tawny saw
at once that reality could far surpass her fantasies. And when he
took her in his strong arms, she thrilled to the desire in his searing
caresses . . .

SAVAGE FURY   (2676, $3.95/$4.95)
Lovely Gillian Browne was secure in her quiet world on a remote
ranch in Arizona, yet she longed for romance and excitement.
Her girlish fantasies did not prepare her for the strange new feelings that assaulted her when dashing Irish sea captain Steve Laf-
ferty entered her life . . .

TEMPTING TEXAS TREASURE   (3312, $4.50/$5.50)
Mexican beauty Karita Montera aroused a fever of desire in every
redblooded man in the wild Texas Blacklands. But the sensuous
señorita had eyes only for Vincent Navarro, the wealthy cattle
rancher she'd adored since childhood—and her family's sworn enemy! His first searing caress ignited her white-hot need and soon
Karita burned to surrender to her own wanton passion . . .

*Available wherever paperbacks are sold, or order direct from the
Publisher. Send cover price plus 50¢ per copy for mailing and
handling to Zebra Books, Dept. 4030, 475 Park Avenue South,
New York, N.Y. 10016. Residents of New York and Tennessee
must include sales tax. DO NOT SEND CASH. For a free Zebra/
Pinnacle catalog please write to the above address.*